The Nightclub Owners Wife

Maggie Parker

http://www.facebook.com/maggieparkerauthor

The Nightclub Owners Wife

Maggie Parker

Paperback Edition First Published in the United Kingdom in 2019 by aSys Publishing

eBook Edition First Published in the United Kingdom in 2019 by aSys Publishing

Copyright © Maggie Parker 2019

Maggie Parker has asserted her rights under 'the Copyright Designs and Patents Act 1988' to be identified as the author of this work.

All rights reserved.

No part of this book may be reproduced or transmitted in any form or by any means, electronic, mechanical, photocopying, recording, or otherwise, without prior written permission of the Author.

Disclaimer

This is a work of fiction. Names, characters, businesses, places, events and incidents are either the products of the author's imagination or used in a fictitious manner. Any resemblance to actual persons, living or dead, or actual events is purely coincidental.

ISBN: 978-1-07-076483-2

aSys Publishing
http://www.asys-publishing.co.uk

For my sons, David and Jamie, my worst critics, my biggest fans, you both make me proud every day of my life.

INTRODUCTION

Message from the author

Thank you taking an interest in my book. I hope you enjoy it; my writing is not for everyone. I write about issues and although the settings and storylines are fictitious; all of the issues have and do happen in real life.

I live and work in the beautiful Dumfries and Galloway region of Scotland, although I was born and brought up in Irvine Ayrshire. I have grown up children and now am a proud Grandmother.

I am an independent author, I keep the cost of the eBooks and the paperbacks as low as the distributers allow. I do not make a lot of money from my writing and have no great desire to. I am fortunate that I am in full time employment and have a career I enjoy. Writing remains a hobby, I love doing it and when I stop enjoying it, I will stop writing.

I write because I have a vivid imagination and I find it a great relief from stress. I have always written and never had the confidence to allow anyone to read it. Somehow, I reached the point where I felt it was time. This happened after some life changing personal events, and a period of major stress. Writing became my escape from a difficult time in my life. I allowed some friends to read my stories, then published my work because the feedback was mainly constructive and positive.

I also write in a plain style which I hope makes it a readable story. I have no great desire to be clever and use language where you require a dictionary to understand. I will leave clever writing to others, if I hope for anything, it is that the reader will come away from the story with empathy for the characters and an understanding of the complexity of the issues involved.

Because I write about real life issues, some of the subject matter is taken from experiences, personal and vicarious. The result is at times the stories can be emotive and explicit. Real life is like that, I do like some twists in the storyline and a happy ending though. I have seen people recover from the most terrible tragedies and traumas, I wanted to highlight this into my work.

If you enjoy this book, can I ask that you take the time to provide feedback? This can be done on Amazon, Goodreads, Good Kindles or where ever you like. If you are reading in eBook form, click on the last page. Can I also direct you to my other books, which are listed?

I also can be followed on my Twitter and Facebook pages *(Maggie Parker Author)* and Instagram *(magswritesfiction.)* This also provides a public forum for you to ask any questions you may have.

Thank you again from the heart

Maggie Parker

CHAPTER

ONE

Island of Mykosis, Greece, May 2018

'Oh, dear god, I don't believe this?' Rosie Gibb's shock and distress was evident to the handful of tourists having their last drink before closing time. People averted their eyes, trying to pretend they weren't interested in the scene unfolding before them.

'Rosie, please just let me explain!'

Tears welled up in Rosie's eyes, and she fought hard to stem the flow. 'Explain? Explain what? That you lied to me? How could you have pretended for two years to be someone you are not? You ... you ... bastard, you knew how this would go down. Why? Why have you done this to me?'

'Rosie, just give me a chance darling. Nothing has changed, everyone lies on on-line sites. It's only my name I lied about, not how I feel about you!' He put his hand on her arm, but she slapped it away.

'Please don't dare, try to ... I can't even start to tell you how much I hate you.' Her body shaking now, Rosie turned her back on him, she moved away trying to compose herself.

'Please listen, it wasn't intentional. Well maybe it was at first, it started because I was bored. I didn't know who you were, it wasn't because of you I pretended to be someone else. When you and I became close, I wanted to be that ideal man, until you put up the picture . . . I swear, I didn't know it was you. I knew if I told you, there was no way you'd come over here. I couldn't come to you because you wouldn't have spoken to me.'

Rosie turned back to face him, her eyes bright with unshed tears. She looked around the bar and then straight back at him, the disgust she felt obvious, her body shook, and she struggled to speak. When she did however, there was no mistaking her anger. 'You are a liar and a fraud,' she hissed, embarrassed by the situation she found herself in. She swallowed hard. 'You got me here under false pretences. After what you did? How else did you expect me to react? I'm leaving, don't ever contact me again.' Rosie picked up her bag and rushed from the bar.

He watched her go and then turned slowly to look at the man behind the bar. 'Double, Keith, what an idiot I've been, I need to get drunk.'

'No Jimmy, you need to go after her, who the fuck did you tell her you were?' Keith Arnold looked at his friend and sighed, shaking his head he turned to the gantry, pressed the whisky optic twice, then placed the half full glass on the bar. 'That's not the answer, please mate don't go back to the bottle. Go after her and make her listen to why you did it. I take it there's a reason you didn't tell her who you were?'

Jimmy nodded and took a long drink from the glass, 'too hard to explain mate. She's had horrific experience of men, been really traumatised and hurt. I'm a prick for thinking she would react any other way?'

'Fuck sake Jimmy, who did she think you were?' Keith repeated.

'Wasn't that obvious?'

The Nightclub Owners Wife

Keith looked at his friend, realisation dawning, 'she thought I was you? You used my photo? What a fucking prick you are! Did you use my name too?'

Jimmy shook his head slowly and sighed, he put his hand out as though awaiting a handshake. 'Wilson Anderson, aspiring travel writer? I put up your picture, one where you're dressed as a Viking. I was using the name Trygve, which ironically means trustworthy, we got talking on line. Her handle is Sigrunn. Fuck Keith, I told you it started as a bit of fun and escapism. Then I began to enjoy talking to her. She's funny, kind and intelligent. I had pretended to be a writer, no one in the game questioned it. She actually is a writer, so we kind of gravitated towards each other.'

'Why Jimmy? Why not just tell her? If you liked her that much? Was it about Kim? Surely if you'd told her the truth she would have understood?'

'When I started using the site, it was just after the accident, and oh . . . I don't know? It was like everyone wanted a piece of me. I was laid up in the hospital when I found the site. There was so much interest in what had happened. Then when I came home, I started talking to some of the players privately in the chatroom. Well I was taking pain killers, and as you well know; drinking on top of them.

'Okay I get that, but two years? Let's not get into why you were using my photo?'

'Oh fuck, I just got carried away. I found a picture of a guy from an obituary and I was going to use it. Then I remembered the photo from the fancy-dress thing Kim did for your 30th. It wasn't about hiding who I was from Rosie specifically at the start. It was about being able to be someone else.'

Keith scratched his head, 'so why keep lying? If you got interested in her, went as far as getting her to agree to meet you here on your turf? This is so not like you Jimmy. You really didn't think this through. If you had been talking to her, knew that she hated lies, why do this?'

'I only lied about what I did for a living, I was going to own up. I got close to her, she took ages to put a picture up for me to see what she looked like, then a few months back she finally did it. Then I couldn't use my own.'

'I don't get any of this mate ... I have so many questions. I don't know where to start?' Jimmy said nothing, he stared miserably into his glass. Keith shook his head and began washing glasses. 'Okay folks times up, we are closing in five minutes, finish your drinks.' He called out to the few stragglers who were lingering in the shadows.

'It was a kind of defence mechanism I think Keith. Only she believed the fictitious persona, I didn't intend to hurt her. It has taken me four months to get her to agree to come out here. Fuck I need to go find her, but, you saw her reaction.' He drained his glass and put it down on the bar. 'Pour me another bud?'

Keith put another drink in front of his friend, he looked around the now almost empty bar and then leaned forward. 'She came on the last ferry, so she can't get off the island tonight Jimmy. There is no service tomorrow because it's Sunday. So maybe let her calm down and then go wait at the ferry terminal on Monday.' He shook his head and then smiled. 'You are a fuckwit, you must be the only guy who has wooed a chick on line and then ... Fuck sake, most men put a better-looking picture on their profile. I don't get why you didn't just fess up, especially when she agreed to come out here to meet with you?' Keith took a drink from his own glass then sighed. 'I don't get it Jimmy? Why is she so upset?'

'It's so not funny mate,' Jimmy said smiling wryly. 'You saw her reaction? We've been talking online for nearly two years, I really looked forward to speaking to her. At first it was just the game, I told you why I was playing. I was laid up at home alone after the accident and I was drunk most of the time.'

Keith waved as the last of the drinkers left the bar and walked over to the doors, sliding the bolt across he returned to the bar and pressed the button on the wall. The electric shutters rattled

The Nightclub Owners Wife

as they came down on the outside of the bar. 'So how did you get from playing a Viking game, to wooing a woman like Rosie?' Keith scratched his head. 'And how did you manage to upset someone that much? She looked devastated?'

'I had started playing when I was in hospital. I was looking for escapism, browsing on line and saw the game, started playing and got a bit hooked. Rosie and me, we were in the same clan and well, she showed leadership qualities, to be honest Keith, at first I wasn't even sure if she was female.'

'Did you tell her about the accident, what happened? Who your wife was?'

'No, I just said I was widowed, why didn't come up. She's too nice to ask. The only thing I lied about was my real name. I was going to tell her then she put the photo up. She wouldn't have spoken to me if she had known.' Seeing Keith's quizzical look, he added quickly. 'Oh, there are reasons mate, I don't feel like talking about them, but anyway it was all a bit weird. For the first few months it was about the game, because of all the different time zones there was always someone on. After I cut down on the drugs and booze, I couldn't sleep, and it helped to take my mind off stuff. I used to enjoy talking to her, but it was kind of well ... impersonal like, we didn't share personal information. I carried on playing even after I was back on my feet. It was last Christmas when it started to be something else. Remember, I left you and Michael and went home with that American doctor, Karen, who was staying here? I kind of messed it up, she left and ... Well, I went online because I was upset. Rosie was on and we started to talk in a private chat room. I asked her why she was on-line at Christmas. She said she was alone, didn't trust men. We started to talk about sex, and I suppose there was some flirting. Then she logged off suddenly in mid-sentence. She came back on a couple of weeks later and well the talk started to go off in another direction ... we kind ... we kind of started to have virtual sex. It wasn't all about sex, we talked about other things, found we had a lot in common. The more we talked ... well I got really into her. I liked her personality, we had become friends playing. I'm not sure how it happened but...Fuck Keith, I shouldn't be telling you this, but I wanked a lot.'

'Seriously? On line? You never saw her? Heard her voice? Wow Jimmy, that is... Fuck, weird, even you must see that?

'You know what a private person I am...'

'I have never got why you do the...'*I want to be anonymous.*' I don't get the private person thing? I can understand it when you and Kim were together, the media circus she lived in. Afterwards...well...I always thought that for someone with your looks and talent it was all a bit strange. Has this got something to do with it? Rosie...her accent, it's very like yours, she knew who you were, you and her, you have a past?

Jimmy nodded his head slowly and handed Keith the now empty glass, 'there is so much I should have told you mate. So much...I...I just couldn't talk to anyone. I did try after Kim died, that first day you came to the hospital, but you were grieving too, so we kind of left it hanging. Time passed and well I suppose I dealt with it my way.'

'So, what happened with Rosie? You were playing that daft game? You were happy to be anonymous having what? Text sex? Getting casual sex here and there? So, what changed? Why did you ask her to come out here?'

Jimmy sighed and looked at Keith. 'We began to play the game less and talk more in private chat rooms, and well I kind of looked forward to those chats. I haven't been with a woman in a while because of it. I tried, but, I just kept thinking about her, at the same time I felt so guilty about being disloyal to Kim.' Jimmy hung his head in shame, at the pain on his friend's face. 'And to you mate,' he added quietly.

'Jimmy, you know I want you to move on. Kim's gone, she wouldn't want you to be alone. Now she's here, Rosie? Do you still feel like that? Keith refilled the glass and placed it on the bar. 'It's what we all want for you...to be with someone else, be happy.'

The Nightclub Owners Wife

'Why do I sense a but here?'

Keith sighed and took a drink, he hesitated for a second, 'it's just that, well, she's not who or what I thought you would go for. She's pretty, but she's not, well mate... she's not exactly what you are used to is she?'

'I think she's beautiful, she was honest with the picture she put up and oh fuck you don't need the details. I was shocked to the core.' Jimmy took a drink from the glass he was holding and looked at Keith. 'She wasn't entirely honest either... oh, look can we just leave it? I need to go home to bed... try to work out what I'm going to do.'

'I do need the details Jimmy, I don't understand why you did it mate, I'm really confused. I'm also not sure what she's so upset about really? If you didn't lie about your feelings, and you mostly told the truth? Surely you just need to talk to her, explain? Fuck sake you'd think she would be pleased about how good looking you are? Who wouldn't love a guy like you? Just how well did you know her?

'Keith, it's not just about me pretending to be someone else... like I said... there's stuff, things I've never told anyone, things I wanted to forget. I well... oh this is just not the time to go into it all. She has more reason than most to hate me.' He finished the drink and held out the glass.

Keith took the glass from his friend. 'You can't leave it like that mate, what stuff? I've known you what? Ten years? Jimmy, come on mate, nothing can be that bad? Is this about your first wife and child? Did Rosie know them too?'

'Yes, no... sort of.'

'Jimmy, If you like her that much you need to just tell her, make her listen. I'm not sure I understand what you did or why? But you must have had reasons? Just make her listen.'

'I need to find her first, I hope she's okay.'

'She got back into Michael's taxi. He'll have taken her to the Blue Bay if she was looking for somewhere to stay... Sleep on it and go see her tomorrow.' Keith smiled, 'I really can't believe you did it?'

'What part don't you believe?'

'The picture of me.'

'Well I did and I'm now going to bed with a bottle, so give it a rest tonight Keith. You're always telling me I'm a fanny, I don't know why you're shocked?'

'No chance Jimmy, not this time, you need to tell me what's going on? Lizette and Harry are in the residents' lounge. I'll go ask one of them to come through and finish up here. We'll go upstairs then you can tell me all about it. I know there's a story here, surely it can't be that bad?

'Okay, okay, but Keith, I need you to understand mate, this is not easy for me, and it is bad. I did try to tell you after the accident, but you said you didn't want to know. I'm not who you think I am. You might not even want to know me after I tell you this.'

'You're my family Jimmy, and families accept each other's limitations and mistakes. Family forgive each other.'

Jimmy sighed, nodded and lifted his glass. 'You might want to bring a bottle too, because I need to be drunk. You'll want a drink too when I tell you this story.'

***

In the Blue Bay Oyster hotel, Rosie Gibb put her bag down on the floor and looked at the Greek woman who had shown her to her room. 'Thank you Madam Katsoulis, you have been very kind. I was a bit worried I wouldn't be able to find a hotel room at short notice. Especially when it is just two nights...It's a beautiful room, so Greek and it has a sea view. Too many hotels lose their identity, this is wonderful thank you.' Rosie knew she was speaking to stop herself from crying, she needed the woman to go, so she could let go.'

The older woman handed Rosie her passport back. 'It not as Stylish as the Hotel Angelica, Mrs Gibb, my husband Sandro, he not as handsome as Mister Jimmy. We very comfortable, you stay for a few days, you like the island? You are not married?'

'No, I'm not.' Rosie struggled to contain her emotions, she needed to cry, she was however an expert at hiding her feelings. Still reeling from her lack of control earlier, she knew she needed to be by herself. 'not anymore.' She added quietly.

The Greek woman smiled and patted the beautiful white woven bedspread. 'My son Michael, he bring you here? You like? He need a wife Mrs Gibb. Michael, he very nice you think? He very handsome, has all his teeth and he is good to his Mama! He been to university, very clever, he be a very good husband. Make beautiful children, no? You like?

'Thank you!' Rosie said smiling despite her internal misery, 'I'm very flattered, but I'm afraid I wouldn't make a very good wife. I've tried it before you see and well... it didn't work out. Your son is a very handsome man Madam Katsoulis. I'm sure he will meet the right woman some-day.'

'Many time he meet the right woman Mrs Gibb, but Michael he never think they be the right woman. I worry I never be Yaya, he is now going to be forty. He spend his time when he no work, gambling and drinking with the two English devils. Mister Keith and Mister Jimmy, they tell him he no need a woman, *don't listen to your Mama!* they say.'

'I'm sure when the right woman comes along he won't listen to them.' The mention of Keith and Jimmy immediately made Rosie blush, her embarrassment acute. She couldn't believe she had been taken in, made to look a fool. Her stomach was turning, she felt sick. Unsure of what Michael Katsoulis had told his mother, she turned away desperate to change the subject. 'Is this the bathroom? Oh, it's lovely and it has a spa-bath. I feel so grubby, I really need a long soak in the tub. Thank you Madam Katsoulis, if you'll excuse me.'

'Excuse!' Both women turned, Michael was standing in the doorway, holding a tray with a wine carafe and glass, alongside a platter containing bread, cheese and olives. 'I thought you may be hungry.'

'How kind, thank you.' Rosie said smiling, embarrassed about how she had behaved in his taxi she tried to make conversation. 'Your English is very good Michael, you have almost no accent.'

'I studied in England Mrs Gibb. I was at Oxford with Keith, he and I shared lodgings there. I'm co-owner of the Hotel Angelica.' Michael looked at his mother. 'Now Mama, you must leave Mrs Gibb to rest, she has had a long journey.' Winking at Rosie he ushered his mother from the room.

Rosie ate some of the bread and olives whilst waiting for the large bath to fill. Eventually she climbed into the warm water and lay back. Tears which had been threatening all afternoon finally came, she sobbed quietly, unable to believe she had been taken in. She had finally found someone she thought she could trust and again she had been deceived. The worst thing for Rosie though, was that he must have known how she would react.

Unable to relax she got out of the bath, she opened the doors onto the balcony, she could hear the sea, normally this calmed her. She poured the wine into the glass, took a large gulp and got into bed. As she lay there listening to the sound of the ocean outside, she was transported back to another time, how long was it? Imogen had turned twenty-one six months before. So long ago, so many tears, an ocean of sadness and regrets. She remembered the time before she had been hurt, when she had been able to trust. Remembered that saying, the one that many years ago had been her mantra, *'nothing hurts more than being let down by the person you thought could never hurt you!'* More years than she cared to remember had passed and it all still hurt. Imogen had been just one month old when their world turned upside down and changed their lives forever.

CHAPTER TWO

Kilmarnock, Scotland, December 1996

'Rosie, will you hurry up babe, how long does it take you to get dressed? You look fine, stop worrying, so you are still carrying some baby weight. Everyone knows I have a young baby. How many outfits have you tried on?' Carl Ranmore looked at the pile of clothes on the bedroom floor, he began to pick garments up. Shaking a green dress from its outside-in discarded state, he put it on one of the black velour covered hangers hooked over the wardrobe door handles.

'Carl this is important, I look like a heifer and you know it. All those skinny models, I'm going to look even worse. Will you stop tidying up after me? I'll put them all away later.' Rosie pulled a red evening gown over her head. 'I'm going to embarrass you I just know it. I'd be better staying at home. Can't you just say I'm ill?'

'No, I need my wife to be there. Stop worrying, no one is going to be looking at you. Its opening night, I've worked hard for this. The club looks brilliant and the PR is costing a fortune.' Carl Ranmore smiled, 'you will be the most beautiful woman in the room. You are the mother of my daughter and the wife of the most successful night club owner in Kilmarnock. What more can you aspire to? Hmm, I'm not sure about that dress babe, you do look a bit porky in it. I think the blue sparkly one looked better. He held up a royal blue sequin covered dress, 'put it on babe.'

'It was too short Carl, you said so yourself.'

'No, you said it was too short, I just agreed to make you feel better. I think it's the best of them all, shows off your lovely legs, your best feature Rosie. Used to be your boobs, but I can't say that now, can I? When you are feeding our daughter with them. The cut of it gives the impression you're slimmer. Carl tightened his blue striped silk tie and smiled at his wife. 'I like your hair that way Rosie, you really suit it that length. Told you it would look good, didn't I? The way it was before you looked like a little girl.'

'It was a bit naughty of you to tell the hairdresser to do it like this after I said I just wanted a trim. Still I suppose you are right, I'll get used to it. I did like my long hair though Carl.'

'You look all woman now.' He watched her pull the flimsy blue dress over her head and nodded, smiling as his wife turned around examining herself critically in the full-length mirror. Carl put his hand into the pocket of his suit jacket and pulled out a long black velvet jewellery case. 'This is for you darling, it matches your dress, and your eyes.'

Rosie opened the case, nestled in the silk lining lay a necklace and earrings, ornately fashioned in white gold, the blue green stones sparkled like an ocean on a summers day. 'Carl it's amazing!' she gasped, 'it must have cost a fortune, it's...oh, it's so beautiful, so unusual. From the same jewellers as my engagement ring.'

'Sweetheart, the stones are rare blue green Ceylon Sapphires, and yes it cost a fortune, but you're worth it.'

'I don't deserve you, after all the moaning I've done about the new club. I've been such a cow about it all.'

The Nightclub Owners Wife

'I've deserved some of the abuse, I've been neglecting you. You've got a four-week-old baby, I think you had a touch of the blues. It's all going to be fine, you and I we are going to have it all. Now put on your shoes, no not those ones, put on the silver sandals I got you.'

'But they hurt Carl, they dig in and ... oh, you're right, they will be perfect with this dress and the jewellery. Help me with the necklace?' Rosie shivered as Carl fastened the ornate necklace and kissed her neck.

'Just you wait till you see the club, it's amazing. Julie and Moira have done an amazing job with the décor. It was difficult with you being so ill before the baby. I had to be with you so much. They worked with the builders and decorators in the last couple of months. I owe them so much for all their hard work. They've both worked hard for the business. I'm really disappointed Moira is leaving.' He stopped and sighed, 'thing is ... I had to sack Julie this afternoon, so they are both going.'

'You sacked Julie? Why?' Rosie gasped, 'you always said she was an essential employee and the place couldn't run without her. I never liked her, but she was good at her job.' She looked at her husband, 'has this got anything to do with Moira and Elaine?

'No, we had a row, she's got ideas above her station, she threw a tantrum. I asked her to leave. Now you are better, you can play a role in the club if you like? You don't need to worry about the old guard. I know you don't like them, so maybe it's all for the best.'

'Oh, I don't know why I don't like them, maybe I was a bit jealous, I was ill and wanted to be involved, they kind of took over. I don't mind Moira as much, she was always nice to me. I'm still angry about what she did to Elaine though. I think Elaine isn't talking to me because she thinks I knew.' Rosie's face clouded over, 'I've tried everything, if she doesn't come down this weekend Carl, I'm going to Stirling. I need to find out why she is avoiding me. She can't possibly think I knew and didn't tell her.' She looked at her husband, 'Carl I know what Alex said, and I mostly agree with him. They weren't exactly Romeo and Juliet. Elaine knew it was never going anywhere. This reaction is just not her, she was fine until I had Imogen, she saved our lives, Carl. We should never forget that.'

'Rosie, sometimes childhood friendships don't last into adulthood. It happens it's sad but . . . Fuck . . . Lex and Moira? He says that's over too. I would imagine her leaving has something to do with Elaine and her fucking behaviour.

'I thought it was Julie, thought Alex might be having a thing with her, so did Elaine.' Rosie looked at her husband and she could see the veiled anger on his face. 'Julie well she's always been funny with me. I thought it was because Alex and I are friends, she never liked me, I think she fancied you. Like I said, I got a bit jealous too, I suppose. I'm not sorry she's gone, but you will give her a good reference, won't you? She has kids, with Ronnie in prison, she'll need a job.'

'You're a good person Rosie, you don't have a vindictive bone in your body sweetheart. Always thinking of others, you are too good for me babe. Can't believe you were jealous of Moira and Julie?'

'I wanted the club to be our dream, build it together, but then with me being so sick at the beginning and what happened at the end.' Rosie saw Carl's gaze soften, she smiled, thinking about the baby upstairs in the nursery. 'Imogen, was worth it, wasn't she? Even if she wasn't planned. Come on, let's go and say bye to her, our beautiful daughter. Get us with an au-pair? Makes me feel a bit redundant. Can we afford this lifestyle Carl? I worry all the time. The house, the cars? Not to mention the huge loans and overdraft. I know you told me not to read the business papers I signed, but I couldn't help noticing the figures.'

'Babe don't worry your pretty little head, this club is going to make us rich, there's nothing like it in Ayrshire. I've got a 3am licence from the council, some of the out of town pubs and clubs are going to run buses at their closing time. We can't

The Nightclub Owners Wife

lose here. So, stop worrying Rosie, I know what I'm doing. Even without Julie and Moira, I've got great staff, three pubs and now the club. The Red Rose is going to be the flagship of our empire. It's all going to be good, you, me, our little family and loads of cash. Hopefully you and I will have a wee boy soon. I want the company to be Carl Ranmore and son. Just watch this space babe. You are married to an entrepreneur, we are a long way from the council estates now. The invitations went out early and we have had a lot of acceptances. It's going to be very busy.'

Rosie was irritated, she had had the discussion about Carl's obsession about having a son many times, but she realised she couldn't change the mindset of her husband. Instead she ignored his misogynist thinking and changed the subject. 'Did you invite Elaine? I put her on the VIP list, I put her Stirling address on it too.'

'No, I didn't invite Elaine, look, I know you go way back, but she's a liability Rosie. I get she was mad at Lex and Moira, but I don't want her around especially if she is going to cause a scene in the club. Rosie, the friendship with her, it's not something I want to encourage. Yeah, she was good when you were pregnant, but she said some horrible things to me and I'm still quite hurt. She had no call to blame me for what Lex did. She also said she wouldn't come to the opening if I paid her. So, she's not expecting to be invited.'

'Phone her right now and invite her or I'm not going. It sounds as though you were very rude to her too. Her and Alex, well, he was cheating on her, you know he was. She's my best friend and I want her there tonight.'

'No, I told you I don't want her there. Rosie, I don't want to fight with you. I'm not calling her now, she'll know it's down to you if I do that.' Carl moved towards the door, 'let's go see our baby, we need to leave soon.' He turned at the doorway. 'If it means that much to you, call her and invite her, but I'm not doing it.'

Rosie lifted the telephone and grimaced as she saw the dark look on Carl's face. She knew he would bring it up later, but Rosie didn't want to be one of those girls who dropped their friends because of a man. Elaine had been distant, avoiding Rosie since Imogen was born, which had confused and hurt Rosie. She knew that it was probably a bad idea to call her, given how much Elaine disliked Carl. They had mainly tolerated each other, but Rosie was not sure what had happened to change that to out and out hatred, because she hadn't seen Elaine in a month. As she left a message with Elaine's gran, Rosie looked at Carl, sighed and replaced the receiver.

Carl put his arms around his wife and kissed her, gently wiping away the stray tear with his finger. 'Babe I'm sorry about you and Elaine, but it happens, people just grow apart. You and her, your lives are going in different directions. I think she's just jealous you know? Now come on, shift that sexy ass and let's get going.'

Rosie sighed, nodded and then kissed her husband, she thought about him to herself, *'I love him? Don't I?'* This was her life now, and it was a good life. Rosie knew she was fortunate. She just wished she had been able to share it with her best friend. Rosie realised her life had changed direction, things were different now, she was a wife to Carl and a mother to Imogen.

***

Carl and Rosie had met when she and Elaine had started working in his pub as Saturday girls. Waitressing during the day serving meals, collecting glasses at night, still too young to be serving alcohol. Nobels had been the trendy place to be. Sixteen-year-old Rosie had been initially interviewed by Bobby the bar manager. On her first shift, she had met twenty-seven-year-old owner Carl. It was love at first sight he always said, reckoned he knew she was special as soon as he saw her.

Carl Ranmore was arguably the most handsome man in Kilmarnock, initially Rosie had been shy and overawed by this older man's interest in her. The much more streetwise Elaine had disliked him immediately. Six months older than Rosie, Elaine had been in a very casual relationship with another childhood friend Alex Lockwood. Alex lived in the same street as Rosie, three years older than the girls, he had gone to the same school. Rosie loved Alex, their mothers had been best friends. Both girls had known him all their lives and idolised him.

Alex had always been there for Rosie, she couldn't remember a time when she hadn't known him. He was her friend and protector. As young teenagers, she and Elaine had, with their group of friends, got drunk down the Scott Ellis in the winter and hiked to Craigie Woods in the summer. Alex had looked after them. He'd never taken advantage of them and always made sure they were safe. He had been a best friend of Rosie's dead brother Simon and felt a responsibility towards her. It had been Alex who told them about the job in Nobels. He had been working as a door steward to supplement his university course. Alex had secured them an interview with Bobby the manager and driven them to work that first day. It had also been Alex who introduced Rosie to Carl.

From that first week, Carl had pursued Rosie, knowing she was an innocent abroad. He had never met anyone quite like her. Carl had grown up in a neighbouring estate with a mixture of local authority and privately-owned homes. His parents had not been affluent, but they worked hard running the local public house. Carl had been about to leave for London to take on the lease of a brewery owned hotel, when his father died suddenly. An only child, Carl had felt obliged to take on the pub with his mother. He had strived to make the traditional public house a trendy watering hole and had increased profits tenfold in that first year. Two more pubs followed, he began to see profits from them too.

Tracey his then girlfriend, an aspiring model had left him when he took the decision not to leave for London with her. Tracey relocated to London alone, Carl remained in Kilmarnock.

Carl never admitted to even his closest friends, he was in truth relieved when the relationship ended. Tracey was high maintenance, she wanted the finer things in life. She was gorgeous and Carl knew they made a beautiful couple. He had no intention when Tracey left of entering another long-term relationship. A succession of women ensued, mostly older married ones, safe women who didn't want anything more than a good time from him.

Everything changed for Carl Ranmore when he arrived at the pub after a holiday abroad and met the teenage girls Bobby had hired as waitresses. Initially it had been the more outgoing gregarious Elaine who'd caught his eye if he was honest. Then that first night there had been a fight brewing in the pub just before closing. He watched astonished as the tiny, slightly plump Rosie, talked down two drunk young men about to fight. Afterwards he bought her a drink whilst the others cleared up. He knew she was a virgin before Alex warned him off.

Carl had been sure Alex was attracted to Rosie, but Alex explained the relationship. He told Carl about her brother Simon. The friendship, the three wild fourteen-year olds, the stolen car, the police chase, the crash, the dead driver. Alex in the back seat had been mostly unhurt, whilst Simon in the front passenger seat minus a seat belt, had been thrown from the car. Carl vaguely remembered his mother telling him about the youth who had grown from a child to a man in a coma. Simon was, Alex told Carl, visited daily by his parents for five years, before he died from a chest infection. Alex relayed his survivor guilt and told of his promise to his unconscious dying friend to look after his baby sister. He told of his friendship with Rosie's parents, who had never blamed him for the accident. How he had become a changed person after it happened. Allocated a social worker, who helped him to turn his life around, encouraged his love of art, drawing and reading, got him a membership at a gym, where he learned to love himself by working out.

Alex also worked harder at school. Now at university, working in Nobels at weekends to supplement his student loans, he had become a loyal trusted friend of Carl Ranmore. Carl was astute enough to realise, the physical presence of the big handsome mild-mannered bodybuilder, allowed him a degree of protection.

Despite his youth, Alex was now head of security for Carl's company. He was going to be an architect, he was also determined to look after little Rosie who had been just eleven years old at the time of the accident. Alex was antithetical to most of the stewards Carl had employed, he didn't appear to Carl to have an aggressive bone in his body. His calm composed presence was the very essence of Alex. Everyone liked him, his physical appearance belied his personal strength and emotional intelligence. When Carl began seeing Rosie, Alex had at first appeared annoyed, this left Carl with a dichotomy, he needed Alex for protection. He wanted Rosie.

Carl had assured Alex, that his intentions towards the young girl were honourable. He had wooed her and her family. Her parents had, Carl realised, neglected their daughter for years and knew it. Alex had told Carl, during the time Simon was in the coma, their focus had been visiting their son, hoping against hope despite the medical prognosis of limited brain activity, he would wake up. Rosie was mainly left to her own devices during the week and spent Sundays at the hospital. If she resented the time her parents had given to their comatose son, she never said. She did say, after Simon died she found it hard when her parents wanted to parent her.

Rosie had not rebelled though, she had done well at school and intended to go to university to study English Literature, her love of reading amused Carl. Other young staff went to parties and enjoyed the kudos and social life that went along with working at the trendiest waterhole in town. Rosie spent her breaks reading and went home alone at closing time. Carl was aware being more than ten years older than Rosie, he was in a very privileged, if not precarious, position. She was not his normal type, but he knew she was marriage material. Despite having an endless supply of women willing to sleep with him, Carl Ranmore wanted to marry someone only he had been with.

It had taken him just three months to seduce Rosie, Carl had carefully planned it all. The weeks of waiting he had supplemented with the ever-willing group of females he knew from the pubs. They all knew about Rosie and she was well liked in the town. No one wanted to hurt her, and Carl suspected it was loyalty to her rather than him, which bought their silence.

The first time with Rosie hadn't actually been planned. However, when the opportunity arose it turned out to be memorable. Carl had rented a secluded log cabin with a hot tub and had taken Rosie away to celebrate her passing her exams with distinction and obtaining an unconditional place at University in Stirling. The university place worried Carl, he was sure that once she started she would get caught up in the social life. Many of his staff were students and Carl had heard their stories of university life. Carl knew he had to find a way to stop her. For the first time in his life Carl Ranmore felt insecure, he knew Rosie was too intelligent for life in a small town. He was in love with her, he wanted her in a way he had never wanted anyone. She was becoming more confident and he liked it. The realisation he loved her came as a shock for Carl. His love life was varied, and he was an experienced lover. Seducing Rosie was easy for him, he now wanted her so badly he was afraid he wouldn't be able to wait.

Carl had booked the weekend away for him, Alex and the girls. Aware of how Alex viewed Rosie, Carl had been careful to include him. He knew Rosie felt safe when Alex was around. However, he had been delighted when Alex had come down with flu shortly before they were due to leave, and he and Elaine had decided to stay at home.

The hot tub had been the perfect place to seduce the teenager, she had initially resisted him. Rosie wanted to finish her

The Nightclub Owners Wife

degree and be a virgin bride. Carl loved this about her, but he also knew he couldn't wait that long. He had decided weeks ago Rosie would be a perfect wife, he hadn't planned to propose, but some heavy petting and frustration had overtaken his plan to marry at thirty, and he had done it. Got down on one knee and asked her to marry him, Rosie had melted. He knew she was needy, after all the years of being second best to her brother, she wanted to be loved. She also read books about romance with strong male characters, she loved the classics, the Bronte's, Jane Austin. Carl didn't read much but he knew enough to realise he had to be the male hero. He'd approached the seduction of Rosie as a project. Had watched the film versions of some of the classics she read, and couldn't decide between Heathcliff, Mr Rochester or Mr Darcy. He knew Rosie wanted a romantic love affair and strived to be what she wanted him to be.

Carl hadn't expected to enjoy sex with Rosie as much as he did. He had, after proposing on the Saturday afternoon, taken her to Glasgow. Visiting the Argyle arcade, with its array of sparkling window displays, they chose the platinum diamond set trilogy ring. They returned to the lodge at Loch Lomond as an engaged couple. Rosie shy and inexperienced had given her body to him. Carl had, to his knowledge, never had sex with a virgin. He held back and was gentle, performing oral sex until she climaxed, before making love to her. He knew she found it uncomfortable that first time, Rosie never realised he had neglected to wear a condom. The next morning, he made love slowly and gently bringing her to climax several times. His father had told him once, when you made love to a woman you cared about, a man should try to make sure she enjoyed it too. He knew enough now, to know that his father had been a wise man.

Carl considered himself a thorough and experienced lover, he liked to know a woman enjoyed sex with him. It was important he thought, made him feel masculine. As he held Rosie as she reached orgasm, he knew she wasn't faking. Afterwards still trembling she had lain in his arms as he told her about his plans to open the new club in the town. He told her he was going to name it after her, the Red Rose. He was sure it would be a success, and the start of his empire of clubs throughout the country. *'Oh yes!'* he told the impressionable teenager, *'Carl Ranmore is going to be a tycoon.'*

The pregnancy discovered eight weeks later had come as a shock to Rosie, Carl was delighted, however he contained his joy and was supportive. Her parents initially wanted her to abort the baby. However, Margaret and Davie Gibbs had been as seduced by Carl Ranmore as their daughter. A wedding was hastily arranged. Carl saw it as a way to keep the lovely young girl with him. She was curvier than he normally liked, but her body was soft and beautiful. He also knew he could mould her to his will, and she would be a good wife. Carl loved the way she looked at him with stars in her eyes. His mother Rowena who had disliked previous girlfriends, particularly Tracey; had loved Rosie from their first meeting. Carl had been sure their life together would be perfect.

CHAPTER
THREE

September 1996

'Fuck sake Rosie, you're skin and bone. I thought you looked thin at the wedding, but you have lost so much weight and you're so pale. Is he not feeding you, your new husband?' Elaine shook her head, 'I thought you were supposed to get fat when you are pregnant. What's the doctor saying? You have seen a doctor?'

'My mums a midwife Lainey, it happens, severe morning sickness, only it lasts all day. I've got an antenatal appointment on Thursday, hopefully they will be able to give me something for it. Apparently, it's called hyperemesis gravidarum, it should have stopped when I got to three months. Mums quite worried, she said it should be tailing off by now. I feel like shit Lainey and I can't sleep, I keep being sick. All those diets I used to go on, all I actually had to do was get pregnant.' Rosie smiled slightly, 'Carl likes me a bit thinner, but I can't even, you know... Do it with him, because I vomit all the time. Mum wants me to go back home so she can look after me, but Carl won't hear of it, says he'll do it. Don't make a face, he's lovely Lainey. I don't know why you can't accept it, but he is, and he loves me. I told you before you went to stay with your mum. I need you to accept this is what I want Lainey. I hate that you two don't get on. I hoped after your holiday you would try to ... please, just try for my sake. He says he will if you will?'

'Oh, I'm sorry babe, it's just, well ... all those stories about him with girls before you got together.' Elaine sighed and shook back her red curls. 'Are you sure he's faithful? I don't know ... I can't explain it but ... there is something cruel about him. Rosie, you would tell me if he hurt you? You're too good for Carl Ranmore, he's a prick.'

'Elaine Lamont, will you stop it? He's my husband now and may I remind you, still your boss! I wish you wouldn't keep arguing with him, he's going to end up sacking you.'

'Don't care, I'm going to be leaving soon anyway, I'm just waiting to hear about a job in Stirling, then I'll tell them. Moira's my supervisor, Carl doesn't interfere with her decisions. She's a bitch but she's fair. I'm sure she fancies your man by the way, it's all Carl this and Carl that. As for that fucking Julie, who does she think she is? She's a fucking trollop. She was all over Lex like a rash last weekend. I said to her, *'he's spoken for.'* He thinks it's funny that I get jealous.' Elaine grinned and nudged Rosie, 'Lex and I, we do have great sex, he's good at it. I'll miss that. We did it in the cellar the other night, don't tell Carl? It was the night he was at the antenatal class with you. Lex was locking up, everyone had gone and well we did it over the beer barrels. We had been arguing and I got mad at him then I was really turned on. It was brilliant, he's got a big willy you know!'

'Elaine Nooo ... I've told you before, he's like my big brother Alex is, please don't tell me about his bits. I can't think of him like that.' Rosie hoped she sounded as though she was being truthful, in reality she had always felt sad that Alex never thought of her that way. Now she was with Carl, *'till death do you part,'* the priest had said. Any longing she had felt in respect of Alex, needed to remain in her head, she tried hard not to think of him as anything other than her friend. Rosie smiled and looked at

The Nightclub Owners Wife

her best friend. 'He is gorgeous though, I suppose I've always thought he was a beautiful boy. Do you love him Elaine, he needs to be loved?'

'No, I don't, but I like him as a shag, he'll never manage to be faithful, he would never want to be tied down with me. I actually don't want that either. I've got my university place and well... I'm going Rosie. I'll be a journalist, and a good one. Maybe in a few years I might want marriage and kids, but not yet, and not with Lex Lockwood.' Elaine smiled and nudged her friend, 'I've got a lot of partying to do first.'

'So, you don't mind if Alex sleeps around? I'm sure he's faithful Lainey, he likes you a lot.'

'Yes, I mind, he's not making a fool of me! I don't go with others, so neither should he. Oh, I know it's not love story. He's at Glasgow, I'm going to Stirling, so there's a distance problem right away. Who knows in a few years once we are both finished, maybe? It's not love, I do like him Rosie, but I'm not you babe. I don't believe in marriage, I think it's slavery. It's not what Lex wants either, he's three years older than us, this is his honours year, I'm just starting. I can't believe you are not going to uni with me? I'm still going to apply for camp America next year too, even though you're not going to be there. I want to travel, I know once I go to uni, it will be curtains for me and Lex I expect. But I'll always have good memories of him. I'm sure he's a tart Rosie, none of them are exactly celibate in that pub, so why would Lex...' Elaine looked at the floor, 'or Carl be any different.'

'I'm going to be sick!' Rosie cried rushing from the room.

Elaine followed her friend into the bathroom and stood watching. 'Here clean yourself up, I hate sickness, I hate being sick when I'm drunk. That's why girls should be being sick at our age.' Elaine handed a wet flannel to her friend and smiled. 'I think I'd be shit at being pregnant Rosie.'

Rosie sat back against the bath and wiped her mouth with the flannel, 'yeah cos I'm great at it, aren't I? Honestly, I want to cry every time I'm sick. I feel awful, each time I think that's it... it comes back. I've no energy and I just want to sleep. Mum says I have to keep drinking, so I don't dehydrate, but it's hard.' Rosie sighed and brushed away a tear from her face. 'I see all these other pregnant girls at the antenatal clinic, and they look wonderful, blooming they call it. I'm nearly six months gone and I'm starting to look like something from a concentration camp. Chiseled or what? Look at me, I hardly have a bump, but you can see my ribs.'

The two girls looked up as the bathroom door opened and Margaret Gibbs wearing her nurses uniform put her head around the door. 'Not again darling?' She sighed, 'I spoke to Dr McDougal this morning, she's going to see you this afternoon, that's why I'm home. So, get yourself onto your feet and clean up. Do you want me to call Carl?'

'He's in Leeds mum, I told you he was going to that brewery thing, because of the sickness I couldn't go with him. Rowena is staying with me tonight, but she's at her sisters, I'm not sure what the number is, I think she wrote it down and put it beside the phone.'

'Oh well,' Maggie said helping her daughter to her feet and handing her a clean towel. 'Elaine do you want to come with us? They'll probably do a scan, you'll get to see the baby. Is Lex away with Carl?'

'No, he has exams next week, so he couldn't go. Not sure who went with Carl, maybe Bobby? I'm sorry Maggie, I can't go, I'm working this afternoon. I'm already on a warning, so I'd better go, I'm on the lunch shift today, then a few hours rest and back out tonight for the quiz night. I owe Ashleigh a shift. I need to keep my job until I start Uni.'

***

Selina McDougal looked at the emaciated body of the young girl in front of her. 'My goodness Margaret, thank god you thought to ask about an earlier appointment.' She looked at Rosie, 'I can't believe this? You've lost ten pounds in a week. You are going to have to come in for a few nights and have some fluids intravenously. Is your husband not with you?'

'No, he's away for a few days. Can't mum look after me at home?'

'No Rosemary you need to be here. With your mum on nightshift this week though, you'll be well looked after. Hopefully it will only be for a few days. When is Mr Ranmore expected back?'

'Sunday afternoon, he only left this morning. He had to, it's a brewery thing, they're funding some of the new club.'

'I saw the plans in the Standard, Rosie. Very adventurous to turn that old eyesore into a club. I'm a bit old for that sort of thing but he's a bit of a local hero your husband, and so handsome. Right let's get you admitted, soon have you feeling comfortable. Margaret, can you go home and get her things? We can put her in 1C, I want her in the side room and kept quiet. Do you knit or read Rosemary?'

Maggie answered for her daughter. 'She's usually got her nose in a book, but she writes too Dr McDougal, all the time. She was going to Stirling University to study English Literature, but well, my grandchild got in the way. Davie and I are happy about it now and looking forward to a new life, but that's it for her until her children grow up.

'Not necessarily Margaret, lots of young women who have children go to university. These days it's pretty common, they just need a bit of support, perhaps Stirling is out of the question now, but there is Paisley or Glasgow. That's where I did my first degree, she could travel every day.

'She has responsibilities now Doctor, a husband, a house and soon a baby too. She'll be too busy for studying. How can she study for a degree with a small baby? Rowena her mother-in-law and I, we both work so we can't be looking after the baby for her. No, she's made her bed she will have to lie in it for now. As beds go though it's a pretty good one. Their new house is amazing, Dundonald Road no less, beautiful home. Carl, he got in an interior designer to do the baby's room. They are going to have a nanny too, really posh, she's landed on her feet with him. He is such a good husband, he's old enough to know how to treat a wife.'

'Sounds as though you should have married him Margaret.' Selina McDougal grinned and nudged Rosie. 'Better watch her Rosemary, she sounds as though she's after your man.'

'Right now, she can have him, I just feel so tired, I want to sleep, oh no I'm going to be . . . sick!'

***

'Hey babe, how're you feeling?' Carl sat down on the edge of the bed and kissed Rosie's cheek. He looked at his mother-in-law. 'What's in the drip, hope it's nothing that will harm my son?'

'It's just fluid to hydrate her, the other one is an anti-sickness drug.' Maggie said smiling and checking the cannula in her daughters' hand. 'She'll be fine, Dr McDougal says we'll will just keep doing this if the sickness persists, sometimes it does, how was your trip Carl?'

'Oh, it was enlightening Maggie, really good. They are well impressed with the new club, and even more impressed I managed to get the late licence, a first for Kilmarnock. It's going to be great, I've got good staff and should be opening around the same time as we have the baby. It's not every girl who has a club named after them. Hey, guess what Maggie? I got Lex a start with the architect who's doing the club for me. So that should help. I showed him the drawings he did when we first started talking about converting the old hanger. He was well impressed with the boy, he's going to work for him just now as a placement. Then if he does well, he'll get taken on full time. He should hear if he's passed his exams any day now.'

'He came in earlier to tell Rosie, it's brilliant news, he's so excited. I worried about his future, after losing his mum, I was afraid he would give up uni, but it made him work harder.' Maggie sighed, 'imagine our Lex being an architect he's worked

The Nightclub Owners Wife

really hard at university.' Maggie repeated. Tears pricked at her eyes, 'he still visited Simon every week too, apart from holidays, and he came every day near the end, he was helping look after Rebecca too. We always hoped that he and Rosie would be a couple, but now I'm glad they're not. She's a lucky girl Carl.'

'Comes from good stock Maggie.' Carl said hugging his mother-in-law. 'How long is she likely to be here?'

'Another day or two Carl, you should have her home soon. Back to wifely duties and a bit stronger, the drugs are starting to work now. Baby is fine, have you seen the scan picture?

Carl frowned and shook his head, he was annoyed at his mother-in-law's remark about Alex and Rosie. He knew Maggie didn't mean anything, however he also felt jealous of Alex and Rosie's closeness. Rosie was one of the few people close to Alex who actually called him by his name, to most people he was Lex. Carl had noticed that Alex often corrected people who called him Alex often saying 'Lex, he also introduced himself to new people as Lex Lockwood.' However, Carl had noted he never corrected Rosie. Carl knew from Rosie, that Alex's mother had been the only other person who called him Alex. The other thing that annoyed Carl was the fact Alex Lockwood was popular, and it was difficult to find anyone who disliked him, he was useful to Carl and he supposed a good friend, Carl did not really have any close friends, he didn't trust many people.

Maggie unaware of having upset her son in law, looked at him. 'No? Rosie show him the picture, where is it?'

Rosie, who had remained silent, listening to the interaction between her mother and husband, smiled, took out the polaroid picture from under her pillow and handed it to her husband 'here it is, they know the sex, but I said we don't want to know. I know you do, but I don't, and you said I could choose. Apparently, they can tell from scans, but I think a surprise is nice. Anyway, Doctor McDougal says it's all good, baby is growing well despite my sickness. I've got to rest a bit, but I should be fine.'

They turned around as the door opened and Rowena Ranmore came into the room. She was carrying a bunch of flowers. Her face clouded over when she saw her son. 'Oh, so you are back? I left three messages for you at your hotel. You were out partying when this wee soul needed you.'

'Got to earn a crust mum, I didn't get the messages till this morning some mix up with the staff at the hotel. I'm here now,' Carl frowned at his mother then turned to his mother-in-law. 'By the way Maggie, she won't be doing any wifely duties when she comes home. I've hired an au-pair instead of a nanny. The house is too much for one person, and Rosie needs to look after me, herself and my son. Her name is Giselle, she's French and she can start right away.'

'An au-pair, why? I don't need one, I told you I didn't want a nanny, but I'm going to have nothing to do at this rate Carl!' Rosie looked at the three people in the room and she could see her mother and mother-in-law were impressed by this news.

'You are going to sit back, rest and grow my son to be big and strong.' A bell sounded in the background, Carl stood up. 'Visiting is over, come-on mum let's go and I'll treat you to tea, can you wait outside whilst I say goodbye to my wife? You'd better get back to work Maggie.' Carl watched as his mother and mother-in-law left the room. He kissed his wife and smiled, 'You do look a lot better Rosie, there's some colour in your cheeks. What's with the note pad?'

'I'm going to write a book, I'm really bored, and I always meant to do it, I think I'm going to write a best seller. How does that grab you, your wife the author?'

'Yeah, a little hobby is probably a good thing for you just now, until you can make me your hobby again. I love you so much darling. Is it weird that I'm finding you very sexy just now? You look beautiful, the bit of weight loss suits you. I didn't realise you had such beautiful high cheekbones because your face was a bit chubby before.

The Nightclub Owners Wife

'I don't know what to say to that Carl, I'm a bit hurt you thought I was fat. I think I look awful. I have no boobs or hips I weigh less than seven stones. Everyone is saying I need to gain weight.'

'I bet Elaine said you looked too skinny? She was in the pub apparently, telling Moira how awful you looked. I think she's jealous of you, you're nicer looking and you're married to me. I had a bit of a row with her, she's a cheeky cow Rosie, she needs to go. She is good with the punters, but Moira and Julie are really pissed off with her giving them lip.' Carl sighed, 'the only reason she still has a job is because of you, the others are starting to resent her because she is getting away with murder. No one else gets three weeks holiday, she then argued over the rota when she got back. Hopefully she will hand in her notice soon.'

'No Carl, she's my best friend and she cares about me, don't you dare let them sack her? She'll leave once she finds something in Stirling anyway. Elaine isn't being nasty about my weight Carl, she was worried. She's never been jealous of me, she doesn't want to be married, she wants a career. Besides your mum and mine also keep telling me I'm too thin and my consultant says that if I don't put on weight the baby could be damaged. I don't want you thinking I'm going to stay this thin. I have no clothes and now I'm going to be really self-conscious you think I'm a heifer!'

I didn't say you were a heifer babe, you are a beautiful sexy girl, maybe just now you are a wee bit on the thin side. You've never been fat. I think it was because I was with Tracey for all those years, she was slim, obviously, her being a model, she had to be. Probably made me think you were a lot heavier than you actually were.

Rosie began to cry, and Carl immediately sat down and put his arms around her he kissed her head and looked into her eyes. 'You're just hormonal babe, look at me darling, you are a beautiful woman. You are the mother of my child and you're special. You're mine all mine, I love you and you love me.' He kissed her lips and smiled. 'I didn't mean to upset you, you are the love of my life Rosie Ranmore. Now you get back to your scribbles and cook our baby. I'd better go and take mum out to tea. If she comes back in here and see's you are crying like this, she'll think I've upset you.' He kissed her and quickly left the room.

Rosie stared at the window, she lifted her note pad and began to write, within a few minutes she had immersed herself in her story and her husband's thoughtlessness was put to the back of her mind. Rosie knew she had been a little overweight before she was pregnant. Although no one had ever said to her. '*Rosie you're fat!*' She realised that she'd always been a little heavier than she should have been. At her first antenatal appointment, her consultant had said she was within normal weight range for her height. She had warned Rosie though about gaining too much weight.

***

'Right Carl, you have some explaining to do? What the hell are you playing at?' Rowena Ranmore was furious, she pushed her son, who looked at her and then started the engine saying nothing. 'I want to know what you've been up to?' Rowena cried.

'I have no idea what you are talking about Mum!'

'Where were you Carl? Because you sure as hell weren't at a meeting. You also weren't staying where you said you were. You were with a woman, I know you were. Please tell me it wasn't Tracey again? I told you when you brought her to my house, stay away from her.

'Don't talk rubbish mum, it's over between Tracey and me. I told you I needed to talk to her, it was because she was upset. She'd only just found out I'd got married. I couldn't be seen in town with her. I could hardly take her to my own house, could I? I wasn't with her this week, as far as I know she's in New York. I was in Leeds for meetings with the brewery. The venue was changed at the last minute and I moved to a hotel nearer it. That's all that happened. I can't believe you're accusing me of this?'

'Carl, stop it, don't lie to me, I'm your mother and you might be a grown man, but I know when you're lying. You are married to a beautiful young woman, who is having your baby. You are going to risk all that for sex with a bimbo, because that's what Tracey is? Do you think I didn't know you had been in the bed in the spare room? It's not big or smart son. Please stop it now.'

'Mum, it's not what you think, it honestly isn't. Look can we just forget it? I did have a meeting in Leeds, and I haven't been with another woman.'

'You were in Leeds with Julie Muir, yet another tart, Carl. I checked when I realised you weren't where you said. I heard she's split from that thug she was involved with. If Tracey wasn't with you then ...?'

'What are you a fucking detective? It was business mum, I'm not sleeping with Julie. You are being ridiculous now. I'm her employer, of course I took her with me, she's doing a lot of the work for the new club. I had been going to take Rosie, but she wasn't well.'

'So why didn't you tell your wife Julie was with you?' She looked scathingly at her son, 'if there's nothing in it, why not admit she was there?'

'Because Rosie's young, pregnant, hormonal and, like you, she would jump to the conclusion there was something going on. Now can we go and eat please? I'll take you somewhere special. Then I must go home, get changed and go to work. Stop worrying mum everything will be fine. I love wee Rosie you know I do.'

CHAPTER

FOUR

'Hey bud, how was your trip?' Alex Lockwood looked up from the book he was reading. 'It's been busy in here today by the way. Now you and Julie are back, Moira and I can get a break.' He watched as Moira Jameson disappeared into the storeroom at the far end of the bar, 'mate you're not still doing Julie, are you? Why didn't you tell anyone she was going with you? You fucking promised you would finish it. I mean, I couldn't stand back and do nothing if you were. Rosie and her parents are more family than my own.

'Just say it as it is mate.' Carl replied, he lifted the bar hatch walked around and stood in front of Alex. 'Hey, there's nothing to worry about, I'm in love with Rosie, but it's just well... she can't because of the pregnancy who wants to be shagging someone who is spewing all the time. I'd be pushing my balls in a wheelbarrow if I didn't get a shag now and again.' He nudged Alex and grinned. 'You never worried about me fucking around before I got married? Julie, she doesn't want a relationship, she's quite happy to be my bit on the side. I was a bit worried when she finished with mad Ronnie. She assures me she's happy with our arrangement. Why the concern Lex? Hey, you are not exactly an innocent abroad either, you and I have had a lot of adventures. Surely you're not going all moral on me?'

The Nightclub Owners Wife

'I'm not mate, what we got up to before was one thing, but you weren't married to my little sister then, were you? You are now and Rosie, well, she would be devastated if she found out. She's a romantic wee soul, and you are going to struggle being Mr Darcy, aren't you? I told you when you got involved with her Carl! I told you I wouldn't be able to stand back and watch you hurt her. If she were to find out, she'd hate me for not telling her.'

'Well we best make sure she doesn't Lex.' Carl poured a drink from the vodka optic on the bar. After pouring a second measure in to a glass for himself and splashing the two glasses with draft cola, he walked back around the bar and sat down.

Alex pushed his glass towards Carl, 'I'm driving mate, and I need to study tonight.' He stood up lifted a clean glass and walking around the bar he opened the chill cabinet and picked up a bottle of apple juice. 'I mean it Carl,' he said shaking the bottle, 'I don't want to know because, Rosie, well, she's important to me, she's like my sister.'

'She's not your wee sister Lex though, is she? She's your girlfriends' best friend, your mate's wife. I don't want Rosie to know what I do, any more than you would want Elaine to know what you get up to. You and Moira, I know you were at her house the other night. How can you face her man when he comes in here? You watched the footie with him last time he was home on leave. She's a very attractive woman, but she's old enough to be your mother? I'm a bit shocked I've never known her to be with anyone else. I've always thought her, and Dougie were pretty solid, they've been together a long time?'

Alex smiled and shrugged, 'none of your business Carl, it's just, oh... just convenience. I'm not married either, so it's not like you and Julie, that is so wrong Carl, on so many levels.'

Carl looked slyly at his friend. 'Hey, don't knock it, fuck she's adventurous mate, she almost wears me out, sometimes my cock feels as though it's going to drop off. So, Mr Morality what is it with you and Moira? It seems the same thing to me?'

Alex shrugged then smiled. 'For Moira, I fill a gap for her when Dougie is away, suits me, she is an experienced lady and I don't really go with anyone else. I can if I want though, because I'm not married. Elaine and me, well it is what it is. I used to think it was mutually casual. She's always said she didn't want a serious relationship, but recently she's gone a bit nutty. I think it's the stress of starting uni, but she's taking it out on me. She got really fucking angry last week thinking I was with Julie. She knows Julie is doing someone but hasn't worked out it's you. She'll be away soon anyway, she's got a job in Stirling lined up, so hopefully she'll leave before she finds out about you. Or before Moira sacks her. Bobby is the only one stopping it. Elaine well she's a bit of a free spirit and I like her a lot, but it's hardly a love story, is it?'

'I hear Norrie Weston spoke to you?' Carl said picking up the glass of Vodka Alex had refused and scooping ice into it.

Alex grinned and patted Carl on the back. 'Thanks for speaking to Norrie, I'm really fucking chuffed about the job, means I can still work here too, fill in when you need me. I thought I was going to have to relocate to Glasgow or Edinburgh.' He looked Carl in the eye, pleading. 'Please mate don't keep asking me to cover for you with Rosie, its fucking hard I don't know what I would say if she asked me if you were doing it with someone else?'

'She won't, it's never occurred to her that I might be shagging elsewhere, partly probably because she's been so unwell, but she is a bit naïve about these matters. You're a good friend Lex, thanks for keeping schtum, I'll need to be careful though.' Carl sighed and shook his head. 'My mum, she worked out I was away with Julie! Colombo has nothing on Rowena Ranmore when she's on a mission.'

'Why are you doing it with Julie mate? Rosie and you, it could be something special?' Alex took a sip of the apple juice and made a face. He pushed the drink away, 'she's a sweet wee thing, and very loyal.'

The Nightclub Owners Wife

'Oh, it's the illness I think, I want to, be faithful, I mean to be, but you know . . . there you are jogging along getting excited and she starts spewing. Kind of off-putting that is. She's still got another three months to go. As I said, I wouldn't be able to put on my strides if I don't empty my balls.' Carl sighed, cupped his crotch through his trousers and grinned. 'It's a bit like you and Moira probably, perk of the job. Rosie, well, she's kind of shy, not very adventurous . . . It's great knowing I'm the only guy she's been with. The downside is, no experience, means you need to teach them. She's been pregnant and so sick, it will all need to wait till she's better, the training.' He winked at his friend before continuing. 'Although Lexie-boy, you don't want them too well trained because you end up with a Moira or Julie, then don't you? I know my wee Rosie will be faithful, she looks at me with that hero worship thing. The way your dog looks at you mate, when she does the *'Carl you are such a wonderful husband!'* I feel bad about doing Julie.'

'Obviously not enough to stop doing it mate!' Alex observed, 'What're you going to do about your Mum?'

'Oh, I'll just need to stop seeing Julie, mum she loves Rosie. Well she is a lovable wee thing, but I'm kind of hoping her first loyalty will be to her one and only. She went nuts at me last month, I panicked when Tracey turned up. I took her to mums, cos I thought she was out. Mum caught us together,' Carl grinned again and whispered, 'thankfully after I'd shagged her. She had a go at me tonight, apparently I forgot to straighten up the bed, she knew we'd been in it. At least she never actually caught us. Tracey, she's really flexible mate, fuck she can get into some interesting positions.'

The two men looked up as the heavy storeroom door creaked opened and Julie Muir came through to the bar. She was wearing a black jumpsuit which was opened at the neckline, showing a hint of her ample breasts, a wide leather belt emphasised her tiny waist. She smiled at Carl, 'you free for a few hours from babysitting?' She tossed back her bleached blond hair. 'I need to go over to the club and let the electricians in, fancy coming?'

The emphasis on the word coming, was not lost on Alex, who raised an eyebrow. He looked at Julie then turned his gaze back to Carl, 'well don't think I'm covering here for you two. I need to study, I worked all weekend when I should have been at the books. All so you could go on your jaunt.'

'So, you are doing a degree on Wilbur Smith?' Carl asked turning the cover of the book on the bar.' He looked up at Julie and shook his head, 'sorry Angel I can't, I've got to go visit my wife.' He downed the alcohol in his glass and put it down on the bar. Standing up he smiled, 'Lex seeing as you are sober, and keen to get back to studying, can you give me a lift? I got a taxi to come in here, I had to drop the car off for a service, Colin is doing it first thing. Julie you've had three days in a posh hotel, been wined and dined at the company's expense. You'll need to work tonight, so don't stay too long at the club.' Without waiting for a reply, he walked towards the gent's toilet. 'Lex, I'm just going for a slash and then I need to get home.' He called over his shoulder.

Julie turned her back and busied herself sorting out glasses. Alex watching her in the mirrored bar, noticed she was upset. 'Jules be careful babe, he's a great guy, but he's never going to leave her, you're going to get hurt.'

'I have no idea what you are talking about!' Julie said quietly. 'Carl is my boss and a happily married soon to be family man, Lex. It is what it is.'

'Julie I'm a man of the world doll, but this is hard, Rosie is my friend too.' He could see Julie was close to tears. 'Walk away before anyone gets hurt.'

'Why should I Lex?' Julie turned around and she looked angry, 'I was with him first, Rosie muscled in on me, not the other way around. Miss fucking innocent, he fell for her little girl thing.'

She stopped talking as the toilet door swung open and Carl came out zipping up his trousers, he lifted his suit jacket from the bar stool. 'See you tomorrow Jules.' He said as he walked towards the doorway.

Alex jumped to his feet, took car keys from his pocket and rattled them, 'okay mate let's go, I need to get back to the text books. See you next week Julie.' He lifted the novel from the bar and carried it outside.

'Fuck, this car is a mess Lex.' Carl said looking at the mud splattered paintwork. What have you been doing, rallying? The inside is as bad,' he pushed a hamburger box away with his foot, 'it's a fucking health hazard this car.'

'Julie's upset Carl,' Alex said ignoring the comments about the car, as Carl slid into the passenger seat of the BMW.

'I know, I noticed, I probably need to calm it down, don't I? I like her Lex, but she's just . . . a shag.' Carl sighed and then shook his head, 'she's too self-obsessed and despite the make-up and designer clothes she's a bit rough. She doesn't get why I married Rosie. Can't see what any man would see in her. Julie thinks looks are everything. She told me she loved me the other night but was happy just with what I could give her. Fuck sake . . . a tart with a heart, just what I fucking need, isn't it?'

'You really are a devious misogynist bastard Carl.'

'Yeah, you can talk, pot, kettle, mate? Now take me home Alexander Lockwood.'

'Thought you were going to visit your wife?'

'I'll go tomorrow with mum, I need to fucking sleep for a few hours. Just as well I'm not shagging Rosie just now, I'm exhausted.' He grinned, 'it's not easy being a stud Lex!'

'Yeah my heart is pumping pish for you!' Alex said grimacing as he glanced in the wing mirror and drew out into the street. 'Three beautiful women, three pubs and a club, you're hard done by mate! I'll drop you and nip over to Irvine to see Rosie if you're not going to. Maggie and Davie are going out for their anniversary, so she will have no other visitors if you're not going.'

'What a kind boy you are Lex,' Carl sneered, 'can you come in and take some stuff to her if you are going?'

CHAPTER FIVE

November 1996

Carl wrapped a blanket around his wife, he placed a glass of water on the small table beside the sofa. 'Do you need anything else darling? I'm sorry about leaving you on your birthday, but I need to go to this meeting at the club. Opening night is only a month away now, you've got the pager? Even a twinge, I want you to page me. I can't believe mum is staying over with Auntie Jessie again, she said she would stay here until the baby is born. I knew you shouldn't have given Giselle the time off to visit her mum.'

'It's fine Carl, I'm pregnant not an invalid. Your mum is worried about Jessie. You knew she was really sick after the chemo, well she still isn't right. Giselle's mum isn't well, and she hasn't had any leave since she came here. She's an Au-pair not a slave Carl. It's fine, I told you Elaine dropped in earlier with my birthday present, I was asleep, mum didn't want to wake me. Mum asked her to come over to sit with me tonight. I've still got a month to go. I feel like a great big turkey, look at me I'm huge.'

'You heard what the doctor said, it's mostly fluid and will go once our boy is here. So, stop it, you are beautiful, and I love you.'

The Nightclub Owners Wife

How can you love me looking like this?' Rosie held up her hands, 'I'm all puffy and swollen, you can't even see my wrists for fat now. I've put my wedding ring on the chain Elaine gave me for my birthday.' Rosie smiled, 'I can't believe you bought me a car and driving lessons.'

'Well you'll find it much easier with the baby if you can drive. Phil, the driving instructor, reckons he can get you driving in a few months.' Carl smiled 'did you like my other surprise?'

Rosie nodded, she looked at the envelope on the table in front of her. 'Thanks for the voucher for the personal trainer. As soon as I have the baby I'll get back in shape, I promise. Then we can make love again. Can't believe I started bleeding when we had sex, I'm so sorry. I promise I'll make it up to you when I'm better.

'Oh, you will too, six months without nookie, I'll be rampant.' Carl smiled.' What's Elaine up to? Thought she was in Stirling?'

'No, study leave, she's home for a couple of days. Will you see Alex tonight?'

'Not sure, he's been away for work, he might come in, he was in yesterday sorting out rota's I think. I never saw him because I was at the hospital with you.'

'Tell him I want to see him, I need to know what's going on. Elaine just said it was over, she never said why. Do you know what happened? Elaine was upset on the phone, she said she would tell me when she came over.'

'No idea babe and I don't want to know, whatever it is remember it's none of our business. Elaine's had this coming, she's treated him like shit recently.'

'Had what coming? Thought you didn't know what it was?'

'I don't, but I have a fair idea what's caused it.'

'Has Alex got someone else Carl? Tell me if he has? You would know if he was doing anything. I know you would.'

'Rosie, I don't know, I think he might be seeing someone. You should be glad for him if he is. Elaine and him, they're not good for each other. He's one of these guys who wants to be with one woman, a bit like I am now. If he is seeing someone I don't think it's serious, not that he ever discusses his love life with me, or anyone, the other stewards get up to all sorts, and openly discuss what and who they do. Lex is oh . . . I don't know, discreet, you know him better than I do.' Carl shook his head and looked at his wife, 'you always go on about him being like your brother, be happy for him when he does meet someone.'

'Who? Who is he with? I know you know something Carl. Is it Julie? Elaine thought they were doing it. Don't you think it's strange she never goes with anyone? She's been away from that Ronnie for months. She dresses and acts like a tart, but you never see her with anyone.'

'Julie isn't a tart Rosie, she is a really attractive girl with a great figure, and she dresses to show it off. Maybe she has got someone and just keeps it private. With Ronnie in jail maybe she maybe doesn't want his family finding out she has someone new? Look its none of our business. You rest up and I'll see you later.'

As Carl made towards the door he heard a car in the driveway. He walked quickly through the hall, putting on his jacket as he moved. Elaine rushed in through the door. Carl grabbed her by her wrist, pushing her back outside and closing the door behind them, he put his hand on her chin and squeezed. 'You say anything to upset her and you'll have me to answer to Elaine,' he hissed through gritted teeth. 'Fucking stupid cunt, how dare you cause a scene like that in my pub.' He grabbed her arm and pulled her around the side of the house to the kitchen door.

Elaine shook herself away from Carl and turned to face him. 'You knew he was having a thing with her, you fucking knew you prick. I'm going to tell her man, so I am, soon as Dougie comes back I'm calling him. He's away fighting for his country and she's whoring and touring. She's practically fucking old enough to be his mother. It's disgusting.' Putting her hand on his chest she pushed Carl, 'and you, I have your number pal. If

The Nightclub Owners Wife

Lex isn't shagging Julie Muir, you are. Do you do foursomes? I heard her and Ronnie were into all sorts. She's a common tart just like Moira, and I'll say what I like to Rosie, she's my friend.'

'You fucking dare tell Rosie anything and I'll fucking bury you Elaine. She's pregnant and has high blood pressure.' Carl hissed in Elaine's ear, 'do not tell her anything about any of this, it's all just rumours and hearsay. Don't you dare tell my wife. I swear I'll fucking swing for you if you do.'

'Don't threaten me, you don't fucking scare me Carl Ranmore. I won't tell her the rumours,' Elaine made a quotation mark gesture with her fingers, 'about you and Julie, only because I won't hurt her.' Elaine looked Carl in the eye before continuing. 'But, if you don't stop it I will tell her Carl, you're making a fool of her. She's my friend.'

Carl sighed, looking worried, he whispered 'Elaine, I swear I'm not doing Julie, there's nothing between us. Yeah, there was something briefly before I met Rosie. Convenience really, Tracey left town, I was lonely, Julie was there for me. It was a casual thing.' Carl looked at Elaine and made a face, 'I suppose she got a bit obsessed with me, but I only want Rosie and the baby now. You must believe me! I'm telling the truth.'

'You wouldn't know the truth if it bit you on the bum Carl. You don't deserve Rosie, you know she's too fucking good for you?'

Carl moved closer, 'Elaine please, I'm begging you, don't tell her about Julie and me? I don't want her upset.' He sighed, 'Elaine I told her I didn't know what you and Lex fell out over.' Carl leaned in towards Elaine, she could see he was upset, his eyes were pleading. 'I will tell her about Julie, I promise, just not yet, she's been so ill.'

Elaine shook her head, 'I won't for now, but you'd better not still be shagging Julie? If I find out you are, I'm telling Rosie, I swear Carl, I will tell her.' Elaine took a cigarette from Carl, they stood outside the door, their shadows falling across the gateway backlit by the streetlamp on the other side of the garden fence.

Carl sighed with relief, he looked over at the lamppost the light shining down on his face exposing the fact he was composing himself before he spoke again. 'When are you going back to Stirling?' He finally asked, his voice shaking a little.

'Tomorrow, I have exams. I won't be home much after this, I've got a job in Stirling now. Apart from my gran, there's nothing other than Rosie here now. I'm going inside to drink your booze. Then I'm going to sleep with your wife.' Elaine looked up her eyes moist, she made a face, 'I'll need to tell her about Moira and Lex, Carl. I can't keep that from her, she could find out from someone else, I won't tell her you knew.'

Carl nodded. 'Thanks, Elaine I do know how hard this is for you. I promise there was nothing serious with Julie. All I want is Rosie and the baby, I swear.'

'Are you going in to work now?'

'I need to, we are so close to opening the club now. I have a meeting with the council planners to go over the final building warrant check.'

'Can you take some stuff to Lex please? I have it in the car, I don't want to speak to him, and I think it's better if I don't come to the pub just now. I'm sorry about the scene I caused. I didn't see that coming, never thought he was seeing anyone else, and I certainly didn't think he would be into Moira. They were doing it in your office when I walked in.' Elaine sighed, 'they should have locked the door, you'd have thought they'd have been careful?'

'I'm sorry you got hurt Elaine, couldn't have been nice catching them like that?'

'Shit happens Carl, I've had better days, but I'll live. I know you don't like me. I'm not overly keen on you either, but we both love Rosie. Can we just try to get on for her sake?'

Carl studied the young woman's face. 'Yeah, I suppose, just don't come home from Stirling too often' he said smiling looking relieved. 'Now you'd better go in before she comes looking for you.' He shook the keys to his Audi, 'need to go and earn a crust. Come on open your car and I'll take the stuff, it better not mess up my cream leather upholstery?'

When Elaine entered the living room, she smiled, Rosie was sitting up in the big reclining armchair wrapped in a blanket with a book in her hand. 'Hey chick, what are you reading?'

Rosie smiled at her friend, she held up her book.

Elaine read the title 'Watermelon? What's it about?'

'Me, I'm feeling like a big watermelon ready to burst and I'm also a bit weepy I'm afraid. I can't get comfortable, my back is really sore, probably because of all the extra weight.'

'You look wonderful, big and fat, but wonderful. Happy birthday, not what we planned for your seventeenth still never mind.' She nodded at the chain around Rosie's neck. 'I see you got the present.'

'I love it, I've put my wedding ring on it, thank you, it's just what I wanted.' Nomee, Rosie's big ginger tom stood up and stretched, he looked at Elaine and walked towards the door. 'Can you let him out Lainey? He's been lying here all day, if he wees in the house again Carl is threatening to get him put to sleep. Elaine can you bring me in two paracetamol there's some in the kitchen drawer, the one under the side window. I have a headache I had to wait until Carl was gone, he doesn't want me taking any drugs because of the baby. The doctor said occasional paracetamol was fine.' Rose rolled her eyes, 'but Carl he gets worried, he thinks he knows better than the doctors. Get yourself a drink from the kitchen, you look as though you need one. I'm going for a wee.' Rosie stood up and walked towards the door. 'Then you can tell me what happened between you and Alex.' She looked at the cat now rubbing himself around Elaine's legs. 'You dirty stop out, behave and stay off the road.'

'God, you talk to that cat like he's human, come on bagpuss get out so I can tell your mummy my tale of woe.' Elaine nudged the large cat with her foot as she pushed him towards the kitchen door.

'That's what Carl says, I think he secretly likes Nomee. He did keep going and bringing him back from mums when we first moved here. Honestly, I think he likes him but can't let on. He does get upset about him, he sleeps in his wardrobe, pees in corners and things.'

'Who Carl? Thought he was house trained.'

'Oh, ha-ha, he's a bit OCD... Carl, not Nomee. Always cleaning up after me. Right, go get me some drugs, honestly my head is thumping and put Nomee outside before he has an accident. Carl's going to go mad if he does his business in the house again. Says he's a health hazard.'

''Well Carl and I agree on one thing at least,' Elaine said scooping up the big ginger tom as she moved in the direction of the kitchen. Elaine threw Nomee outside and shut the back door. She opened the drawer, smiling at the organiser inside she lifted the packet of pain killers then took a glass and poured herself a generous measure of southern comfort and opened the freezer. She concentrated on shaking ice into the glass. Hearing a scraping noise, she opened the door again, 'where are you? Fucking ginger fleabag?' She hissed, before realising the noise was coming from behind her. She rushed through the kitchen door and gasped. Rosie was lying on the hall floor, her body convulsing, eyes rolling, white foam was spreading across her mouth and chin. Elaine dropped the glass on the hall floor it smashed, the amber liquid spilled out over the black and white parquet flooring. Grabbing the telephone, she dialled 999, screaming at the operator she gave the address, as she dropped to her knees on to the floor. Rosie's teeth were chattering, her body shook, then stopped. Elaine shook her friend, then leaned in closer. 'Rosie, no, please don't do this to me.' She realised there was no breath. Rosie her face deathly pale, lay motionless on the floor.

Remembering long ago first aid training from school, where she and Rosie giggling like the young school girls they were, had practiced mouth to mouth resuscitation on each other. Elaine went into auto-pilot, just as their biology teacher had assured the class of teenagers they would. Elaine opened Rosie's mouth and pulled her tongue out, wiping away the froth on Rosie's chin with the edge of her cardigan, she began to breath into her friend's mouth. After what seemed like an eternity, Rosie coughed and gasped, her breathing although laboured was steady. Elaine stopped, checked Rosie's pulse then rolled her over onto her side.

Cradling the now still but very pale Rosie's head in her lap Elaine waited. Checking her unconscious friends pulse in between silently praying, *'please god don't let her die?'* and crying out. 'Please babe don't die, I can't be without you, you need to be okay.' Elaine knew she should call Carl, but she was afraid to leave Rosie's side, the telephone dangled from the hall table and Elaine became aware in the silence of a distant voice calling from it. She did not dare move away from Rosie though, terrified she would stop breathing again. Elaine heard an ambulance siren, faint at first and then louder she saw the blue light through the glass window of the door across the hallway. 'They're here babe just hang on in there, it's going to be fine. You're going to be okay.' Gently laying Rosie's head on the floor, she ran outside, leaving the door ajar.

A green jump suited female paramedic appeared and hurriedly followed Elaine back inside the house. 'Bert radio the control room, she's heavily pregnant.' She shouted over her shoulder. 'How long has she been out?' The paramedic asked, dropping to her knees and gently cradling Rosie's head in her lap. 'What's her name? How far along is she in her pregnancy?'

'I came in here just as East Enders was ending, so seven thirty, it happened just after that, her name is Rosie Gi...Ranmore. She's had high blood pressure and been ill. She's...she's about eight months, please save her, is she going to be alright? I think she's had a fit, she was convulsing then she stopped breathing and I didn't know what to do, so I gave her mouth to mouth.' Elaine began to shake the trauma now real, tears welled up in her eyes.

'Look Miss you need to stay calm, we need to get her to hospital, looks like something has gone wrong. We'll do everything we can for her. Are you her sister?'

'No, her friend, her mum is a midwife at the hospital, Maggie Gibb, I need to call her.'

'Has the baby got a father? She isn't wearing a wedding ring?' The second paramedic asked softly.

'Her fingers were swollen, she couldn't wear it. It's around her neck on a chain. Her husband, he's at work.'

'Call him sweetheart, he needs to know. We'll get her comfortable and into the ambulance. You try to get her husband, she's going to probably need a section tonight. The female paramedic put a stethoscope to Rosie's swollen belly and raised her hand for quiet.

Elaine lifted the dangling telephone receiver and dialled Nobels, to her horror Moira answered. 'What the fuck do you want? Haven't you called me enough names?' She said as she recognised Elaine's voice.

'Moira fuck off, this isn't the time, can you get Carl for me?'

'He's not here, he wouldn't want to speak to you if he was after the abuse you gave him, so you fuck off.'

'Moira please don't hang up,' Elaine said, her voice breaking. 'If he's not there he's on his way, he left here ages ago. Rosie is ill, she needs to go to hospital, it's bad, she stopped breathing, so don't hang up.' Find Carl, tell him he needs to get to the hospital quickly.'

'Elaine, he's not here,' Moira cried, 'If he comes in I'll tell him, but I really don't know where he is?'

'Well send your fucking boyfriend, my fucking ex to find him, because he'll know where he is. Then go take a fuck to yourself, and take Lex Lockwood with you, rabid old tart.' She banged the receiver back down and began to cry.

The male paramedic raised an eyebrow as he and the other paramedic strapped Rosie, now with an oxygen mask covering her mouth and nose, and a drip in her hand, onto the stretcher.

The Nightclub Owners Wife

'Okay sweetheart, keep breathing, in and out.' He said quietly to the still figure on the stretcher. He gently put his hand on Elaine's shoulder as she stood in the middle of the hall now shaking and crying. 'Can you lock up here and come with her? It may help if she sees your face when she comes around.

Elaine climbed into the back of the ambulance, the female paramedic strapped her into a fold down seat and then shut the door behind her, leaving Elaine with the male who was tending to Rosie. 'Boyfriend trouble?' He asked sympathetically, looking around at Elaine.

'You could say that, I caught my man with a woman old enough to be his mother. I've just had to speak to that woman, because she works for her husband.' Elaine said nodding towards the still figure on the stretcher. 'So, this isn't a great time for me, but this puts it all into perspective.'

'Plenty more fish in the sea!' the paramedic said smiling, 'he's a stupid man darling.' He added, looking Elaine up and down. 'You work at Nobels don't you? I live in Irvine, but my ex lived in Crosshouse, so we used to go out in Killie quite a bit. You served our lunch a couple of times.'

'Used to. I'm at Uni in Stirling now, so I work in a pub there now. Rosie's husband Carl, he owns Nobles. I'm just home for a couple of days, study leave.'

'What you doing? At university?'

'Journalism.'

'Wow, clever stuff, you going to be writing for the Daily Record some day?'

'No, I'm going to be presenting the news pal, that's where I'm heading, media, hopefully in London.'

'I'll watch out for that then,' the paramedic said winking at her. He continued to check Rosie every few minutes as the ambulance, its siren blazing, roared down the A78 towards Irvine.

'Is Rosie going to be okay?' Elaine whispered, 'it's her birthday today, she's seventeen.'

'Hopefully, if she got enough oxygen she will recover, the baby is okay we could hear his heartbeat. Nice and strong, I think you might just have saved your friend and her baby's lives. This young lady is going to share her birthday with her baby, I think.'

CHAPTER

SIX

'Where is she?' Carl Ranmore rushed into the hospital waiting room. 'What happened? She was fine when I left.' Two women in blue hospital scrubs sat with Elaine who was crying into a pile of tissues.

The nurse sitting next to Elaine stood up. 'Mr Ranmore, I presume? I'm Carole Caven, sister of the labour suite.' She nodded in the direction of the other nurse. 'Flo here will take you through to the relatives waiting room, I'll go get an update. Elaine good to see you, tell your gran I was asking for her. Mr Ranmore if you will just go with Flo here, I'll go and find out what's happening. I know you are worried, your wife was very ill, she's in theatre, we couldn't wait for you to get here.'

'What the fuck happened Elaine?' Carl shouted, ignoring the nurse, 'what did you do?'

The sister looked at him, 'Mr Ranmore!' She said sternly.

'What?'

'Please calm down, shouting will achieve nothing.'

'Did I fucking ask for your opinion?' Carl snapped, 'did I speak to you? I was talking to her.' He stood in front of Elaine. The rage on his face unmistakable. 'Where is my wife, where is Rosie? What have you fucking done, Elaine? I told you she was ill.'

Elaine began to sob, 'nothing Carl, I went to let the cat out when I came back she was on the floor she was ... she was rolling around, she almost swallowed her tongue. I was so scared. The paramedic thinks it's something called eclampsia. It's to do with her blood pressure. Carl please can I come with you to speak to the doctor?' They looked up as Maggie Gibb in her blue hospital scrubs rushed into the room her face white and shocked, she was followed closely by her husband.

'What happened Carole?' she asked the sister, 'I just got a call saying she was in here and to come quickly. I had just about finished my shift. Davie was picking me up. I went out to the car park to tell him I was running late, when Angela came out and told us Rosie was here.'

'She's in theatre Maggie they are sectioning her, eclampsia, her BP was off the scale. Luckily Selina McDougal was on duty, she just went straight to theatre. I'll go and find out what's happening, can you take Mr Ranmore and Elaine into the relatives' room?' She turned at the door, 'hopefully there will be some news.'

Seeing his mother-in-law's shocked face, Carl began to panic. 'Is it serious?' he asked, 'what is wrong, what is this eclampsia thing?'

Maggie looked at him, 'it's really serious, Elaine, was she conscious? Tell me what happened? How long was she fitting for?'

Before Elaine could answer the door opened again, the sister put her head around it. 'Little girl five pounds three ounces. Mums doing well too, Selina is still in theatre, but the baby is in the recovery room and she appears to be fine. Terry is just checking her out, then you can see her. Congratulations Mr Ranmore you're a father.' She hugged Maggie, 'and you, glamorous granny or what? You're not even forty yet, are you?'

'You'd better call your mother Carl.' Maggie said composing herself, 'Carole, can he use the staff phone?' She turned to her husband, 'Davie, call our lot and let them know. Carole, you are sure my granddaughter is all right?'

The Nightclub Owners Wife

The nurse sighed, 'the baby is doing well they say, hopefully Rosie will be fine too. She's young and strong the pressure will drop now it's out. You know all this Maggie, we just need to wait. The paramedics think she got enough oxygen and Elaine here probably saved her life. She is a wee star, remembered her first aid training from school stopped her choking, opened the airway gave her mouth to mouth as soon as she stopped breathing and put her in the recovery position.'

'I was really scared though,' Elaine said quietly. 'I've never seen anyone in a fit before.'

Carl put his arm around Elaine and hugged her. 'Thanks Elaine, for saving them both, Rosie and my daughter. I'm sorry I shouted at you.' He looked at the sister, 'I'm so sorry I was rude to you. I was really stressed. I'm a father, wow, can I see her, the baby?

'Yes, I don't see why not, come with me and I'll take you along to the nursery. You can use the phone first though, let her other granny know.'

Maggie hugged her son-in-law, tears in her eyes. 'I'm a Granny!' She whispered. 'I'm going to take Carl along to the nursery, Carole will you let us know when they bring Rosie out of recovery? Elaine come on love, if anyone deserved a cuddle of this wee baby it's you. Davie, you go and call everyone else. Tell them all not to visit until I tell them they can, especially my mother.' Maggie kissed Davie, 'go papa' she said, gulping back tears. 'While I take Miss Hero here to see the baby she saved.'

Elaine shrugged and followed them from the room. 'I honestly didn't know what I was doing, but at least it worked. It was like auto pilot. When can I see Rosie? She will be alright Maggie wont she?' Elaine began to cry again, Maggie stopped and swept her into a hug.

'Elaine, you heard what they said, you saved her and the baby, they are both alive because of you. So, you're my hero, stop crying and come see her.' Maggie looked around at Carl who looked a little crestfallen. 'Did you decide on a name? There were so many, and they were all boy's names you had. Did you even discuss a little girl? Are you disappointed it's not a son, Carl?'

Carl smiled and nodded, 'a wee bit I suppose, we were sure it was a boy. He was to be Carl, Tobias. She wanted to call him Toby, but I put paid to that, it's a dogs name, so I said she could have it as a middle name. She can call the baby whatever she likes Maggie, I'm just glad that they are both okay. At least we will never forget her birthday? Maybe next time eh? Girls names? Well we had it down to Miriam or Imogen, but who knows? I'll wait until Rosie is able to hold her, let her decide.' They stopped as they reached a door marked nursery. Maggie rang the bell and the door opened.

'Maggie, congratulations,' a nurse in white plastic apron and mask air kissed Maggie. 'Come see her she is perfect just a little small, and her temperature is a bit low, we are heating her up. She's a good weight and doing fine. Got loads of black hair, almost a pony tail. Now scrub your hands and put on a gown, is this Dad? You must be proud Mr Ranmore, you have a beautiful perfect baby girl. It should be two in the nursery at a time, so we won't count you Maggie, but be careful you might end up doing a shift.'

'Oh, she's beautiful Carl so tiny.' Maggie said a few minutes later as Carl Ranmore cradled his brand-new daughter in his arms. The tiny baby wrapped up in a white hospital blanket wearing a little pink wool hat, opened one eye and looked up at the man holding her. Then moved her little head following Maggie's voice. Both eyes opened, and Maggie gasped. 'She looks so like Rosie with her eyes closed, look at her little cheeks? When she opens her eyes though it's you Carl, she has your eyes.'

A nurse put her head around the door, 'Mr Ranmore, Sister Caven asked me to let you know, your wife is doing great. She's come around and is in a natural sleep now, she's going to be taken up to the ward in about ten minutes. I'm afraid you will be the only one allowed into see her tonight. Sorry Maggie, she'll be fine, you can see her in the morning when you come on shift.'

Carl kissed the baby's head and then handed her to his mother-in-law. 'Elaine, I'm going outside for a smoke, then hopefully they will let me see Rosie for a few minutes want one?' He held up a cigarette packet.

***

'I gave Lex his stuff, he said to say thanks. I'm sorry about you and him,' Carl said, as he and Elaine stood outside in the hospital car park. 'It must have been rough finding out like that?'

Elaine shrugged and blew a long thin line of smoke into the sky watching it as it rose. 'I've had better days, you knew, didn't you? Don't bother to lie Carl, it's not that I'm devastated, it was never a love story. I'm more worried about you being with Julie?'

Carl rolled his eyes, 'I told you there is no me and Julie, Elaine, well, not any more. Ok yes there was something, but it was before me and Rosie got together. It wasn't serious, more habit than anything else. Her man he's a vicious thug, he beats her up quite a bit, but luckily, he's in prison where he should be for the next wee while. She's talking about divorcing him and getting some sort of restraining order whilst he's away. I wasn't lying about it all Elaine, it was over as soon as I met Rosie. Me and Julie, like you and Lex it wasn't a love story,' Carl sighed. 'Like I told you it was convenience, a casual thing I thought for both of us. It was after Tracy left, well I didn't really want to get in to anything heavy, but you know? a guy needs sex. Julie, she was willing, and I suppose it was easy because of Ronnie being away. It was just sex, for both of us I thought. Julie got a bit possessive, I got scared and ended it. Then I fell for Rosie and because no one knew, you know? I never told her.' He took a long drag from the cigarette and then blew the white smoke up into the air, watching it rise into the night sky he sighed. 'I swear Elaine, Rosie and the baby, that's all I want now.'

'You'd better not be lying Carl, after what she's gone through tonight. She could have died. Both of them could have.'

'Thank God you were there Elaine, I don't even want to think about how this could have ended if you hadn't. Look, stick around till I go see Rosie and I'll buy you a drink. I don't know about you, but I could use one. Your car is at our house anyway, so let's get Maggie home, get a takeaway then you and I can talk. I want us to be friends Elaine, you're important to Rosie. Despite what you think, I do love her Elaine, I will make her happy.'

'Yeah well, you'd better Carl, because she deserves to be treated well, she really loves you. I love Rosie too, I want her to be happy. We've been best friends forever and I won't stand back and let you hurt her.'

'I swear I won't, I'm going up to see her, please wait downstairs with Maggie, we can talk, yeah?' He looked Elaine in the eye and smiled sadly. 'I promise Elaine, I love her, she's the best thing that ever happened to me. Look I need to go, I'm not going to believe she's alright until I see for myself.'

Elaine nodded and watched as Carl made his way back inside the building. She sighed and looked around her. She really didn't trust Carl Ranmore, but as she had just alluded to, Elaine loved Rosie, the sister she never had, and Rosie loved Carl. Elaine was sure it was just because Rosie had never really had a boyfriend before. Elaine just didn't think that Carl was right for her friend.

Elaine sat in the back seat listening as Maggie chatted happily to Carl as he drove her home. Elaine had not been able to see Rosie but had been assured by Carl that she was doing well, and in a natural sleep. Carl had been advised to go home get some rest and return to the hospital in the morning. Elaine was aware of him watching her in the mirror as he drove home. She rested her head on the soft leather interior of the car and sighed. The baby had been beautiful, and Elaine's heart had melted as she held the little girl, she had been startled when her eyes opened and Carl Ranmore's eyes looked back at her from the tiny infants' face.

The Nightclub Owners Wife

'Thank God she's gone,' Carl said smiling, as Maggie ran off down the path to her house. 'She never shut up the whole journey.' He looked sideways at Elaine who had replaced his mother-in-law in the front seat of the car. 'You look thoughtful Elaine, we'd better not go to the club tonight, I'm sure you don't want to see Lex or Moira?'

'Am I barred? You said yesterday not to come back in.'

'Of course, you're not barred, but I don't want any more trouble from you. Perhaps its best you stay away for a while, I take it you have to get back to Stirling tomorrow anyway?'

'Yip, I have exams starting Thursday I need to hit the books, I was going to go back in the morning, but I really do need a drink after what's happened. I'll have a couple with you and then get a taxi back to grans, get some sleep, then I can go see Rosie in the afternoon before I go back. I'd better not stay at yours now, people will talk.'

'I doubt if anyone would think there's anything between you and me Elaine, everyone knows you hate me. You've made your feelings clear on a number of occasions.' Elaine blinked as Carl drove into the driveway of his home and the big security light came on momentarily blinding her. Elaine's little six-year-old green Clio was parked in the garden next to Rosie's brand-new red Golf.

Elaine laughed, 'I kind of said some nasty things, didn't I? The whole of Kilmarnock must know you and I don't get on. Carl, I don't hate you, I just love Rosie. I told you earlier I don't want her to get hurt.' She followed Carl in through the garden gate and watched as he opened the front door taking them into the hallway. The shattered glass still lay on the floor, the brown liquid had dried into a sticky looking mess in the hours since Elaine had left in the ambulance with Rosie, she had a flashback to watching in terror as the paramedic had worked with her best friend, the siren and blue flashing lights still imprinted on her brain. She picked up her cardigan which had been discarded on the floor and shivered, remembering putting it under Rosie's head.

'I'll clean this up Elaine,' Carl said handing her the carrier bag from the Chinese takeaway, 'you can put the food onto plates then pour us a drink. I have a couple of bottles of Cristal in the wine fridge for this celebration, bring one out babe and pop it will you?' He looked kindly at Elaine, 'I owe my wife and baby's life to you right now. Let's be friends tonight?' He grinned, 'we can go back to disliking each other in the morning.'

Elaine shook her head but said nothing as she went off in the direction of the kitchen. She took two crystal glasses from the glass wall cabinet, found the champagne and popped the cork. Carl appeared in the kitchen with a dustpan and brush. The sticky looking glass clinked as he emptied it into a small box, then taking a large gulp of the champagne and putting down the empty glass, he disappeared outside to dispose of the box. When he returned to the kitchen, Elaine was seated on a high stool at the island stirring her curry with a fork, staring at it. She had poured them both a second glass. Carl took it from her and sat down opposite his wife's friend. He looked at the clock on the wall the clock hands pointed to midnight. 'Let's get pissed Elaine, properly wet this baby's head, do you want some blues?' The telephone rang before Elaine could reply and Carl reached over and answered it. She knew from the expression on Carl's face before he spoke, the person on the other end of the line was Alex. She said nothing as Carl gave the other man a very quick account of the evenings events. Pulling a small clear bag from his jacket pocket he tossed it on to the table. He smiled as Elaine took a pill and swallowed it, then repeated this, she washed them down with the champagne, all the time watching Carl. 'Yes, they are both fine mate, thanks for looking after things at the pub. Elaine? No idea mate, her car is here so I expect she will come back and get it in the morning.' He looked over at Elaine as he spoke. 'No thanks bud, I got a takeaway, I'm going to eat it, have a couple of drinks and go to bed. I'm shattered I'll catch

The Nightclub Owners Wife

up with you in the morning. Rosie? I'll let you know mate, I expect it will be a couple of days. They said she was fine, but I kind of need to see for myself. Okay, I'll tell her Lex, I'll go in and see her in the morning. She didn't know if it was New York or New Year when I was in earlier. Poor wee soul, she was lucky, the doctor who spoke to me said if Elaine hadn't been there, Rosie could have died. Yeah thanks mate I appreciate that.' Carl picked up the bag and shook out two pills, he popped them in his mouth and swallowed. 'Catch you later Lex.'

'What was he asking? Not that I actually care, but he was asking if you'd seen me, wasn't he?'

Carl nodded, 'obviously Moira told him about you calling looking for me.' Carl sighed, 'I was parking the car when you called. Elaine, I think he wants to apologise to you, he feels bad about you catching them like that.'

Elaine looked upset, she quickly turned away to gaze out of the window, standing up she opened the door and lighting a cigarette she stepped outside and leaned against the wall. The pitch black of the night became less frightening as her eyes grew accustomed. She jumped startled as the security light came on, Nomee strolled casually across the patio and in through the open door. Elaine threw away her cigarette composed herself and followed the big ginger tom inside. 'So, tell me?' she said sitting back down opposite Carl, 'what did he say?'

'He said he'd not come to the hospital because he knew you would be there. You heard me, I told him I hadn't seen you. I just wanted to be able to talk to you Elaine. In any case, you and Lex, it's probably for the best darling. It wasn't exactly a big romance, was it?'

Elaine took a large gulp of the champagne and pushed the still full plate away, the noodles spilled out onto the worktop and Carl immediately took a cloth from the sink and cleaned it up. 'No Carl it wasn't, but he made a fool of me with Moira, she never liked me, did she? Now I know why. How could he do that, she was at the high school at the same time as our mothers, just a couple of years below them. So, she's what 36, 37? She's fucking ancient. She's married too, I wouldn't fancy Alex's chances if Dougie finds out, he's a big man and he has access to guns. Different from Ronnie Muir, he's a coward and a bully, you could blow him over, but Dougie? Lex is a big guy, and he can fight, but I wouldn't like to put money on that battle, would you? Give me another pill Carl, it will help take away the urge to call Lex and give him abuse or try to phone Dougie. I bet I could get his number if I wanted to, his sister lives near my Gran.'

'Don't be stupid, you really don't want to do that do you?'

Elaine shrugged, 'what would happen if Dougie finds out?'

'He won't find out if you keep quiet though, leave it Elaine, it's not about you. It's what guys do, Moira is an attractive woman. Lex is young, he's sowing wild oats, I'm not too happy he was sowing them in my office, but I'll speak to him about that. Forget about him and all this. You have your course and you are going to be this big hot shot journalist. You're only seventeen, do you want to end up getting charged, you won't get much work with a criminal record? Elaine, if you do what you did on Thursday in the pub again, Moira will call the cops.' Carl sighed and touched Elaine's arm gently, 'look I shouldn't be telling you this but, Moira, she's leaving.'

'Really since when? Is she splitting from Dougie? Is she moving away? She's not leaving him to be with Lex is she'

Carl shook his head. 'Her and Dougie, he's coming out of the army and they're moving abroad, Cyprus, they've bought a bar there. She gave me a months' notice today. She's staying on until the opening but then she's off.'

'Can't say I'm sorry, do you think it's because I caught them Carl? I mean it's kind of sudden is it not?'

Carl shrugged, 'it's probably connected, but she's spoken about going abroad before. He's taking a package from the army, redundancy, and they are using the money to do it. You need to stay away till she's gone Elaine. I'm not kidding, you really have got to leave this alone and just get over Lex. Moira will call the cops if you come around shouting the odds again.'

Elaine finished her drink and poured another, she held the bottle out to Carl who drained his glass and allowed her to refill it. 'I know, I was just so angry, I couldn't believe he was doing it with her. Oh, I know him and me, we weren't exclusive, well, there was never any promise and it wasn't forever, but I feel stupid I didn't know. Feels as though you were all laughing at me.'

'I actually didn't know about them Elaine, it's not something he was doing a lot. I don't think anyone else knew. I think it was just one of those things that happened. You know what it's like working in the club, you get drunk, do something daft and that's it. Then working together, it can be hard to end it.'

'Was that the way it was with you and Julie? Just one of those things? If it was and it was over, why didn't you tell Rosie about it?'

Carl shrugged, 'I meant to actually, then she got pregnant so quickly, she was ill, and I just didn't know how to tell her. Everyone knew about Tracey and me, well Julie, it just kind of happened when Tracey left town. Ronnie got jailed, my Dad died, Tracey went to London, we just got into a habit. Ronnie is never out of jail for long, so it was safe, and I suppose convenient for both of us. I wasn't serious about her, I like her she's funny and great in the pubs. I know she's a bit rough and tarty, but I was never going to marry her. Was I? Rosie came along, I fell for her and she got pregnant.'

'How do you know you will be faithful to Rosie? I mean she's really sweet Carl, but naïve, she loves you. Did you know right away? That you loved her?'

'No, I didn't,' Carl smiled slyly, 'actually Elaine, it was you I fancied when you two started, not Rosie, you caught my eye.' Then I realised Lex and you were having your thing, he's a mate, and he's bigger than me.' He laughed, 'no I just kind of fell into it with Rosie, she's not the type of girl I normally go for.'

He leaned back and reached into the wine fridge and took out a second bottle of Cristal champagne, popping the cork, he filled both their glasses. 'You are more my type than Rosie.' Carl smiled and sighed, 'life is funny at times isn't it? If I thought about it at all, it was you.' He watched as Elaine downed the glass of champagne and refilled her glass.

'I better make this my last, I'm really drunk, and I've had four vallies now,' Elaine giggled, 'Who'd have thought it, you and me drinking as friends?' She drained the glass and jumped down off the stool, 'I'd better call a cab and go to my grans Carl. I'm really wasted cos I'm starting to like you.'

Elaine wobbled and fell against Carl who smiled and caught her. He kissed her on the mouth, she returned his kiss then pulled away, 'Carl I can't, and you can't either, fuck, I need to go home.'

'Elaine, I'm really sorry, I've been a bit sex starved lately with Rosie being ill, haven't done it for a while. I forgot myself there.' Carl sighed, and then looked at Elaine, 'you don't need to go home Elaine, you can have our spare room, or you can take Rosie's place in mine sweetheart. Come on I'll put you to bed?' Carl still holding Elaine up grinned. 'I'm joking Lainey, told you I love my wife.'

Elaine pushed Carl away, 'I can't stay here Carl, people will talk,' she said, her speech slurred. 'I'm pissed, really pissed, I need to sleep before I'm sick. I've never got drunk on champagne and I usually only have a couple of blues.' She staggered laughing as she fell onto the kitchen floor. Sitting up she looked up at Carl. 'What have you put in my drink Carl? You've got me drunk, and I kissed you. I'm going to tell your wife, soon as I see her.' Elaine giggled, 'help me up please? I just need to sleep.'

Laughing, Carl scooped her up and carried her along the hall to the stairs, at the top he opened the spare room door and put her down on the bed. 'I'll go and get you a bucket, babe, you might need it when you waken up.'

The Nightclub Owners Wife

'No, no I'll be fine, if I get to sleep, I will be okay. I won't feel sick if I just get to sleep. I just need to get my clothes off, and you can't look at me. I'm your wife's friend it's against the rules, so just go, I'll be fine.'

'I don't believe you Elaine, and I'm not cleaning it up, I'll lock up and get a bucket. You get into bed.'

When Carl returned to the bedroom after locking the doors and washing up the two glasses. Elaine was sprawled on the bed, lying on her stomach wearing only her bra and knickers. He placed the bucket beside the bed and threw the quilt over the sleeping girl. Then returning to the kitchen he opened a bottle of vodka, lifting his wallet he took out a credit card and a twenty-pound note, he cut a line of cocaine on the worktop and snorted it through the rolled-up note.

CHAPTER SEVEN

Carl crept into the hospital room. Rosie lay asleep, her face pale, and he was sure she was in pain. He had just come from the nursery, where he had held his baby daughter again. He looked at his young wife and bent and kissed her forehead. Rosie stirred and opened her eyes, she groaned as the pain in her abdomen shocked her fully awake.

'Hi babe, how are you feeling? Do you know where you are?

'Carl, the baby?' Rosie cried. 'What happened? Have I had the baby?' Rosie tried to move her hand but realised she had a drip attached to it. She looked up at Carl, 'what happened?' She whispered, she tried to move and groaned as the pain in her abdomen cut in to her like a knife.

'What do you remember?'

Rosie stared at Carl and then her brow furrowed as she tried to recall events. 'Elaine went to put the cat out and get a drink, and then I went to the toilet, my head hurt a lot. Now my stomach hurts. Carl where is my baby?' The confusion on Rosie's face was obvious, she tried to move and then cried out in pain again. Carl immediately sat down on the bed and put his hand on her head.

'Shoosh babe, we have a wee girl, she's 5 pound something. I can't remember how many ounces but she's beautiful she looks just like you darling. She's perfect and in the nursery downstairs, your mum is there. You had a fit and they had to deliver the baby by C-section, do you remember anything? You did wake up and look at me when they brought you back from theatre last night, but you were out of it. Then you had some serious bleeding during the night, and they took you back to theatre. So, you've had two anaesthetics in a few hours that's why you're so groggy. Are you in pain? The doctor said they had given you an injection of morphine, but when it wore off you would be in a lot of pain, you need to rest darling, our baby is fine. She's had loads of attention, lots of visitors, she's gorgeous, just like you babe. When you are feeling better tomorrow morning, they will bring her up beside you and we can give her a name.

'Can we call her Imogen I like that best. You're not lying are you, she is alright? Have Elaine and Alex seen her? Where is Elaine? Is she here? She was at the house, when was that?'

'Lex is coming in to pick me up for work. Elaine, well I'm not sure, she was upset after what happened. She saved your life the doctor says, but she was a bit stressed when we went back to the house. She was drinking she had a couple of blues, got a bit mad with it and I put her in the spare room. They called me back to the hospital about 5am, they needed me to consent to take you back to theatre. When I got back to the house she was gone, I just had a quick shower and came back. She must have taken her car, if she got stopped she would still be drunk I think.'

Carl stopped speaking as a nurse came into the room, she looked at Rosie. 'Mrs Ranmore you are in pain? I'm just going to give you some more morphine that will help and you should be able to sleep.' She opened the cannula in Rosie's arm and put a syringe of clear liquid in it. 'Just relax now and breathe slowly.'

Rosie, did Elaine say to you when she was going back to Stirling, did she have something on?' Carl asked stroking his wife's hair gently.

Rosie looked at Carl then closed her eyes, 'I think she had exams, she'll have gone back to uni likely. She had exams,' she repeated, as she drifted off.

Carl sat watching his wife sleep, wondering when it would be acceptable for him to leave. He had so much to do with the new club opening, he'd had an argument with Julie earlier. Carl knew he had to end it, but he also knew Julie had the potential to be a loose cannon. With her husband in prison, and her divorce from him underway, she felt that there was nothing to stop them seeing each other. Julie had told him she accepted his relationship with Rosie and would not interfere, however she had made it clear she expected them to also remain in a relationship. Carl knew there would be a lot of gossip if he was seen leaving her house which was in the middle of a housing estate. He was well known in the town now and his car very distinctive. He had been at Julie's house a few times but always late at night, he usually parked at the supermarket across the road and walked the hundred yards there, he always left before it was light.

Carl looked up as the door opened and Alex stood in the doorway, his large frame momentarily blocking the light. 'Maggie said it was okay to come up Carl, I saw the baby, she's beautiful, really like Rosie, but so tiny.' He looked at the still figure on the bed. 'Poor wee thing she's had a terrible time, she's so pale. She looks really like Simon lying there like that, it's scary how much like him she is when she's asleep, makes me shiver, must be worse for her parents.'

Carl sighed, 'yeah Maggie was crying all over her earlier, it's hard for Rosie the way they all talk about Simon, it's like she's always second best in their eyes. She told me once that she felt her parents would have rather she'd died than him.'

'I don't think that's how it is Carl, it's just that they had to focus on him for so long, Rosie kind of got forgotten.' Alex glanced at Rosie, he lowered his voice, afraid she would hear. 'Simon was their golden child I suppose, because they needed him to be, he wasn't though, he was just a normal boy.'

The Nightclub Owners Wife

'What was he like Lex? I've never really asked about him, she gets upset. They talk about him like he's some sort of Demi God. There's photo's everywhere in their house. Gives me the creeps, his bedroom has been left as it was and everything.'

'I think they always hoped he would come out of the coma, I watched it Carl, it was strange. We were just kids when it happened. I suppose him and I, we were always a bit wild. But Billy, well he was involved in a lot of other stuff. You know he was Ronnie Muir's younger brother, don't you? I don't remember much about the crash, we had been drinking, taking Valium Si had stolen from his granny. Billy took the car I was scared I suppose, but just went along with it. I do remember the police pulling me out and them working with Simon giving him mouth to mouth. Billy, well, it was pretty gross, he was already dead, so they just left him in the car. Alex shook his head, 'I see it sometimes in my head, not so much now, but the first couple of years were bad.'

'What was it like? The family before Simon got hurt?'

'They were a bit unusual I suppose, they were close, I suppose a bit spoiled. They were better off than the rest of us. Davie and Maggie both worked so Simon had a new bike when I had a second hand one. His room was decorated the way he wanted, they had quite a big house, so with there just being two kids they had their own rooms. They had a holiday every year, usually I got to go too. He was a great laugh, Simon, really funny, you know the type? witty answers to everything. Rosie was ... I suppose, quite shy.' Alex sighed and looked at the still figure on the bed, 'Rosie was always really quiet, always had her head in a book. It's weird, her and Elaine they are so different, but they have been inseparable since they were at nursery. Maggie, Elaine's mum Ingrid, and my mum were best friends since their schooldays. Elaine was always more outgoing. Rosie is as intelligent as her though, but it was always in a kind of dreamy way. Elaine was, a lot more in your face. I never really meant to get involved with her you know? I thought she knew it wasn't serious. Rosie never noticed guys the way Elaine did, she was always aware of her sexuality. Rosie was kind of sweet and that's I think why I feel so protective towards her. Davie and Maggie, they weren't the kind of parents who ignored their kids, well not before the accident anyway, I can't say I noticed anything. I think it was just you know? Scottish mums and their sons? Kind of like your mum is with you Carl?'

'What about after the accident? Did they just ignore her? Rosie never really talks about it, but I know it hurt her.'

Afterwards? Rosie, well she just got forgotten, she was always in the house on her own. Davie and Maggie, well they spent every spare moment at the hospital. Rosie, she spent a lot of time at our house, she got on well with my mum. I suppose that's why I think of her as my sister. Davie and Maggie, they were distraught about Simon.' Alex shook his head and his eyes were shadowed in regret and sadness. 'They had birthday parties every year for him, but not for Rosie you know? I always thought that was unfair, she was just a little girl. I remember my mum and Ingrid discussing it, you know in whispers. They tried to make Davie and Maggie see what they were doing. I guess their grief was just too much. It became all about Simon. He grew from a boy into a man in that bed, never waking up, I remember noticing that they started to shave him about the same time I started shaving. Funny the things that I remember about it. Sometimes I felt I just didn't want to go. I had a lot going on, my mum was ill too by then, but I went twice a week, most of our other mates stopped going.'

'So why did you?'

'Davie and Maggie . . . I couldn't do that to them, and well I just kept going. I think after he died they started to live through me if that makes sense. I became Simon, they were interested in everything I did. It's still a bit like that I suppose. They are nice people Carl. They just had that awful thing happen.'

'Rosie talks about you as though you are her brother Lex, it's kind of weird sometimes. I honestly did think you had a thing about her. How come you don't think of Elaine as your sister, if you all grew up together?'

Alex looked again at the still figure on the bed and sighed, 'no it was never like that, Rosie she was just a kid. It was different with Elaine I wasn't as close to her when we were growing up. We didn't see as much of her, she lived in Crosshouse. Elaine's mum took off just about the same time as my mum's health deteriorated. Ingrid, her mum, she met a guy and moved to Spain. Elaine was about fourteen at the time, didn't like the boyfriend, so she just moved in with her Gran who still lived beside us. That's when I kind of started to notice her. Before that I only ever saw her if she was with Rosie.'

'So, you never ever thought of Rosie that way?'

'No, well…not whilst she was young. To be honest just before she started in the club, I kind of thought about it, but then I started to see Elaine.' He glanced at Carl, 'then you and her got together, she loves you, so that's it. I'd never try it on. I do want her to be happy, I know you'll think this is a bit mad, but I value her friendship.' He smiled at the figure in the bed. 'She has grown into a beauty, hasn't she? Si, he used to tease her mercilessly, she was plump, and he was always calling her names, you know the way brothers do? If anyone else did it though, he got angry.' Alex stood up. 'I'd better go Carl, I'm kind of worried Elaine will come in, I really don't need another scene.'

'Okay mate, I'll just come with you, she's not going to waken again tonight.' Carl dropped a kiss on his wife's head and picked up his jacket. 'Did Moira tell you she's leaving, she and Dougie are moving abroad, fucking Cyprus…is it something to do with you?'

Alex smiled and shook his head. 'Nope, they are moving to the sun, think they've always wanted to do it. Dougie is coming out of the army and it's a new start for them.'

'Wish fucking Julie would go with her, save a lot of heartache if she did.' Carl sighed, he watched as Alex gently kissed Rosie on the cheek moving her hair away from her face to do so.

Carl, like Alex was an only child, he wasn't sure how you treated someone who you thought of as a sister. However, he thought Alex lingered just a little too long when his lips touched Rosie's cheek. Carl felt a pang of jealously as he followed his friend from the room.

Alex watched in silence as Carl flirted with the nurses, handing them complimentary tickets for the opening night of the club, now only a month away. He knew it wasn't just Julie, Carl wasn't capable of being faithful. Alex on the other hand felt that when he met the right woman, she would be all he wanted. He declined Carl's offer of a drink, didn't want to drink with this man tonight. Alex felt responsible for Rosie and Carl being together. He had never for one moment thought that Carl Ranmore would be interested in Rosie. Alex had encouraged her to spread her wings and had told her and Elaine about the jobs in the pub in order to watch over his pseudo sister. He had always thought of Rosie as just that. Recently however he had begun to feel things for her, things he knew he shouldn't, he realised he wanted to be more than a brother to Rosie, but this was impossible. If he couldn't have her himself though he wanted her to be loved and cherished, he doubted that Carl Ranmore was capable of loving anyone but himself.

***

After five days, Carl brought Rosie and the baby home. They had decided on Imogen as her name. She was a beautiful baby, quiet and content, Rosie was besotted with her. She was upset when Elaine didn't visit her during her time in hospital. She didn't respond to any of Rosie's attempts to contact her. She did send a card and a gift; however, it was addressed to Rosie alone. Carl told Rosie about Elaine appearing at the club and causing a scene. She had he said been very rude to him calling him names and making accusations about him covering up for Alex's behaviour.

CHAPTER
EIGHT

Club opening night

'Hey what's up? Carl was mildly annoyed, Julie stood weeping in the corner of the staff room. Moira was handing her a tissue from a box.

'Ronnie got parole, he's back in town. He came around looking for her earlier.' Moira said sighing.

Carl gasped, 'What? I don't want any trouble, not on fucking opening night, I don't need him here Julie, I'm serious I can't have it. Did the bouncers have to deal with him? I need to go home get changed and pick my wife up, so sort it out the pair of you. If Ronnie Muir is here, get him out. He's barred, and you better fucking make sure he remains away from here. I've got loads of important folk coming tonight.'

Moira shook her head, 'he had a right go at Lex, brought up all the stuff about Billy, trying to say he was the reason he died. Everyone knows Billy Muir was a wee toerag. Trouble from the day he could walk so he was.' She put her arm around Julie, 'you make sure you stay away from him, you should talk to the cops again, you might not be safe. If you want, you can stay with me tonight.'

'That's not the answer Moira, I need to face up to it.' Julie shook her head, then blew her nose loudly. 'I knew he would get out early, he's such a bullshitter with authority, he probably grassed someone up to get parole. I'm sorry Carl, Lex put him out, I think he's a bit scared of Lex now, he accused him of sleeping with me. Says one of his mates told him.' She looked at Carl, her eyes pleading. 'Maybe I should just book into a hotel or something. What do you think?'

Carl waited until Moira left the room before he answered. 'Julie, I think you should just go to Moira's tonight and stay away a few days. Ronnie is bound to fuck up and get lifted again. He's going to go back to jail sooner or later.' He made a face, 'Julie, I'm sorry babe, I don't want to add to your problems, but I just can't see you anymore, especially not now. I've got Rosie and the baby to think about, I want to be a family.' Carl sighed and started to walk towards the door. 'I just think you and me, have come to a natural end.'

'No Carl, you can't do that, you don't want to, what about this morning? What you said? I know you have feelings for me. I've been there for you, you are not going to just walk away.' Julie grabbed his arm, tears running down her face. 'You are not fucking doing it Carl, I need you. I've never asked for anything from you, you can't do this to me, not now. I need you.'

'Julie, what you need is to calm down before any of them out there hear. I don't want anyone to know about you and me. I'm sorry but it's over, and I think you should go to Moira's just now and chill, we can manage without you.' Carl was beginning to feel irritated. Julie, mascara running down her face dripping off the end of her nose, disgusted him.

Julie reached out to Carl, but he pushed her roughly away. She fell in a crumpled heap on the floor sobbing dramatically. 'Carl don't leave me, I promise I won't tell anyone, it can go back to the way it was. You know we are good together, please Carl don't do it. I'm begging you, I love you and I know you love

The Nightclub Owners Wife

me.' Julie grabbed Carl's leg and held on to it, Carl now furious, kicked her away.

'Enough Julie we open in three hours, go home... stop your drama queen nonsense, we'll talk in the morning I promise. I need to go and pick Rosie up, you are in too much of a state to be here tonight.'

The door opened, Alex appeared in the room, seeing Julie sitting on the floor he moved over and gently helped her to her feet. 'Carl what have you done?' He gasped. 'Jules, come with me, I'll take you to Moira's. That's the best place for you just now.'

'I haven't touched her she's lost the plot, I so do not need this tonight of all nights.' Carl was now so angry he could not contain himself. He pointed at Julie and then turned to Alex. 'Get her to fuck out of here Lex, take her home, drop her and get back here. Just get her out.'

'Carl stop shouting, everyone can hear you, go pick up Rosie and I'll take Julie to Moira's. You can talk in the morning, sort this out... in private.'

'There is nothing to fucking sort out, its fucking over, now get this mad bitch out of here.' Carl shouted, his face red and angry, he turned and looked at Julie, 'don't come back. I don't want to see your face around here anymore, I'll pay you till the end of the month, but find yourself another job.' Pushing Alex aside he made for the door.

Julie jumped in front of him, 'don't you fucking dare, you are not just dumping me, acting as though I meant nothing to you. I'll go out there and tell everyone about us. The whole fucking world Carl, including your little wife. What makes her different from me? She got herself pregnant to trap you, you are a fucking fool Carl. Little fucking virgin my arse, she took you from me, and I will fucking tell her I swear I will.'

In response Carl grabbed her chin and squeezed he pulled her face close to his, 'you say one word to my wife or anyone else, you fucking trollop, and I'll fucking bury you on the Moor Julie. You are a tramp babe, a piece of rough, my wife has more class in her little finger than you have in your whole fucking body. So just try it Julie and I will fucking have you, you mean nothing to me, you were a ride nothing more. Just a fucking spunk bucket, so just fuck off and don't come back.'

Alex moved towards Carl, 'you are right out of order Carl, stop it, don't speak to her like that.' He pushed Carl away and handed Julie a tissue.'

Carl looked at Alex, 'Lex, it's none of your business, keep your big nose out of it. I won't say it again, get her fucking out of here. I don't care where you take her, preferably the fucking station, better still the fucking airport, but get this piece of shit out of my club.' Carl left the room slamming the door behind him. 'Get back to fucking work!' He roared at the staff milling around in the bar area outside the staff room. 'I pay you to fucking work, and if one word of my business leaves this club, heads will roll. There are plenty of people on the dole who would love to work here.'

Alex led Julie who was still crying out into the car park, 'Jules, I don't know why you are in this state babe? You must have known he was using you? I don't get why this is a shock. You shouldn't have threatened to tell Rosie. This has nothing to do with her, she's the only one in this mess who hasn't done anything wrong, and she's going to get hurt, Jules don't do it. Don't tell her, you need to get on with your life, find another job, you are a good barmaid. Walk away and hold your head up. There's nothing to keep you here now, get away. You could have your own place, there are plenty of breweries who will offer you a tenancy.' He looked at Julie, 'you're not going to tell wee Rosie, are you?' This has nothing to do with her. You know Carl seduced her as well?' Alex handed Julie a clean white hankie.

Julie shook her head, 'I'd no intention of telling her Lex, I was just angry at him. He has really used me, and I've let him. I don't know why I thought he would eventually realise he loved me, I honestly did think he cared about me.' She blew her nose then smiled, 'you are as bad as him, with your crush on wee

The Nightclub Owners Wife

Rosie. What is it about her Lex? She's got a nice enough face I suppose, but she's a chubby wee thing isn't she, and she is just a little girl really, what is she? 17? She's not even age to drink in pubs yet.'

Alex unlocked his car door and held it open. 'Get in Julie and I'll take you home. Walk away and don't look back if you want my advice. I do think you should stay at Moira's tonight, at least you will be safe. If the kids are at your mums then you don't need to go back to yours, do you?'

Julie shook her head, 'It's okay Lex, I think I'll just walk home, I need the fresh air and the thinking time.' She kissed Alex's cheek and smiled through tears. 'You are a gentleman Lex, nothing like your mate. What about you and Moira? '

'There is no me and Moira, we are friends, friends with benefits, I suppose, but surprisingly she loves Dougie. I think she just gets lonely and I'm more than willing to keep her company. There's no strings with us, I enjoy her company and I like her. It's not a love story though. Now she's moving on, I'll miss her but it's time for her and Dougie to sort things out and move on to a new life.'

Julie smiled, 'what about Elaine? She was raging, aren't you worried she'll tell Dougie? He's a big guy Lex, I know you are too, but not sure who would win in that fight?'

'Oh, I'm younger and stronger Jules. I don't think it'll ever come to that. There are things you don't know about Moira and me.'

'Like what?'

'That's for her to tell you, not my tale to tell. Let's just say Dougie is not as blind to my arrangement with Moira as you think.'

'He knows?' Julie gasped. 'How? You're not into weird stuff surely? You know Ronnie used to make me do stuff, threesomes and the like, he's a bit I suppose kinky. I kind of did it when we were first together would you believe, because I was afraid of losing him. Then later what I'd done disgusted me. He began to force me to do it, used to bring his mates home, to you know? I never thought Dougie was like that.'

'Oh Jules, I'm sorry, I'd heard rumours about it, but I just thought you were into it too. Each to their own if no one is getting hurt. It wasn't anything like that with me and Moira.' Alex put his hand on Julie's shoulder and squeezed. 'You really need to realise you are worth more than that. Get your shit together, guys like Carl are only interested in themselves. Ronnie is just a poor version of Carl babe.'

Julie wiped her eyes and nodded. 'I know but it's hard to get out of these things. Ronnie, I was a kid, just fourteen when we got together. Carl, well he made me feel special, anyway it's all over and as you say time to move on. What happened with you and Moira? I can't believe she never told me. Wont Dougie come after you if you were having an affair with his wife?'

Alex shrugged, 'no it's nothing like that, we had an arrangement. Look forget about it, I'm in no danger from Dougie.' He smiled and kissed Julie's cheek, 'and he's in none from me, besides it really is over, and we've all stayed friends. Right, for now though, I'm more worried about you. Should you be alone with Ronnie about? Do you want me to give him a doing? I'd love to, he brought up the stuff about Billy tonight, that was difficult. If I do anything public, I'll lose my stewards licence and I need to keep myself clean with my new job and everything. However, there are plenty of dark alley's I could pull him into, just him and me. I would just give him a few slaps nothing more.'

Julie shrugged, 'he thought you and I had something going on, so he got a bit territorial I suppose.' She looked at him sadly then touched his cheek. 'I wish it was you and me, I don't think you would ever treat a woman the way Carl has treated me.'

'You are a special lady Jules, but you need to find a man who loves you back. Are you sure you'll be alright? How do you know Ronnie won't bother you again tonight?'

The Nightclub Owners Wife

'I'll be fine Lex, he's just out, he'll go and get drunk and fall asleep somewhere. I've changed all the locks on the doors and the kids are at my mums so I'm not worried. If he's out on parole, he won't want to bring attention to himself, he's ended up back in jail before for breaching his licence.' She turned and closed the car door then looked at Alex. 'The stuff with Billy, the Muirs, they blame you and Simon for it, yet they all know Billy was wild. He was the one who led you two astray not the other way around. Ronnie's mum she's an old cow, going on about her perfect son.

'We were kids, the Muirs house was fun to be in, she let us do stuff our parents didn't. All the lads used to go there. When you are that age you think someone like that is a cool mother. She did love Billy.'

Yeah, she probably did, but if she had maybe laid off the gin and parented the boys, instead of trying to be a cool mum, he might not have been the wee shit he was.' Julie shook her head, 'be careful though Lex, Ronnie, well, he's not like the others, there is a cruel streak in him, don't underestimate what he will do. He's a coward and a bully, he will target the weakest link.' Julie smiled stood on tip toe and kissed Alex's cheek. 'See you around big man.'

Alex smoked a cigarette as he watched Julie head off in the direction of the town centre, then returned to the club. Moira told him Carl had gone. Alex was glad. He realised that he had to rethink his friendship with Carl and possibly with Rosie, which meant leaving his job. Carl's behaviour recently had become erratic. Alex wasn't sure what was causing it, Carl did take a lot of drugs mixing them with alcohol. Uppers, downers, coke, party drugs, Carl did them all. Alex worried about Rosie and still felt the overwhelming need to look after her. He knew he should be thinking, '*she's made her bed she needs to lie in it!*' However, he felt however that with Rosie's naivety, it could all end in tears. He was forced into a dichotomy, could he protect Rosie and separate himself from Carl?

CHAPTER

NINE

'Did you call Elaine?' Carl asked as he drove towards the town centre. He glanced at his wife, 'is she going to behave if she comes?'

Rosie knew Carl was irritated, she didn't care. She was deeply hurt and confused by Elaine's behaviour, however she was angry with Carl. feeling he was in some way to blame for Elaine's absence. Rosie had always shared her life with Elaine, and she wanted to see her. 'Oh, you don't need to worry, she didn't answer. I called her Gran's and she wasn't there either, so she won't come to the opening. I know you hate Elaine, but she and I ... she's always been there for me. I don't have a lot of friends Carl, and well ... it gets lonely.'

'You don't need friends you have me. Now the club is open, I can spend more time with you. We can get a wee holiday booked, get some sunshine. Tell you what, you get your baby weight off, get your bikini body babe, and I'll book us our honeymoon. How do you fancy Mauritius? Or the Maldives?' We can take Imogen with us, some bonding for us and for her, but if we have Giselle with us we can get some time to make a little brother for her too.' He changed gear and put his hand on Rosie's knee. 'What do you think babe?'

The Nightclub Owners Wife

'You think I'm fat, you want me to look like Julie Muir?' Rosie felt tears gathering at the corners of her eyes.

'I've just said I'll book us the holiday of a lifetime, make another beautiful baby and that's what you heard? Me saying you'll enjoy it more if you feel good about yourself? Julie has a great figure, but she's naturally like that, you have a cuddly body babe, you'll always have to watch your weight. You're my wife and I can't have the staff in the club looking better than you, can I? Now stop crying before your make up runs. I think this is post-natal depression babe. Moira was saying that her sister was bad with it. Apparently, the side effect of the tablets they gave her was weight gain though, so you don't want that. It's all that sitting about scribbling, you need to do something where you are using up energy, last night when we were making love you weren't interested, you were in tears, it's that thing babe. Men need sex to feel good, women need to feel good to have sex. You were just conscious of how much baby weight you're carrying?'

'I was crying because I was in pain Carl, I don't think my scar is healed properly, and it hurt. I told you I just wasn't ready, it wasn't you, I know you were being gentle, but it has only been four weeks.'

'I know babe, but I wanted you so much, I just couldn't wait to be with you again. You said yourself . . . I have been more than patient. You also knew I wanted another baby quickly, hopefully if you fall, this one will be different, and you won't be as ill. Dr McDougal said that you had just been unlucky, didn't she? Hey, the bright side is if you are sick again the way you were with Imogen then you will look great when we are on holiday.'

Rosie tried not to cry at her husband's insensitivity, she knew Carl had her best interests at heart. Knew she was conscious of how much weight and how flabby the baby had left her. She had been, she realised, writing quite a lot, but she hadn't felt well enough to do anything else. Carl was right, he had said he wanted to have another baby quickly. Imogen, he said needed a brother or sister to grow up with. Carl had hated being an only child, but he was also desperate for a son. He had admitted to her he was disappointed when Imogen wasn't the longed-for son.

Rosie missed Elaine, she was confused and hurt by her disinterest in the baby and her keeping her distance. Until the night Imogen was born she had spoken to Elaine every day. Neither Alex nor Carl would admit to knowing why Elaine was ignoring her. Rosie was sure that if she could just talk to Elaine find out what happened, then she could sort it all out. With her mother and Rowena both working, Rosie had felt starved of female company for the last month.

'Hey, stop it babe, stop crying, we are nearly at the club, and they have put the red carpet out. The local paper photographer is there, we're doing it Hollywood style. You are a beautiful woman, I don't know why you don't realise how gorgeous you are babe.' He drew over to the side of the road and pulled Rosie into a hug, kissing her wet face. He held her and looked into her eyes. 'Darling I just want you to be happy, I want what's best for you. I love you and I'll love you whatever you look like. Now sort your make up and let's arrive looking like the happy couple we are.'

'Carl, I really don't feel well, can you take me home? I'm sweating, and my heart is beating really fast.' Rosie grabbed his arm. 'I can't breathe ... Carl I'm scared. I feel really hot and I can't breathe!' Opening the door, ignoring Carl's protest, she unfastened the seatbelt and stumbled out onto the road. She leaned on the fence at the side of the kerb and vomited, unaware people walking past were looking at her.

'It's okay folks!' Carl called out walking towards Rosie, 'she's having a moment, she's fine aren't you babe?' People walked on, some looking back, many of them Carl knew were heading to the opening of his new club. 'For fuck sake Rosie, you're making a show of me, take a fucking long slow breath, silly cow,' he hissed. 'You're having a panic attack. I know cos my mum used to have them after my dad died, fucking women, you are all fucking mad.' Carl grabbed her arm roughly and pulled Rosie towards him, 'breathe slowly and let yourself relax, get back in the car. I've got some Valium in the glove compartment. Get back in and keep breathing slowly, I'll give you a pill that will help. You need to be there tonight, Rosie, it's important. I promise you if you just come with me for the opening ceremony, I'll ask Lex to take you home afterwards.'

Aware now of people passing and staring at her, Rosie gulped and got in the car, she still felt her heart beating wildly and she needed the toilet. Shaking, she leaned forward. Carl opened the glove compartment and took out a small bag with several blue tablets in it. Rosie didn't care where they had come from, she quickly swallowed two and took a drink from the bottle of water her husband held out. She'd had Valium before, after the accident when Simon was hurt, her mother had given her one, she remembered sleeping through the night. Rosie knew Elaine often took pills, but she never did. Breathing slowly and with difficulty, she felt calmer after a few moments. By the time they drove into the car park under the club she felt herself drifting away, as the champagne she had drunk with Carl earlier mixed with the Valium. Closing her eyes, she leaned back on the head rest and to Carl's dismay she slept.

***

'Lex?' Carl hissed coming in from the staff entrance to the club, I need you to take Rosie home for me. She's fucking nutted. She had a panic attack I gave her two blues, I had some in the car, she's passed out. Can you take my fucking car and get her home! Just throw her into bed and come back.'

Alex took the set of keys from his boss, 'where are you parked?' His eyes narrowed as he looked at Alex, his face showing he was concerned, 'if she's sparkled, surely someone should be with her? Was she drinking too? Rosie's not used to drink and drugs, it could be dangerous. I can't just leave her and come back. What about Elaine, can't you phone her to go around.'

'No, I'm not phoning that psycho, she's been staying away from Rosie and it suits me for that to be the case Lex.' He nodded in the direction of the door, 'the car is underneath in the staff car park. Just go get it and take her home, the au pair can see to her.' Seeing Alex look of disgust Carl sneered, 'If you're that worried, you fucking stay with her, it's not as though you will be needed here, there are other bouncers. Did you take Julie home by the way? Was she calm? She'd better not be going to cause a scene? Where is her fucking man? Did you warn him off?'

'What?'

'Did you take Julie home? Simple question Lex, needs a simple answer, yes or no?'

'No, she didn't want a lift, she wanted to walk. She's not bothered about Ronnie, she says he was really drunk and will just fall asleep somewhere. Why are you bothered? She told me she had no intention of telling Rosie anything.'

'I need a hostess, if Rosie is out of it, I'll need to ask Moira, so Julie will need to cover for her.'

'You fucking sacked her Carl, I don't think she will be back here tonight, and anyway it's all for the best. You are going to end up with Rosie finding out about you if you don't stop it. You are fucking losing it mate, lay of the fucking drugs for a while and you might remember stuff. Leave Julie be, she will get over you quicker if you just get out of her life.'

'If I need your advice Lex, I'll fucking ask for it . . . Bobby . . . where the fuck are you?' Carl called out.

Bobby appeared from the store room, followed by Moira who was carrying a magnum of champagne. 'What?' He asked putting a box of wine glasses down on the bar.

'Have you got cover for Julie?'

'Of course, I have.'

'Moira, my wife is ill, so you need to be hostess tonight, you'll probably do it better than her anyway. Right fuck off Lex and get Rosie home, don't hurry back.'

The Nightclub Owners Wife

Alex slid into the driving seat, the leather recently vacated by Carl still warm, he nudged Rosie, she stirred and opened her eyes looked at him and then closed them again. 'I'm so cold,' she murmured. Alex looked around he couldn't see anything to cover Rosie with, Carl had just taken delivery of the brand-new Range Rover Sport and Alex breathed in the new car scent. He took off his dinner jacket and put it over the sleeping girl.

Starting the motor, Alex turned off the radio and flicked on the heated passenger seat switch. He drove up the ramp and out onto the street, as he passed the entrance to the club he smiled and raised his hand in a wave. Moira, wearing a long dress stood beside Carl posing for photographs. Smiling broadly, she waved back as Dougie, standing a few feet away from the door with a cigarette in his hand, saluted Alex.

Rosie slept throughout the journey, Alex tried to waken her when they arrived at her home. The security light came on and he could see she was in a deep sleep. Eventually, unable to rouse her, he scooped Rosie up and carried her through the front door. She sighed as Alex laid her down on the king-size bed, he took off her shoes and decided against removing her clothes. As he put the quilt over her she opened her eyes. 'Where am I?' She whispered, 'where's Carl? Alex is that you?' she said struggling to keep her eyes open.

'Yes, it's me, Carl had to stay at the club, you were out cold, so he asked me to make sure you were safely home.' Alex sat down on the edge of the bed, 'are you okay babe? I'll go get you a drink, you might want to take that dress off, where are your jammies?'

Rosie rumbled around with her hands trying to put them under the pillow, Alex helped her sit up and lifted a pair of pyjamas from under it. 'Rosie babe, you will need to undress yourself babe, I can't, it wouldn't be right.' Seeing her trying to unzip her dress he moved over and pulled the zip down for her handed her the flowery patterned pyjamas and then quickly left the room. When he returned with the mug of warm milk, she was on the floor, the dress around her head. Alex took a deep breath as he helped her up. He sighed, and quickly pulled it over Rosie's head, seeing the control underwear she wore, he quickly stripped it from her, trying not to look at her body. He helped her dress in the pyjamas, whispering in her ear, 'this stays between us Rosie.' He realised though he was aroused at the thought of her, the softness of her skin, he breathed in her perfume and the sweet scent of her hair as he put the quilt around her. 'Drink this babe, it will dilute the Valium hopefully,' he said handing her the mug and helping her to drink.

'Alex, I'm sorry, you're missing the opening because of me,' Rosie whispered becoming aware of her circumstances. 'I'm so sorry you got left with looking after me when you should be partying. Thank you. Look just go back to the club, I'll be fine.'

Alex smiled he bent down and kissed Rosie's cheek, then looked at her. 'No, I'm fine babe, I think I'll raid your fridge and have something to eat. I'll wait till you're settled, your au-pair is upstairs anyway. Alex looked at Rosie who was already closing her eyes and drifting back to sleep. 'I don't think me missing a couple of hours will make much difference, I've kind of lost any enthusiasm for the party anyway. There's a good film on so I'll go downstairs and watch it on your big telly if that's okay?'

***

The door was tapped lightly, and Giselle the Ranmore's French au-pair stood in the doorway. Alex lifted the remote control and turned down the sound on the film. 'Hope this is important there's only five minutes to go.'

'Monsieur Carl, he call, you had the television much loud you no hear the telephone. He say, I must go to the party, you mind Imogen. Is okay? He said you call the club.'

Alex shrugged, 'I don't mind staying longer, but what about the baby? I don't know what to do with babies.'

'She fed and changed, she sleep through night now, she angel, good baby, never cry.' Giselle already heading back out

The Nightclub Owners Wife

the room called, 'I've made a bottle, yes? It in the fridge. Put in warm water, you make it how you say ... tiède.'

'Tepid?'

'Tepid yes? Test ... How you say ... poignet, yes?' Giselle made a gesture of shaking onto her wrist. 'Remember you must call Monsieur Carl, he say it important. I going to make me beautiful. Call me taxi, yes? You call Monsieur Carl? Yes?' She added as Alex reached for the telephone.

'What the fuck are you playing at?' Alex hissed down the phone, 'I know jack shit about babies. I can't babysit, what the fuck are you all about? Giving the nanny the night off? It's nearly fucking midnight. Your wife is still out of her face because you gave her drugs and you think I can babysit for a four-week-old baby?'

'Lex listen, please I don't have any choice. I had to get Giselle out of the house, there's been a problem.'

Alex realised Carl was worried, he knew him well enough to recognise the fear in his voice. 'What's happened? You're shitting yourself, what is it?' Hearing a familiar sniffing sound, 'Alex said, 'lay of the coke Carl and tell me what's wrong?'

'Your fucking ex ... fucking psycho bitch, Elaine, she's only told Ronnie Muir about Julie and me. He came around here again, he got right into the club earlier looking for Julie. He started fighting with Bernie and Iain when they tried to put him out. They got him out of the club. I took your car and went to Moira's, to make sure Julie was alright and to tell her, but she wasn't there. I thought it was over and he had gone, then he came back, said he had been talking to Elaine. Fuck Lex, not sure what he was taking, but he was out of his tree, said he was coming to see Rosie. I needed to make sure Giselle didn't hear it, her and I well, you know, you've seen her, we kind of you know?'

'For fuck sake Carl, you're doing the Nanny?' Alex hissed, 'you really are a bastard.'

'Never mind that for now Mr Moralistic, that's none of your business. I need you to stop Ronnie getting to Rosie. I don't think anyone here realised what he was saying, the music was too loud. He's lost the fucking plot; the only good thing is the cops are looking for him now, cos he's breached his licence. There were some off duty cops in for the party. They've let the station know.'

'What the fuck do you expect me to do Carl? I need to make sure I keep my nose clean. I have my career to think about.'

'I need you to make sure my family are safe. Don't need you to do anything drastic Lex, just call the cops and try to keep him quiet, couple of smacks to the mouth should do it. Is Rosie alright mate? Is she still out of it? If not there's some blues in the back of my sock drawer give her a couple. It's been a few hours since the last two she should be okay to take more. Then hopefully she'll sleep through it if he comes around. With a bit of luck though he's driven off the fucking road or something. Fucking nutcase. Whatever you do, don't let him near Rosie. He threatened to rape her, said he was going to do her cos I've been doing Julie. I've sent a cab for Giselle, it should be there soon, get her fucking out. Lex please, look after my family? I do love Rosie, I swear I do. Mate, please don't let anything happen to her.'

'Okay I'll stay, but I'm not giving Rosie any drugs,'

'Lex please just give her a couple of blues, you know what she's like, she's a fiery wee bird when she gets going. She will confront him if he comes and fuck knows what will happen. Please mate, if she won't take them, crush them up and give her something to drink.'

'No not unless she is distressed and panicking, are they real Valium or street ones?'

'Of course, they're real, straight from the NHS. I have a reliable source, doctor with a gambling habit. I'd never buy them untested, I'm not that fucking stupid.'

Alex hearing a noise looked outside, a taxi sat in the driveway. 'that's the taxi for Giselle, need to go get her . . . no need.' He said quickly as Giselle fully made up and wearing very little, rushed through the hallway. Relieved he had a reason to hang

The Nightclub Owners Wife

up, Alex assured Carl he would remain at the house replaced the receiver and followed Giselle out.

After watching the taxi leave, Alex returned to the house, Rosie was sitting up in bed sobbing, gasping for breath. When he couldn't calm her, he asked where the sock drawer was and took out the bag of blue pills. 'Here babe, it will help you sleep,' he said holding out two pills with a glass of water. Rosie looked at him, her eyes huge she nodded and swallowed the pills. 'Thank you,' she whispered. 'Alex you are always there for me, can you hold me please? I need someone to tell me it's all going to be alright, please don't leave me?'

Realising how confused Rosie was, Alex whispered. 'It's okay babe, Carl will be home soon.' Alex sat holding Rosie till she fell asleep, he kissed her head and lay her back on the bed. Lifting his jacket, he took his cigarettes from the inside pocket and stepped outside the kitchen door, Nomee sauntered past him as he stood smoking, thoughts rushing around his head. The evenings events had made up his mind for him, he decided to leave Carl's employment and concentrate on his career. He realised for his own sanity, he had to distance himself from Rosie and Carl.

Hearing a smash behind him Alex stubbed out his cigarette and went inside thinking Rosie had probably dropped the mug containing the milky drink. He put his head around the master bedroom door. Rosie lay sleeping peacefully on the bed the quilt crumbled at her feet. Alex heard a noise from the kitchen below, he realised it was probably the cat but walked downstairs to look. 'Where are you puss?' He hissed, he put his head around the kitchen door, the side door lay open. Nomee lay on the floor, his legs spread out, red blood spreading over the tiled floor. In the same instance Alex realised there was someone behind him he felt something hit his back and spun around. Ronnie Muir stood holding a knife, a bloody knife. He plunged it into Alex's stomach and then kicked Alex in the head as he fell to the ground.

'Who is the tough guy now!' Ronnie growled as Alex tried to crawl away.

CHAPTER
TEN

Rosie wakened she heard a noise, she moved, and felt a sharp pain in neck, her vision blurry her head fuzzy, she looked down at her flowery pyjamas then blushed as she remembered her dream, Alex undressing her. The blue dress lay on the floor, she struggled to raise her hand to her neck, as she did she realised she was still wearing the new jewellery Carl had bought her, the left side of her neck ached where the earing had been digging into her as she lay on it. Taking a drink from the mug on the bedside table she made a face as the now cold milky coco slid down her throat. She tried to put the mug down but missed the table, the sound as it fell seemed to be miles away and echoed. 'Alex, she called out, Alex are you still there?' Rosie looked up as the door opened and gasped when she saw Ronnie Muir in the doorway. Even in her confused state she automatically pulled the quilt around her although she was not naked. 'what are you doing in here?' Rosie stammered, she wondered if she was dreaming, it felt as though she was in a dream, 'please get out of my bedroom? Alex, where are you? Alex?'

Ronnie jumped onto the bed and kneeling he grabbed Rosie by the hair and pulled her from the bed. 'You want big Lex, do you? Well tough shit Rosie, he can't help you. He's kind of busy, bleeding all over your lovely tiled floor darling.' He pulled Rosie roughly towards him and held her arms, dragging her downstairs to the hallway. Rosie gasped. Alex lay on the hall floor, blood was spreading across the black and white tiles, he was clutching his side. Rose took in the bloodstains on the wall and the dark red blood spreading across Alex's hand.

Rosie knew she was dreaming she had to be. She called out, 'Alex, oh dear god Alex...somebody call an ambulance, please don't let him die.' Rosie tried to get to Alex, their eyes met, and she could see the pain on Alex's face. Rosie shook her head trying to wake up.

'Let her go Ronnie,' Alex gasped, you have no fight with her, she's done nothing, except be married to Carl. Please, don't hurt her. You'll go back to jail, please Ronnie?'

'Hey, I'm going back anyway, Ranmore called the cops. Did you know he was shagging my wife? I thought it was you, your ex though, she told me, you and Moira, and Carl was doing Julie. She didn't deny it, my wife, said he was better than me. So, I thought, what's the fairest way to deal with that? Why don't we let wee fat Rosie here be the judge? In a swift movement Ronnie let go of Rosie and ripped her pyjama top from her body. She tried to move away from him, but he held her firmly by the arm.

Rosie looked at Alex her eyes pleading, suddenly aware this was no dream, she moved her free arm to try to cover her naked breasts. When she spoke, her words were slurred, as she fought the effects of the Valium. 'Alex...it's...alright, don't move, you are losing blood, too...much blood.'

Suddenly she pushed Ronnie hard, he fell over, she stumbled away in the direction of the front door, he caught her and slapped her hard. Pulling her back into the hall he forced her onto her knees, why don't we let Lex here watch, it can be the last thing he sees his 'wee sister' getting fucked by a real man, not his fucking mate.'

'You better hope I fucking die Muir, because I'm going to fucking kill you if I don't!' Alex gasped, he tried to move, however the blood loss had made him weak and he couldn't. He watched in horror as Ronnie forced Rosie to take his penis in her mouth. Ronnie grinning at Alex's distress, wrapped his fingers around Rosie's hair and held on to it.

'Fuck I can't perform with an audience, even a dying one,' He said pulling Rosie by the hair he dragged her upstairs. Alex took a deep breath and managed to move across the hall on his knees, reaching the staircase he crawled up the stairs. Exhausted, he reached the top, he heard a loud slap as he collapsed exhausted on the hall floor. The bedroom door at the end of the corridor was ajar and he tried to crawl towards it, he knew he needed to try to rescue Rosie. He heard another slap and Rosie cried out in pain. Alex realised Ronnie was forcing Rosie to have sex.

In the bedroom, Rosie struggled to comprehend what was happening, her head still fuzzy from the drugs she had ingested earlier, she tried to separate herself from reality, focusing on the bedside photograph of her and Carl's wedding. As Ronnie Muir raped her, she retreated into the little girl who nobody noticed. Rosie looked at the wedding photograph, she concentrated hard on it. Happy times, she saw Carls smiling face looking back at her.

Alex knew he had to stop what was happening, he could hear Ronnie Muir shouting out. The noise of the bed moving, the headboard hitting the wall every few seconds as Rosie was violated. Terrified the lack of sound from Rosie meant she was dead, Alex took his hand away from the bleeding wound in his abdomen and tried to move. The pain in his back and side immense, he struggled to breathe, but the sound of Ronnie Muir shouting out what he was doing to Rosie, gave him the strength to move. Ignoring the pain and dizziness he managed to get on to his knees, crawling across the floor aware of the trail of blood spreading out on the light wood floor, his life ebbing away, he lifted the discarded knife. Alex somehow managed to struggle to his feet, he staggered into the bedroom. Ronnie was on top of Rosie having sex with her from behind, pushing her

The Nightclub Owners Wife

face into a pillow, holding her down, Alex could see blood on the white cotton sheets.

Suddenly the door flew open and Carl Ranmore appeared in the room, crying out, he grabbed the knife from Alex who slid on the pool of milk on the wooden floor and fell over hitting his head on a chest of drawers, he passed out.

Rosie suddenly aware of her surroundings, crawled away as Carl pulled Ronnie from her. Unable to make a sound, she cowered on the bed as Carl plunged the knife in to Ronnie Muir repeatedly. Blood splattered covering the white bedspread and Rosie. She stared at the thick dark red life blood of Ronnie Muir spraying out over every surface as her husband continued to stab him long after Ronnie stopped fighting. Rosie found her voice and screamed as Carl took the knife and slit Ronnie's throat, the blood bubbled as he gurgled towards death. Rosie became aware there were others in the room, policemen, someone grabbed Carl and pulled him from the blooded body on the bed. A female officer wrapped Rosie, still naked, covered in blood, and now silent, in a blanket and led her gently to the chair on the far side of the room.

The next few minutes passed in a blur, Rosie wasn't sure if she was dreaming or awake. She was outside of her body, watching the scene unfold. The paramedics rushing in and working with Alex, unconscious on the floor he lay still and pale. Carl in handcuffs blood dripping from him being led from the room. 'Rosie, I love you, I love you!' he cried out as he struggled with the uniformed police officers.

Rosie locked her thoughts in a different place, a calm place, she told herself she was dreaming, she knew someone had given her pills, who was it? Carl, she remembered, he gave her two blue pills, she knew she must be dreaming. Told herself this was all a dream. The journey to hospital in the ambulance the medical examination, the endless questions from the police. Rosie unable to utter a sound, stared at them as they asked her question after question. She knew she would wake up soon, and she would be back in her own bedroom, back in her and Carl's house.

It was morning when they took her to see Alex, hoping for some reaction. Alex lay covered in tubes and wires, unconscious on the bed. The policeman sitting beside the bed looked at her as she stood staring, tearless, just staring. Alex so pale, so still, slept on. She saw the doctor and the police man talk, their voices blended into noise, Rosie couldn't make out what they were saying, she began to panic, her body shaking she struggled to breathe. They noticed her gasping, the doctor lifted her onto a trolley. Rosie was sure she was going to die now as she fought them. Struggling to breathe she felt them turn her over a sharp prick in her bottom, then nothing.

***

The door opened, and Rosie's mother entered the hospital room holding a baby car seat. Imogen slept peacefully, blissfully unaware of the drama surrounding her. Rowena followed Maggie into the room. Rosie loosened the straps then took Imogen from the car seat. She sat down staring at her baby daughter, Carl's eyes looked back at her... finally the tears came. Maggie took the baby from the room as Rowena wrapped her arms around her daughter-in-law as she sobbed silently, no sound. 'Oh god Rosie, I don't know what to say. The police are saying that, he was having an affair with Julie Muir, and that Elaine told Ronnie. They won't let me see him I've tried. He's being charged with murder, he stabbed Ronnie thirty times the procurator fiscal says. Julie is missing, no one knows where she is. Oh, dear god sweetheart, please say something? You must speak Rosie, please?

Rosie's mother minus the baby, re-entered the room, she sat down on the bed. 'Rosie, please listen darling? The police, they need to know what you know? It's been two days darling, I know you are in shock, but you need to try to speak.'

Rosie lay down on the bed and sobbed silently into her pillow. Crying herself, Maggie took the sheet and blanket and pulled them over Rosie, she kissed her cheek, 'try to sleep darling.' She whispered as a medic came in holding a syringe.

***

'She still hasn't spoken? Rowena said quietly, as Maggie and Christine Caven the female police liaison officer came into the relatives' room. 'This is frightening, it's been four days now, I thought seeing Lex might help, but it made things worse.'

Christine sighed and looked at the two women. 'They think Ronnie raped her Maggie, the DNA from her is his, the lab has confirmed it. There's pelvic trauma and anal injuries that they say are consistent with a brutal sexual assault.

'What did Carl say happened Rowena?' Maggie whispered tears running down her face. 'Did he do it because he caught Ronnie raping her? Who hurt Lex? Surely that wasn't Carl, they are friends?'

'Carl told the police he got to the house and when he saw him on top of her, Ronnie that is, he just lost it. I managed to see Carl this morning, they've got him up at Kilmarnock prison. Remanded in custody they call it. I'm so sorry for what my son has caused Maggie, but he ... he ... is still my son. I need to ... I need to be there for him too Maggie.'

Maggie looked at the other woman, she nodded. 'We need to take Rosie home, she's not badly physically injured. So, it might be better if Davie and I take her to our house. She can't go to her own, it's still a crime scene. The good news is though, Lex has come around, he's still critical, but they reckon he will recover, he lost a kidney and his spleen, and there was serious blood loss. The police are about to interview him. He's asking for Rosie, maybe he will be the one to get her to talk. He will at least be able to tell us what happened.'

The three women looked up as a male detective came into the room, 'Christine can you come out please? I need to speak to you.'

The policewoman was gone a few moments and then returned to the room. Rowena and Maggie looked up expectantly. 'Has something happened? Rowena asked.

'They've found Julie,' Christine said sadly, 'they just fished her out of the river at Dean park, looks like she has been strangled.' The young police woman shook her head and sighed, 'I knew Julie, I was at school with her. She was alright until she got in tow with Ronnie, there are three kids orphans now.' Christine shook her head, 'Julie's mother is distraught, the kids, well, they are too young to understand what happened they have just been told she's dead.' Alex appears to have been the last person to have seen her, so hopefully he will be able to tell us what happened to her.'

'You can't think Lex has anything to do with Julie dying? Maggie gasped, 'he's not capable of that kind of violence. He's is a real gentle giant, Christine you know that, you know us, know Lex and Rosie.'

'We're not thinking anything just yet, this is a mess, it will all come out in the wash, ladies. For now, you must look after Rosie, she's been through so much.' Christine sighed and looked at the two women, 'we have to put a jigsaw together. Carl has been helping with the facts, and well, you know it doesn't look good for him either Rowena. We can't do anything but charge him with murder. D.I Jones asked me to thank you for your help this morning, he was a lot better and talked more after you saw him.'

'He was worried about Rosie and the baby, once I told him they were alright, he calmed down and complied with the questions. Rowena looked at Maggie. I did tell him about Rosie being in shock, but not that she hasn't spoken since it happened.' Tears ran down Rowena's face, 'I can't believe he was cheating with Julie Muir? He said it was something that happened after him and Tracey split up, then he met Rosie and Julie wouldn't accept it was over. He says it was Elaine who told Ronnie about them though.' She looked up and wiped the tears away from her face with the tissue Maggie handed her. 'The police have gone to Stirling to speak to her, to find out what she knows.'

CHAPTER
ELEVEN

'Rosemary can you tell me what happened? What you remember? You went to the new club with your husband. Then you went home with Mr Lockwood before the party, leaving your husband at the club? Why did you go home Rosemary?'

Rosie looked at the doctor, he was a psychiatrist they were trying to assess her they said. She knew they wouldn't let her go home until they had, they said, made sure she wasn't a risk to herself or others. *'Why do they speak behind curtains?'* she wondered, *'and think you can't hear'* she stared at the doctor, he was good looking, his dark hair was cut fashionably, and his eyes were dark brown, kind eyes, his facial expressions showed he was concerned. He looked like someone she could speak to. Rosie opened her mouth, but nothing came out. She shook her head and tried again, 'he said I was fat!' she whispered. I had a panic attack, I think he gave me a pill, a blue pill.' Rosie spoke slowly showing no emotion, as though reading from a book.

'Mr Lockwood? He said you were fat and gave you Valium?'

'No Carl did it, he said it would help me get through the night. Wait, maybe it was Alex? I think I fell asleep, I don't know what I dreamt and what was real. The next thing I remember was ... I was wakened, and Carl was there.'

'Where was Mr Lockwood?

'He was on the hall floor, oh my god, the blood ... Alex was bleeding.'

Rosie sat forward and the Doctor seeing the panic beginning to take hold, put his hand gently on her shoulder. 'Mr Lockwood ... Alex ... he's fine Rosemary, he's out of high dependency, conscious and doing well. Rosemary this is important, can you talk to the police? Tell them what happened? What you remember? I can sit through it with you, but they need to interview you.'

Rosie, however, was back in her house, in the bedroom seeing it all again. 'Carl, he was there, he was stabbing him, he had this look on his face, he was stabbing and stabbing him.' Having now found her voice she began to speak faster, the fear and pain apparent to the doctor and to the detectives watching from behind the two-way mirror. 'Ronnie was gasping, then he took the knife and he, he slit his throat there were bubbles and the blood sprayed all over me, it was on me. So much blood so much.'

'Rosemary ... Can you focus, where was Mr Lockwood? When your husband had the knife, where was Alex?'

Rosie her brow furrowed, straining to remember, shook her head and pursed her lips and let out air, as though trying to blow away the memory. Eventually she spoke again. 'I think he was still on the hall floor, he was holding his stomach there was blood running through his fingers, he was gasping, trying to breathe, and I tried to get to him. No, wait, he was lying on the bedroom floor. I remember when the police came and stopped Carl. Alex was on the bedroom floor, I thought he was dead.'

***

Well its consistent with what Ranmore said, and with Alex Lockwood's account of events.' D.I Michael Jones said to

Christine Cavin. 'I'm still a bit worried that she doesn't seem to remember being raped. Docs say that can happen, she has shut it out. All her injuries are consistent with a brutal violent rape. She has agreed to speak to the psychiatrist, he's with her now. Maybe we will get something from that.

'Do we have enough to get a murder conviction Mick? I believe what they are saying, but I still think Carl is a dangerous man. We need to put him away for this. I'm worried that he will change his mind and blame Alex Lockwood. Say he admitted it under duress.'

'I think you are worrying unnecessarily Christine, and I don't think that Ranmore is as dangerous as you think. If anyone was provoked it was him. Best mate dying in front of him, lowlife raping his wife. He's admitted it all, so it will be up to the fiscal to decide what they go for. I think it's going to be reduced to manslaughter, but we will go for murder, we have a confession. I think Alex Lockwood is off the hook. They are not trying to hide anything.'

'You believe Carl Ranmore?'

'Well you heard Alex's account Christine? He managed to crawl up the stairs and got into the room. He saw Muir raping Rosie, couldn't get to her. Then you have Ranmore's story, Alex standing in the room dripping blood with the knife in his hand. He admits he lost the plot, took the knife and killed Ronnie. Alex was definitely stabbed in the downstairs hallway; the forensics show it's his blood on the wall and floor. All the evidence points to them telling the truth. You heard Alex, he managed to get up and tried to go stop Ronnie. He picked up the knife because he was too weak to fight. He knew Muir was raping Rosie and was trying to stop him. Carl took the knife from him and he passed out, said he never saw Carl kill Ronnie. What was it he said though? *'I suppose if it was my wife, I might do the same.'* Michael sighed and shrugged. 'You know what Christine? I might too, if I came home and found someone raping my wife.'

Christine looked at him, 'Carl Ranmore stabbed Ronnie Muir thirty times, he almost decapitated him, that's a frenzied attack, not someone trying to get a rapist off his wife? Not a normal reaction . . . yeah, you'd want to kick the shit out of him, but it must be someone in a blind rage to be capable of that amount of damage. Do you think he killed Julie too?

'After interviewing Elaine Lamont, I think Ronnie might have. She claims Carl Ranmore raped her you know? The night his baby was born, she says they were drinking together, and he raped her in his house. She's given forensics her clothes from that night she put them in a bag at the bottom of a wardrobe in her Grandmother's house. I don't get her logic? She didn't do anything she says, because she didn't want to hurt her friend Rosie. 'Then she goes and tells Ronnie Muir about Ranmore doing his wife, causing Rosie to be raped. Do you think she's involved?'

Christine looked closely at her boss and sighed. 'What a fucking mess, I just can't take this in. Could Elaine Lamont have had other reasons?'

'It would seem likely, don't you think? I just doesn't add up. I can't understand why she wouldn't tell her friend that her husband raped her, if he did? Do you think they were having a thing? Fuck it's crazy, they all appear to have been humping each other? Alex Lockwood, he was Elaine Lamont's boyfriend, but Elaine says he had a thing with Moira Jameson the under manager of Carl's pub. Alex was really worried about Rosie, he's been asking to see her. You don't think?

'Rosie and Alex? I doubt it, but, who knows? I'll tell you one thing Mick, Ronnie Muir, he was a fucking little thug, worlds a better place without him. I lifted him you know, for the one he's just finished serving. Proper charmer he was, he groped me then spat in my face, called me some lovely names, proper misogynist, he has given Julie a doing more times than I care to remember. Was Rosie having an affair with Alex? I don't know, it wouldn't be like her, but Alex is a good-looking guy. In terms of attraction, Carl Ranmore would be quite a catch too. Maybe her and Alex were having a thing. They go back a long way, so, who knows?'

Michael sighed, 'she doesn't seem the type though, she's a bit quiet and shy, she is so fucking traumatised. She is a cute wee thing though Christine. Very young she must be about ten years younger than Ranmore. You know some of them, don't you? Alex and the Gibbs. What's their story?'

Christine sighed, 'yeah I told you I know them all, Maggie, she's a friend of my mums, they work together. Rosie and Alex, they are more like brother and sister I think. He was a bit of a tearaway when he was younger. I don't know him that well, but what I do know is he's a nice guy. Rosie had a brother who died, he was in a coma for years after a car crash, his name was Simon. Alex was his best mate. They were teenagers, stole a car and crashed it. The driver died too he was one Billy Muir, Ronnie's kid brother. A real wee toerag, but a likeable rogue, not creepy like Ronnie. Alex he was the only one who lived, well, they say it was the making of him, he turned things around started studying, he's just finished university, qualified as an architect and was only working as a steward to supplement his grant. He has a job now with an architect firm in town according to Maggie.

The door was tapped lightly, and a police officer put his head around the door, 'Sir, you asked for the tox reports as soon as they came in? He handed the paper to Michael and then left the room.

Michael read it and then looked at Christine, 'Rosie Ranmore was full of Valium enough for us to doubt what she says. The psychiatrist who saw her reckons that it may have wiped out the memory of what happened. That means that we cannot use much of her statement.'

'What does that mean for us then?'

Michael looked around and he shuffled the papers on the desk, he sighed and looked at Christine. 'Carl's not implicating anyone else, is he? He says he went home fearing for his wife's safety, after Ronnie Muir came to the club off his face. I'm sure there's more, but he's holding his hands up to it all, saying he just lost it and when he saw Alex, who's his mate on the floor and Rosie being raped. We know Alex was in that bedroom he was unconscious on the floor when the police got there. He says Ronnie sneaked up on him and stabbed him in the back.'

'Who called the police?'

'DC John Lowe, he was off duty and at the opening, he saw Ronnie fighting with the bouncers and threatening Carl, he ran off shouting '*I'm going for your wife!*' John says Ronnie was like a man possessed, tox will tell us what he's taken. The uniform boys were taking statements. They had called it in, let CID know. Unfortunately, Carl Ranmore got to the house before they did. Guy protecting his wife? He'd been drinking, he was full of cocaine when they swabbed him.' Know what, we have a confession, and maybe we just need to go with that.'

'Do you think he killed Julie? He's admitting to Ronnie's murder, so are we just going to accept that Ronnie killed Julie and leave it?'

'Christine, you know as well as I do once the lawyers get involved the confessions mostly become retractions. He's denying he had anything to do with Julie Muir's murder, he reckons that was down to Ronnie. Carl Ranmore well ... crime of passion or what? You know him better than me, would you have thought he was capable of murder?

Christine shook her head sadly, 'no to be honest I wouldn't have thought it. He's a womaniser, so I'm not surprised about him and Julie, violence no. He was really rude to my mum the night the baby was born, but he would be stressed out most likely then. The last time I saw him he was buying drinks for everyone, telling us all about the baby, poor wee soul, she's only weeks old. Daddy is going to be away for a long time, and fuck Mick, poor wee Rosie, she's only just turned seventeen. How do you recover from what she's been through? That family have had their fair share of tragedy.'

The Nightclub Owners Wife

***

'Carl, you can't be serious? You can't just hold your hands up, you must plead self-defence or temporary insanity. You'll get life for this. You caught a man raping your wife, your best friend was dying on the floor, you lashed out. Yeah you totally lost the plot, but fuck me Carl? If anyone was provoked, it was you, but thirty times?' Tommy Halliday stared at Carl and shook his head. 'They will need to pour what's left of him into the coffin.'

Tommy, you're my lawyer, I respect you... I know you have my best interests at heart, but I'm not going to put Rosie through a trial. I did it, they caught me, my wife is a fucking wreck, my mum says she hasn't been able to speak for days now. You can go with the defence of I lost it.' Carl looked at his hands, 'I killed Ronnie Muir and I would do it again, he must have killed Julie, he almost did Lex in, and he would have killed my Rosie too. The bastard was holding her down and raping her, he had to die. I'm not insane, I knew what I was doing. I just don't think denying it is an option, all I want is to see Rosie.

'You are not denying it, you are asking to plead to manslaughter. You will get a much lower sentence if we can prove that.' Tommy sighed, 'it will get you back to your wife a lot quicker if you are convicted of manslaughter and less licence conditions too.'

'I need to see her, hold her, make sure she's okay. They'll find me guilty and I'll get longer if I don't admit it. So that's it, that's my life now, please Tommy. Try to get them to let me see Rosie and Lex. Tell whoever you need to tell I'll plead guilty to whatever. As long as I get to see my wife and my mate. I'm not going to contest it.'

'Carl, they are implying you killed Julie because she was going to tell Rosie about your relationship. People heard you shouting at her that day, you threatened to kill her and bury her. If they want to go down that route, we need to be prepared. I think I probably know the answer to this but... Will they find your DNA on her?

'Yes of course they will, I was shagging her, I had been at her house that morning, in her bed. I always used a condom cos I never really trusted her, but yes, I did it that morning. I'm not lying about the fact we had a thing. I was stressed out, when I got back to the pub that afternoon I lost it with her. I was worried about her telling Rosie, it was opening of the club. I had a lot on my mind. Yes, I was shouting at her, I ended it with her because I didn't want Rosie finding out and she threatened to tell her. I was a real bastard, and that's the last time I saw her. Do you think I don't have that on my conscience? I cared about her Tommy, you know I had been having a casual thing with her for years, but I certainly did not kill her. That must be down to Ronnie. I need to speak to Rosie myself, tell her what I've done. You tell the police and the fiscal I will plead guilty to all the stuff about Ronnie, if you can get it down to manslaughter great, if not I'll plead to murder. The condition is however that I get to see Rosie and Lex in hospital? Today? Yeah?'

'Okay I'll try, they were kind of hanging towards manslaughter given the circumstances. That was because there was only the charge in respect of you doing Ronnie in. I think there are a lot of people who feel that they don't know what they would do if they came home to what you did. If they can tie you to Julie, there's no way they will go down that route, its double murder. Now there's this ridiculous accusation that you raped Elaine Lamont, what is that about?'

'I never raped her, oh fuck Tommy, it was moment of madness, Elaine was wasted, came onto me I was drunk, we did it. I felt like shit after it, I thought she did too. Rosie was in the hospital, it was the night Imogen was born. Elaine and I got wasted in my house, it happened once.'

'What the fuck Carl? You are not exactly making this easy for yourself, Elaine Lamont? Your wife's best friend? You slept with your wife's best friend the night your kid was born?'

I told you, we were wasted, it was a mistake. I don't even like the crazy bitch. She caught Lex shagging Moira in my office,

The Nightclub Owners Wife

and she was upset, she went around to the pub and caused a scene. Then she came home with me after the baby was born and we got drunk, took some stuff and one thing led to another. I thought she was feeling as bad as me. Maybe she doesn't remember she started it, she came on to me. I hadn't seen her since the night we did it. I got up in the morning and she'd gone. She waited a month then came to the pub that day, started shouting the odds at me, accusing me of raping her. I told her to fuck off and reminded her she started it.'

'For fuck sake Carl, this is all you need, we need to shut her up, do you think she will take money to keep schtum. I mean you are not exactly skint, are you?'

Carl banged his fist onto the table in front of him. 'She fucking caused all of this. She told Ronnie Muir about me and Julie, she couldn't stand to see Rosie happy. She should be up there for murder too. I will not admit to things I didn't do Tommy. So, there will need to be a trial for that accusation.' Carl shook his head, 'I will not plead to fucking rape. Let them try and prove it, it's my word against hers, isn't it? I'm willing to admit to killing a man in cold blood, but I never raped Elaine Lamont. I need to speak to Rosie though, tell her what happened.'

'What about Julie? What are we going to do about that? You were heard threatening her shouting at her and someone saw her on the floor when Alex opened the door to your office. Everyone saw Alex taking her out to the car, she was crying? You went out looking for her, the boys at the door of the club said you were angry.'

'No, I told you I didn't kill Julie, you know I cared about her. I was angry at her for the way she was carrying on. I'd finished it with her, I went looking for her to make sure she was okay. I didn't find her, I didn't kill her, must have been Ronnie. If she was in the water though there will be no forensics, so there will be no evidence to prove it either way. Look I trust you Tommy, you've always been straight with me. I need you to go to the police and get me a deal. I'm going to jail mate, hopefully the judge will get the fact that I was a man in a terrible situation and go easy on me. But I am going to go down for this, so we also need to make sure that Rosie is looked after financially. Get me to that hospital so I can see Rosie and Lex.'

***

Carl entered Rosie's hospital room. He looked at her sitting on the bed fully dressed. Baby Imogen slept peacefully in her car seat. A holdall sat on the floor, Carl had been told she was being discharged that afternoon, into the care of her parents. 'Can I be alone with my wife, please? I swear I'm not going to do anything stupid. Please take the handcuffs off?' He looked at the officer and raised his free hand. 'Please? The chief constable said you could, if it was safe. It's the fourth-floor guys, I'm not going anywhere, you can watch through the glass. Please just ten minutes to speak to her in private, you have everything you need. I've cooperated with your enquiries just let me have ten minutes alone with them. Let me hold my daughter, fuck knows when I'll be a free man again.'

Rosie said nothing as the female police officer took the handcuffs from Carl's wrists, she and the other officer moved out of the door, closing it behind them. Carl sat down beside Rosie and put his arms around her. 'Sweetheart there is so much I need to tell you, so little time to do it.' Tears welled in his eyes, he took her chin and gently moved her head to look into her eyes. 'After I've said this, I hope you can forgive me babe. I need to tell you some stuff, need you to know some things. I hope you will be able to forgive me and wait for me. I'm going to go to jail for at least eight years babe. I need you to know some stuff.'

Rosie sat silently watching, her eyes dry, she stared at him, then nodded and looked away.

'I've done some bad things to you babe, I'm not proud of it but you need to know.' Carl took a deep breath, he reached out and took Rosie's hands in his. 'Babe, I well, I had a thing with Julie Muir, it was after Tracey left, I never told you. Oh, I don't know why I didn't tell you because it was over. I just wanted things to be perfect. Then you got pregnant and we got married, I wanted to tell you, but oh I don't know I thought she was good for the club, and if you knew, I would have to lose her as a member of staff. I was scared babe, frightened if I told you, you would leave me. I was scared she would tell you about us. I was with her in her house the morning it all happened. We were in her bedroom, it was just because her kids were in and I didn't want them to see me. She was threatening to tell you about us. I swear Rosie it was over as soon as I met you, she wouldn't let it go, kept pestering me. I sacked her that day and I was going to tell you, then you had the panic attack that night and I couldn't.'

'Were you sleeping with Elaine too?' Rosie took her hand away from his and continued staring out of the window. 'The police, they said Elaine told them you raped her?'

Carl began to sob, he tried to take Rosie's hand and she pulled away from him still not looking at him. 'Did you rape Elaine?' She repeated.

'Babe it wasn't rape, I swear. It was I don't know . . . too much alcohol after you had the baby, I . . . I don't know why. You and me, we hadn't had sex in so long, I was drunk, I know it's not an excuse. We got drunk that night, she took quite a lot of drugs. I put her to bed because she was wasted, then I had more to drink and went to bed myself. She and I had talked quite a bit and agreed we would never like each other, but, would be friends for your sake. I went to bed and I wakened she was in our bed. Fuck Rosie I don't know what happened, but we did it. Afterwards she said she was going to tell you about it. Said she did it because she knew I would cheat on you. Rosie I'm sorry I should have told you, but I was so afraid of losing you. She instigated it, oh I'm not saying I didn't, but I was wasted, it was stupid, it meant nothing. I did it and pretended it was you. I'm so sorry babe, I need you to say you'll wait for me?' He tried to put his arms back around her, but she moved away.

'Did you kill Julie?' She asked looking at him for the first time.

'No, I didn't, Rosie you have to believe me,' Ronnie that was different. I would do it again if someone hurt you or Imogen. Please Rosie listen to me,' he grabbed her arm and pulled her towards him.

'Don't touch me Carl, I want you to go, I can't bear to have you near me. I never liked Julie, but now she's dead and her kids are orphans. You killed a man, you slept with my friend and you want me to wait for you. No Carl I can't, I won't, I loved you, I thought you loved me.' Rosie began to sob, she buried her head in her hands and wept. 'I thought you were perfect, I thought you loved me. I've lost everything except my child,' Rosie took her hands away and looked at him. 'I've lost my husband, my home and my best friend. I can't not see what I saw Carl, and I can't ever forget what happened.' She stood up and looked Carl in the eye. 'When I close my eyes I see it, the blood...when I sleep I dream about it? I see Alex covered in blood, you...you are cutting Ronnie's throat.

'Please Rosie no, no, don't do this, I love you, I need to make sure you're safe. I need you to believe me I love you, I can't lose you.'

'Safe? How can I ever feel safe with you again? You and your behaviour you started the chain of events that led to our home and me being violated. I thought my life was perfect Carl, I thought I had it all. I worried that I had too many good things, that I wasn't good enough for someone like you.'

'Rosie no please don't give up on me? We can still be together after this is over. Rosie please darling I did it because I love you. Please Rosie.' Tears ran down Carls face he tried to hold Rosie, but she moved away and stared ahead.

Standing in front of him she shook her head. 'I worshipped you. I thought I had everything I would ever need. Now all I have is my baby, and she will always be the child of a murderer and a rape victim.' Rosie, seeing a look on her husband's face added. 'Oh, I don't remember the actual act Carl. I felt the pain afterwards, I know it happened. The world is going to know it all Carl, and it's your fault. Now please Carl go please? If you love me, please just give me that?' Rosie turned away from him, still sobbing she made for the door of the shower room. Not sure where to go but needing to get away.

'No, please Rosie, don't give up on me, please don't. I've nothing to live for if I lose you and Imogen.' Carl lunged forward and grabbed Rosie knocking her off her feet. Imogen startled and began to cry. Carl however did not appear to notice the screaming baby. He held Rosie down on the floor trying to kiss her, 'you can't do this Rosie, you are my wife, I love you and Imogen is my daughter. Please darling don't do this to me? Carl remained on top of Rosie, pinning her to the ground. The two police officers rushed into the room and pulled him away from Rosie, who was now crying hysterically, shuffling along the floor on her bottom.

'Rosie please don't do this to me!' Carl shouted, he began to struggle violently with the two officers punching and kicking them. A third uniformed officer ran into the room and assisted the two police officers to overpower Carl. 'If you had just gone to the fucking opening, none of this would have happened,' Carl shouted as they dragged him from the room. 'Think about that when you fucking sit there wondering why it happened.' A fourth officer tried to pull Rosie to her feet, but now terrified, she cowered in the corner shaking violently.

A nurse rushed in to the room she lifted the car seat and the screaming baby, pushing the policeman away she knelt on the floor in front of Rosie. 'Get him out of here!' She cried over her shoulder, before putting her hand gently on Rosie's head. 'Mrs Ranmore it's alright, you're safe, no one will harm you here.' Rosie was distracted by Imogen who was now red in the face her little arms and legs jerking as she cried. Moving across the floor on her knees, she took the baby from the car seat and held her close to her chest, kissing her little face holding her, sobbing into the soft bundle. The baby calmed down quickly, safe in her mother's arms.

Carl continued to struggle, beyond reasoning now, he cried out. 'Rosie please, don't do this, I did it for you. I love you don't do this to me, please Rosie, you need to listen. You are mine, you cannot think I will ever let you go. You don't make that decision Rosie. You are my wife and Imogen is my daughter, I will not accept you don't love me.'

Rosie shook her head, she tried to talk, but no words came out, the nurse held her and Imogen firmly, as Carl, who was still shouting, was dragged from the room. 'Okay, okay, stop dragging me, I'll come with you, I will not be treated like this.' Carl stopped struggling, he allowed the police officers to put the handcuffs on him and lead him towards the door. People stopped and stared and for the first time, Carl realised that the implications of what he had done were far reaching and long lasting. He looked back at the door he had just exited, he could see Rosie holding the baby, she was sobbing sitting alone on the bed. Carl looked at the officer handcuffed to him. 'Can I see Lex now? You said I could, I need to see he's alright, he's my friend. I will stay calm I promise.'

CHAPTER
TWELVE

Alex lying on the bed hooked to machines opened his eyes as the door creaked open. The two police officers entered the room. Carl, handcuffed to the second officer, met Alex's gaze and inclined his head. 'How're you doing mate?' He asked moving towards the bed.

'I've been better bud, have you seen Rosie? Is she all right? I've asked but they won't let me see her.'

The female police officer brought over two chairs and gestured to Carl to sit. Carl sat down and looked up at the police officer. 'Can't you just take the cuffs off me?' He asked looking down at his wrist attached to the male.

The female officer shook her head, 'sorry Carl after your escapade earlier, we shouldn't even be letting you see Alex. The chief agreed it as long as we kept you handcuffed. Please just sit down, you have five minutes, we've been ordered to get you back to the prison.'

Carl sat down, saying nothing he looked up at Alex who had with the assistance of a nurse, been pulled into a sitting position propped up by pillows.

'You're in a right mess Carl, I can't believe what happened, any of it.' Alex shook his head, remembering what had occurred, everyone in the room could see the distress Alex felt, his voice shook, emotion high. 'Carl, I couldn't stop him, he stabbed me, I couldn't get up, when I did he was...doing what he did. I managed to crawl up the stairs, but I couldn't stand up. I'm so sorry Carl, I tried to stop him, I don't remember anything else, I never saw you do him, but he deserved it. He was a bastard, but I can't believe...you?'

'Stabbed him thirty times?' Carl said, quietly finishing Alex's sentence. 'What was it you always said about me?'

'A lover not a fighter!' Alex replied, 'I would have killed him if I could have Carl,' he shook his head sadly. 'Oh, fuck Carl, what are you going to do? You'll be facing a life sentence.'

Carl shrugged and sighed loudly, he looked Alex in the eye as though carefully considering his words, his voice calm and flat he said. 'I'm going to plead guilty and hope they are lenient with me for admitting it. I couldn't stop, I just saw him on her, and I lost it. I don't regret it, I killed a man and I don't care. Lex, I need you to look out for Rosie, help her, she's my wife and I need you to make sure she's alright. Guys are going to start chasing her with me away, please make sure she's safe. Make sure they all know she is still my wife.'

'Carl, you know I think of her as my sister, I will do the big brother thing and look after her. Her and I, well, we're friends.' Alex wondered how he could do this, given his growing hope that Carl being in prison would give Rosie the opportunity to get him out of her life. He said nothing though, being astute enough to know this wasn't the time. Carl was his friend, Alex wondered briefly who he would align himself with if Rosie did decide to end the marriage. He realised immediately his affinity with Rosie, was far stronger than any loyalty to Carl.

'Thanks bud.' Carl looked at his friend, 'there's more mate. I need you to help Bobby with the club and the pubs. Now Moira is going, he'll need help. Rosie, she's just a kid, too young to take on all that responsibility. My mum well, she could probably run Nobels again, but the club and the other boozers...it will

The Nightclub Owners Wife

be too much for her. She's not been too well. The pub was my dad's thing, not hers. I know you have plans, but I need you to do this mate. Bobby will do most of it, but someone needs to be in control you're the only one I trust to do it.' Carl reached out his hand, and Alex, clearly fighting tears, took the other mans outstretched hand and held it for a few seconds.

'I can do it bud and still work with Norrie. I'll help run things instead of carrying on as security. Kev is good enough now to take over as head of security. I'll use the time to run things. With your mum and Rosie helping, we should manage it. If we can get it into a way of working, then I will be able to do it and keep my daytime job.'

"Thanks Lex, I knew I could rely on you. Rosie, she is pretty upset with me just now. I had to tell her some of the stuff I've done. I'm kind of hoping she'll come around if I give her some space. She's been through a lot and well...I suppose I haven't exactly been honest with her.

'Do you want me to speak to her? I wanted to see her, but they wouldn't let me. The doc says I'm going to be well enough now to get up and about soon. Maggie reckons they're going to take her home. What about your house Carl? She can't go back there, not after what happened.'

'Well I'm not going to be able to sell it, am I? Even if I could, it's all in Rosie's name anyway. My accountant advised me to do it that way when I was setting up the club, so if things went wrong she and the baby would still have a home. Rosie is probably better with her mum and dad anyway, they'll hopefully look after her. I'll just leave it for now, once the police are finished with it can you organise for it to be cleaned up? There's quite a mess there I would imagine.'

'We can put you in touch with someone Alex,' the policeman handcuffed to Carl said looking up. There are companies who specialise in that type of thing. Once forensics are finished then they will notify your wife Carl, it can be done then. Now I'm sorry pal, but we must go, you need to say your goodbyes and we will get back in time for your tea. Once you've been up in court tomorrow you can make decisions. You know you'll not get bail, don't you?'

Carl nodded, 'I've pled guilty I need to get it over with. I want it ended, there's no point in prolonging it.' Carl laughed bitterly, 'I need to put my faith in the justice system. My lawyer is attempting to get it reduced from murder to manslaughter. Hopefully that will cut the jail time.' He and the police officer stood up. 'Look after her for me?' Carl said looking into Alex's eyes, and can you come and see me from time to time?'

Alex nodded, he watched them leave then lay back on the pillows, still fighting tears he shut his eyes and dozed off.

***

Alex wakened as the door opened again, he realised it was dark outside and a few hours had passed. He was expecting it to be his evening meal, he had been vaguely aware of the sound of the trolley bringing the meals from the kitchen far below in the bowels of the hospital. He looked at the door and Rosie stood watching him. Dressed in a black sweater she had her hands inside the sleeves she looked like an urchin in the oversized jumper. Alex sat up, wincing at the pain in his back and disturbing the tube draining his chest. Rosie said nothing she moved over and sat down by the bedside still looking at him. Alex realised she was very pale and tired. 'How're you doing sweetheart?' He asked reaching out and touching her shoulder.

'I'm . . . I don't know how I am Alex, I'm scared, really frightened, and I can't sleep or eat. I keep seeing it all, you on the floor, Ronnie dragging me upstairs . . . then Carl doing what he did.'

'You are safe now babe, it's all right, it must have been awful for you. I'm so sorry I couldn't . . . couldn't stop him. Rosie I will be there for you help you get over it.'

'I don't remember Ronnie raping me, just being in the hall seeing you. The next thing I remember is Carl being there and you on the bedroom floor. I thought I had dreamt it. At first, I didn't want to believe what had happened, then I thought I had just blocked it out, I do that sometimes when things get bad, just block it out. When I saw the psychiatrist, he thinks that it has something to do with the mix of alcohol and diazepam, says it can permanently delete some memories. When I told him the time frame... he said that from when I took them, till everything happened the effect would be at an optimum.' Rosie looked at Alex, her face showing her sadness. 'You gave me two more at that point, he thinks it could be a mixture of trauma and the effect of the substances.' She looked at Alex then shook her head. 'I'm okay Alex the pain from it is wearing off. I've been so worried about you, I thought... I thought you were dying.'

Alex reached out and took her hand in his, 'well I didn't die, and neither did you. We both lived through it and we will be fine.' He gripped Rosie's hand and squeezed. 'We can get through this Rosie, get over it, you just need to have faith.'

'Did you know he was sleeping with Julie Muir?' Rosie asked quietly, her eyes sad. Alex could see the tears building up.

'Yes, I knew babe, he was doing it before you and him got together, he stopped at first, I think. He told me he wasn't still doing it. I didn't know what to do, he kept telling me it was over, then I would see them, know it was still on. He did end it the night of the opening, he told her he wanted you and the baby. Rosie, I think it carried on longer because he was afraid she would tell you about them. He didn't love her or anything. It was just hard for him.'

'Were you going around as couples, you and him and Moira and Julie?'

'What? No? It wasn't like that, oh there's so much we need to talk about Rosie, but not now. I don't think Moira knew about Carl and Julie, it was well hidden. Carl said some horrible things to Julie when he ended it with her. Moira heard him, she looked shocked, so I don't think she knew. Me and her well it was just one of those things that happen, it's over, she and Dougie are going abroad and that's it. Moira and me it was just sex, I'm not proud of it but well ... it's done, and we parted friends.'

'What about Elaine? You really hurt her.'

Alex sighed, he looked at Rosie, 'It was never serious, me and Elaine, it was just oh, I don't know? I like her a lot, but I never made any promises to her. I told you all this ... it was just good fun to be with her. I kind of enjoyed her company, but well it was never going to lead to anything, we both agreed that. It wouldn't have bothered me if she had gone out with other people. We never really discussed it, but I just assumed that casual meant casual. If I'm honest, I still don't understand why she was so upset with me. Maybe I didn't understand it at all. I thought it was her being a drama queen when she got upset about stuff. Rosie, I never meant to hurt her, I am still dead embarrassed that she caught me. Her reaction, wow? Even for Elaine it was weird. You know she told Ronnie about Carl and Julie?'

Rosie nodded, her eyes sad. 'Carl said he slept with her the night Imogen was born.'

'Julie?'

'No, he said him and Elaine, they had sex.'

'What? Elaine? No way babe, Elaine and Carl hate each other.'

'She told the police he raped her.' Rosie bowed her head and began to cry, tears ran unchecked down her face dripping off the end of her nose. 'He says they got drunk and slept together.'

Alex tried to sit up and move forward, groaning and wincing breathing through the pain, he put his hand out to Rosie, but she ignored him. 'Fucking hell Rosie, why would she say he raped her if he didn't? Elaine's angry at me, but she loved you, she would never have done that to you. She might have been too drunk to realise it was him.' Alex blushed, 'she gets really horny when she is pissed, especially if she is partaking in chemicals too. You know Carl indulges in the old Columbian marching powder and he does take blues to come down from it, if they were together?' Alex sighed loudly, 'I just don't think she would do anything to hurt you. Maybe I don't know her as well as I think I do though? After what's happened recently, I just don't know Rosie?'

Rosie despite her distress realised Alex had said Elaine wouldn't hurt her, which implied that her husband would. She said nothing though, realising that this was for another time. 'Carl said she told him she did it to prove he would sleep with someone. He says she told him she was going to tell me.'

'Did she? Tell you?'

'No, that's where it doesn't add up, she hasn't been near me since the night Imogen was born, probably too ashamed. Alex I've lost everything, my marriage, my best friend and my home.'

'You haven't lost me sweetheart, I know you're confused and angry but I'm on your side. He's asked me to look after the business for him.'

'Are you going to?'

'He's my mate Rosie.'

Rosie moved forward, hovering over Alex, she put her hand on his shoulder and leaned in. 'He doesn't have any loyalty to anyone. He killed Ronnie in a fit of rage, I saw him. It wasn't about what he had done to me. It was because Ronnie had taken his woman. It was about a possession not about me.' Rosie took the tissue Alex held out and held it to her face. 'I didn't know him, I've kept trying to shut it all out, but I can't forget that part, it's so clear in my head.' Alex could see the pain on Rosie's face, feel her trauma.

'Do you want to talk about it.'

Rosie nodded, 'I think I need to tell someone I trust, he kept stabbing the knife into him. It was as though he couldn't see anything, there as so much blood, Lex, and the expression on his face... he slit Ronnie's his throat and kept on stabbing. He was like a monster. I was so scared, I didn't know him I never knew he was capable of that kind of violence. Alex is everyone going to blame me? I feel that I should have done something.'

'Hey, hey, stop it babe,' Alex pulled Rosie towards him and she sobbed into his chest. He held her close, kissing her head, sobbing with her. 'I feel that way too, I think it's probably a kind of normal reaction to what we both experienced.'

When Rosie spoke again it was a whisper Alex had to strain to hear what she said. 'He said he did it for me, it's all my fault, if I hadn't got myself upset and had the panic attack, I would have gone to the opening. I would have been there, and Ronnie wouldn't have come to the house. You would have thrown him out of the club, and it would have all been all right. It all happened because he said I was chubby.'

'You're a beautiful girl Rosie, and you're being silly now, it's not your fault it happened. If it's anyone's fault its Elaine's, she told Ronnie about Carl and Julie. She started a chain of events. If he raped her then I can understand it Rosie, why she would want to hurt him. It ended up with you getting hurt though, and I can't see Elaine wanting to do that. Whatever you think now, she loves you.' Alex sighed and looked down at Rosie making eye contact. 'Carl loves you too babe, he killed Ronnie because he was hurting you.'

Rosie wiped away tears with the back of her hand and shook her head. 'Alex, Carl killed a man in cold blood, he threw me aside never stopped to see if I was hurt. He just kept stabbing Ronnie. I hate Ronnie for what he did to me, but two wrongs don't make a right. It wasn't Carl's right to take a life because I was raped.'

'Rosie, I would have done it, killed Ronnie if Carl hadn't taken the knife from me. I picked it up, I meant to use it, I knew I was too weak from the blood loss to fight. I was out on the landing and I could hear what he was doing to you, I got up and came into the room.' Alex gripped Rosie's hand and looked sadly at her. 'I remember Carl taking the knife from me, I don't know if I slipped or fell over, but I passed out, didn't see the rest.'

'It was . . . was gruesome Lex, don't think I can ever forget what Carl did.'

'Give yourself some time babe, I want you to be happy, and Carl did make you happy, didn't he? You're not thinking straight just now, just don't do anything rash. We will get through this Rosie, you and me, we need to talk about the club and the pubs babe, as his wife, you need to help run them now. If you can't do it for yourself, do it for Imogen, she needs to be looked after, it's going to be hard enough for her with this happening. It's always going to be there. She needs to be financially and emotionally secure. The pubs and club will allow you do that.'

'I can't go back to the house Alex, I can't live there, all I'll ever be able to see is the blood. I need to get his permission to sell it.'

'The house Rosie, it's in your name. I witnessed it with the lawyers, he wanted it to be yours. I think because he didn't want it to be part of the business. So, they couldn't take it if it all went wrong. So legally it's yours to do with as you please. You might be better though to wait a while, you won't get market value just now because of this. The other option is we remodel it, I could do some drawings and totally change the layout, that might help. Like I said Rosie don't make any plans just now, you just concentrate on getting better babe, and back on your feet.'

She nodded and kissed Alex's cheek, 'you're a good guy Alex, thank you, for everything. For being there for me and him, I'm not sure either of us deserve your friendship. I love you Alex, you've always been there for me.

CHAPTER
THIRTEEN

Elaine Looked up as her flatmate put her head around the door. 'Lainey there are two men here to see you. Fucking hot men, wow!'

'Who is it? What do they want?'

The other girl shrugged, 'One is called Lex, he said you would know what it was about. Fuck he's hot.'

'Tell him to fuck off, I don't want to see him Gail. I want nothing to do with him.

'Fuck if you don't want him, can I have him? He's so good looking. Who is he? You've had a lot of visitors this week. Come on Elaine spill the beans what's going on?'

'Yeah spill the beans Lainey, what's going on?' Alex stood in the doorway, he was pale and drawn looking. Elaine realised he was in pain. His voice and actions were however strong and direct, he looked at Gail, 'can you make us a cup of coffee babe? Two and a coo for Tommy here, and black, one sugar, for me.' He looked at Elaine, 'you need to speak to us Elaine. This is Tommy Halliday, Carl's lawyer.'

Gail looked at Elaine, who nodded, 'can you make coffee Gail, I need to talk to them.' Seeing Gail's confused look, she added, 'it's okay they're friends of mine, no worries. Can you give us ten minutes? Sit down gentlemen.' Elaine said nodding

The Nightclub Owners Wife

at the two chairs in the room. She sat back on her bed and stared out the window. 'What do you want Lex?' Elaine asked quietly as her flatmate closed the door behind her. 'Why are you here? You look awful by the way, I heard about you being hurt ... my gran told me. I'm glad you are okay. It was only two weeks ago, should you be here?'

'I'm fine, healing up nicely, I got out of hospital last night. Look I'm here because Rosie needs to know the truth Elaine. She needs to know about what happened that night, why you told Ronnie Muir about Carl and Julie. Two people died because of what you did.'

'Two people died because of fucking Carl, Lex. When you get over your fucking bromance, you might just see that.'

Tommy Halliday leaned forward. 'We need you to drop the rape claim? He's going to go down for killing Ronnie, but they are trying to blame him for Julie too. He never did that Elaine, it must have been Ronnie.

'What did you tell Ronnie Muir and why?' Alex asked looking at Elaine. 'If he raped you then you carry on,' he looked at Tommy and shrugged. 'I'm not interested in what he gets charged with. I need to help Rosie, I get you were angry at me, why did you do it? What on earth made you tell Ronnie about Carl and Julie, why not just go and tell Rosie?'

'I told him the truth, Lex, I told him about his fucking wife shagging Carl, I told him because I wanted Carl hurt. I wanted him hurt because he raped me.' Elaine stared out of the window, her eyes tearless and her face showing no sign of emotion.

'What about Rosie, Elaine, did you even think about her when you did it? What it would do to her?' Alex stood up and walked to the end of the bed, he looked at Elaine, and he could see nothing in her eyes. 'She's supposed to be your best friend Lainey.' He continued to look Elaine in the eye. 'She didn't deserve any of this, you once told me that other than your Gran, she was the most important person in your life. Do you have any idea what this has done to her? What happened what she had to go through? What she will need to go through if you persist with this story about him raping you. Carl says you were gassed and slept together. If that's true then you made a mistake, but Rosie doesn't deserve this. Carl doesn't matter, it's a mess, but that girl has done nothing wrong.'

'Oh, fuck off Lex, sweet little Rosie everybody loves her, what I did was do her a favour, he will go to prison and not be able to hurt anyone else.' Elaine stood up and looked back at Alex, her face angry. 'You have no idea what it's like to wake up with someone having sex with you. I went to sleep in his house and wakened up with him doing it to me. Your mate, my friends' husband, he was having sex with me. I never invited him to do it, I got drunk with him and fell asleep. He took it from me, I didn't give it.'

'I don't believe you Elaine, I know what you are like when you are drunk and taking stuff, you're horny. I'm sure you're mistaken, why would he rape you?' Alex's brow furrowed, he shook his head. 'Carl Ranmore can have any woman he wants. Why would he bother with someone who hates him and who he hates? Why would you lie there and let him? I don't understand Elaine.'

'No, you wouldn't, would you? You are a fucking man, you are his friend and you are her fucking ... I don't know what you are to Rosie? What is she to you, your sister? Your friend, or the woman you really want?' For the first time Elaine showed emotion she quickly wiped away a tear and grabbed a wad of tissues from a box on the bedside table and held it to her face. Shaking her head, she moved towards the door. Opening it she took a tray from her flat mate and made to shut the door again.

'Are you alright Chick?' Gail asked looking around the room.

'I'm fine, I promise I'll tell you everything later. Just go back to doing your revision. I'll tell you about it later.' Elaine repeated.

'Okay if you're sure.'

Elaine put the tray on a table, she made no attempt to hand out the mugs. She returned to sitting on the bed and looked at

Alex, ignoring Tommy. 'I always thought that if someone tried to rape me I would put up a fight. I didn't, do you know what Lex? I was so fucking shocked I didn't fight. I said stop, he didn't, and I just let him do it. I just let him, then got up and left the house. I drove home to my Grans and then got in the bath and scrubbed myself till I bled.' She turned and looked at Alex seeing the shock on his face. 'I went to the club looking for you, I needed to tell someone, I wasn't going to tell Rosie, I... I never wanted to hurt her. You weren't there so I drove back here, I never told anyone.'

'Oh, fuck Elaine, you should have told me, should have told someone. Rosie, your gran, we could have helped.'

'You believe me then?'

Alex nodded, 'I believe it happened, but Elaine, why did you wait a month then tell Ronnie? You might have been angry at folk, but Julie died because of you, and Rosie, she is such a mess. He raped her Elaine; Ronnie Muir took Rosie because you told him about Carl and Julie.'

'What?' Elaine asked her eyes now wide and shock obvious on her face.

'Didn't they tell you Elaine? Ronnie Muir stabbed me and then raped Rosie, brutally, on her own bed. I was lying out in the hall listening, have you any idea what that's like? Knowing someone you love is being hurt and feeling helpless, all because you told him about his wife and Carl.' Alex looked around at Tommy Halliday, who was nodding.

'Rosie, was raped by Ronnie? That's why Carl killed him. I thought they had been fighting over Julie. Oh fuck... Is Rosie? Is she alright?' Elaine gasped, looking for the first time at the other man in the room.

'She's doing better now, she's home with her parents. Elaine?' Tommy asked, 'I need you to drop the rape allegation, say you were mistaken, or something else. Carl killed Ronnie Muir because he had stabbed his best friend and raped his wife, he caught him in the act. We may be able to get them to reduce the charge to manslaughter if there's nothing else.'

'Why should I? He raped me I just told you.'

Tommy nodded, 'I can understand you being angry, but if you persist with this, you are leaving yourself open to an investigation as to your involvement with Carl. He says you got drunk and slept together, perhaps he misread the signs? He is admitting killing Ronnie, but he will not admit to raping you. This could force a trial. What good will it do you? What if the jury believe him, it puts you in the frame for at the very least being an accessory after the fact in the murder of Julie Muir? If he is convicted of murdering Ronnie and Julie, then you could be implicated.'

'I don't give a fuck what happens to Carl Ranmore. Why should I care what happens to him? I was in Stirling when it happened. There is no way I will be implicated, I've told the police everything I know.'

Alex nodded, 'okay let's try it from another angle? Do you want to put yourself and Rosie through a trial? She has been through enough. There would be some question about whether you were raped or not, given the fact that you got drunk and took drugs with Carl, then slept in his house. Rosie, she was attacked brutally violated and then witnessed the death of Ronnie Muir. If you care about your friend, then you need to know how affected she has been. She didn't speak for over a week. She had multiple injuries, she is traumatised beyond belief.'

'Is she going to be alright? She is not thinking she will stay married to that monster, is she?' Elaine stared at Alex. 'Surely she's not going to wait for him?'

'She's refusing to have anything to do with Carl,' Alex said quietly, looking Elaine in the eye he nodded. 'She's ending the marriage anyway, so you got what you wanted, her away from him. Elaine, I believe you, Carl Ranmore was my friend, but I know he is capable of doing what you said he did.' He reached out and touched Elaine on her arm. He sighed when she moved quickly out of reach, he swiftly began to speak again. 'Rosie is also hurt and vulnerable, and I need to protect her too Elaine. You must realise there will be doubt about what happened to you, but if you want to go ahead with the rape allegation then I guess you need to do it. Elaine, for what it's worth. I'm sorry about what I did, I'm sorry about what Carl did.' Alex inclined his head to Tommy, 'come Tam let's go, we've said all we came to say.'

'Wait' Elaine cried, 'what about Rosie? I didn't want to stay away, I didn't know what Ronnie had done to her Lex. I feel responsible now for her being attacked. I was in shock and I was afraid, I just reacted, please tell her I never intended her to get hurt. Lex will you look after her? Make sure her and the baby are alright. Does she believe he raped me?

Alex shrugged, 'I think she's been through so much, she can't think anything right now. Carl, he told her you got drunk and made a mistake.'

Elaine looked sad, 'best leave it like that I suppose. I don't want her to go through any more than she has already. I can't come back to Kilmarnock, I hope someday I'll see her again.' Elaine looked at Tommy Halliday, 'I'll tell the police I don't want to proceed with the rape prosecution. I'm going to say I can't face going to court and want to get on with my life. They won't charge me with wasting police time, will they?'

'I don't think so, if they try to pressure you, give me a call Elaine. I'll get someone to represent you.' Tommy put out his hand, but Elaine ignored the gesture, she turned to Alex.

'What about your plans? What are you going to do? Will you have to run the pubs for her?'

'No, there are staff who can do that. Rowena can run it all for now. I'll help, but in my spare time. Rosie is all over the place, so I'm not sure what her plans are.' He smiled sadly, 'I'm still going to be an architect Elaine. Norrie has been great about me being ill, so I'll start back as soon as I get the all clear from the medics. What about you are you going to carry on at uni?'

'Yeah of course, I've got my future all planned. Lex I'm sorry, you and Moira, it was such a shock, I never saw it coming. I know we never promised each other anything and it wasn't for ever, but I was really hurt. I just want you to know, I don't hate you or her, but you need to be careful about Dougie finding out.'

'Dougie, he knows Elaine, he always has, I'm not going to go into it all, it's their business. Suffice to say it's not what you think, it's not serious or anything. After what's happened though I'm not going to be doing that anymore. Elaine can I give you a hug?'

'I'd rather you didn't Lex,' Elaine shook her head, 'I'm not ready for physical contact, not sure if I will ever be again.' She looked at him and sighed, 'I certainly don't want you to touch me.'

'Are you going to be alright Lainey?' Alex asked, 'have you got support?'

'Yeah, I told my personal tutor, she's arranged for me to speak to a counsellor from rape crisis. Carl Ranmore isn't going to be allowed to ruin my life, Lex.'

'Lainey if there's anything you need, anything I can do?'

Elaine shook her head. 'No thanks Lex, I don't want your help.' She opened the door, 'if you don't mind I have things to do, I'm sure you have too, it's a long way back to Kilmarnock.' Elaine held the bedroom door and let them pass. As she unlocked the front door, she turned and looked at Alex. 'Have a good life Lex, look after Rosie and the baby, but please do not contact me again.'

'If that's what you want.' Alex said quietly without turning to look at her.

CHAPTER
FOURTEEN

May 1997

'Carl Johnstone Ranmore you are charged with manslaughter of Ronald Kenneth Muir, how do you plead?'

'Guilty.'

The Judge looked sadly at Carl, 'this is a tragic case. Carl Ranmore you have admitted causing the death of Ronald Kenneth Muir. You will be remanded in custody for background reports, sentencing, four weeks from today. I do intend to hand down a significant jail term Mr Ranmore. It is only due to your circumstances, and your admission of the offence, you are not being convicted of murder.

As he was led away Carl searched the public gallery, hoping to see his wife. His mother sat in the front row, with Davie Gibbs, his arm around her, Alex on her other side. Rowena looked as though she had aged ten years. '*I love you!*' she mouthed as he was led down from the dock. Carl had been in custody for five months, when he finally appeared in court. Rosie had not had any contact with him, Alex had visited weekly with Rowena; however, their conversations were mainly around the business.

They had told him Rosie was recovering, and now taking an interest in the pubs and club.

***

'Rosie, he is going to get a significant sentence, the top whack his lawyer reckons. Probably ten years, he won't be sentenced for a few weeks. Can you not just go and see him?' David Gibbs looked at his daughter. 'He killed a man for attacking you darling, you owe him at least a visit. He also needs to know about the baby.'

Rosie shook her head, 'I don't know if it's his Dad, I could be pregnant by my rapist, the man he killed.' Rosie put her hands protectively on her stomach. I'm not telling anyone yet, though the way it's growing, I won't be able to hide it for much longer.'

'Darling please have an abortion, given the circumstances they would do it right away.' Maggie Gibbs shook her head her eyes filling with unshed tears. 'Even if you were sure the baby was Carl's we'd be encouraging you to terminate. He's going to be in jail for years. It's hard enough with one baby you will be a single parent with two children there will only be ten months between them. Imogen needs you to be a mother, if you are ill again what will happen to her? You were in and out of hospital with the hyperemesis gravidarum with Imogen and you were really ill towards the end, if it happens again you will not be able to look after her.'

'Mum, I have been keeping well, I've seen Dr McDougal she said I won't develop sickness now it's too late and you know it. I'm sorry it's come as a shock, I don't want to hurt you two. You have been great, I didn't tell you until I had sorted it out in my own head first. You are clutching at straws, the one thing that is sure is ... it's my baby, it doesn't matter who fathered it, it's mine. I'm its mother and I owe it to the baby to love it and look after it. It's not its fault it was conceived.' Rosie looked at her parents and sighed loudly. 'If I had realised sooner I was pregnant I might have terminated, but it's too late, I feel it moving,

The Nightclub Owners Wife

I can't kill it. So please both of you, be happy for me. This is my baby, your grandchild, who fathered it doesn't matter. I'm twenty-four weeks pregnant and I'm having this baby.'

Are you going to have tests done to see who the father is?' Maggie asked. 'Surely you need to know? Why on earth didn't I make you take the morning after pill they offered you. I should have insisted, you were not in a fit state to make that decision. You don't even remember being asked to take it. You were so traumatised. I should have realised you'd got pregnant from the rape? I should have been looking for it, should have realised sooner.' Maggie repeated, wiping away tears.

'Why? I never even noticed my periods had stopped. Mum stop it, this is not your fault. They said when I wouldn't take any drugs, I had capacity to make the decision, you disagreed. You were overruled. Mum you were right they were wrong. I don't remember being asked.' Rosie shook her head and sighed. 'It's a baby I'm carrying, not a fucking bomb. It makes no difference, I will love it no matter what, mum, please respect my wishes.'

'Have you told Lex? About the baby?' Rosie's father asked.

Rosie looked at her father and nodded, 'I told him before I told you. He's my friend, he was a little shocked, but he's accepted what I'm doing, not that it's any of his business. Now I need to go to the club, there's a problem with the wine rep Bobby reckons she is not giving us as good a deal as she can. I'm going to meet her, Alex is in Cyprus this week with Norrie, they're looking at some building technics there. I think it's just a boy's week away, what is it about Alex that everyone wants to adopt him? He always lands on his feet.'

'Are you coming straight back darling? Your mum's working tonight, remember, first nightshift? She needs to get a few hours' sleep. I'm not great with the nappies and stuff.

'Yes, I'll be back late afternoon. I'm also meeting the social worker who is writing the report on Carl, yes dad, I returned her call. I've arranged to see her at Nobels, I can use the office for privacy. Then I have a meeting with the builder about the house.

Alex and Norrie have done a brilliant job with the plans, and the planning permission has been granted so that should be done in about eight weeks. Alex has got someone lined up to rent it too.'

'Rosie, you need to go see Carl, tell him about the baby, what if he finds out some other way? He hasn't seen Imogen in five months. If you won't go, then let Rowena take her in. You don't even open his letters. He phones every Friday, but you won't talk to him.' Maggie looked at her daughter pleading with her eyes. 'He's been very patient with you Rosie, but he's talking about getting legal advice to force you to let him see her. Rosie don't let it come to that.'

'My daughter is not going to a prison, mum. I want nothing to do with him.'

Maggie Gibbs looked at her daughter and shook her head, 'Imogen is his daughter too. She deserves to know her father, she's a baby now, but she will grow up and want to know about him Rosie. He's also still your husband and he should know about the baby. He has rights, you need to get over this, get counselling or something, you loved him enough to have a child with him.'

Davie Gibbs shook his head at his wife and then turned to his daughter. 'Sweetheart I get it, we both do, we understand how you feel about Carl. We are not suggesting that you should have a relationship with him, if it's over its over. He won't be in jail forever, he will want to have a relationship with Imogen when he gets out. How will you support yourself without a husband? If he stops you getting money from the business?'

'I intend to go to university once this one is born. I've got a place, I deferred when I got pregnant and I still have the place. I've already investigated the university creche for the babies. I'll oversee the business with Rowena, but that's it.' Rosie looked sadly at her parents, 'my marriage is over. I won't divorce him whilst he's waiting to be sentenced, once it's over I'll decide what to do about the business. Alex and I discussed hiring a business manager to oversee it all. That will allow us to have careers away from it all but leave a business for Carl when he gets out.'

'Rosie, you and Lex, are you? You know?' Maggie asked her voice wavering. 'Your dad and I well we noticed you're spending a lot of time together. You're still a married woman Rosie.'

'What? No, we are friends, that's all, I . . . I don't think of him like that, and he doesn't think of me as anything other than his little sister. He's my closest friend . . . that's all.'

CHAPTER
FIFTEEN

Rosie looked up from the computer as Alex came into the office. 'Well?'

'Ten years! Exactly what Tommy thought.' Alex loosened his tie and took off his suit jacket. 'I need a drink; do you want something?'

'Glass of red wine, a small one,' Rosie stood up and walked to the window, she stared outside.

Alex returned to the office carrying a glass in each hand a bottle under his arm. Seeing Rosie with tears running down her face he put the glasses and the bottle on the desk and rushed to her side. 'Babe it's okay, it's over, he's alright. You need to cry Rosie, you've lost so much. I know you loved him, this must be hell for you?' He glanced down at her stomach, she saw him look and turned away from him.

'Alex please don't, I can't bear what you and my parents are thinking just now. I want this baby to have a happy start in life. Not everyone wishing it hadn't been conceived. It happened because of the state I was in. I couldn't give consent for the morning after pill. I wouldn't take any drugs and they said I still had capacity to choose. I don't know what I was thinking Alex, I just don't remember.'

The Nightclub Owners Wife

'Rosie it's okay babe, I'll be there for you, whatever you choose, the social worker said there were lots of options. It will be okay babe. I'm just worried about you making the wrong decision. You've been so strong right from the start. I don't want it all setting you back. What's worrying you? Talk to me Rosie?'

'I don't want everyone hating the baby, I don't want everyone upset. The way it was when Imogen was born, everyone worried, I was so ill. Then there was joy, new baby everyone loving her. I want to be happy Alex. Yet how can I be after what's happened? Someone has got to want this child you all think it's going to be a monster. I've looked at all the information . . . I think I want to keep it, I don't want it going to strangers, however desperate they are for a baby. Alex what if . . . you know nature nurture . . . this baby is either the child of a murder or a rapist?'

'No Rosie, it's a baby, new life, it has a wonderful beautiful mother. It's just that I don't want to see you do this alone.'

'But I am alone Alex, when it becomes known I'm pregnant, do you think that Carl is going to be overjoyed. He is going to want me to give the baby up.'

Please don't think like that, you're not alone. If you want to give it up for adoption, I'll be there for you. If you don't I'll still be there for you. Rosie,' Alex whispered, 'it's not just about you though, the baby it needs to be loved you need to be sure you are doing this for the right reasons, that you can bond with it. I'll help you through this, I promise Rosie.'

'What about Carl? I don't want him to know about the baby. If I do this?' Rosie put her hands protectively on her swollen stomach and looked down. 'I need to be prepared for how he will react, I just don't know if I want him to know.'

'Carl needs to know, you're going to have to tell him you're pregnant. Is that why you won't see him?' He handed her the glass of wine and she took a large gulp of it. Alex looked into Rosie's eyes, for all you know the baby could be his anyway. You said you had sex the day before it all happened. Carl wanted another baby darling.'

'Alex if I tell you what I'm thinking you will think I'm a terrible person.'

'Rosie, I could never think that.' Alex said softly, moving closer to Rosie he reached out and touched her cheek gently.

She looked up at him, her eyes sad, he knew she was struggling with her emotions, biting her bottom lip trying not to cry. 'I don't want to be with him, because I don't love him. I don't think I ever did. I think, oh I think I wanted to love him, I couldn't believe someone like Carl wanted me. Lex, you know him, there is a cruel streak in him.' They stood, neither of them moving or speaking, when she spoke her voice wavered and he could feel the sadness and regret. 'He was controlling me, telling me what to think, what to wear, who to be. I was okay with it because I wanted to be the woman he wanted. I thought he loved me.' Her eyes searched Alex's face, looking for a reaction, he sensed it and said nothing. Rosie looked away and continued to speak. 'I saw him kill a man and I can never forget that. He either slept with my best friend or raped her. I can't forgive that. Rosie began to sob, and Alex instinctively moved closer wrapped his arms around her and held her. She looked up at him and then her lips brushed his cheek. He looked into her eyes and kissed her back. She moaned softly and turned her head towards him. Their lips met, and they kissed, Rosie pulled away first, but she didn't move from his arms instead she buried her face in his chest her arms reached out and she held him.

'Rosie, Alex whispered, I've wanted to do that for a long time. I never realised I had those kinds of feelings for you until you started going out with Carl.'

'Alex, I've never you know ... been with anyone, only Carl. Then when I was raped, I might not remember it happening, but it hurt so much afterwards. I felt so dirty and used. I need time, I don't know if I can you know? It's not about Carl. I don't want anything to do with him now, I don't think I could ever be with him again and not see what he did. I try to see it all from his point of view, but it was, oh this is going to sound mad.' Rosie gulped away tears, she buried her face in Alex's chest and he had to lean forward to hear her. 'He was angry, and I get that, but he didn't need to kill Ronnie. He could have pulled him off and then looked after me. He kept stabbing, all the time he was... doing it, he was... oh, I don't know it was the same look... almost the same... As when he is having sex. Alex, it was as though he was enjoying putting the knife into him.'

Alex continued to hold her and whispered in her ear, 'it's okay darling to feel frightened and confused.' He kissed the top of her head, 'You were raped and then you saw a horrible thing, in a place where you should have been safe. You've been let down by people you love and who should have been there for you. It's okay to be angry.'

'Rosie sighed, and shook her head, I'm not angry Alex, just achingly empty and sad. I don't feel anything for Carl, I don't miss him. 'He blamed Elaine, you all did, but if he hadn't been sleeping with Julie then none of it would have happened. People will talk if you and I... you know? Get together?'

'It's no one's business babe, just yours and mine.' Alex gently lifted Rosie's chin and looked at her. 'Rosie it's alright darling. I'll wait until you are ready.'

'What if I'm never ready? Right now, I can't imagine ever wanting to have sex again.'

'That's okay too, it's not important now sweetheart there are a lot of things we have to work out. If we end up with something intimate, then we do.' He kissed the top of her head, 'if we don't then that's okay too. We are friends before anything else. If it works when we've had time to get our heads around it, then great.'

'When did you get to be so wise?' Rosie said smiling sadly, she looked up at him. 'You and I could we... you know, be together without it always being there? Could you be with me, he's your friend Alex?'

'I don't feel great about doing this either, but I do care about you Rosie, I want you, in a way I never thought I could. Carl was my mate, I've tried to understand some of the things he did, but you're right there is a cruel streak in him. There's stuff I have to tell you darling, I don't want there to be secrets between us.'

'Alex, I told you when you came out the hospital, I don't want to know anything about your past. I know you had other women, I know Carl did too, but please, don't tell me about it, can you just hold me? I just want to be held. Suddenly I want to be held, I couldn't bear any physical contact until you kissed me. It feels right Alex.' Rosie shook her head and paused composing herself. 'And...'

'So wrong.' Alex finished for her. They stood there for a long time, arms locked around each other neither wishing to move away. Suddenly the baby kicked, Alex looked down at Rosie and smiled. 'I think your son is going to be very possessive of his mummy. He's telling me to let you go.'

'How do you know it's a boy?'

'Oh, I'm sure that kick was a boy, going to be a footballer I reckon. You and I will make sure he has everything.' Alex kissed Rosie's forehead, 'Rosie, I meant what I said, I want to be there for you.' He moved away slightly and looked down at her. 'If you'll let me?'

'Alex...I well I don't know if I'll ever be able to be intimate with anyone again. I want you to hold me, but oh I don't know. I feel that I couldn't, you know? With anyone. They keep offering me counselling, I don't know if I could talk about what happened. What I just told you about his face when he did it. I've never told anyone, not even the police, I couldn't say it. My husband, the man I married is a monster.'

'Rosie, I'm not asking you to be intimate sweetheart, I know that will be difficult for you,' Alex smiled, 'I'm not going to pretend I wouldn't with you, but we can deal with all that stuff later. Let's just take it slowly, spend time together. No one needs to know just now, we can just be together, be friends yeah?'

'What about Moira? Aren't you missing her? I take it you went to see her when you were in Cyprus?'

The Nightclub Owners Wife

'Yeah, I dropped into their bar for a drink, she is doing fine, it's a lovely island and they are happy. Dougie is enjoying being out of the army and the business is doing well. I had to go see her ... there was some unfinished business between her and me.'

'You and her you're not?' Not that I've any right to tell you who you can be with, but if she and Dougie are sorting out their lives?

Alex smiled and shook his head. 'Not any more. We weren't, oh it's complicated, we well it's not what you think I swear it's over, I just don't want to be disloyal to her babe. It was a casual stupid thing we did, I can't discuss it without telling you other stuff. You said you don't want to know.'

Rosie nodded, 'I don't want to think bad of you Alex, I want you to be my knight in shining armour. Is it important to you to talk about things you did?'

Alex smiled and shook his head. 'There are more important issues just now than what happened with me and Moira. We need to discuss Elaine, I do need to tell you this, you need to know. Tommy and I went to see her, got her to drop the rape charge.'

Rosie looked at Alex, 'did he rape her? I can see by your face, you are struggling with it. Did he? Did he rape her? She whispered.

Alex's face clouded over, and he looked away, 'yes I think he did Rosie. She says that they got wasted together that night, the night the wean was born. She admits that he kissed her in the kitchen, she responded. I don't know, she says she realised what she was doing and told him no. She should have gone home, but she says she was really drunk, he put her to bed in your spare room.' Alex sighed, 'babe I'm sorry, but I believe Elaine, I know she wasn't lying. She says that she wakened up and he was on top of her, finishing off really. She thought she was dreaming. I know it sounds crazy, but she was drunk and done some drugs, she admits that she wasn't hurt physically, she just let him do it, says she didn't fight, she reckons she was in shock. He had given her blues too. She says she remembers him carrying her to bed, so he wasn't as drunk as she was if he managed that. He also managed to have sex, so he must have been straight. Anyway, she just waited until he went back to his own bed, then left. She didn't know what to do, she came looking for me. I think I was with Carl at the hospital. She went to her Gran's, got changed and went back to Stirling.'

'Why didn't she tell me? Why did she just go back to uni and ignore me? She was my best friend almost the sister I never had. Alex, she just acted as though I was nothing to her.'

'Would you have believed her, if he'd said they slept together?'

'I don't know?' Rosie admitted, 'but she never gave me the option. It's been five months and she has never been in touch with me.'

Alex gazed into Rosie's eyes. 'She said she was afraid of losing you, however the more time that passed, she got angry. I think she . . . oh I don't know, she said you left a message for her inviting her to the club opening. She came through to Kilmarnock intending to go to the club. She says she didn't want to let you down, because she knew you had gone against Carl to invite her. She had no intention she says of saying anything to you or anyone else.

'So how did she go from this to telling Ronnie Muir about Carl and Julie, when she hadn't told me?'

'She says she got here and started panicking. She was sitting on the bench outside the car park at the town centre, trying to decide if she could go in and she met Ronnie. He asked her what was wrong, and she told him, she told him the lot. There isn't really a defence other than she was probably traumatised, angry, upset, she thought no one would believe her. She was all mixed up I think, it's all so unlike Elaine, which would make you think she's been through major trauma.'

'Alex is it bad I don't want to see her? She and I, we've been friends our whole lives, but I just can't bear to see her just now.

The Nightclub Owners Wife

If he did rape her I know I should be there for her, Alex I just can't, is that wrong?'

Alex shrugged, 'if I'm honest I don't want her around either sweetheart, it's just too soon.'

'The person responsible here is Carl, but she kissed him, got drunk with him. Then she didn't tell me? I . . . I just feel that I never knew her. Just like I never knew him?' Rosie wiped away the tears now streaming down her face. I just can't deal with anymore stuff Alex, I need to sort everything out in my head.

'She doesn't want to see you either just now Rosie, or me. I'm trying to understand, but I can't stop blaming her. That's not good either is it?'

'I hate the idea of her going through this alone, I've got my family . . . and you. Who has she got?'

'She has a good friend at Uni, Gail, she said she was going to tell her. She is being supported, the university have arranged counselling for her too. Rosie don't feel guilty, you've been through a lot recently, you need to get your head around it all. You have a lot of decisions to make babe.'

'I'm keeping this baby Alex, thank you for not telling me not to have it. You never have, despite everyone else saying it, you've supported me.' Rosie looked up at him, 'what do you really think, you must have an opinion?'

'It's a baby sweetheart, your baby, your decision, your body.' Alex smiled at Rosie and kissed her gently. 'Whatever you decide I'll be there for you, but like I said, if you keep it you have to be able to love it as much as Imogen.

Rosie nodded. 'Promise, me that's the last you will say on the subject?'

Alex nodded, 'yeah, but if you do want to talk . . . you know you can tell me anything?' he looked at Rosie and smiled, 'quite like being a knight in shining armour.'

CHAPTER

SIXTEEN

September 1997 Irvine Central Maternity Unit.

The noise of the fan whirring appeared to Rosie to be loud and shouting at her, *'it's coming the monster is coming!'* The plaster cracks on the ceiling of the room appeared as faces shouting with the fan. She'd tried hard during the pregnancy to want this child, she hadn't been as sick this time and there was, to everyone's relief no sign of the eclampsia. She had been in labour for seventeen hours, her choice, they had wanted her to have a caesarean due to there being only ten months between babies. Rosie had asked to try labour and a normal delivery. She'd hoped if she could experience this child being born, she might stop feeling the way she did. She wanted to experience labour, however she had now been forced to take the painkilling drugs they offered her.

Rosie heard a voice, she stared at the fan on the ceiling she could hear it talking. 'Rosie, focus, can you hear me?' Her mother's face appeared before her. 'Rosie, they are going to have to do a cesarean, the baby is in distress, there is no other choice. Rosie focus darling, we need to get it out.'

'I'm having a monster!' Rosie cried out, 'mum, what if it's a monster, what if I can't love it? I don't want it to come from the same place as Imogen.'

'Rosie you're in pain and distraught, they are going to give you a general anaesthetic. I've signed the consent forms darling, you are in no fit state to decide. Lex is outside, is it okay to let him in? Rosie, he's in a right state, he just got back from London.'

'Let him come in, mum him and I we...I don't know how to say this we are...Argh!' Rosie cried out in pain and as the contraction subsided. She whispered, 'I love him mum, we haven't you know? Argh...it hurts, I need him.'

'It's okay darling, I know...you and Lex, your dad and I worked it out. Rosie this is not the time to discuss this. I'll go get him.'

'Mum, I'm sorry, I really am,' tears ran down Rosie's face as another contraction took hold she gasped and cried out again. Rosie closed her eyes and panted as the contraction ended, she opened them, he was there. Rosie could see the worry on Alex's face as he took her hand and held it, kissing the top of her head. 'Alex, I'm sorry so sorry, I can't do this, I can't do it alone, what if I hate the baby? What if it is his? What if it looks like him?'

'It's a baby Rosie, your baby, you are going to love it as soon as you see it.' He leaned forward and whispered in her ear, aware of the nurse and doctor in the corner of the room. 'He's going to be our baby, yours and mine, we will love him, okay babe?' Alex kissed her gently, hoping beyond hope he sounded calmer than he felt.

'It's time Rosie, they need to take you to theatre darling, Doctor McDougal has come in especially,' Maggie coming up behind Alex whispered over his shoulder. She looked at Alex, 'we'd better go wait in the waiting room.' She touched his arm, 'we can wait together, Davie is looking after Imogen, so I'm all alone.'

Alex watched as the porter and nurses wheeled Rosie along the corridor before putting his arm around the woman beside him and gently leading her into the empty waiting room. 'Thanks for calling me Maggie, I appreciate how hard it was for you to do it. I'm so scared, what if something goes wrong?' I'm trying to go along with her wishes to keep it, but what if that's the wrong decision for her? What if we ... she can't love it? The social worker says they can put it with people who will look after it for a short time. Foster parents, so she can decide but she was adamant that she wants to keep it. Maggie, Rosie and I ... I'm so sorry.'

'Lex, this is not what we wanted, well not now, years ago after Simon ... well Davie and I kind of hoped that you and she would be an item. Then she met Carl, we knew you were friends you and Rosie, what is going on? You're not, are you? She's been through so much, she won't even speak about it, hasn't since the day she told us she was pregnant. I've tried to talk to her, but she just blanks it and says, *'it's my baby!'* after tonight though, I'm really worried, can she love it? Does she know who the father is? Imogen was only four weeks old, so it surely isn't Carl's?'

'She doesn't know Maggie, Carl he wanted her to have another one, they had sex, once, the night before the rape ... she doesn't know, and I don't think she wants to know. That's not why she doesn't want to speak to Carl, it's a lot more complicated than just her being pregnant. Her and I well we're not you know? I want to Maggie, I want to be with her, I love her, I think I always have. I want to look after her and the kids, but it all needs to be her choice.' He looked sadly at the older woman and sighed. 'It doesn't matter who the baby's father is, it's her baby, she's been so strong throughout this, but I think tonight she is just panicking. It's all becoming real, isn't it? I know she'll love the baby when its born. She thought if she told anyone she was struggling you would all make her give it up, the social worker has also given her all the info about adoption. Maggie, I'm going to be there for her. I think she needs to tell him, tell Carl about the baby.'

'Carl knows about the baby, son.' Maggie gently touched Alex's arm, 'Rowena told him, I understand why. She was afraid someone else would do it. I think someone needs to go and see him. Rowena isn't well Lex, Rosie told you? The cancer is terminal, she shouldn't have all this stress. You and Rosie have helped her but, well, the club, it's too much for Rowena, she needs more help with it all. I know you have your career, and Rosie well she has the babies. It's even more difficult now Moira has gone as well, she was good for the clubs Lex. Imagine her and Dougie deciding to live in Cyprus just like that?

Alex shrugged, 'oh Dougie and her just fancied a change I expect. I think what happened changed a lot of people's way of thinking Maggie, not just us.' Alex looked thoughtful, 'Bobby does a good enough job Maggie, holding it all together. He's really loyal to Rowena and Carl, he was Carl's dads' mate. Rosie has been doing all the accounts for Rowena too. She reckons Carl's little empire is worth a small fortune now, the business is doing well. Perhaps this is the time for them to let it go.'

Maggie nodded, 'it is most likely the best thing, Rowena knows that, but, Carl won't give permission for her to sell up. Someone needs to explain to him how hard it all is. Davie says they won't let Carl run the business when he gets out anyway. He's a convicted murderer he'll not be able to have the licence.'

'Maggie, can we talk about all of this some other time? Rosie is in there having the baby delivered, I just need to focus on that just now.' Alex looked at the ceiling as he spoke, 'Carl Ranmore killed a man in cold blood, I know he was my mate, but I ... oh ... I don't know?' He brought his gaze back to Maggie and looked her in the eye. 'For now, ... I ... I just want to look after Rosie and the kids ... both of them, if she'll let me. At least Rowena managed to talk Carl out of going to court for access to Imogen, that was a lot off Rosie's mind. She is going to have to let him see her some time, she knows that, but she just wants to have the baby and get herself psyched up for it all. Maggie can we just? Maggie I need to . . . Alex wiped away a tear from his face.'

Maggie put her hand on Alex's, she gripped it. 'Let's change the subject?' she whispered, 'how was your trip? Did you pass your exam?'

'Yes, with distinction, but it was bad timing.'

'The baby wasn't due for another ten days, you got back very quickly. Davie said you only phoned this morning.'

'I flew back instead of getting the train. I called your house and Davie told me you were here.'

Alex and Maggie looked up as the door opened, Selina McDougal put her head around the door. 'She's through with flying colours. It's a little boy folks, eight, four, and he has all his bits in the right places. Rosie is doing well, we'll take her up to the ward in about thirty minutes, she's going into room thirteen if you two want to go up and wait. The baby is a little cold but otherwise alright I think. We will warm him up a bit and then bring him up. Has she got a name for a boy?'

Maggie shook her head, 'not that I know of Dr McDougal, she has, well you know, she's been really traumatised. It's the circumstances.' Maggie began to cry, and Alex immediately wrapped his arms around her and held her. 'She wants to call him Tobias Simon' He said, looking over Maggie's head at the doctor. 'Toby for short.'

Selina McDougal came into the room and closed the door behind her, keeping her hand on the handle as though to prevent anyone else from entering. 'I know she isn't sure who the father is, she told me. I offered her DNA tests as soon as it was born, we can use Imogen to compare. She doesn't want it done Maggie. She says she feels that neither is a good prospect, so she doesn't want to know.' She looked at Alex, and then added, 'if she does later then let me know? I can get it done without any hassle. Maybe once she has settled and made decisions she will feel more able?'

The Nightclub Owners Wife

***

'He looks like Imogen,' Alex said looking down at the baby in his arms, 'hopefully that's a good sign Maggie.' Alex kissed the baby's head and then sat down beside the bed cradling the infant close to his chest.

Maggie shrugged and then sighed, 'I suppose I would rather he was Carl's than Ronnie's, although I wish he wasn't here at all if I'm honest.' Maggie nodded at the still figure on the bed, 'I can't say that ever again.' Lex do you think she will manage to love him? I mean no matter whose child he is, it's still a reminder of a very unpleasant time. Selina wants her to have some counselling. She's going to speak to her about it later, I don't know Lex, it's going to be so hard.' Maggie gently moved her sleeping daughters' hair from her face then bent down and kissed her forehead.

The door opened, a nurse put her head around the door. 'Mrs Ranmore is on the telephone Maggie. Can you come and speak to her?'

Maggie stood up, 'I think she is wakening now Lex, so this is probably the best time to go and leave you to it.' Maggie kissed first Alex then the tiny baby who screwed up his little face and opened his eyes for the first time. Maggie looked at the baby and smiled through tears. 'I'm sure he's Carl's, look at his eyes? I remember when Imogen was born as soon as she opened her eyes we saw Carl.'

They stopped speaking as Rosie opened her eyes slightly, sighed, muttered something and then went back to sleep.

Alex nodded and gulped back tears, 'I don't know if that's good or bad Maggie... for her,' he nodded at the still figure on the bed. 'I think for him,' he said kissing the top of the baby's downy head, 'it's the lesser of the two evils. I'm not going to try to convince her to have the DNA done, she is adamant she doesn't want to know. I'll stay here until she wakens.

As Maggie closed the door behind her, Rosie stirred and opened her eyes. Alex moved in closer. 'Hey, how are you?' He whispered kissing Rosie's forehead. 'This is your son Rosie, eight pounds four ounces. Isn't he a handsome little devil?' He smiled and moved the baby closer holding out the little white bundle.

'Oh my god he's beautiful!' Rosie gasped, taking the baby in her arms, she held him close and suddenly she was crying loud sobs holding the baby, kissing him, telling him she loved him.

Alex let her cry he sat on the edge of the bed and held her, the baby squashed against them began to cry. Alex moved back and kissed the baby. He looked at Rosie his eyes filled with tears his heart full. 'Rosie, we will look after him, he is ours, yours and mine.'

CHAPTER
SEVENTEEN

November 1997

'I'm not doing it Alex, I've told you, mum and dad and Rowena, I don't want to know. If he wants to know when he's older then that's his choice.' Rosie kissed her two-month-old sons' cheek and smiled as he opened his eyes and looked up at her, she put him to her breast and he immediately fastened and began to suck. I'm sorry Alex, but I just don't think it matters. She suddenly looked at Alex her face showing the horror of the situation, 'you don't think he will force me to do it, Carl I mean? If he's not Carl's, then the Muir's could try to get him.'

Rosie no, they won't, and you heard what Rowena said, Carl he won't do it because he thinks you've got post-natal depression or something. He thinks that's why you won't see him.' Alex hesitated and sighed, I'm going in to see him next week, oh I won't say anything about us.' He smiled wryly, 'there is nothing to tell anyway, Rosie, I'm happy just to be with you, I love you babe. I'll always be there for you and them. He lifted Imogen on to his knee and she snuggled in. Alex kissed her cheek and smiled, 'she's worn out from her party. Who's a big one-year old?' He said softly as Imogen closed her eyes, her mouth making sucking motions her lips holding on to the pink sparkly dummy in her mouth. Her little hand gipping Alex's shirt. 'Rosie, he was asking Rowena about me, he was wondering why I hadn't been in.'

Rosie nodded, normally when Alex suggested seeing Carl she became upset, however she looked at him and agreed. 'I think you are right, he could cause problems now though. I'm still a bit scared, because he'll get out some day and I don't know what he is capable of now? Murder? Rape? What else could he do? I need to sort some stuff out, Alex I'm going to move in with Rowena, she's so unwell just now and I want to look after her.' She sighed and looked down at the baby in her arms. 'I know it will make things difficult for us, but I need to do it.'

'Rosie, I would be more worried if you didn't want to look after her, she's an amazing woman, isn't she? You and I Rosie, if it's going to happen, our time will come,' Alex moved the sleeping child in his arms on to the couch and moved to sit beside Rosie, smiling as she rested her head on his shoulder. Happy birthday babe, eighteen today. I know you didn't want a fuss, you said not to spend any money on you. So, I didn't, but I had to do something to mark the occasion.'

Rosie smiled sadly, 'I loved the painting Alex, thank you it's so original. I'm going to hang it in my bedroom. I wish I could show you how much I care about you?' She sighed and looked around at him. 'Wish I could . . . you know?'

'Someday, you and I will be able to be open and honest about how we feel. I told you I can wait. How did it go at the hospital? What's the news?'

Rosie moved the baby who was now sleeping from her breast and began to rub his back gently. She avoided looking at Alex, but he knew she was struggling with her emotions. Her shoulders hunched as though being pushed down into the depths of despair. Rosie took a deep breath and when she finally spoke he could hear the raw emotion. 'She hasn't got long, maybe as little as six months. They are going to try some treatment or other,

The Nightclub Owners Wife

an experimental one, it may give her a few more months. I just can't contemplate her not being there. From the moment I met her, she has been like a second mother to me. Alex, I need to do this, need to help her. She doesn't have anyone else, her sister lives so far away and has cancer too you know? Their mother died from it, some families just have such terrible luck. I'm sure it's all related to what happened with Carl in Rowena's case. The oncologist said it was a very aggressive type, all the treatment so far has failed. It's this new treatment then palliative care, but I don't want strangers looking after her. Mum is going to help, now she is part time and has finally passed her driving test, she can assist in providing the nursing care, just like she did with your mum. Rowena and mum are really close friends.' Rosie sighed and looked at Alex, 'I'm also going to defer university for a year, I've spoken to them explained and I can start next year.'

'You need to be careful you're not taking on too much babe, I'd like to help more, but...well I...I can't be around her as much as I would like to be. I don't want to hurt Rowena by her finding out what you mean to me. She loves her son, and I know she's hoping you and him will sort things out. Then I think well...we haven't done anything wrong, have we? Well maybe a few impure thoughts. Carl and you, well it would be over anyway, wouldn't it? Rowena, she loves you and both the kids, but Carl he's her son, it must be so hard for her to accept what's happened.'

'Oh, I don't know Alex, I think she realises what he has done, it must be hard, he's her only child. But Rowena? I think she of all people knew what Carl was capable of, we've talked a lot about it. You know she guessed about him and Julie, but he denied it. She was in a difficult position, she now lives with that guilt. She feels she spoiled him, and his Dad, well apparently, he was the type of person who couldn't see any faults in Carl. He thought he had a perfect son. Rosie looked thoughtful, 'they were both good people, but they loved their son too much, gave him everything. It's all a bit like my parents and Simon, I wonder what he would have been like?'

Alex smiled. 'Oh, I think Si would have been just like you, he had a good heart Rosie, and a great family. I know we were just stupid teenagers, but he was like me, he knew some of the stuff we did was wrong.'

I often wonder is it nature or nurture? What turns someone into a monster? I honestly don't know anymore. I'm so afraid for Toby and Imogen, I mean if Carl could turn out like he did, selfish and controlling, with a mother like Rowena. What chance do they have?' Rosie kissed the top of her little son's head and looked over at her sleeping daughter her red chubby cheeks vibrating as she snoozed, her dummy now lying on the cushion beside her.

'No Rosie, we will bring them up to be respectful and loving, look at me. Even when I was a teenager getting up to all sorts, I knew the difference between right and wrong. Simon, he did too, we did things for kicks, but oh . . . I don't know, the night of the accident. I was really scared. I remember most of it, I vowed whilst we were in that car to sort my life out. I knew it was wrong.

'Alex what if it's an inbuilt thing? You know nature not nurture, look at the Muir's? They are mostly into bad stuff aren't they. Billy, he led you two into loads of stuff. I was young I know, but I remember Mum telling Simon she thought he was a bad lot. She and Dad were always going on about you and Simon being friends with Billy. They blame the Muir's for Simon dying. I remember their uncle coming to the house after the accident and asking if mum and dad would go to Billy's funeral. Mum was really upset. The uncle started shouting at them because they refused.'

Alex sighed and looked away, remembering what for him had been a very painful time. 'Billy was wild, but he was likeable, their house was fun to be in. His mum let us do things our parents wouldn't. We thought she was a really cool mum. She was a bit like Carl's dad, she couldn't see any wrong in her boys, blamed everyone else. Ronnie, well he was always a nasty person even as a kid, I remember him being a real bastard. Billy used to keep chickens and Ronnie once went in and chopped the heads off them, over a fairly minor row with Billy. There were three boys in between them you know? There is not much in age between them, because they were all at primary school at the same time. Gordon the second eldest got out, he's doing fine, he's a nurse up north. Andy well you know he's a drug user, sits down the precinct most days; his mum still bales him out all the time. Pete is Andy's twin, he's just like Ronnie. Thing is they were all really scathing about Gordon it's as though getting away from it all is a bad thing. Simon used to say the Muir's got extra pocket money if they got charged by the police.' Alex smiled remembering, then frowned. 'My mum, bless her, she was really upset when I got into bother, she had so much to contend with being a single parent and then being so ill. She tried hard with me, but she couldn't shake off the council scheme mentality, she worried about me not having a manual skill to fall back on.

'She was a lovely lady your mum, it was so sad her illness, you had to do so much for her, didn't you?' Rosie touched his arm and looked up, 'she was so proud of you getting into university, at least she knew all that before she died.'

'Your mum and dad, Rosie, I owe them so much, they helped look after her, so I could go to uni. I had to do things for her, personal care. Things a young boy shouldn't know about his mother. I didn't mind, but she hated it. When your mum started helping it was good to hand some of it over.

'I think it helped mum to look after her Alex, when Simon was ill she could focus on something else, then afterwards she was able to throw herself into caring for her it helped her deal with Simon. Motor neuron is a horrible illness she was kind of dying from the inside out, wasn't she?'

'I miss her Rosie, but I have you and the kids now.' Alex bent forward and kissed her on the mouth. She began to return his kisses initially, then as always, she pulled away from him.

'Alex, I'm sorry, I just keep trying, please forgive me?'

Alex sighed, 'it's okay babe, you need to take time, you've so much on your mind right now. The babies, Rowena, I can wait, when you are ready we can talk.' He stood up, right let's get you round to Rowena's. She will be desperate to see these two. You finished feeding him?'

Rosie knew Alex was talking to avoid how aroused he was, she liked that he never pushed her to have sex. Walked away, perhaps frustrated, but never putting any pressure on her. Rosie couldn't think about intimacy, she knew she wanted to with Alex, but she wasn't able. She wasn't sure if she would ever be. She also was afraid of losing the friendship she had with him. They did a lot together, there was very little she didn't share with him. The issue of them as an intimate couple came up from time to time, however usually as soon as it got to a point where a decision about progressing intimacy loomed, Rosie retreated. Rosie wasn't sure whether Alex saw other women, she didn't think he did, however she knew she had no right to prevent this. He spent most of his spare time with her and the children. They both knew that now she was going to live with Rowena this would be even more problematic.

Rosie had also decided that she needed help to deal with what had happened to her. She didn't want to discuss this or anything from the past with anyone close to her. She had spoken to Selina McDougal at her post-natal appointment and had been referred to a counsellor.

CHAPTER
EIGHTEEN

November 1998

'You okay babe?' Alex said putting his arm on Rosie's shoulder.

'Yes, I'm okay, she looks lovely doesn't she, they really have managed to make her look the way she did before the cancer took hold.' Rosie bent down and kissed her mother-in-law's forehead. She nodded at the undertaker, 'has my husband arrived yet?'

'Yes, Mrs Ranmore, he's decided he didn't want to see her, he's in the chapel. They apparently took him to see her in the hospital just before she died. We thought it would be better for him to be seated first given the circumstances.'

Rosie looked at the undertaker and then at Alex who put his hand on her shoulder and squeezed, knowing what Rosie was thinking, 'probably for the best, I take it he's handcuffed to the prison officers?' He asked.

The undertaker nodded, 'that's always the case when they are allowed out of prison for the day Mr Lockwood. They won't let him stay, they'll take him straight back after the service.' He turned to Rosie. 'Now about the seating arrangements in the chapel, we've put Mr Ranmore in the front row on the right, if you go in the side door you can go straight into the left-hand front row, I've told your parents to go there. Your Dad has spoken to your husband, let him know the arrangements.'

'Alex can you go sit on the same side as Carl please? That might make it look better for him,' Rosie asked quietly. 'Are his cousins there?'

Alex nodded, 'Bobby and Dessie from the club are here too babe. I've spoken to Carl, Rosie, told him that you can't sit with him, but I will. They have left a seat for me on his right-hand side'

'You're a good man Alex Lockwood, a real gentleman, thank you. I haven't seen him since I was in the hospital it seems so long ago. I have no wish to see him now, but you are wonderful doing this, you are sitting there to block his view, aren't you?

Alex nodded, Rosie took one last look at her mother-in-law. She placed one of the roses she was carrying in the coffin and turned away as the undertakers slid the lid on top. When Rosie turned back she put the remainder of the red roses on top she kissed her fingers and touched the brass nameplate then turned and left the room with Alex, his arm around her shoulder.

Alex dropped his arm to his side at the door, then walked beside Rosie into the chapel, she sat down beside her father, Davie Gibb put his arm around his daughter and pulled her closer kissing the top of her head. Alex walked on and sat down beside Carl Ranmore. Rosie did not look over at her husband, afraid of what she would feel if she looked at him.

The service felt endless, Rosie was aware of Carl in the pew to her right flanked by two men in uniform. She knew he was watching her, sensing him rather than seeing. She knew Alex was standing nearest her and when she eventually glanced over it was Alex she could see.

The Nightclub Owners Wife

When the service was finally over, they quickly took Carl away and it was Rosie and her father who shook hands with the other mourners.

She saw Alex coming along the line of people and when he reached her, he hugged her and whispered into her ear, 'you did great babe!' He looked around before adding, 'I'll see you back at the house later. I'm not going to come to Nobels darling, I don't think I can hide how I feel.' Rosie nodded and watched as Alex disappeared into the crowd of mourners outside the crematorium. Suddenly Rosie knew she wanted to be with him, the months of discussion with her counsellor had proved fruitful, suddenly it was all clear. Although she now wanted everyone to know, Rosie resisted the urge to run after Alex and tell him there and then.

***

Rosie stepped into the hallway closing the front door, Alex was in the living room packing toys into a box. He stood up and walked towards her. 'How did it all go? I take it you got the message about the kids?'

'Thanks for going for the babies Alex, I phoned Jodie to arrange to collect them and she said you had been.'

Alex smiled, 'I wanted to spend some time with them, but they are both sleeping now.' He sighed then stood up and walked towards her. 'It was hard seeing you so upset, I wanted to hold you darling. I know you are struggling with us, but I just wanted to fucking hold you, make it all better.'

In response, Rosie put her arms around his neck and pulled him closer, she put her lips to his and melted into his arms. 'Make love to me Alex Lockwood, make me feel good. I love you and there is no reason to hide anymore. It's been so long, I want you here and now, thank you for being patient with me.'

Alex looked into her eyes and then not taking his lips from hers he turned the key in the door behind her, picked Rosie up and carried her in his arms still kissing her, upstairs to her bedroom. He laid her gently on the bed before he spoke again. 'Are you sure?' He asked his voice husky and emotional. 'Are you sure you're ready?'

Rosie nodded, 'I think I've been ready for a while, but I had so many other things to think about.' She put her arms around his neck, they kissed Rosie felt her body react. 'Let's just see how it goes?' She whispered in his ear. 'There are condoms in that drawer next to the bed. I got them when I was up at the university last week, someone handed me a bag, you know what they are like at freshers week.' Rosie giggled and then nudged Alex. 'I saw the condoms in it and thought, must be a sign.'

'I love a lady who is prepared.'

The first time they made love it was over quickly, emotional and crying as they moved together. 'Rosie, I will never stop loving you, I swear I will love you till the day I die,' Alex whispered.

Rosie shivered as two years of pent up emotion exploded within her, she knew that she loved him, wanted him and all the bad memories were gone as she climaxed. Shivering, crying out as the tidal wave over took her, when she looked up Alex was lost in his own orgasm.

Afterwards she lay in his arms feeling more content than she had in a long time, he stroked her hair, gently kissing the top of her head as she snuggled into his muscular chest. 'Alex that was wonderful, oh my god you are good at this. Can I keep you?'

'You sure can, I've never felt like that before babe, it was . . . you were wonderful. I want to be doing that for the rest of my life.' He kissed the top of her head again then looked into her eyes. 'You look tired Rosie, try to get some sleep, I know you've had a lot of running around to do, you're exhausted. It's time someone looked after you properly. For starters I'll see to the kids when they waken.'

'Alex, I love you.'

'Yeah, yeah, as a sex slave now!' Smiling broadly, he kissed her again, 'I adore you Rosie Ranmore, you are going to be my princess. Know what?

'What?'

'I'm glad we waited, I think we have something special and it can only grow from here.' Alex rolled over and stood up lifting his trousers from the floor. He bent down and kissed the tip of her nose. 'I love you so much, I always have.' Alex pulled on his trousers, lifted the used condom and walked towards the door. 'Now get some sleep!' He said over his shoulder.

***

Alex looked up as Rosie came into the room, Imogen and Toby were eating breakfast. 'You've slept for thirteen hours babe. Your mum's just been around looking for you. I said you had fallen asleep after the funeral and I would get you to call her when you get up. Tommy Halliday phoned too. He needs to speak to you about Rowena's will apparently.'

Rosie frowned, moved over and put her arms around Alex and kissed him. 'Why didn't you come back to bed Alex, after yesterday I thought I had made myself clear.' She nodded at the blanket and pillow on the sofa. 'You slept down here?'

Alex looked bashful, 'I didn't know what to do to be honest, I wanted to get back in beside you but ... you know ... I hadn't been invited. I know we said some stuff, but I don't want you to feel you have to.'

'Alex, I want you to live with us, I think we've spent far too long skirting the real issue here.' She looked him in the eye, you've kept saying you would wait for me, till I was ready, well I think I kind of proved I was ready. I love you for having waited for me. This is our time now Alex, you and me and ... well.' Rosie grinned, 'what you did to me earlier, wow, you're good at that sex stuff. Have you been practicing?'

Alex frowned. 'I ... I don't quite know how to put this but ... I don't want to live here with you, this doesn't feel right, its Rowena's house, this is where Carl grew up. I would imagine he'll get it in the will. I want us to have our own place. Besides when Carl finds out, he might not want you living here. Rosie,

I haven't been with anyone, you know... for a long time. I only want you,' Alex sighed, 'I want us to be a family, but I need you to let me tell Carl about us. I want to look him in the eye and tell him we are a couple. I need this Rosie, I just don't feel right about it. I understand you didn't want to ask him for a divorce because of Rowena, but she's gone now. Rosie, I want it all with you. Marriage, the works, I love the kids like they are my own, but we both know they're not and someday they are going to ask questions. They're so young, we could be a family. I just don't want it to be here. Rosie I've been hiding some stuff from you. About a year ago I bought a plot of land and designed a house, it's almost finished, and I want you me and the kids to live there.'

'Where is it? You've never said a thing, you've built a house and never said?' Rosie smiled and shook her head, 'you're full of surprises Mr Lockwood. How did you manage to keep it a secret? When can I see it?'

Alex laughed and pulled Rosie closer, he kissed her and looked into her eyes. It was easy, you had so much to do looking after Rowena and the kids, going to uni, I had so much time on my hands. Well when I wasn't using them to make up for having no sex. Every time I kissed you good night I wanted you and well I had to use a lot of self-control.' He grinned, 'but you asked about the house, our house I hope. It's along the coast from Ayr, I'm not telling you where, but I will take you and the kids there this afternoon. Rosie if you don't like it or don't want to live there I can sell it, it was a project to keep me busy. You need to be happy about it all. I just want to be with you, it doesn't matter where, as long as it's not here and just us.'

CHAPTER

NINETEEN

'Okay now you need to keep your eyes closed, I want you to get the whole picture. The front isn't finished so keep them closed till I stop and take you inside, Rosie I mean it, I need you to see the view from it first, and then use your imagination.'

Rosie could hear the uncertainty in Alex's voice, she did as she was told. 'Alex, if you made it I'll love it, why are you so scared? I put on the blindfold as we passed the airport, so I don't even know where we are?' She held on to him as he put his arm around her and led her away from the car. She knew she was near the sea as she could hear waves crashing. She heard him turn a key and then open and close a door as he led her inside. Immediately the noise of the sea disappeared.

'Keep them closed, just through here, another ten seconds and you will get the best view. Step coming up, lift your feet now another, here let me guide you. Keep your eyes shut,' Rosie felt him let her hand go and stand behind her, his hand on her waist pushing her. Right there are a few steps now, so just keep going I won't let you fall. She realised he was taking her upstairs and she did as she was told. She felt him push her through a doorway then he leaned in and opened another door, immediately she could hear and smell the sea. Okay you can open them now.' He said, pulling her scarf away from her face.

Rosie opened her eyes and gasped, she was on a balcony, a large concrete area with white walls and floor, a canopy over a corner area with a hot tub. She could see the Isle of Arran across the water and Ailsa Craig in the distance. Oh my God Alex, what a view, where are we? Is that Prestwick, Troon? How on earth did you manage this?'

We are in between them, there was a small house here and I just expanded it. I'm hoping so much you'll like it, I made it for us.' He wrapped his arms around her. Come see the rest of it. Through here is the master bedroom.' He led her into the large room and then through a mirrored corridor. 'This is the ensuite, I haven't bought any furniture yet. I hoped you would do that with me. I also haven't decorated. I wanted us to do that together too. Rosie I'm earning good money now, and I can afford to live like this. I've also insured my car for you to get to university, so you won't need to go on the train as much. If we move in here I can work from home more, so I can be here with the kids.

'Alex, I love it, I can't believe you did all this, it's perfect. I can't wait to look around.

'Looks like our little people are awake!' Alex looked out of the window as the car alarm went off. 'You have a wander and I'll go get them, I think it's Toby, I can see his arm moving. Do you really like it?'

'I love it Alex, I can't believe it's ours.'

'Well it is Rosie, all ours.' Alex kissed her and then went off down the stairs.

Rosie peeped into the four other bedrooms and the large family bathroom. She walked downstairs and smiled as Imogen toddled into the hallway towards her.

'Mama, house,' Imogen cried running around the large hallway.

Alex carrying Toby who was wriggling in his arms walked out after her. He looked up at Rosie who was standing on the last stair. 'Well?'

'When can we move in?'

Alex smiled broadly, Rosie could see the relief and joy on his face. 'As soon as we buy some furniture babe. I've got some you've got some, but we will also need some that's just ours, like a bed. Come let's get a coffee and you can see the kitchen and lounge, it has a conservatory and looks out over the bay. The kitchen is over there, he kissed Toby then handed him to Rosie and scooped Imogen up. The play room is through here big girl.' He kissed the little girl, she smiled happily back at him.'

'uv ooh,' Imogen giggled, kissing Alex's face.

'I love you too.' Alex said, putting her down at the door of a large bright room with a brightly painted toybox open to disclose age appropriate toddler toys. A large ball pond was built against the wall, a small area in the corner housed large soft play bricks and a fort. Imogen giggled and followed her brother who was already crawling across the floor towards the brightly coloured foam bricks and arches.

'Can you take me into town on the way back?' Rosie asked as she watched the children playing, 'I told Tommy Halliday I would drop by, he wants to see me in person. He needs to discuss it all with me. I think Rowena has left me her jewellery, she always told me she wanted Imogen to have it when she is old enough. I expect that's it. Are you going to arrange to see Carl?'

'Only if you are okay with it?'

'Yeah, I'm fine with it, he needs to know, I just don't want to be the one to tell him. Do you think I should let him see Imogen? I want to forget he exists Alex, is that bad?'

'He's her father Rosie, she doesn't know him. I know you don't want her taken into a prison. I can't help thinking babe that it's going to be worse when he gets out and wants to see her. She won't know him at all. At least if you let him see her monthly or something she will know who he is as she grows up. Then there's Toby babe, you and I know he's most likely his son.'

Immediately Rosie snapped into defensive mode. 'No, we don't Alex, and I don't want to find out, what if he's not Carl's?' She looked sadly at Alex tears building up, 'I keep hoping we offer to take Imogen in to see him and he refuses. Does the decent thing and lets us go?'

'I don't think he will do that babe, he did want the baby, and he has been happy enough with the photo's you've sent him up until now.'

'Did he say anything to you at the funeral? I saw you talking before you stood up. What was he saying, was he asking about the children? You know he never wanted a girl, he wanted a son. He wanted a mini me Alex and I'm so afraid that well . . . if Toby is his then he will only want him. I'm scared Toby will turn out like him. What was he asking about, he looked over at me, I saw him?'

'He asked if you were seeing anyone, I said not as far as I was aware . . . Then he asked about the club Rosie, and about the rental for the house, he wants the mortgage paid off. The pubs and the club are doing well, he's a millionaire on paper now. He knows it, so he wants you to have some extra money from it all. Alex looked sad, and he touched her arm gently. 'He never even mentioned Imogen, he asked about Toby, who he looked like, so you may be right. Bobby had been to visit him and said the boy looked like him, he asked about him not her.'

'What did you say?'

'I said he looked like you, which isn't strictly true, you know he looks like Imogen, who looks like Carl.' Seeing a familiar look come over Rosie's face Alex sighed, 'okay, I'll shut up. I'll drop you in town and take the kids round to the soft-play in King Street, you can either call me when you come out or just walk around. I wonder why you have to go in to the office?'

***

The Nightclub Owners Wife

Alex looked up as he saw Rosie come through the turn-style and enter the soft play area. Imogen was playing on a mat in front of Alex, Toby lay asleep in his pushchair. Alex could see she was emotional before she reached him and sat down. 'Well?' He asked looking at her, 'what is it?'

Rosie choked back tears, 'she left me all her jewellery, the caravan, her house and the insurance money half between me and Carl. It's almost two hundred thousand pounds cash. Tommy says Carl knew and agreed. As you said, he has plenty of income from the club and pubs, and the rental from the Dundonald Road house. I had to sign some papers, sign it back over to him, he's bought it back from me, for the market value. I'm not bothered I never wanted to go back after it all happened anyway, and the tenants have been in it for 2 years now. I wasn't expecting anything from it, he can have it, I've never touched the rental. As soon as its cleared though the money well... it will go into my account, along with the insurance money. She took an envelope from her bag this is the deeds to Rowena's house. There is a letter from her too, but I need to wait until I get home, I can't read it here.'

'I've arranged a visit for next week babe, I called Bobby when I got here, he had a pass so he's called the prison and asked if it can be changed to my name,' he smiled, 'Imogen is really tired now, so let's go via Nobels and have dinner then go home to bed.'

'Will you stay with me tonight?'

'Yes, but Rosie, I don't want to move in there, are you going to be able to sell it?'

Rosie shrugged, 'I don't want it, the house, I thought I would just rent it out and keep it for Imogen her legacy from her grandmother.'

'What about Toby?'

'Rowena left both the kids fifty thousand in trust for them when they are twenty-one, I'm going to match it from the money she left me. With interest, it could be worth a lot more by the time they are adults.'

***

'That's the weans settled,' Alex walked into the living room where Rosie sat, her face buried in a pile of tissues her mother-in-law's letter in her lap. 'Do you want to talk darling? I'll understand if you want to keep it to yourself'

Rosie nodded and handed Alex the letter, she watched as he read it stopping frequently to look at her. 'She knew about us Alex and she has given us her blessing. I thought I was hiding how I felt about you, and she knew.'

Alex smiled, 'she was an incredible woman, I'm proud to have known her.' He sat down beside Rosie on the sofa and putting down the letter he pulled her into his arms and held her kissing the top of her head. 'I love you so much Rosie, I can't believe she thanked us for being so discreet and sparing her feelings. I've just spoken to Bobby about the visit, its all arranged. I need to do it, I want us to be able to be honest about our relationship.'

'When are you going to see him? You need to be careful Alex, he is going to be angry, he won't let go of me easily. I'm really worried he forces me to send the kids in to visit now.'

'Thursday morning, ten o'clock. You need to think about him having contact if he asks. The social worker who wrote the report when he was sentenced, she said they would need to assess him first. Look Rosie don't worry about that just now, we can deal with it when we have to. He leaned over and kissed her gently. 'Right now, I want to make love to you. I want to see what else you have to offer.' Alex stood up and pulled Rosie to her feet.

CHAPTER

TWENTY

'How are you Lex?'

Alex knew Carl well enough to realise that he was concealing anger, but he answered, his voice even and calm. 'I'm good Carl, you're looking well?'

'I've been working out, using the gym a lot, not much else to do in here. Okay what do you want? I know you want something.'

'I'm here to tell you something... not sure where to start though?'

'Oh, now let me see, what can that be?' Carl put his thumb and forefinger on his chin. 'Could it be that you are feeling bad, you've been cutting my grass? Did you think I wouldn't find out?'

'Who told you?'

Carl looked at Alex he shook his head, 'does it matter? You bastard, you sat there at my mum's funeral when I asked you if she was seeing anyone? What did you say? *'No mate she has never even looked at another man.'* His eyes showing his anger, he hissed, 'No fucking wonder you haven't been here for months. When did it start? Was it before I was in here? How fucking long Lex?' He looked around him and noted that people were politely pretending not to hear him. His voice rose as he looked at Alex who remained tight lipped. 'What a stupid cunt I've been trusting you to look after her. I always thought you fancied her, but when you came in to the funeral with her it was fucking obvious. So, I asked the questions I needed to ask.'

Alex sighed and shook his head. 'I'm sorry Carl, I knew there was no easy way to do this. I wanted to tell you myself, it's a fairly recent thing, me and her. I know you are hurt.'

'Hurt, fucking hurt . . . that doesn't even touch what I'm feeling, you expect me to just accept this? You are having a thing with my wife. Shagging a mate's wife Lex . . . how fucking low is that? How could you? I trusted you, fucking believed you.' People around stopped talking and stared.

A prison officer moved towards them. 'Carl calm it down please or this visit is over. I realise you are angry,' the officer looked at Alex, 'and it seems you have reason to be. You know the rules Carl . . . calm it down now.'

'Carl,' Alex said quietly, 'this is not just an affair, I love her and the kids, I want to look after them. I didn't mean it to happen, but I'm not sorry it did. I will look after them Carl, I have been looking after her and the kids for two years, ever since you've been here. I haven't laid a finger on her, it wasn't about that. Me and her, it just happened but we both want it, so we wanted you to know. I never slept with her until this week, but we didn't want to hide it from you. We never wanted you to hear it from someone else. She wants you to give her a divorce Carl.'

'You can fuck right off, I'm not giving her a divorce. I can't stop you shagging her, but I can make sure you can't marry her.'

'I'm sorry Carl, but that doesn't bother me, I just want to be with her. I will look after her, I promise.' Alex stood up, 'I'd better go.'

Carl looked up at Alex and leaned in, 'oh that's okay then, you are shagging my wife, she's my fucking wife, mine, and you are shagging her.' All eyes in the room were on them as Carl's voice rose, 'She's my fucking wife, mine!' he repeated 'and you think you can just do this.' Carl jumped to his feet and grabbed Alex's jacket, 'I killed the last bastard who touched her, so don't you ever forget it, she is my fucking woman. Mates don't do that, I asked you to look after her, that didn't include fucking her.' Two prison officers jumped forward and tried to restrain Carl, he began to fight. He jumped forward and head-butted Alex before they could stop him. A bell rang, and everyone was ushered out of the room. The two prison officers held Carl on the floor, he looked up at Alex. 'I will fucking get you Lockwood you bastard you dirty bastard. She will always be mine I love her. I will get out of here someday, and I will have you, I swear you will fucking pay for this.'

Alex took the pile of tissues from a female prison officer and held it to his nose which was bleeding profusely. 'If you loved her, you'd want her to be happy Carl, that's how I saw it when you married her.' Alex said as he walked towards the door.

CHAPTER
TWENTY-ONE

August 2003

'You look wonderful babe,' Alex said kissing the top of Rosie's head. All the studying and working hard, its paid off, a first in English Literature you so deserve it. Hey Toby, where are you? Imogen?

'I'm here Dad, Imogen is putting her shoes on.' Five-year-old Toby Ranmore came into the room carrying a huge bunch of flowers. 'These are for you mummy because you are clever and beautiful and lovely. Happy grandutatian day mummy.' He smiled as Rosie hugged him and immediately she saw Carl in him, she had no real doubt now that her son was the child of her husband. His dark hair flopped over his eyes and his brown eyes so like Carl's sparkled.

'It's Graduation day Toby!' six-year-old Imogen cried coming through the door, she was carrying a small package which she handed to her mother. 'It's a bracelet! I picked it Toby wanted to get you a necklace, but Daddy and me, we thought you would like a bracelet better. Happy Graduation Day mummy! We have to go to school and when we come out we are all going out for tea.'

The Nightclub Owners Wife

'Two presents how lovely, I'm so lucky, can I open it now? Or do I have to wait till I come home?'

'No silly you have to open it now, so you can wear it to your wear it to your granduation!' Toby said pushing his sister. He stamped his small foot and looked at his mother. 'I picked the blue car bit on it she wanted a pink bow,' he smiled as he climbed up to the table and took the bowl of cereal from Alex who was dressed in a dark suit.

'Toby that's not how you put milk in your coco pops!' Imogen said shaking her head. Let me do it?'

'Darling eat your own breakfast and let Toby do his,' Rosie smiled and kissed the top of her daughters' head. 'He won't learn if you keep doing things for him.' Rosie opened the package and looked at Alex shaking her head, as she lifted out the bracelet nestling in the black velvet box, knowing how expensive it had been. 'It's beautiful my darlings thank you it fits perfectly,' she said holding it against her right wrist.

Alex moved over and fastened the bracelet. He looked at his watch a silver Rolex, a gift from Rosie on his last birthday. 'Okay let's get this show on the road, leave mummy to get dressed for her big day, get your bags and out to the car. You don't want to be late for assembly, do you?' He dropped a kiss on Rosie's head, then winked at her, 'we have two hours before we need to leave babe. I'll be back in ten minutes.' Taking a drink from his coffee mug he said, 'okay let's go troops,' as he ushered the children from the room.

Rosie walked upstairs to their bedroom, and down the mirrored corridor to the ensuite, she smiled at the black dress hanging on the outside of the wardrobe door, ready for her graduation. The last four years living here had passed in a flash she thought. Still married to Carl, Rosie knew she would have to do something about that someday, however since Alex had told Carl about their relationship, Rosie had heard nothing from her husband. He had sent her a letter at the time outlining how he felt about their relationship, said as long as she remained married to him he would not interfere. Her pain at the circumstances of their separation less vivid now, however recently she had realised that she would have to face Carl coming up for parole in the next few years. She turned on the shower and dropping her robe on the floor stepped under it.'

When Rosie came out of the shower Alex was in the bedroom. Seeing Rosie, he dropped onto one knee in front of her and took her hand. 'Marry me Rosie?' He said, looking up at her, 'please?'

Rosie smiled and shook her head, 'Alex? We can't get married yet? I need to be divorced first for a start, I promised you the other night I would do it soon. I don't need a wedding ring to prove how much I love you? I'm just scared Alex, I don't want to rock the boat with him babe. That letter, he said if I stayed married to him he would leave me and the kids alone. I need the kids to be older, so I can explain it all to them. We just can't do it yet, you know we can't.'

'No not yet, but you can wear this, and we can be engaged can we not?' He opened a box and Rosie gasped as she saw the Ruby and diamond ring nestling in it. 'Rosie our life together is perfect, but I just want to make it into a fairy-tale too, you know like one of Imogen's princesses.'

'Alex it's... it's exquisite I don't know what to say, I wasn't expecting this today. I was going to be the one with the surprise.' Seeing Alex's quizzical look, Rosie smiled and walked over to the large dressing table and lifted a small gift bag. She handed it to Alex and then stepped back, 'this is for you, something I think you've always wanted but never said because of my circumstances.'

Alex laughed and pulled her close, 'you have given me so much, what else could you possibly think I would want?'

'Open it?'

Alex moved away slightly and broke the seal on the bag, he looked inside and gasped. 'What? How? When? Oh my god darling does this mean?' He lifted out the pregnancy test wand and looked at her, his eyes filling with tears.

'Yip you've knocked me up Lockwood, not sure how it happened, but I thought I might be. Apparently, my coil has fallen out. I never realised right away, last week I felt a bit queasy, then it dawned on me I hadn't had a period for a while. I saw Dr Linton yesterday after I did that test, he sent me for a scan right away because of the missing coil, so I also have this? She handed him a scan photograph, that's our baby Alex, that little peanut, I'm nearly three months, it must have happened around the time we were on holiday in May. It's pretty good timing isn't it? I've finished my degree? I won't be able to do the post grad teaching qualification this year but I'm sure they will defer me for a year or two if I ask.'

'When is it due, oh my god darling, I'm so . . . I don't know . . . I thought I was the one with the surprises today. Oh, you have no idea how happy I am?' Tears ran down his face, 'I always hoped we would, but having you and the kids was enough. This is just the most unbelievable wonderful surprise babe.'

'I'm giving you something you didn't have, a child of your own, I think that's special, isn't it? It's due February. We are pregnant. So, I've got the upper hand on surprises today. Okay my mum and dad will be here soon, so you'd better dry your eyes and then you can tell them. They'll be over the moon.'

'Will you marry me Rosie? I want you to be my wife, especially now.'

Alex I'm still not going to file for my divorce. I know there will be nothing Carl can do to stop us now, but you know it doesn't matter to me babe. I love you, you are the love of my life and a wedding ring won't change anything.' Rosie's face clouded over.

Rosie no court will allow him contact with Imogen she's six years old and doesn't know him? He hasn't asked for years and he made it clear it was you he wanted not the kids, besides you heard what Tommy Halliday said, Carl would need DNA to get contact with Toby, and you would need to give permission.'

'Alex please I just don't want to tempt fate, I love you and nothing can change that. I've asked Tommy to ask him to sign the consent form for Imogen's passport so hopefully he will sign it this time and once we have the baby, we can have a holiday abroad. Alex please, I don't want to fight today, you always told me you would never pressure me? I'm his wife in name only, my heart is yours and now we are going to have a baby. Alex please can we just enjoy what we've got? You are the senior architect with your firm. You're winning awards for your designs and we have this beautiful home, money in the bank and two healthy children and now a baby on the way. Please Alex, today is so special.'

Alex sighed, 'okay you win again, I know I have so much, you, the kids, a good job. My darling you have made me so happy, I'm the luckiest man alive. We have it all don't we?'

CHAPTER
TWENTY-TWO

February 2004

'Hey how are you babe?' Alex walked into the hospital waiting room. 'Told you I would make it, didn't I? Are you okay darling? You look worried.'

'Oh, after two emergency sections, I'm a bit scared about the planned one would you believe? I never knew what had happened with Imogen, and I was in so much pain after all the hours of labour and so worried because Toby was in distress.' Rosie smiled. 'How was the museum, is it looking good?'

Alex grinned and patted Rosie's baby bump, 'Best thing I've made, apart from the bump. Hey, guess what? It's already been nominated for awards. It could open a lot of prospects for me, the architect of the Scotland Museum, Norrie reckons he won't be able to pay me what I'll be worth after this. However, nothing can top our baby being born today. In a couple of hours, we are going to know whether it's a brother or sister for the kids.'

'Hmm I think I'd like another boy myself, but I think it's a girl, it feels the same way it did with Imogen, and I was really sick again too. Just as well you can afford to keep me in the style

I've become accustomed to, because I would have never managed to work feeling the way I did.'

***

'Darling she is perfect, Alex sighed cradling the tiny girl in front of Rosie, allowing her to see her new baby. Are you okay with the names we chose? I'll understand if you don't want to call her after my mother.'

'No, I love Rebecca Margaret, it's a name for a special child. She looks like you Alex, she is so much fairer than Imogen and Toby were, they were both so dark when they were born.'

The baby opened her eyes and looked at her father, Alex gasped as he looked back at her. 'Christ, she has my mums' eyes Rosie, it's like seeing my mum looking back at me.'

Rosie smiled and nodded, 'so she has, your mum was a very beautiful woman Alex, so it's good.' She looked at her watch. 'You're going to have to go soon and pick the kids up. They were so excited this morning about their new baby.'

'How are you feeling darling? Was having the epidural easier than the other two? It was really good of them to let me come in too, but it was a bit scary knowing they were cutting you open behind the screen.' Alex kissed the top of Rosie's head. 'I love you and the kids Rosie, more than life itself and she is so perfect.'

'Hey, you two, I'm still here stitching her up,' Selina McDougal said looking over the screen separating the medical team from Rosie and Alex. 'Of course, it's better to be conscious, but we had no choice with the other two babies. Okay I'm almost done so we'll check you out and get you up to the ward in a little while. You need to stay in bed tonight and hopefully your feeling should come back as you sleep. Everything went brilliantly, and she is perfect. Six pounds eleven ounces, your mum will be delighted Rosie. I'd love to see the other two when you bring them in Alex? It's not often I get to see the babies I deliver grown up. Question is, are you going to make an honest woman of her? We have to label her baby Ranmore I'm afraid, hospital policy, mothers surname.'

Alex's face clouded over, and he frowned, looking down at Rosie, who could see the pain on his face. She looked at Selina McDougal who had walked around from behind the screen and was looking at the baby. 'I'm afraid we haven't resolved that one yet, I would like all the children to have the same name. I don't know we keep going around in circles. I also want the children to have the same name as me. I'm not divorced so it would be fraud, would it not? To call myself Mrs Lockwood, so I thought I could go back to being Rosie Gibb.'

Alex sighed, 'not today babe, let's just leave it for now, can we just have one day without having this discussion? You know how I feel about it Rosie so don't keep bringing it up expecting me to say anything different.' He kissed the baby in his arms and then handed her to Rosie. 'I'm going to go now whilst they take you up to the ward, I promised Imogen I would come get her and bring her to see the baby.' Alex bent down and kissed Rosie, 'I love you, thank you for our daughter, now I'd better go and get our other daughter before she dies from excitement.' Alex laughed, 'Toby is going to be in a major strop when he realises he has another sister, he was convinced she was a boy, so was I.'

'Are you disappointed she's a girl?'

'God no Rosie, I love Toby, but I prefer girls,' he whispered bending down and kissing both Rosie and the baby. 'I'm a lady's man, babe, you know that. I was secretly hoping for a daughter, let's have six girls?'

'Eh no you won't,' Selina McDougal said, you need sections and four's usually the maximum we recommend.'

'Sections? What's the limit? Will we be able to have any more? Rosie asked. 'I'd kind of like another one.'

'Not impossible to have four.' Selina smiled, 'You are still so young Rosie and your wound healing is better the younger you are. If your family is not complete, then we can talk about it.'

Alex smiled, 'oh our family is complete, she is not risking her life for another child. Three is fine, I have two daughters and a son. That's enough.'

'Let's have one more Alex? She is so beautiful isn't she, so perfect. I have beautiful children Alex, I'd love another boy though, even if you want to be a lady's man.'

'Let's just get you recovered from this one first, we can think about it later.' Alex smiled, 'we can add it to the list of things we don't talk about.'

Rosie smiled and kissed the top of the baby's head. 'You know I'll get my own way here, don't you?'

CHAPTER
TWENTY-THREE

June 2005

'Daddy's here, mummy, daddy's here it's time for our holiday.' Imogen jumped up onto the couch as Rosie came into the room. She glanced outside, Alex was getting out of his new black Range Rover. He saw her looking and waved through the patio doors. He opened them and Toby, his hair neatly cut after his trip with Alex to the barbers, ran into the room. Becca looked up from her dolls pram and ran towards Alex. He scooped her up and kissed her before dropping a kiss on Imogen's dark curls.

'You're cutting it neat, the taxi is coming in twenty minutes, we have to be in Greenock in two hours. You'd better go get the bags down.' Rosie smiled, as Alex pulled her towards him and kissed her. She looked at him, 'did you get everything sorted at work last night? I can't believe we are going to be away for six weeks. How will they manage without you?'

'They'll manage just fine. Are you feeling better? Your colour is back, hopefully it's just the stress of the move? And of the worry of you know what?'

Rosie smiled, 'I drank a bottle of red wine with Sue, Alex, that's why I was sick. I'm fine now, well a bit hungover, not looking forward to getting on that boat. Sue says Norrie is really upset at us going, he understands, but is going to miss you. I'm going to miss them too, but she says they will visit us in New York. Mum came over, she gave the kids some holiday spending money. Becca has hers in her pram, apparently baby Becky needs it for sweeties. She won't put it in the purse you got her. That has her jewellery in it.'

'I see they've been and put the for sale sign up whilst I've been out. I'm not sure we should have done it before we go, but I suppose we only have another three months before we move. Imagine us in New York. No regrets babe? Is your mum still crying?'

'No, thank god, she gets it Alex, I think now she's thought it through she realises it's time to move on. She says she knows it's a fabulous opportunity for all of us. Can't believe what they are going to pay you. Dad said they are pleased I can concentrate on my writing.'

'So, no regrets babe?'

'Nope, none now mums okay with it. The people we love will visit so it's onwards and upwards. You are so worth it Alex Lockwood, aka sex god.'

'Hmm I like it when you call me that, makes me feel all manly and important. I'm glad babe, when you were drunk last night you were upset.'

Rosie glanced over at the bureau in the corner where the envelope containing the letter from the parole board lay. Informing them that Carl Ranmore's parole had been decided and he would be allowed a phased return to Kilmarnock. Which would commence in three months. 'We won't be here when the you know what happens.'

The long holiday had been booked many months before. Timed to coincide with several of Alex's long-term projects ending. They were starting with Florida and Disneyland, then they would cruise from Florida to the Caribbean. They were now joining a third ship along the east coast of America stopping off for a week in New York where, now their move was confirmed, they would see the house the company Alex had been offered and accepted a partnership with, had found for them to rent. The children would visit the schools and nursery they would attend. They would return to Ayrshire and then make the permanent move in September.

Rosie had collapsed in tears when she had received the letter. They had known it was a strong possibility that Carl's parole application may be granted this time around having been declined on two prior occasions.

Alex had come home from work after hearing his wife's voice on the telephone. He knew that the life that they had led would need to change and had already been considering the offer of a partnership from a leading North American company. They had decided that they would leave Scotland to preserve the family life they had built up. The children were now seven and eighteen months, so Rosie and Alex felt that this was the time to make the move, before they got any older. The two older children had been made aware they had another daddy who had gone away, and they had been shown photographs of Carl, but neither Imogen or Toby had shown much interest. Alex and Rosie however realised that as the children grew, they probably would begin to ask questions. They had been told a lot about their Granny Rowena and how much she had loved them.

***

The holiday began with a wonderful fortnight in Florida where they stayed at the Disney resort, the children met their cartoon hero's. The 21-day Caribbean cruise had left them sun tanned and happy and the visit to New York and their new home and school in Pelham was also a source of excitement for the two older children. Becca was too young to understand the situation; however, her siblings' excitement was infectious, and all three children were happy and excited as they boarded the cruise ship for the journey back across the Atlantic.

The weather on the sailing was magnificent and the children enjoyed the kids club, allowing Rosie and Alex time to themselves. Although they knew they faced a major life change, both Alex and more so Rosie, were feeling more relaxed than they had since the letter had come from the parole board.

***

'Are they sleeping?' Rosie sitting up in the king size bed in their stateroom asked, as Alex tiptoed back through from the adjoining bedroom. He smiled as he turned and closed the door behind him.

'Oh yes!' He said grinning, he sat down on the edge of the bed and pulled Rosie towards him. 'I seem to remember someone promising me a night of passion for our final night onboard this beautiful ship although, I don't know if it can get any better than it was last night. We've just approached the coast of Ireland, so we'll be in Greenock in the morning. We can sure try though.' Their lips met, and Alex slid his hand inside her nightdress his gently cupping her breast. 'I'm just jumping into the shower, you keep reading your book babe, I hope it's erotic enough to start you off? Miss Rosemary Gibbs.'

'Oh, with you around, who needs erotica,' Rosie said smiling up at him as he stripped off his jeans and shirt and walked towards the bathroom. Rosie picked up the book she had been reading during the holiday. The final proof of her debut novel, Rosanna Gibson being the name she had decided to publish under. The book was to be released in time for the Christmas market. So, don't be too long in the shower Mr Lockwood, because I might get a better offer.'

Five minutes later Alex reappeared from the bathroom in a cloud of steam, he dropped the towel on the floor and climbed back onto the bed still damp from the shower. He pushed Rosie back onto the bed and taking her book from her he tossed it onto the floor and pushed the thin straps of her nightdress down over her arms. 'I'm so proud of you and your book Rosie, but it's not getting more attention than me tonight.'

Rosie sighed, as Alex's lips formed around her nipple, she moved her hand in to his hair, as he kissed his way down her body. 'Oh no Mr Lockwood, you are doing all the work tonight. My erotic scenes in the book are all based on you.'

'Mummy, daddy, Becca is being sick, and Toby is crying. He's got a sore tummy.' Imogen's voice called out, she opened the door, Alex sprang away and lifting the towel from the floor he wrapped it around his waist as Rosie straightened her nightdress and got out of bed, her body tingling from his touch she followed her daughter from the room.

'Oh dear, she has been sick. Okay Imogen, you get into our bed with Daddy and I'll clean this up.' 'better calm yourself and put some clothes on,' Rosie hissed as she passed Alex. 'Cos this is going to be a long one. Think it might be a bug, I've been feeling kind of seedy too.'

Rebecca sat on her bed a pile of sickness around her and her little body retched as she continued to vomit. Toby lay crying on his bed holding his stomach seconds later he sat up and he too vomited over his bedding. Rosie looked up as Alex still with the towel around his waist came into the room. 'This is your fault,' she hissed, 'filling them up with ice cream sundae's just because they ate salad, not that cucumber and chips is a healthy option for a toddler. Bribing your children with unhealthy food to make them eat healthy gives this result Lockwood. You can clean it up whilst I put them in the shower. At least Imogen had the sense to say she didn't want ice cream if it meant eating salad, as she said, we weren't having salad so why should she.'

'So much for our night of unadulterated passion!' Alex whispered in Rosie's ear as he began stripping the sheets from the beds, he lifted the pile of soiled bedding. 'I'll go and find the steward and get them to bring some more bedding,' he said leaving the room. Returning a few minutes later dressed in Jeans and a t-shirt, 'do you want me to ask them to send the ships doctor?'

Rosie smiled, 'no I expect it's just too much rubbish, Imogen is fine, is she sleeping?'

Alex frowned, 'yeah in the space where you and I should be right now, making love.' He looked at the two children, both looked extremely ill, 'Rosie I'm worried. 'Are you sure we don't need the doctor?'

'No, I think they will be okay, I think they are just really sleepy now. If you can get clean bedding, we can put them down and sleep with them in case they need us during the night. Get us some more bottled water too, the secret to kids with tummy bugs is to keep hydrating them.'

***

Alex returned to the room followed by a steward the two men carried bedding. 'Half the ship has it babe! They think it's either a vomiting bug, or food poisoning. The doctor is coming in to see them in a couple of minutes, just as a precaution because of how young they are.'

Rosie nodded, she was becoming increasingly worried, Becca was listless and sleeping, wakening only to vomit, running a high temperature and extremely unwell. 'Alex the wee soul is really ill, I'm getting scared. I've put a nappy on her twice, diarrhoea is just running from her. Toby has fallen asleep but he's really restless, he made it to the toilet but...'

'It's okay I'll go clean it babe.' Alex took the pile of bedding and towels from the young steward. 'Thanks Kevin, can you close the door on the way out?' He walked towards the bathroom just as Toby sat up cried out and vomited over the bed.

'Sorry daddy, it just keeps jumping out... daddy I've pooed myself.' The little boy was obviously distressed. Alex frowned he looked at Rosie who was cleaning up yet more vomit from

Becca, who was lying listless in her mother's arms looking up, her little cheeks flushed and her eyes bright.

'That's okay Tobes, let's get you into the shower and cleaned up. Alex lifted Toby up and carried him into the bathroom. When he returned Toby was asleep in his arms wrapped up in a fluffy white towel. Rosie had laid Becca on Imogen's clean bedding and remade Toby's bed whilst Alex had been in the bathroom.

***

'Mrs Ranmore, Mr Ranmore, we are going to have to get them to hospital I'm afraid.' The doctor looked worried, and Rosie was now terrified at how ill her children were. 'They have I think got food poisoning. There are quite a few others, we are not sure where it has come from, but you two and your other daughter appear alright, so we are asking that everyone fills in a form with what they ate. Then we can try to narrow it down.'

'They will be alright? Doctor, please tell me they will be okay?' Rosie asked, sounding she knew, calmer than she felt.

'Mrs Ranmore, children are very resilient they can go from deaths door to the playground in an afternoon. Your children are very unwell, and we need to get them to hospital. We have permission to dock at Cairnryan in about ten minutes and we will take them by air ambulance to Glasgow children's hospital. Now one of you will need to stay with your healthy daughter the other can come to hospital with the children.'

'Air ambulance? That bad? Why can't we ... why can't they go by ordinary ambulance?' Alex gasped.

'Mr Ranmore ...'

'My name is Lockwood, Alex Lockwood, my daughter is Rebecca Lockwood.' Alex snapped, 'the older two are my step children.'

'Mr Ranmore both children are dangerously ill, I'm going to put a fluid drip line in to try to hydrate them, but this has come on very quickly and hopefully with the right treatment it will go just as quickly. Do you have anyone you can contact to come get your daughter? To allow you be at the hospital with your wife . . . girlfriend?'

'Partner!' Alex said calmly, 'Rosie is my life partner.'

Rosie her face pale and showing how frightened she was, looked at the doctor. 'My parents live in Kilmarnock. They could meet Alex on the A77 and take Imogen home, but what if it's a bug and she gets it too?' she asked.

'The doctor shook his head, 'I think it's food poisoning, so if she had eaten whatever caused it she would have it. We can deal with all this later. He put a cannula into Becca's hand, she didn't make a sound, Toby cried out seconds later as his was fitted, the doctor linked both children up to fluids and instructed the ships nurse to stay with them until the boat docked. He turned to Alex. 'Mr Lockwood do you have your driving licence with you? We can get you a hire car from the terminal to allow you to get home with your daughter and luggage? Your wife can go in the Air Ambulance with the children. There are several people needing treatment, they will mostly go by road but I'm afraid both your children are gravely ill.'

'What's likely to happen Doctor?' Alex asked his voice a mere whisper, Rosie could see her own terror reflected on his face. 'They can't . . . they won't die, will they?'

'As I said Mr Ra . . . I'm sorry, Lockwood, children are very resilient, let's just wait and see how it goes. They are going to the best place

***

Alex watched as the helicopter took off carrying most of his family, he made his way back to the car. He knew he had to try to remain calm for Imogen's sake. He had told her that Granny Maggie and Papa Davie were going to meet them on the road. As he drove Alex prayed for the second time in his life. The first time having been when he lay on the floor of Rosie and Carl Ranmore's house feeling his life ebbing away.

CHAPTER
TWENTY-FOUR

'Rosie, thank god you're alright, they said you were here, how are they?' Alex ran into the waiting room, having been pointed in the direction of the high dependency unit as soon as he arrived at the Glasgow hospital.

Rosie jumped to her feet and fell sobbing into his arms, 'it's bad Alex, really bad, they are both so ill. The consultant says he says ... He says that the next 24 hours are crucial, you are sure Imogen is alright? My mother knows to get the doctor if she gets sick? They are working with them, they asked me to wait here. They are saying that ... oh god, they say their organs are shutting down ... I can't bear this ... I can't lose them,' Rosie sobbed into Alex's chest he held her close, crying silent tears with her, her sobs gradually became quieter, they huddled together both terrified of what the morning would bring.

It was light outside when they finally came for them, the consultant white faced and shaking his head. Rosie heard the words, she looked at Alex his face reflecting how shocked and scared she herself was. The consultant telling them that there was very little hope for Becca, she was just too weak. Her little body failing, as her organs shut down. Toby less so, his liver compromised, his kidney's failing and him being put on dialysis to try to prevent the build-up of toxin in his body. He'd made no improvement, but his condition hadn't worsened either.

Alex spoke to the doctors asked questions but there were no answers. The days passed slowly, one, two, three. Each day Becca failed a little more, the machinery surrounding her increased and the little body on the bed grew weaker. They heard the words E. coli, possibly from the salad on the cruise ship. All the victims had eaten from the salad bar, all were recovering, apart from the little blond girl fading away on the hospital bed, and the little boy who made no progress. On the fourth evening, Rosie and Alex held their baby as she passed quietly from their lives. Hours passed, Alex held the child's body, crying out, refusing to allow them to take her from him. Rosie despite her own grief engulfing her, eventually managed to persuade him to let her hold Becca. Tearless, Rosie kissed her still warm body and allowed the doctor to take her from them. She sat down beside Alex and let him sob in her arms. His grief all consuming. Unable to believe that in a few short days their lives had been altered forever.

Over the next few days, Rosie retreated more and more into herself. No one could reach her. She went through the motions of living. The only time she could cope, was when she was sitting by her sick son's bedside.

***

'Rosie, Lex, this is the worst thing that has ever happened to you I know, but you have to make a decision about Toby. He needs a kidney and liver transplant. Davie Gibb his face white and his eyes red from crying, sat down beside his daughter and her partner. Maggie sat in the corner her face buried in the large wad of tissues she held in her hands. Rosie looked at her father, I've told them they can take mine, I had the blood test. I can't understand why they won't just take mine. I said they could have my kidney and take part of my liver too.'

Maggie took a deep breath, like her husband, her eyes were red and sore, her face pale. She put her hands on her daughter's shoulders and gently shook her. 'Rosie, you heard them, you are not a match, we're not either, your dad and I have both been tested. Rosie, you have to find out who his father is, you know he looks like Carl.' Maggie took a deep breath and paused before she addressed her daughter again. 'Rosie, I phoned the prison this afternoon, he has to know, you know it probably was Carl who fathered Toby. Rosie darling, you cannot let him die, you are grieving both of you, you're not thinking straight.'

'You had no right to do that Mum . . . no fucking right. Carl Ranmore is nothing to do with us,' Rosie cried. 'Do you hear me, nothing?'

'Rosie listen to yourself?' Davie cried, 'it doesn't matter what he's done, we need his help.' Davie looked around him. 'Lex tell her please? That child could at best face years of being hooked to a machine getting weaker and weaker, or he could die. For Christ sake Rosie, you have lost one child, you can't sit back and lose another. Just because the one man who just might be able to save him, hurt you years ago.'

Alex who had been staring out the window stood up and walked towards Rosie, 'they're right sweetheart, you need to at least ask him to be tested. If he is Toby's father, then I'm sure he'll help. Even Carl wouldn't let a child die.'

'No . . . I can't, there has to be some other way.'

Alex knelt in front of Rosie, 'babe, you have no choice, you don't need to see him, you just need to give permission. If you don't and he offers to help Toby, they will do it anyway.' Alex began to sob. 'Darling I know you are in pain, I am too. I feel as though my heart has been ripped out, but I love all of our children and we can't go through it all again. Rosie, tomorrow we have to bury our baby girl. Please Rosie you need to listen, we can't ignore this, if there is a chance that Carl can help, then we need to let him. We need to Rosie and you know that. Don't you?'

Rosie nodded, she jumped to her feet and ran to the bathroom vomiting into the toilet.

Alex knelt beside her rubbing her back, sobbing uncontrollably he tried to hold her, she pushed him away. 'Rosie please you have to . . . have to consider this as an option.'

'I don't want him here, I know I have to allow it, but I just need time. I need to be able to face it.'

'Rosie, Toby ... he's getting weaker babe, it has to happen soon. He is not as sick as Becca was, but if he gets any weaker they won't be able to do an operation. We'll lose him to babe. I'm going to go and call the prison, they must have asked him by now.'

What if he refuses? He could Alex, he hates me and you, he could be cruel enough to say no. You know he could say no, don't you? Just to make us suffer. That's what I'm afraid of Alex. I can't do it, I can't watch my son die, my heart is broken for my beautiful baby girl, and I can't do it Alex. I never thought I would need Carl Ranmore again and I do. What will we do if he can save Toby and he won't?' Rosie stood up, she wobbled, and Alex caught her as she fainted, she opened her eyes and vomited.

Alex carried her through to the room and sat her down on the small couch. 'Sweetheart you are exhausted, you need to go home and get some rest, your mum will stay here with Toby, he's stable. You heard the doctor, he's sedated and will just sleep. You and I need to get some sleep too. We also need to go and see Imogen, we must tell her about Becca darling. She still doesn't know, we can't keep this from her much longer, Rosie she knows about death. We need to tell her and support her. The wee soul has been left with whoever has been available for the last few days and she will be realising ... working out its serious.'

Davie Gibb stood up, 'okay Rosie, you and Lex come home with me, your mum will stay here. After you've told Imogen about Becca, I'll stay with her. We've arranged for her to be at her wee friends for the funeral, so we need to tell her tonight. Lex is right, you need to get some sleep,' Davie looked at Alex, both of you need to sleep, you also need to grieve. You have been here constantly with Toby since ... since the wee yin went,' Davie began to sob, 'I can't say it, I can't say that wee angel is dead, it's not fucking fair. It's so not right, no one should have to bury their child.' He looked at the two-people standing in front of him. 'I know how that feels.' He said quietly.

The door opened and the consultant treating Toby, put his head around the door. 'Mrs Ranmore, Mr Lockwood. Can I speak to you both?' He looked at Davie and Maggie. 'In private?' He added.

Davie stood up and led his sobbing wife from the room. 'We will wait outside,' he whispered over his shoulder.

The consultant cleared his throat. I'm so very sorry, this is an unbearable tragedy for you I know. Given our discussion earlier, I know this is going to be difficult for you to hear.' He cleared his throat before continuing. 'We have a match for the kidney and liver, Carl Ranmore is the best option. The prison contacted us this morning and we had him brought here and tested. If you agree, then we can approach him.'

'Carl's here? In this hospital?' Rosie gasped, Alex reached out and pulled her towards him he held her, kissing her head and she could feel his tears making her hair wet. He said nothing, merely holding her. Rosie unable to cry stared at the consultant and repeated her question.

The consultant shook his head, 'they've taken him back to the prison now. He needs to think about this too, it's a big step for him to donate a kidney. The liver not so much, we take a small part and it regenerates itself, both in the recipient and the donor. We have given him all the information and talked him through the procedure.'

CHAPTER
TWENTY-FIVE

Rosie stood watching as Alex and her father carried the pink coffin into the church, both weeping openly, her thoughts were about Toby. She felt nothing as though playing a part in a film. She shook her head, the coffin looked too big. She had always thought Becca was so small, probably because of the six years gap between her and Toby. They always treated her as their baby, all of them. For Toby and Imogen just six and seven when Becca was born there was no jealousy they loved their little sister and Becca had been a ray of sunshine, a symbol of the love Alex and Rosie had.

Alex still weeping came to stand beside her, Rosie looked up at him, she couldn't comfort him, she couldn't feel anything. Rosie felt she was outside her body looking in at the scene in front of her. People crying, she could hear sobbing behind her and beside her. She looked at Alex, tears running down his handsome face. She couldn't cry, since the night she had held her dying daughter in her arms, Rosie had felt nothing, all her energies were with making Toby well. She heard her mother and those around her talking about delayed shock. Heard them speak in whispers about her reaction when Ronnie Muir raped her, and Carl murdered him. She'd stopped speaking for days then, been unable to comprehend what had happened.

Now all Rosie could see was the coffin and church filled with flowers. She knew her baby was dead, knew she would never see her again. She couldn't feel it. Something in Rosie told her to shut down, if she let herself feel, then she wouldn't be able to cope. She went through the motions, Alex wept throughout the service, but she couldn't comfort him, she couldn't feel what he was feeling. Her heart told her she should, but her head wouldn't let her. She needed to get back to the hospital, back to her living child. When Alex reached out to her she turned away, unable to have him touch her.

When they placed the coffin in the hole in the ground Rosie stared at it. People were speaking to her, but she couldn't reply, staring dumbly at them, seeing their lips move. She was aware she should be feeling something, but she couldn't, she tried to force tears out, but they would not come. She turned and walked away from the graveside, leaving the priest in mid-sentence. Everyone turned to look at Rosie, as she moved away from the crowd and out of the cemetery. Alex followed her and got into the car with her, again he tried to hold her, she pulled away. Alex wept into his hands, Rosie stared at him feeling nothing, no pain no anguish just nothing. When she spoke, it was with no feeling. 'I need to go back to the hospital. You should go to the hotel with everyone else, I need to get back to my child.'

'Rosie don't shut me out,' Alex cried, please darling don't do this. I know you are hurting, blaming me. But please babe don't shut me out.'

When she spoke, it was as though she was reading from a script, no feeling, just words. 'I feel nothing Alex, not anger, blame, sadness, hurting. I've just left my child in the ground and I feel nothing. I can't feel Alex, why can't I feel? My baby, my beautiful baby is gone and all I can think is I have to see Carl Ranmore. My brother is in that hole with my baby, is this my punishment for breaking my marriage vows?'

'Rosie stop it please? Let me help you, we can help each other. Alex cried out. He tried to hold her, but she sat still, her hands at her side.

'I know I should be feeling something, but I don't, and I don't know why? You can cry Alex you can feel, all I can think of is about him. Why can't I feel? I know this isn't a normal reaction, mum keeps saying I need to see someone, talk to someone. I need to look after my other children that's what I need to do. Make sure they know I love them. I need to let Toby get better.'

The car door opened. 'Rosie that was a terrible thing to do,' Maggie Gibb got into the car beside her daughter and Alex, she looked at Alex his face red and swollen. Then at Rosie who was pale, tearless and staring out of the side window. 'You walked away from your child's graveside, you haven't cried, this is not normal Rosie.'

Rosie looked at her mother, suddenly she felt angry, she felt emotion for the first time in days, 'what's normal? What is normal? You tell me mother, is what you and dad did when Simon got hurt normal? Should I neglect my other children because one has died? Is that fucking normal?'

'Rosie for fuck sake!' Alex gasped, 'that's not fair. Maggie, I'm so sorry, she is overwrought she doesn't mean it, Rosie stop it.'

Maggie shook her head, she looked at her daughter, 'do you think we don't know we did that, your Dad and I we both know what we did,' She said quietly. 'I love you Rosie and I don't know how to make that up to you. What we did, we focussed on Simon when you needed us too. You were just a little girl and you needed me, and I wasn't there.'

'Mum, I'm not going to do to my kids what you did to me. I loved Becca but she's dead . . . gone forever, she's never going to grow up, go to school, have a boyfriend, get married, give me grandchildren. Do you all think I don't know that, I can't fucking feel it because if I do, I won't be able to cope with the enormity of it. Please I don't want to hurt any of you, please just let me do what I must do to save my living child. Please just leave me alone.' Rosie turned her face to the car window and then huddled in the corner her face against the window looking out.

Alex tried to put his arm around her, but she pushed him away. 'Rosie I'll come to the hospital with you, your mum and dad will go to the hotel. People will understand, get that we need to be with our son.'

Rosie turned to look at Alex. 'My son Alex, not yours, my child. My husband is the only hope that child has, last time he saw you he threatened to kill you.' Rosie's voice was flat again, she showed no emotion. 'Please stay away from the hospital, if you care about me, please respect my wishes. Imogen needs someone to be with her just now. You go look after her and leave me be.'

CHAPTER
TWENTY-SIX

Five days later

'Hello Rosie, you look good.' Carl Ranmore smiled sadly at his wife, 'it's been a long time? I've missed you, never a day went by when I didn't think about you and the kids.'

Rosie said nothing, she in truth didn't know what to say, Carl smiled at her and she looked back. She tried hard not to think of the last time she had seen him. However, she knew he was the only hope her little boy had, the only hope of leading a normal life. She had psyched herself up for this meeting, her stomach was churning, and she felt sick. She knew however she had to take Carl along the corridor to the hospital room where Toby lay wires and tubes surrounding him. It broke her heart to think of the active and happy little boy who had just three weeks before been running around the cruise ship.

'Thank you for coming Carl, they think you are the best hope of a match for Toby. I know I don't deserve it after keeping them away from you for their entire lives.'

'You did what you had to do, I know what I did that night was horrific and I still don't know why it happened. I've spent hours with therapists and psychologists trying to work it all out,' Carl shook his head and she could see the pain on his face as he remembered. 'I can't Rosie, I can't work out what made me do what I did. I don't remember a lot of it, that's the scary thing. Anyway, let's leave that for another time. I don't like talking about it, I killed someone, and I have to live with it. I caused a horrific thing to happen to you then lost you and my children. I probably helped my mum in to an early grave too. So, I have a lot of regrets. Giving our son my kidney, is my chance to do something good for a change.' Carl reached out and took Rosie's hand, he studied it and then raised it to his lips, bringing his eyes up to meet hers. 'Rosie, I still love you and I hope you will grow to love me again.' He held her hand for a moment and then smiled. 'Okay maybe not the way you did before, let's just leave the elephant in the room for now, concentrate on what's important. Can I see my son?'

Rosie nodded and then led him out of the day room and into the corridor. He followed her along the corridor towards the glass walled room in high dependency where their son lay connected to the machinery needed to keep him alive. 'Did they tell you about the liver?' She asked, still not daring to look at this man, the man who was her husband in name only.

'Rosie, I will do whatever it takes to save our son, I always knew he was mine. Mum, she told me she was sure, said he looked like me as a baby. I'm so sorry about your little girl babe, that must have been awful for you. I used to worry all the time in prison about the kids, thinking that if anything happened to them . . . I can only imagine what you are going through.'

'When are they going to operate on you?' Rosie asked, she knew she couldn't talk about Becca, she didn't want to think about it. In her head now, her baby was at home with Alex, in her pink bedroom. Not all alone in the cemetery at the top of the hill.

'I don't actually know I haven't had the chance to see the doctor again to tell him I will do it. They asked me to go away and read all the literature before I made a decision'

Rosie reached for the buzzer and rang; the light came on and she pushed open the door. She led Carl into the corridor and over to the glass wall. 'You can't go in Carl no one except me can just now, the risk of infection is too high, he's been so ill.' She sighed, 'he's quite tall for his age, but he looks so small lying there. He has your eyes Carl, I think I always knew that you were his father. I'm sorry I've kept them from you, it was all tied up with what happened. If I thought about you, I remembered what happened. I hope you can play a part in their lives.' Rosie looked up as the door of the room opened and the consultant came out in to the waiting area.

'Mr Greenslade this is Carl Ranmore, Toby's father.' Rosie said quietly, she looked at the doctor. 'How is he?'

'We've met Rosie, hello again Mr Ranmore.' The consultant sighed and putting his hand on Rosie's elbow he gently led her into a room at the end of the corridor. Carl took a last look at the small boy on the bed and followed. 'Sit down Rosie, you too Carl, I need to talk to both of you. This is not what I hoped for, there is no easy way to say this.' The doctor looked sadly at first Rosie then Carl, he cleared his throat. 'Toby is deteriorating rapidly, it's the liver more than the kidney, which we didn't expect. I'm not sure how much longer we can postpone operating. Mr Ranmore, right now you are the only hope this child has. Did you read the literature I gave you? You are aware there are risks here for you too?'

Carl looked at the doctor and then his gaze moved to Rosie. 'I'm ready when you are,' he smiled sadly, 'I've not exactly got a busy schedule doc. I read it, the prison doctor explained it all to me, there were parts I didn't understand, and I asked him and the nurse to go over it with me.' He smiled sadly and looked at the doctor. 'The thing about being in prison for the last eight years is I haven't abused my body. There are a lot of drugs inside, however I opted for monthly screening, which got me privileges one of which was the use of the gym. I also worked in the kitchen and learned to be a chef. I thought it might come in useful because of the pubs, so I ate well and healthily, and I haven't had a drop of alcohol in eight years.' He turned and looked at Rosie as he spoke, then returned his gaze to the doctor. 'I'm ready when you are.' He repeated.

The Doctor smiled, 'I was, I must admit Mr Ranmore hoping that would be your response. I have a theatre booked for tomorrow afternoon. I'd like you in tonight though, to run the last tests and go over the procedure. Now if you will excuse me I'll take leave of you and go arrange things.' The doctor shook hands with Carl and smiled, 'it's been good to meet you Mr Ranmore, now I suggest you have dinner before you come in as you will be fasting. The prison has agreed your leave?'

Carl nodded, 'yeah they have got permission from the parole board for my unsupervised leave to start now, to allow for this.' He watched the medical staff leave and then turned to Rosie, 'well can I buy you dinner Rosie? Then I'd really like to see Imogen if that's all right? Just in case. Rosie, I take it she's with Lex? I'd rather not see him if you don't mind? I realise you and him fell in love. I see you're wearing an engagement ring. I don't blame either of you, and I'm glad you found someone, I want to be happy for you, it's just I suppose it's kind of awkward and I have so much to think about just now, I don't ... I can't think about that. After this is over, perhaps I will be able to, I don't think Lex and I will ever be friends again. However, I do want to build a relationship with our children.'

Rosie looked at him her eyes filled with tears, 'I haven't seen Alex since the funeral. And no, I don't want to talk about it. I actually have been here most of the week. I haven't seen Imogen either. Thank you for what you are doing Carl. I couldn't bear to lose him, he is a wonderful wee boy. He ... he's so bright and happy, and he was so active.' To her horror she couldn't talk she began to sob as the pent-up emotion she had been avoiding, rushed to the surface. Carl moved closer and held her, letting her cry on his shoulder he kissed the top of her head as weeks of suppressed grief exploded into a flood of tears and hysterical sobbing. He held her for a full ten minutes as she sobbed, he knew because he watched the clock on the wall behind them. Rosie sobbed, unable to stop the flood overwhelming her.

Seeing a figure reflected in the glass, he made to move away, Rosie held onto him, she looked up at him. Holding her tighter he looked into her eyes and moved his lips to hers, they began to kiss. Rosie suddenly pulled her head away, 'Carl I ... I ... can't, I'm sorry, but I love Alex. I know you and I are still married but I have something special with Alex and I shouldn't be here kissing you. I'm so sorry if I gave you the wrong message, it's been such a stressful time I ... I ... just realised how much I need Alex. I've been horrible to him since this happened.' She looked at the ground. 'I'm so sorry, I haven't been able to cry or feel anything.'

Carl held on to Rosie's arm, he looked sadly at her. 'Got a bit carried away there Rosie, I never stopped loving you darling. I see you every time I close my eyes, I missed you so much, and when I was holding you I ... just for that second wanted to believe it was possible you still wanted me.'

'I'm so sorry Carl, really sorry, I ... just.'

Carl smiled sadly, kissed his finger and put it to her lips. 'I just need to man up and accept that you moved on. Look I promise I won't do that again.' He looked into Rosie's eyes, 'not unless you ask me to. Okay babe, just in case I die on the table tomorrow I need you to know you were special to me, the love of my life. I just made such a mess of it all, didn't know what I had until I lost you.' Over the top of Rosie's head, Carl watched the back of Alex's head as he rushed off through the doors at the end of the corridor. He resisted the urge to laugh out loud. When he looked Rosie in the eye though he was composed and hid the triumph he felt.

***

The Nightclub Owners Wife

As they sat later in the restaurant, Carl looked at Rosie over the glass of water he was drinking. He was aware that his wife had merely pushed food around her plate. 'Imogen is so pretty her photos don't do her justice. It was good of your mum to bring her round. She looks a lot like you Rosie.' He looked sadly at Rosie, 'I'm really sorry about your other little girl, as I said earlier I can't imagine how you must be feeling? You must be worried sick about Toby too?' He looked into her eyes, 'Rosie I meant what I said, I will be there for you.'

'Thank you, I can't quite believe she is gone, she was such a beautiful lively little girl, everyone loved her. I'm trying to focus on the other two though and that's keeping me going. It's worse for Alex I suppose, she was his only natural child. He's been so strong, he has tried to be there for me, but I wasn't able to cry. When I cried earlier that was the first time since it happened. Alex is devastated, I know you don't want to hear this Carl, but Imogen and Toby, well he didn't make a difference between them and Becca. We've always told them about you, but they are young, and you saw Imogen she didn't really understand who you are. I hope that you will be able to have a relationship with them both.' She shook her head sadly, 'Alex, well he has had to deal with a lot. I went a bit loopy trying to cope with it and I think I kind of shut it out, forgot how he must be feeling.'

Carl looked puzzled 'doesn't he see his other kids? The ones with Moira?'

'What?' Rosie stared at Carl, she shook her head, 'what do you mean? Alex doesn't have other children, I would know, I've known him all my life.'

'Oh fuck, he didn't tell you? Him and Moira had a couple of kids. I thought he told you? I'm sorry Rosie, forget I said anything.'

Rosie gulped, 'no they didn't, there were no children, Moira didn't have kids. She always said that she didn't want them.' Rosie looked at Carl and shook her head. 'I'm sure you are wrong. Alex and I, we have no secrets, well not one like that, he would have told me?'

Carl looked sadly at her, Rosie I'm so sorry, but he told me himself. He visited me a lot at the start, I asked him about Moira and if he had seen her. There were two kids a boy and a girl. Bobby visited me every month when I was inside, he was in touch with Dougie and Moira for a while. Moira was pregnant when she left, the boy is a little older than Toby the girl is about a year younger I think. Carl took Rosie's hand, 'I'm sorry babe, I honestly thought you knew. It was before you and him got together, it's not as though . . . you know?'

'I need to go Carl, I'm sorry, I need to ask him, he wouldn't, he couldn't have kept that secret. Could he?'

Carl looked horrified, 'Rosie, he's not my favourite person these days, but I care about you babe, I would never have? You know I wouldn't have said anything. I was angry the last time I saw him. Mum had just died, he came in, I'd heard rumours . . . Bobby and some of the other pub staff used to visit. Well they were all saying Lex was around you a lot. When I first got banged up people were talking. They all thought that you had got pregnant from the rape. I did too Rosie, I thought that was why you wouldn't see me, why you didn't tell me about the baby. Bobby had told me about Moira? I asked Lex about the baby because he said he had been out in Cyprus on holiday.'

'He never told me Carl, why would he have not told me that? He went with Norrie, it was work, just before you were sentenced. He told me he had been to see Moira and Dougie, but not that there were children. Why would he not tell me that?'

'I don't know sweetheart, you'll need to ask him. What I do know is Moira was home, not long after my trial she had a very young baby and Bobby said he saw her and Lex together in the club. Bobby was in Cyprus on holiday about seven or eight months later and he naturally went to their pub. Moira was heavily pregnant, he saw the wee boy, said he was the drawn spit of Lex. Bobby was in Cyprus again a couple of years later. He said the wee girl was so like Lex it was unmistakable.'

'Why wouldn't he tell me? Did you talk to him about it? You said he told you himself? Bobby is such a gossip, perhaps he just put two and two together?'

'Bobby asked him and he didn't deny it, he said he was the father of both of Moira's kids. He said Dougie, didn't know they weren't his. How I don't know? If they look like Lex?' Carl looked sadly at Rosie. 'Look go and see him, I'm sure there's an explanation. Rosie, I didn't come here to cause trouble between you and Lex. I don't give a fuck about him, but you have had enough heartache darling I just want you to be happy.'

Rosie looked at Carl her face showing the shock and confusion at what she had learned from him. Suddenly her whole world had begun to crumble around her. She had for most of her life felt safe with Alex, he had she realised, been her rock. She couldn't believe he hadn't told her about Moira having his children. She knew this couldn't be true, she knew she trusted Alex more than Carl. Her mind raced, she struggled to face what she knew she had to do, she knew however that this was not the time, she stood up. 'I need to go back to the hospital Carl, my . . . our son needs me.'

Carl reached out and took her hand again, he studied it then looked up, 'I'm truly sorry Rosie, I didn't know. This must be bringing back so many memories, what I did, what happened because of it. I just want happiness for you.'

Rosie looked at him she saw the pain on his face, she shrugged and then shook her head. 'This isn't the time to discuss any of this Carl. I need you right now . . . I need you to have that operation and save our little boy.' She looked into his eyes, then sighed, 'Anything else can wait until Toby is on the road to recovery.' She looked at this man who was her husband, yet a stranger now to her. 'Thank you for doing this Carl,' she whispered.

***

Alex stood on the veranda looking out to sea, the waves beat against the shore, he heard the crash as the ocean met the white sands. He could hear the telephone ringing, ignoring it he stared out at the darkness his eyes becoming accustomed to it. He could see nothing in the black of the night, his head full of the sound of his own voice. He knew what he had to do, knew now there was no other option. Sobbing quietly, Alex walked back through to the bedroom he lifted the over-night bag from the bed and took it out to the hallway, he placed it beside his case.

The door to Becca's room was opened slightly, switching on the light he entered the room. Her second favourite doll, a stuffed ballerina with yellow woollen hair lay on the bed. They had put her favourite baby doll Becky in the pink coffin with her. Something to keep her company. Alex tried not to think of his beautiful golden-haired little girl, lying with his childhood best friend, in the cold earth of the cemetery on the hill. When he lifted the little ballerina doll to his face he could smell his daughter from it. He sat on the bed breathing in her unique baby scent, his tears dropping on to the little doll. a symbol for him of the lost baby, the beautiful little girl who would never grow up, never be a teenager, never be a bride. She would always be daddy's little girl.

He knew he couldn't take the doll, Rosie would need it. He looked around the pink painted bedroom. So many memories, the pink frilled canopy over the cot bed. Alex smiled through tears at the memory of Becca when he had converted the cot into a bed shortly before the cruise. She had been so proud when the rails were taken off. Wakened everyone the next morning at five am running around the hallway, calling out she had slept all night in her own big girl bed. He stood on the sparkly ballerina rug on the floor, looking at the pink ballerina dangling from the custom-made sparkly nightshade. He and Rosie had chosen this together, at the same time they'd bought their daughter the little golden-haired ballerina doll he now held close to his chest. He walked over to the pile of stuffed animals in the corner, his eye was drawn to the princess trunki case. Left there when he had brought the cruise luggage in from the car. He opened the case and despite his pain, smiled at the stuffed Cinderella doll. The last toy he had bought his daughter on their recent trip to Disneyland. He put the ballerina doll back on the bed and left the room closing the door behind him. He lifted the bag from the floor and moved towards the stairs cradling the golden-haired princess.

CHAPTER
TWENTY-SEVEN

Rosie looked up as the glass was tapped. Carl stood watching, he smiled sadly at her. He was wearing a blue striped dressing gown and he motioned with his head for Rosie to come out. Rosie walked to the door, she took off the gown she was wearing and removed the mask and gloves. Then looked back at Toby lying on the bed so still. They had given him his pre-med around an hour ago. When the glass had been tapped, her heart had jumped, as she assumed that they had come for him.

'Rosie, I just wanted to see you and him for a few minutes, before I go to theatre. I wasn't going to come down because I thought Lex would be here?'

Rosie shook her head, 'no I tried to call him earlier, but he didn't answer. He hasn't been to mums to see Imogen either. I haven't seen him for over a week. He is I think, giving us space to deal with this as Toby's parents.'

Carl made a face. 'Are you all right Rosie? I'm sorry about last night, I never knew he hadn't told you about him and Moira.'

'Carl, I need to speak to him about what you said last night. I have been sitting here all night, thinking about it, and there must be an explanation. Look do you mind if we don't talk about it, I need to discuss it with him. Right now, I need to concentrate on my ... our son.' She looked back at the little figure on the bed.

'Of course, you do, I just wanted to . . . I don't know be with someone for a couple of minutes. To tell you the truth I'm a bit scared. It's not easy being a hero, they're downstairs waiting for me. Rosie, I know I got it wrong last night, but can I hold you?'

Rosie nodded, her eyes tearful, her heart heavy. She wanted to be held, but by Alex. She had felt nothing when Carl had kissed her the night before, she knew she felt nothing for him. Not love, not fear, she wanted Alex. She wanted him to be here, tell her this was all a big mistake, there were no other children. Yet she realised Carl was telling her the truth. She couldn't understand why Alex hadn't told her. During the night sitting at her son's bedside she had realised if Carl was right about Moira's children's ages. She and Alex hadn't been in a sexual relationship when the younger child was conceived.

She wanted Alex, big strong reliable Alex, her gentle giant. Instead she nodded and allowed Carl to put his arms around her and hold her. He kissed her cheek, however the embrace felt wrong, awkward and strange, she was in the arms of a stranger. Rosie needed to speak to Alex, needed to hear his version of events. Hear him saying he loved her. She however stood statue like, trying not to feel anything, trying to retreat into herself. Blending into the background, the way she had always done in time of emotional stress, shut out the feelings.

Carl moved away first, he took Rosie's hand and held it, realising she was miles away, he touched her cheek. Rosie looked into his eyes, Carl moved in and kissed her forehead she could see the tears in her husband's eyes. Saying nothing she nodded and watched as he turned and walked away. Lifting a clean hospital gown and mask, Rosie put them on and returned to her son's bedside.

***

'Mrs Ranmore, it's going to be a long time, this operation is very delicate. Toby will be in theatre for hours. You need to get some sleep, I've prescribed you a couple of sleeping pills. I want you to take them and lie down in the parent room. Mr Greenslade is downstairs preparing, he says you need to sleep, I agree. You are going to have to be rested, we'll need your help when Toby comes back from theatre and wakes, he will look for you. Brenda here,' the young doctor said, nodding at the nurse standing beside Rosie. 'She'll take you down to the room as soon as they take Toby to theatre. Now be brave, kiss your boy and tell him you'll see him later.'

The nurse handed Rosie two tablets and a glass of water. She smiled and patted Rosie's arm as she swallowed the two white pills. 'When you see this wee man again, he will be nice and pink with a new kidney and part of his dad's liver.'

Rosie bent down and kissed her son's forehead, he looked at her, already drowsy. 'I love you mummy!' He whispered, then closed his eyes, unaware of the drama around him.

Rosie's tears fell on his head, she knew they were right, she hoped the pills would work, stop the endless questions going around in her head. Stop her feeling everything she had known to be true was a lie. Alex was a liar, Carl was a hero, Rosie knew that was the wrong order of things, it had to be. Rosie suddenly felt very tired. She watched as the wheeled her boy away, not knowing if she was ever going to see him alive again. Her thoughts turned to the little pink coffin being lifted out of the hearse, Alex and her father sobbing as they carried it, and she began to weep into her hands. The nurse put her arms around Rosie and gently led her away.

***

When Rosie wakened from a deep dreamless sleep, she struggled for a few moments to think where she was. Her head buzzed, and she felt confused, she pulled herself up in the bed and lifted her arm to look at her watch. She was amazed to see that she had been asleep for six hours. She sat up panicking, thinking about Toby. Getting out of bed she moved towards the door. Then became aware of someone else in the room, 'Alex?' she gasped turning around, however it was not him, instead as her eyes became accustomed to the light she realised her father was dozing in the chair by the window. 'Dad?'

Rosie moved towards her father he opened his eyes and smiled sadly at his daughter. 'I came down about an hour ago sweetheart, your mum is upstairs.'

'Toby? Is he?'

'He's back from theatre, it all went well they said.'

'Imogen? Alex?'

'Imogen is with Aunt Lucy, she's come to help out. Imogen is fine, they were going to feed the ducks at the Kay Park. You looked so peaceful we wanted you to have a good sleep. Toby, he's fine darling. I saw him when they brought him back from theatre, he looks great and they said he was in a natural sleep. Your mum is with him in case he wakes up. I sat down waiting for you to wake up and I must have shut my eyes. You go and get a shower and we can go up and see your little pink boy.'

Rosie looked at her father, 'where is Alex? Why is Imogen with Auntie Lucy? What's happened, I know I was horrible to him after the funeral and told him not to come to the hospital. I tried to call him. Do you know where he is? I couldn't get him last night or this morning. Dad has something happened to Alex? I know it was awkward with Carl being here, but this is so not like him... Dad tell me?' She stopped and looked at her father, knowing there was something.

Davie Gibb looked at his daughter, she could see the pain on his face, the confusion. 'Rosie, he has gone, cleared out everything and left the house. After the funeral when you went off, he did too. He brought Imogen over to us, and darling... he handed your mum a bag we thought it was just her clothes. Lucy bought her some new things and well... we didn't look in the bag right away. We didn't tell you because we thought you had enough to worry about. This was in it.' Davie reached over to his jacket and handed Rosie a letter. 'I'm sorry darling I opened it not to be nosey, but we were afraid well... when he didn't come back, we thought he might have been going to harm himself and you were here and were in such a state. I'll go and get us a coffee and you had better read it. Rosie darling I'm so sorry, this is the last thing you need right now. I'm ... so sorry darling ... I need you to know ... your mum and I won't let you down ... I mean, we will be here for you.' Her father stood up, gently stroked her face then his eyes full of unshed tears, turned and left the room.

Rosie stared at the white embossed envelope, her stationery, from the set Alex had bought her last Christmas, he knew she loved to write letters. The stationery was expensive, and she had scolded him about buying such a frivolous gift as an extra stocking filler, knowing immediately how expensive the writing set had been. She ran her fingers over the envelope feeling the bumpy surface of the raised paper, Rosie was afraid. Knowing she was about to learn something, something she didn't want to know. Rosie was still staring at the envelope when her father came back into the room.

Davie put the coffee down, 'I've just spoken to the nurse who is with Toby. He's still asleep, your mum is with him and they don't think he will waken for a few hours. Carl is fine too, minus a kidney and a part of his liver, but he's awake and sitting up eating toast and drinking tea, they said. Rosie have you read it?' He asked nodding at the envelope in her hand.

'I can't dad, I think I know what it says ... he's not here and well Alex has always been here for me. He ... Oh, I don't know? Becca she was his princess and oh god dad, I was so horrible to him. To you all. I couldn't I ... couldn't let myself think about my poor baby ... Dad ... I ... I can't read this, I don't want to read it. I want to sit here and think he is away on a business trip, he's gone away and taken Becca with him, they are both safe and well and this is not happening. Toby is at school and he's not ill.'

'Rosie stop it sweetheart, this is real. Toby is here in this hospital recovering, Imogen is feeding ducks at Kay park. Darling I don't know why Lex has done this now, the letter doesn't explain why. I can't believe it, not our Lex, he was like my son Rosie, so

The Nightclub Owners Wife

I don't know? I'll never forgive him for this Rosie, but I will be there for you. I let you down when Simon got hurt, your mum and I both did. I know what it's like to lose a child Rosie, you need to know what's in the letter though. I can't take away any of your pain ... and that hurts more than anything sweetheart.'

Davie sat down on the bed and put his arms around Rosie he took the letter from her hand and kissed her cheek. Rosie felt the wetness of his tears on her face. 'Dad.' She whispered, 'can you read it to me?'

Davie nodded and opened the letter, 'I'll fucking swing for the bastard if I see him again Rosie. I just want you to know that. What he's done ... and to do it now, we all thought Carl was a wrong un, but this.'

'Dad please?'

'Okay, this is it.' Davie took a deep breath then began to read, Rosie heard his voice impart words, words from the man she loved, the man she thought would never hurt her.

'Dear Rosie, I'm sorry to be doing this to you now. I know this is the last thing you and the kids need, but you are strong Rosie. The strongest person I know. Me I'm weak, I can't cope with what's happened to my daughter. My child, your reaction to me when I touched you. Since it happened you've been a stranger, I know you blame me.

I blame myself Rosie, but I can't look at you without sadness and regret and I don't think there is a future for you and me anymore. I think I might have stopped loving you when Becca died. You need to talk to Carl about you and your children, his children. What we have done Rosie was wrong, we kept a man from his children and now I know the pain of loss I know it wasn't right. I've taken a job abroad, not the New York post, but another one I was interviewed for.

I've sorted out finances, put the house in your name, to do as you wish. All the documents are in the bureau in my office. Rosie please don't think of me with pain and regret, move on have a life, finish your book and get it published. We had a good few years but it's over. Don't try to contact me Rosie that will only cause pain and confusion. Remember the good times and move on. That's what I'm going to do.

Alex.'

Davie looked up at Rosie his face white and angry, 'bastard, how could he?'

Rosie stood up and moved away, she lifted her clothes and went into the shower. She stood under the water sobbing unable to believe the man she had loved, had a child with could treat her this way. She couldn't comprehend what he had done. She knew she could never forgive him. She didn't know how she was going to deal with it all. How she could tell her children that not only had they lost their little sister. The man who had been the only father figure they knew, had also gone? She remembered seeing a quote in a book, it said, *'nothing hurts more than being let down by the person you thought would never hurt you.'*

CHAPTER
TWENTY-EIGHT

Rosie watched as Carl packed up his belongings, the taxi, booked to return him to prison, waited outside. She smiled as Carl carefully placed the picture on top of his clothes. She couldn't believe how well Toby was, and how quickly he had bonded with Carl. She also saw a different Carl, a new man. Changed by his eight years in custody.

They hadn't discussed a future together, however Rosie knew that whatever happened, she would help her children to have a relationship with him. Rosie had answered both Imogen and Toby's questions about Alex by saying he had gone away, he and Becca had gone, and they couldn't come back. She was unable to think what else to say other than they had both loved them and had to go away. The children cried and had grieved, Rosie couldn't say the words *'he just left us without saying goodbye.'* So, she never told them he wasn't dead. When they assumed he was, she did not correct them. Carl proved a distraction for them, meeting the long-lost daddy they had always known about. Toby, young and recovering from his illness, had readily accepted this new adult in his life. Imogen so like her mother was keeping Carl at arm's length, it was Rosie realised, early days.

Carl smiled at his wife, he longed to hold her, pull her into his arms, but he knew he had to move slowly, at her pace. He groaned as he moved, the pain in his side still raw and acute. It was he realised worth it for what he stood to gain from the donated kidney and part of his liver. His rewards would far exceed any physical pain, however, for now, he had to return to the prison. Carl knew he had to prove himself responsible, there was the promise of home leave soon. Now he hoped that this would be to the small woman standing in front of him, watching him as he carefully placed the white paper on the top of his bag. He exaggerated the careful placing and smoothing it out, so's not to tear or crease it. This picture told a hundred stories. Carl was astute enough to realise that not only had he saved his son's life and possibly was on the road to winning his wife back. He also had he knew won valuable points with the parole board.

Carl was, he realised, luckier than most people in prison, he had a good life to return home to. His business, mainly thanks to Rosie and Alex, was thriving. The managers they had put in at the beginning of his sentence, had he realised, been well chosen. Loyal and honest people, who had served the company well. Bobby, still there overseeing things in the club, had visited him in prison monthly for the last eight years.

Carl looked forward to returning to the helm of his thriving company. He looked at the bag in front of him, the child's colourful picture of a family, carefully smoothed on top. Mummy, daddy and the two children a little boy and a little girl holding hands. The bright sunshine and the golden sands of the beach spread out. He took in the two figures floating in the air above the other figures, the man and child with golden hair. Carl smiled and zipped up the bag. 'See you next week?' He said.

Rosie fighting tears tried to look cheerful. She nodded, 'I'm sorry about the home leave. I know I should Carl, after what you've done. I'm so grateful to you, but, I ... I'm just not ready for it. I think it's too soon, and well, with us staying with my parents just now, it would be a bit like being in a goldfish bowl. I will meet you though with the kids, and we can do lunch or something.'

Carl smiled, 'don't be sorry Rosie... I've got a lot of proving myself to do. It's also going to be difficult to be back in the town again. So, I suppose this way is better, it will give us both a bit of space. With your house being where it is I just thought it would be an opportunity to be away from the people who know our history. I never thought how you must be feeling about what Lex has done to you and all the memories in that house.'

Rosie shook her head, 'I want to go back, I think I'll feel closer to Becca there. I don't know if I can live in it, but if I can't I need to look for another house in the area. Imogen and Toby are settled at school, all their friends are there. I don't know whether I want to sell it and have someone else living in it, but I'll need to sell it to move on I suppose?'

I understand Rosie, probably best to be rid, we still have the Dundonald Road house, the lease is up at the end of the year. I've given the tenants the option to buy it. I had this dream when I was in prison, you and me moving back there, but I realise that's never going to happen.' Carl sighed I don't need to sell it, but it's probably time now. There has been enough time passed since it happened... for it not to affect the value.'

Rosie sighed and nodded, 'I just need some time Carl, I never thought this would ever be an option, never considered you and me... I just want to give it time to develop see where this goes.'

'I hope it's us as a family,' Carl said looking into her eyes, *'sad, beautiful, blue eyes,'* he thought. He smiled, then spoke quietly, still watching the expression in them, 'but if it's not as a couple, I hope it can be us as friends? He moved closer, 'can I hug you?'

Rosie put out her arms and moved closer, Carl held her breathing in her scent, the perfume he didn't recognise, it wasn't what he remembered. He wanted it all to be the way it was before. Rosie was very thin just now, pale and thin. Her hair long and not styled the way he liked it. Her face strained the events of the last month engrained on it. She still looked so young, he realised she would be twenty-six this year, she still looked like the teenager he had left almost nine years before. Carl wanted to take away the sadness that hung like a shroud around her, he knew however he couldn't do that yet. She needed time.

Carl sitting in the taxi returning to the prison, studied the photograph of Rosie and the children, Imogen had given him it, he knew she was in her childlike way testing him out. The prison psychologist had spoken to him about childhood trauma, and the need to be accepting of his children's behaviours, told him some of the behaviours he could expect. Carl looked at the photograph and smiled. The little girl in his wife's arms wasn't his daughter, but she was gone and no threat to his developing relationship with his family. Rosie was laughing into the camera, the child in her lap looking up at her mother, was the image he realised of Alex Lockwood. Imogen smiling, Toby serious, looking at the teddy bear in his arms. Carl smiled to himself as he saw the shadow of the big man on the ground in front of the little family group. *'That's what you are now Lexie-boy, a shadow, still in the picture but not able to do anything!'* Despite where he was, Carl chuckled to himself, he saw the taxi driver glance in the mirror, their eyes met, and Carl smiled, realising immediately the man knew who he was.

CHAPTER
TWENTY-NINE

Rosie opened the car door, Imogen jumped out and ran towards the front door. The sea crashed onto the beach beyond the garden and there were a few people on the sand, dog walkers and an elderly couple who walked every day along the beach. Creatures of habit Rosie realised, was she a creature of habit? She wondered. Rosie looked up at the house, she remembered her pride in telling people on the beach her partner had designed and built it. The party's they had held, their friends, their little family, all connected to this house. She had taken it off the market when Alex left. The empty pink bedroom upstairs, was the main reason she couldn't bear now to sell it.

Rosie had come to the house several times over the last few weeks, removing everything Alex had left. Putting items in boxes, she stored them in the attic. She still couldn't believe that the man she loved, had treated her so appallingly. She longed to speak to him, ask him why? She supposed it was grief, but now she knew about the two children with Moira, she didn't know what motivated him. Rosie became obsessed with Moira's children. During breaks from sitting at her son's bedside, she had driven home and gone through Alex's files on the computer. Looking for evidence, pictures of the children, documents, but found nothing. She had however found some details of the bar in Cyprus on the internet, advertising the Scottish themed pub. There were pictures of Moira behind the bar, and to the right of her a little boy sat drawing, his hair his face, Rosie studied it. Zooming in, she saw the resemblance to her dead child and realised that there was no doubt this was also Alex Lockwood's child. She remembered her pride when she had told Alex she was pregnant with Becca, those words she had said, '*I'm giving you something you don't have but have always wanted, a child of your own.*' Rosie couldn't believe he hadn't said anything then. His joy at Becca's birth, she remembered his words that day in the delivery room*, 'god Rosie she has my mother's eyes. I love our other two, but she is part of my mother?'* Rosie could not comprehend the person she had known and loved, with the person who she now knew had other little replicas of him and his mother. Yet she knew Alex's love had been sincere? The love for their little golden-haired girl? Rosie had always trusted Alex implicitly, *why hadn't he told her?* She supposed that Alex had removed all traces of his other children when he left. Standing looking at the house, his house, she was lost in thought.

'Rosie?'

Rosie's thoughts were interrupted she looked up as she heard her name being called. Her eyes opened wide and her jaw dropped. Elaine Lamont stood at the small wall separating the garden from the beach beyond. 'Elaine?'

Elaine walked towards her, 'Rosie I had to come, I'm so sorry about your little girl.'

Rosie shook her head unable to believe that Elaine was there. Not sure how to deal with her ex-best friend who had walked out of her life without a goodbye and never returned. Rosie knew about Elaine's career it had been hard not to be aware. Local girl made good, the job in Canada, news reporter straight out of university. Alex had mentioned whilst they were on holiday he had heard Elaine was returning to the UK as a presenter on BBC news. Rosie had always felt sadness at the loss of this friend, the woman who had accused her husband of raping her, then dropped the allegation and disappeared from their lives. She saw Elaine's glance move to Imogen, who was hoping from one foot to the other on the doorstep. Realising Imogen was desperate for the toilet from her expression, Rosie handed keys to her daughter. She watched as the child expertly opened the front door and ran off.

'What do you want Elaine? I hope you are not here in your professional capacity? I'm not giving a story to anyone. The newspapers have rehashed the whole story. I just want to be alone with my children.' Rosie's voice broke, 'I need ... I need to grieve for my baby, Elaine please, if you have any decency in you?'

Elaine shook her head, she looked at Rosie her eyes sad. 'I'm not here as a news reporter Rosie. I'm here because I know you must be devastated. I saw the coverage on the news and in the newspapers. I just wanted to come and see you.'

'I don't believe you Elaine, you walk back in to my life after all these years and you expect me to believe that you care? Just fuck off Elaine, I don't need you, I don't need anyone. I've always been alone. That's how I'll be now, alone and not depending on anyone. You were my best friend, sister really and you just walked away from me. I don't know whether he raped you or not, Alex always said he believed you, but then Alex was the biggest fraud of all.'

'Rosie please listen to me, I don't know what happened between you and him. Maybe Lex is a liar and a fraud, but you and him you looked happy together, you had a child. I know he has gone, it's all over the news he's walked out. You need to stay away from Carl. Please, you need to be careful. Don't let him back in to your life, he's a bad man. I've been doing some research and he's been involved in some stuff from inside. Rosie, you need to listen, I know you've no reason to trust me, I don't care. Carl Ranmore is a dangerous man. Please Rosie, if you believe nothing else I say, please believe me on this. Rosie can we just sit down and have a coffee or something?'

Rosie shook her head sadly, 'I don't think so Elaine, you walked out of my life and you think you can just walk back into it? No, it's not happening. I need you to leave, please?' Rosie opened the door, she walked through it without a second glance and then closed it behind her leaving Elaine in the garden.

'Mummy, who was that lady?' Imogen asked coming back into the hall. 'She's very pretty.'

'Oh, just someone I used to know darling, come on let's have a snack and we can sit and watch a movie, you get to choose.'

Wrapped in a blanket on the couch with Imogen in her arms watching Toy Story. Rosie's mind kept wandering back to Elaine. '*Why now?*' She wondered, over the years she had thought often about her, wondered what happened? She knew it had something to do with her accusation against Carl. Alex had believed Carl raped Elaine, however they stopped discussing it and Elaine Lamont had become just someone from their past. Rosie however had never been able to make another friend like Elaine. Seeing her tonight, Rosie suddenly wondered if they could be friends again. She dismissed the longing quickly. Her thoughts returned to her children, she held her daughter tightly and kissed the top of her head. The little girl looked up at her and smiled sadly.

'Mummy, do you think Becca is happy without us, all of her toys are in her room, wont she be lonely? Wont daddy be lonely too? Mummy I don't like Daddy Carl, can you ask him to go away?' Before Rosie could answer, Imogen asked, 'mummy did it hurt Becca when she died? I'm scared about Toby, what if he dies, what if daddy wants all his children with him.'

'Darling it's okay to be very sad, but let's think about all the good things about Becca, how funny she was. She has her baby Becky and her unicorn blanket with her to keep her safe.' Rosie gulped back tears, the rawness of the past few weeks, the pain and confusion so near to the surface. 'Darling, Toby is getting better, you will see him soon, I promise!' Rosie wanted to curl up somewhere and die herself. What was stopping her walking into the darkness she felt around her, was the little girl in her arms and Toby who would soon be home.

Rosie's own experience of her parents overwhelming sadness and grief when Simon had his accident. The years where she was pushed into the background and forgotten about, meant Rosie was aware of the need to be there for her children, despite the mountain of grief growing around her. Thinking of Simon, brought thoughts of Alex back and although losing her child was by far the worst thing that had ever happened to her. The loss of the man who had been her rock, always been there for her in one form or another, ran a close second, up there with Simon's accident. In the three weeks since Toby's operation, Rosie had tried to balance her time at the hospital with Toby and time with Imogen, afraid to be away from either of them. When she did come home she had allowed Imogen to sleep in her bed with her. She knew it was alright to let Imogen and Toby see her sadness at the loss of their sister. However, Rosie was also aware she was retreating into herself. Rosie's thoughts were interrupted by her daughter's voice.

'Mummy I love you, mummy did you put daddy in the grave with Becca? Why did they both go away? Papa said it was the cucumbers. Was it like Snow White and the wicked stepmother put poison in the apple?' Snow White came back when the prince kissed her, granny said that can't happen in real life.

Rosie's head began to spin, she felt sick and rushed to the toilet. Next thing she became aware of was waking up on the floor, her terrified daughter crying screaming out.

'Mummy what's wrong Mummy, please don't die mummy?'

'It's okay Imogen, I'm not feeling very well just now, it's alright. Can you go get me a glass of water, I'll be fine in a moment.' Knowing how afraid her daughter was, helped Rosie to compose herself. Suddenly a thought entered her head, she realised that she might be pregnant.

CHAPTER
THIRTY

Rosie looked at her husband, 'Pregnant?' he said looking back at her. 'Were you trying?'

'No, well we had never really consciously stopped trying, after Becca was born we just left it to chance and it never happened. Carl, I can't think about this just now. I'm seeing Dr McDougal on Friday to discuss my options.'

'What are your options? Surely you are not thinking you will have his baby? After what he's done to you? You also said they didn't recommend more than three pregnancies because you needed C-Sections.

'I think that they can consider a fourth one, the decision I have to make is either have it or I don't. My own GP reckons that with care I could have it. A termination is possible too, I'm only about ten weeks, so... there are options. Having another baby feels like I'm trying to replace Becca... With Alex gone, I just don't want to do this alone.'

Carl sighed, 'I'll support you whatever you decide, but I think emotionally it will be too much for you. You're not over losing your baby, and our kids need you. Sure, Toby is doing well but you never know, his body could still reject the kidney and you need to be there for him.'

'I know, but I don't know if I could kill a baby after losing Becca. I think I owe it to her to keep this one. Carl, I don't want it, but my head is all messed up. I keep telling myself I didn't have a termination with Toby when I thought he had been conceived from the rape. Whatever I feel about Alex now, I loved him when this one was made.'

'It is just a bundle of cells just now Rosie, not a person. Look go talk to Dr McDougal, she'll help you decide. You need to know what the risks are, what if something happens to you because of the pregnancy?' He looked at Rosie and sighed. 'What if you keep it and Lex finds out, he might try to get the baby?'

'I doubt that, I...I can't talk about it Carl, I'd rather not discuss Alex or think about him. I thought that you'd hurt me but what he's done? I just never saw it coming, how he reacted after Becca died. I know I was being difficult, and I pushed him away, but, he just changed.'

'You had just lost your child, you weren't being difficult, you were grieving. I know he must have been too, but its different for men isn't it?' Carl sighed, 'He should have been there for you, should have been stronger.'

'Oh, he was strong, he mostly supported me, tried to help me...Oh please Carl I don't want to talk about him. The worst thing he did was...To disappear like that after the funeral, when I needed him most.' Rosie stood up she shook her head and wiped away tears with the back of her hand.

Carl leaned forward and kissed her cheek, wiping away the tears with his finger. 'Rosie, I promise I will be there for you. I won't let you down.'

'Look Carl, please don't think I'm being rude. But you and I, I don't think there is a chance of us being together again, you have to understand I can't even think about that.'

Carl looked sadly at Rosie, 'I've so much making up to do here, please don't rule it out.' He reached out and touched Rosie's arm, 'you know sometime in the future you may change your mind. You've been badly hurt, been through so much. Right now, I'll settle for whatever crumbs you throw me, no pressure Rosie, I promise. I just want to get to know my kids for now, that's all. Do you want me to come to the hospital appointment with you tomorrow? I can get a day release, I'll go with you as a friend.'

Rosie shook her head, 'No, thank you for offering, but I need to do this alone. Carl, I haven't told anyone else about the baby, so could you keep it to yourself please?'

***

'Well Rosie, how are you? Can I just go over what will happen before we take you up to theatre?' Selina McDougal looked sadly at Rosie. 'I know I said it all last week, but you were very emotional, you seem calmer now. Are you sure you are doing the right thing? Four sections is taking a risk, but it's not any riskier than a termination. You are sure this is the right thing? Even with everything else that's happened, you could still go ahead with the pregnancy. Does anyone know you are here?'

Rosie sighed and shook her head she sat in the white and blue hospital gown and looked at the woman in front of her, 'I think I'm kind of detached from it all. I'm sure this is the best decision for everyone. I just can't have another baby now, it's all for the best. No one knows I'm here Dr McDougal, there is no one I can tell. Carl knows I'm having the termination, he doesn't know it's today. He offered to be here for me, but it just didn't seem right, and I don't want to give him the wrong message.'

'Rosie, you should have told your mum, she would be there for you, you know she would. You need to have someone there to look after you tonight.' Selina sat down on the edge of the bed. 'What about friends? There must be someone?'

'There's no one I can tell, most of my close female friends are the wives and girlfriends of Alex's friends. I can't risk him finding out. I honestly don't know if he would care anyway after what he's done.' Rosie stared ahead emotionless and seemingly calm. 'This is all for the best,' she repeated. 'I've booked a taxi to take me home, I'll rest. Mum and Dad think I've gone away for a few days, so they have the kids.'

Selina took a pen from her pocket, she wrote down a mobile phone number and handed it to Rosie. 'Put this in your bag Rosie, if you need anything tonight call me.' She sniffed, 'Okay let's talk about the process. In a few minutes someone will come in and give you your pre-med, then when you are nice and calm they will insert a pessary, that will soften your cervix. She looked at Rosie over the top of her glasses, 'once that is in place there is no going back. You are sure this is the right thing for you?'

'I'm sure Dr McDougal, there is no other way, I have to think about my children. I've thought about nothing else for weeks this wasn't an easy decision but it's the right one.'

'Okay dokey I'll go and get prepared, you will be taken down to theatre in about forty minutes, the procedure is relatively simple, when you come around it will be like a heavy period, perhaps a bit of discomfort. I'll send in nurse with your pre-med okay?'

***

Fourteen months later

'Dad I told you I don't care what Elaine is saying, I don't want to speak to her. It's hard enough to get through Christmas, just let me go to the cemetery and lay my wreaths.'

Davie Gibbs sighed, 'Rosie please just listen, we think you could be in danger in respect of Carl, he has been getting involved in some dodgy business. I don't think we ever really knew him. Darling please? Just think about it all? We are really worried you and him will...you know, get back to together. Please just listen to what Elaine is saying? Hear her out.'

'Dad how many more times do I have to say this, there is no Carl and me. It's been over since Imogen was a month old, he accepts it. He's my children's father and Toby would be dead if it wasn't for him. I see him a couple of times a week, the children are ready to be there overnight. They want to go, it's going to be Christmas night, he knows that I need sometime alone so he is taking the children, end of dad. Carl and I have discussed our marriage and he knows that there is no hope of any sort of romantic reconciliation. In fact, he has a girlfriend, his ex, Tracey is back in town and I think they may have hooked up. Imogen told me she was at the pantomime with them last week.'

'Does he know you are seeing Tommy Halliday?'

'I'm not seeing Tommy, I've been out for dinner with him, that's all, he has been great sorting out all of my legal matters, I bought him dinner to say thank you. He bought me dinner to discuss some other things, he's a friend, dad that's all, no romance.'

'Did you tell Carl about it?'

'No why would I? It's none of his business.'

'Be careful sweetheart, it's not just what Elaine is saying, I've heard all sorts of rumours. I'm worried about you letting him stay on Christmas Eve.'

'Dad he missed all the children's Christmas's, just let him have this one without a fuss. We'll be over to yours for Boxing day as usual, he is having the kids at his house on Christmas night, so it'll be fine. I need to get through Christmas without Becca, she would have been starting nursery after Christmas. I will be sad, but I can hold it together for a few hours. Carl has never had Christmas morning with the children so let me give him that. I promise Dad I'll come over on Boxing day, Carl is bringing them back early, he is going on holiday after Christmas. The Canaries, his parole officer has said it's okay. I would imagine Tracey is going with him.'

'I've invited Elaine and her Gran on Boxing day too, she needs to talk to you, you need to hear her darling.' David Gibb continued to look worried, he looked at his daughter. 'Rosie have you ever seen your mother and I this worried before? Please sweetheart don't let him stay overnight.'

'Dad he has been out of prison for months, and he had all that home leave, things were fine. He gets how I feel and accepts it. I wouldn't let him stay last year it was too soon, you know all this dad. For the last time will you stop panicking about it? It's one night. Imogen, she wants to go to his house, it has taken so long for her to accept him, I don't want to ruin it. You know why I'm not going Dad, they will be fine. He will bring them home on Boxing day. I can't believe you asked Elaine, what are you star struck?'

Davie Gibbs sighed, 'I believe he raped her, there are other things, but she wants to see you face to face to explain. Please Rosie just listen to her?'

'No dad, if she is there I'm not coming, you have your Boxing day party, I'll stay here.

'Rosie, please just see her, Elaine and you, you were like twins since you were babies. Listen to her, you need friends Rosie, you are living like a middle-aged spinster.'

'I can't let Elaine back in to my life dad.' Rosie sighed, tears pricked at her eyes. 'I'm afraid dad, it hurt, I just can't let new people in.'

'She's not new people darling, she really cares about you.'

'Okay I'll think about it, but I don't think I could meet her with other people there.'

CHAPTER
THIRTY-ONE

Christmas Eve 2007.

Rosie knew Carl had something on his mind as soon as he arrived. He said nothing during supper and although he was good with the children, helping them into bed, reading them a story. Rosie realised he was brooding about something. During supper with the children, mainly due to nerves about him being there and not knowing what to talk to him about other than the children, she had mentioned Elaine being in town. she supposed this was what had upset him. Rosie retreated to the living room and poured two glasses of wine. Eventually he came down from the bedroom and sat down.

'What do we do about the presents?' He asked without looking at Rosie, 'I have a car full, for them.'

Rosie smiled, 'go bring them in and then we need to wait until they are asleep to lay them out. Toby still believes in Santa. Imogen is such a smart wee thing, she has I think worked it out, but is a wee bit too unsure to say, but this will be the last year she does. So, have a drink and we could watch a movie or something while we wait.'

The Nightclub Owners Wife

Carl made several trips to the car bringing in brightly wrapped presents of different sizes. Eventually he closed the door and took the wine glass from Rosie and sipped it. He looked away and studied the Christmas tree. Now with rows of presents under it. 'What's this I hear about you and Tommy Halliday?' He asked quietly.

Rosie stared at him, 'what?'

'I heard you and him were at Casa Milano last week, you were seen having dinner.' Carl smiled but Rosie noted the smile didn't reach his eyes. 'Is that why you've agreed to me having them tomorrow night, so you and him can have some child free time?'

'I heard you introduced Tracey Stewart to our children Carl. I don't mean to be rude, but what I do and who I do it with is my business. For the record I had dinner with Tommy to thank him for all the work he's put in sorting out the kids trust funds. He has made a lot of money for them in the last few years, and when I asked for the bill he refused to take any money.' She looked at Carl and shook her head. 'Carl,' she said gently, you do know there is no chance of us ever getting back together. I don't love you anymore. I'm happy for you if you and Tracey have managed to sort things out. You and her, are better suited than we ever were.'

'Have you ever heard from big Lex? I can't believe he just walked out on you. You've not seen him, have you? He's around, he put a wreath on Rebecca's and his mums grave yesterday.'

Rosie gulped down her wine, 'Carl I don't want to talk about it. There has been no contact since the day he left and well, it still hurts. How do you know about the wreath?'

'I went to put one on my mums and I saw it.' Carl put his arm around Rosie and kissed the top of her head. 'I'm sorry babe, what he did was terrible to just leave you like that. What a bastard. I guess I'm just worried that when you find someone else the kids will like him better than me. I love them so much Rosie, I lost so much time with them. I know I'm doing the green-eyed dad thing. Watch Tommy too, he has quite a bad reputation with women.'

Rosie sighed and feeling uncomfortable in Carl's arms made to move away from him. 'Carl you are their dad, I realise that you think that they loved Alex more than you. Carl you know that they think he's dead, they are grieving for him and for their sister. Please just let them develop a relationship with you naturally. I will tell them someday about Alex and what he did to us, but it's not about him, it's about their feelings.' Rosie looked away, 'Carl I'm sorry I hurt you, I never meant to, it was all tied up with what happened. I was so young and inexperienced. I loved you, but it was a young love, first love and we have those two wonderful children ... but ... '

Carl pulled Rosie around and looked into her eyes. 'Rosie please just think about you and me, we are still married, and the kids would love it. I love you enough for both of us. Every single day I was in that stinking fucking prison I thought of you. Just let me make love to you, we were good together, Tracey is just filling a gap, she's not you.' Carl's hand moved to Rosie's breast.

Rosie pushed him away, 'Carl please leave, you can come back in the morning early. I can't have you staying here tonight after this. Why now? Why are you doing this, you told me you understood how I felt. You are the father of my children but I'm sorry nothing more.' Rosie walked to the lounge door and opened it, take your bag and go.' My Dad said this was a bad idea, now please just go.'

'So, your family have finally got what they wanted you and me apart. They never liked me, preferred that bastard Lockwood, didn't they? Your fucking mother was like, 'Lex this and Lex that, he fucking walked out on you, he left you with a dead kid and on your own and he's still the fucking hero. I gave your son a fucking kidney, the son you thought you'd had had with a fucking rapist, but you wouldn't have an abortion you didn't know he was mine. What really happened between you and Ronnie

Muir? Is it rape you want? Do you want me to force you? Is that how you like it?'

Rosie broke away and lifted the telephone just as the door burst open and her father and Elaine ran into the room. 'Carl please, leave?' Rosie's father said through gritted teeth, 'we've called the police so unless you want to go back to prison tonight, you'd better get out of here.'

Carl let Rosie go and walked towards the door, Rosie followed and opened it. 'Don't come back tonight Carl, I don't want you near my children you're not safe.'

Rosie, you are mine and I will not let another man have you. Big Lex, the bastard who ran out on you and your kids, he might have thought he was his father, but Toby is my son, he will not call another bastard, dad. You all better watch out, because I always get what I want.' He looked at Elaine and sneered, 'don't I Lainey?' 'Keep the fucking presents.' He left, banging the door behind him. Rosie hearing a noise behind her turned, Imogen stood at the bottom of the stairs quietly watching the scene.

'How did you know? Rosie asked her father, when she returned from settling Imogen back in to bed, 'how did you know this would happen?'

'We didn't darling, Tommy Halliday called to say he had been threatened by Carl. We tried to call you and the phone just kept ringing.' He walked over to the telephone and lifted it. 'I thought so, it's been unplugged at the wall.' He plugged it back in and turned to his daughter. 'I have to call the police now, I phoned them from the house and to be honest they weren't too interested. You're going to have to give them a statement. They said they would contact social work to let his supervising social worker know. However darling, Elaine here has some information about this.'

Elaine who had remained silent throughout shook her head, 'I've been having him watched Rosie. I think he has an unprofessional relationship with his social worker.' She sighed, then looked at Rosie a sad expression on her face. 'Carl will use people to suit his needs, he's good at it, very convincing. You of all people know how convincing and manipulative he can be?'

Rosie nodded, 'look thank you both for your concern, but I'll be fine, I need to get some sleep. I've put Imogen into my bed for now given that she's just discovered both her fathers are bastards and there is no Santa in the same evening. I need to be with my daughter just now.' She looked at Elaine and smiled sadly. 'We can catch up tomorrow, maybe take some time out of the party with my kids being looked after to talk. What happened between us though, Elaine, it can't be sorted out in one conversation. You realise that don't you?'

Elaine nodded, her eyes filled up with unshed tears, 'I know that babe, but we need to start somewhere, don't we? Rosie I really do hope that we can sort things out... I've missed you so much. Never had another friend like you, no matter how hard I tried.'

Rosie nodded, 'me neither.' She and Elaine embraced and held on to each other. 'Let's start by having a talk tomorrow okay?'

***

Mrs Ranmore, I'm sure this is all a big mistake, Carl Ranmore has been assessed as safe, I've spoken to his supervising officer and they don't think he's a risk to you.' The policeman turned to Elaine. 'As for him having a relationship with his social worker, that is ridiculous, his worker is a married lady and very respectable. Can I advise you what slander and stalking means?'

'I have proof of this constable, and there is definitely something unprofessional about this relationship.' Elaine looked at the policeman. 'Unless social workers have now started doing home visits at midnight?'

'You will need to take that up with her manager after the festive period. Miss Lamont, you can call tomorrow someone will be there.' The police officer turned back to Rosie, 'In respect of the matter in hand, I've spoken to Mr Ranmore. He is a bit upset because you rejected him that's all. He said he was upset because you have been dating his lawyer. He is feeling that it's just like it was when he was in prison. You did take up with his best friend when he was inside, didn't you? The whole town knew about you and Alex Lockwood. You can understand why he is a bit concerned that you have been dating another friend.' The policeman looked at Rosie and Elaine and shook his head. I'm sure you are worried, but we don't think there is any need, it's Boxing day, he is going on holiday tonight, he has permission to go abroad.' The policeman shook his head, 'he's feeling a little embarrassed about mistaking the signs, he says he thought you had asked him over on Christmas Eve for you know?'

'No, I don't know?' Rosie said firmly, 'you tell me? I've been separated from him for ten years. Why would I suddenly want to be with him again? Get out of my house you are a disgrace.' She walked towards the door and opened it. The two policemen stood up and left. Rosie closed the door behind her and looked at Elaine, 'thanks for seeing to the children, I thought at first you had come in with the police. 'Who was the little girl you brought with you by the way?'

'I just arrived at the same time as the police, Rosie. I was at your mums for the party and she asked me to come over and see what was keeping you? Her and your dad didn't want to leave their guests. You told her you were just leaving an hour ago. Then when she phoned, and you said you were waiting for the police well obviously she was worried, just call and tell them you are okay.'

Rosie called her parents and quickly filled them in on the visit from the police. She assured them she and the children were alright, then replaced the telephone on its holder. She turned and smiled at Elaine who had been standing in the conservatory looking out at the waves crashing on to the beach. 'Are the kids alright?'

Elaine nodded and walked away from the glass wall. 'That playroom is amazing Rosie. The whole house is brilliant, what a view. Come on have a drink and we can talk before we go to your parents.'

'I can't have a drink, I need to drive over to mum and dads, there's something I have to do first. You have one if you want there's a bottle of Pepsi in the fridge, pour me one of them. Then you can tell me about the wee girl?'

Elaine looked Rosie in the eye and then sighed, Rosie could sense this was a difficult subject. 'The little girl is my daughter Rosie; her name is Chloe she's nine and she is Imogen and Toby's half-sister.'

'Rosie looked sadly at the woman in front of her, a tear ran on to her cheek. 'I'd guessed that, she looks like him. I saw it as soon as you both came in.'

'I'm sorry to blurt it out like that, I came to tell you yesterday, but with all that happened, it just wasn't the time. I was angry for years about it all, but Chloe, she really is a wonderful child. I wanted to tell you that day after your baby died, but that definitely wasn't the right time. I talked to your mum and dad and they said I needed to tell you. So, when I arrived, and you weren't there today it gave me the excuse to come over.' Elaine smiled, then opened her cardigan to display a baby bump, I can't have much to drink either, because I'm pregnant, this one was conceived through love, not force.'

Rosie stared at Elaine, she took the glass of cola she held out and gulped it down. 'Why did you have his baby? He raped you?'

Elaine shrugged, 'you did it too Rosie, you had Toby.' She sighed, 'I actually didn't know I was pregnant. Believe it or not I had periods the whole way through. I kept taking the pill, I didn't put on much weight. I went to the local accident and emergency thinking I had appendicitis, out came a 4lb baby girl.' Elaine shook her head then smiled sadly. 'If I hadn't been so traumatised I would have been in the papers. I was going to put her up for adoption. Then I saw her in the nursery and realised that whoever her father was, it wasn't her fault. I lifted her up and it was instant the bond. I have never regretted that decision Rosie. Why did you keep Toby?'

'I was so traumatised I didn't notice I hadn't had a period until I was quite far on, I think it was shock. I didn't have an abortion initially, because they told me I would have to deliver the baby, then I kind of bonded with my bump. They had offered me the morning after pill at the hospital after the rape and I wouldn't take it. I don't remember them asking. I was I think just punishing myself. I think I kind of knew the moment I saw him that he was Carl's son. It was instant with him too, I just loved him. You know most people wouldn't have kept their babies? It wasn't easy, but Alex . . . he helped me he made Toby our baby . . . Elaine I can't talk about him. God do you think it was the catholic education, love your rapist's baby?'

'Maybe, but I love my daughter Rosie, more than life itself. She should be a reminder of a really awful time, but she's not. I'm so glad I didn't know I was pregnant because I would have had a termination if I'd realised. There's nothing wrong with termination, or adoption in both of our situations, it just wasn't for me that's all.'

I was just too far on with Toby, I think once I got my head around it not being the babies fault it was a bit easier, you know how I can retreat into a fairy-tale world when I need to block things out. I also think that what my parents did to me when Simon got hurt, made me realise what rejection does and that you can come back from it. Rosie sighed loudly. 'What are we going to tell people? What do we tell the kids? Do we need to tell them?'

'Let's worry about that later, right now we have years of catching up to do. I've missed you Rosie. Like I said, I never could make a friend like you again.'

'What one whose husband raped you and then she blamed you.' Rosie began to cry, she put her hands over her face, and sobbed into them. 'I'm so sorry Elaine, I don't deserve your friendship.'

'Hey, you had been through a very traumatic time babe, it must have been horrible being attacked and then seeing Carl murder him.' Elaine put her arms around Rosie, and they clung together both sobbing. 'Then losing your baby like that and Lex, what the fuck was he thinking to do that to you. Everyone I know said he adored you, doted on you, then just fucked off and left you when you needed him most. What a bastard.'

'Elaine, I . . . I can't talk about it, even to you, the pain of what he's done. This is going to sound mad, it's worse than what Carl did all those years ago. Worse than all the other things, it's the betrayal. I never thought Alex could hurt me like this. It's like I never knew him, I just want to try not to think about him. It's the only way I can cope, just shut him out. It's what I do when I'm in pain.'

'Okay, I kind of get that, I'll not bring it up again, but remember this Rosie? If you ever do need to talk I will be there for you. The way we were for seventeen years, there for each other.'

Rosie stood up 'can we be friends again? The way we were? Can you ever forgive me?'

'There is nothing to forgive Rosie, I don't mean it was my fault, but that night, the night Imogen was born. I got drunk with him, I was seventeen and a half years old. Yes, I was experimenting with drugs, I was young and stupid, he was old enough to know better. I was legless Rosie, really out of it, I think now he might have drugged me, but I did have a lot of champagne too so who knows? Thing is I remember it, I kissed him I realised as soon as I did it, it was wrong. I should have gone home then, not stayed.' Elaine wiped away a tear from her eye and then taking out a tissue she blew her nose. 'I remember him putting me to bed and then I wakened up and he was, you know? Finishing off. I just lay there and let him, I was I suppose so shocked. I pretended to go back to sleep, he went back to his own room . . . I lay there for a while, and then got up and left, went back to my Grans. Oh, I don't know why? Thing is I couldn't tell you and I went around to Nobels looking for Lex, but he wasn't there so I just went back to Stirling. You know the rest don't you, I told Lex what I did. I don't know Rosie, it was shock, I think anger. I was going to confront him and then I just bottled it. So, the question is can you forgive me?'

'We go back a long way, don't we? I missed you so much, it was a difficult time for us all. Let's just try to put it all behind us, these kids are the future. We've both got over worse?'

'Can we start again? Just like that? I want it to be like it was, before Carl. There are children now.' Elaine reached out and took Rosie's hand.

'I would imagine that it'll take time, and a lot of talking but I think I'd like you back in my life Elaine. I hear you've done rather well for yourself. I've seen you on T.V of course everyone has. BBC news, well done you.'

'Know what? I've never touched drugs from that day till now. It kind of wakened me up, stopped me being a party girl. Made me study harder. It was a terrible ordeal, but I think I was able to channel it another way. I got some help from the university. When I had Chloe, it got harder, but I kept going. In some ways it drove me. Rosie, what happened to you, you don't let it bring you down either.'

Rosie nodded, 'that's kind of us isn't it? We keep going, I'm not sure whether there is a martyr streak in us both, what's that saying? That which doesn't kill you makes you stronger. For a long time after Becca died I wanted to crawl into that black hole, it was so unfair. I still feel like that sometimes, I miss her every day and I think a bit of you dies when you lose a child.' Rosie wiped away a tear from her eye. However, at the time though, I needed to carry on, Toby was so ill, Imogen needed me, and I was pregnant. Elaine I just can't talk about that time to anyone, can we just not do it?'

'Okay but I will be there for you if you ever want to? For the record.'

Rosie nodded, 'I had some counselling after the rape, it helped me to move on, learned coping strategies, I had some closure. I think that might be why I'm ... oh, I don't know, not able to get over Alex, no closure. If I talk about him, it happened ... does that make sense? As you know, it's easier for me just to bury it all, not healthy some folk would say but it works for me usually. Anyway, enough maudlin stuff, let's practice what we preach. I need to go to the cemetery before we go to mum and dads. I meant to go on Christmas day but obviously yesterday I was a bit preoccupied. I was also worried that Carl would be there, Dad offered to go but I just need to do this, it makes it real, stops me going into a fairy-tale world where it didn't happen.' Rosie smiled sadly, 'some things I want to remember, how special Becca was, is one of them.'

CHAPTER
THIRTY-TWO

'Does Lex send flowers every Christmas?' Elaine asked reading the card on the flower arrangement made up of red and white flowers to look like Santa.'

Rosie sighed and wiped away a tear, 'he sends flowers every month. Well I suppose it means something, his daughter dying, he was a good father. Becca's death did something to him, he just reacted his way. I reacted mine, but I have never seen or heard from him since the day he left.' She looked at Elaine and the other girl knew she was silently pleading with her to stop asking about Alex.

Elaine watched as Rosie cleared the snow from the small teddy bear shaped headstone in front of the large ornate headstone with Simon's photograph on it. She placed her small Christmas wreath as far away from the floral Santa as she could. 'Why don't I take the kids over to the play park across the road and leave you for a few minutes?' Elaine whispered. 'Babe I can't even start to imagine what it feels like to lose your child.'

'Thanks Lainey.'

***

Elaine looked up from her phone as Rosie sat down on the bench beside her. 'You okay?' She whispered.

Rosie nodded, 'yip, it's hard and maybe someday I will be able to accept she's gone. The grief I feel is overwhelming, I must carry on for them though. I think what my parents did when Simon got hurt, helped me to not do that. In a funny way it made me a better parent.' Rosie smiled at the antics of the children who were chasing each other all over the play park. 'My fantasy with all this . . . is to imagine that she is with Alex, he took her away and she is running around in America. You know that's where he went? He's almost as famous as you now Elaine.' Rosie blew her nose, 'the kids thought he died too, Imogen didn't twig last night what Carl meant, so I've still got to work out how to tell them. Oh, I never told them a lie, I just didn't correct them when they thought he had died and was with Becca. Then when I was able to, I didn't know how to say it. So, I just left it like that. I mean how do you tell a child that the man you loved and was for most of your life the only father you knew, just upped and left. Imogen actually didn't ask last night . . . I think she was more relieved than upset at what Carl did, she said she was pretending to like Carl because she thought it was what I wanted. Toby is such a calm laid back child he will cope with anything. Someday I will tell them, maybe someday when it doesn't hurt.'

Elaine nodded, I get that, I've never told Chloe how she came to be either. She has never really been curious, she accepts my partner as her father, although she does when she is having a strop, often tell him he's not. What are you going to do about Carl, Rosie? I'm sorry for what I've caused, but I know he's a dangerous man babe. I've been gathering stuff on him for a few years now. I think he is a psychopath or has psychopathic tendencies.' She smiled, I kind of became an expert on mental disorders, spokesperson for the people who had mental health problems. However, I also studied the few very dangerous ones who are thankfully in the minority. When I was in Canada I did a documentary where I spoke to offenders in prison who had been diagnosed with psychopathic personality disorder. I also worked with a forensic psychologist, Brian who incidentally is my baby father and now about to be my husband,' she touched her abdomen and smiled.

'What did he think about Carl? I take it he supports what you are saying about him?'

Elaine nodded her face becoming serious again. 'There's a twenty-point checklist and when I started to realise that Carl had those tendencies, I spoke to Brian about what I knew and what I suspected Carl had done. He agreed, I had thought it was a narcissistic personality disorder. He said no, he reckoned it was unlikely due to the fact he had such a stable upbringing. Brian suggested Carl had traits of psychopathy and being spoiled as a kid had added to this. Brian said it's very rare for there to be no trauma involved and it makes him, well it makes him unworkable... you could never fix him in other words. Elaine smiled wryly, Brian got really excited about it, said that type of disorder is really rare... I hate him so much Rosie, I don't want to carry that much anger about with me. I don't know what's worse babe you, ignoring all the trauma, or me getting angry?'

Rosie shook her head, 'Elaine I know why you are angry with him, and I get it now. I don't know a lot about psychopaths, but is there not something about them being devoid of feelings? He was always able to be really loving, yes, he was controlling but no I don't think so. I suppose you and I need to talk, and you can tell me why you think that. I promise I will listen. After his behaviour yesterday, well I know there is something not right, but psychopathic? Is that not the kind of axe murder thing?'

'Rosie, Brian says that if they are really clever, which many are, they can mirror feelings and be very convincing. Carl he's clever and dangerous, and he takes drugs so that makes him even more unpredictable. Think about it, he killed Ronnie, it was a frenzied attack, I read the post mortem report. That wasn't a crime of passion. You do know psychopathy is not always just in criminals? There are loads of successful people who would be classed as psychopaths, but they are not dangerous in terms of physically harming. They just see the world only from their point of view, and this drives them. Carl, well, it's quite rare, he is dangerous, he has already killed, you saw what he did yesterday. The loving bit he does, you know the nice Carl? Well that's an act. You were his possession.'

Rosie sighed and nodded, 'I never really trusted him after what he did to Ronnie. Alex believed he raped you,' Rosie looked at the floor, 'I knew it was true Lainey, I think I just wanted to believe that it was the drugs he was taking, I wanted to believe he had changed. Anyway, he should be at the airport now, going on holiday. He was leaving tonight. I saw the tickets.'

Elaine smiled and put her arm around Rosie, 'babe let's just enjoy what's left of the day. Let's go party then if it's okay I'll come back to yours, we will put the babies to bed and talk about all of this. I have a lot of stuff to tell and show you.'

Rosie shook her head, know what Lainey? Let's just go back to mine and call my parents, I can see them tomorrow. I want to show you the first proof of my book, it arrived on Christmas Eve but with all that happened I couldn't do anything about it then. I have an agent and everything, I'm so excited about it. I had finished it last year, but when everything happened I just shelved it and then this summer I took it back out and re wrote some of it. The agent who had accepted it was really understanding and supportive, she already had a publishing deal lined up for me so ... '

'I can't wait to read it babe, I'm so proud of you, and so happy to be back in your life. Maybe we should go to your parents though. What about Carl? What if he didn't go on holiday? What if he comes around bothering you?'

He won't, he was really looking forward to the holiday, it's all he talked about. He won't miss it, in the very slight chance he didn't go which I doubt, he won't know we are there though Elaine, he'll think I'm at my parents. He knows we always go there Boxing day we usually stay the night too. So, if he is going to cause any bother, he'll go there first. In any case I don't think he'll risk getting his licence revoked, he really will not want to go back to prison, will he?' Rosie sighed and looked at her friend I think we will be safe enough for now. I'll call Tommy Halliday and ask him if he thinks I should do anything legally. No, I'm not having a thing with him, I think he would like it, but well it's too close to home isn't it. I think I'm going to die an old maid now, I'm shit at picking men ... Now come on let's head for home, we can put the kids to bed and then open a bottle of wine, you can have one drink surely?'

Rosie went home to her house with Elaine, they put the children to bed and then opened a bottle of wine. They talked long into the night. By the time they went to bed, Rosie knew Carl Ranmore was a dangerous man.

Elaine with the stealth and dedication of the award-winning journalist she was, had gathered over the last few years a dossier on Carl Ranmore which went back a long way, even before he met and married Rosie. Elaine was convinced that Carl not Ronnie had murdered Julie. She had gathered CCTV evidence that put Carl, driving Alex's car, in the vicinity of the park where Julie was found. Elaine explained how after studying the transcripts of the trial and the post mortem reports the times did not add up to Ronnie having murdered Julie and been at Rosie and Carl's house. She told Rosie she had been speaking to Christine Caven, who had been one of the CID officers at the time of the investigation. Christine had told Elaine she had never believed Ronnie killed Julie, but her senior officer at the time had been keen to conclude the case as the manpower was using a lot of resources. It had been easier to just believe Ronnie killed Julie out of jealousy. As he said, Ronnie was dead, and Carl was going to jail, everyone believed Ronnie did it, there had been no point in using up manpower to investigate further. Now a Detective Inspector in charge of family protection, Christine had agreed to talk to her senior officers about reopening the case.

Elaine had also uncovered drug trafficking when Carl was in prison and money laundered through the clubs and pubs after Rosie and Alex had cut ties with the business.

CHAPTER
THIRTY-THREE

It was 4am when the doorbell rang, having talked well into the small hours, Elaine and Rosie had only gone to bed. Rosie jumped up from her bed and opened the patio doors to the bedroom veranda and looked over the wall. Outside a police car was parked next to her car, and a uniformed police man stood ringing the bell. Rosie ran out into the hall, to be met by Elaine, she looked at her friend 'it's the police Lainey.' She whispered, 'something is wrong for them to come here at this time in the morning.'

'Let's hope Carl has driven off a cliff.' Elaine hissed back.

Rosie opened the door pulling her robe around her, Christine Caven, and a uniformed male police officer stood on the door step. 'Rosie can we come in, I came over because I know you, and I thought this needed to come from someone you knew.'

Rosie nodded 'Is it Carl? Rosie whispered as she led the way through to the lounge, 'has he harmed himself?'

Christine shook her head, 'can you sit down please?' Rosie looked at Elaine and together they sat down on the big leather sofa. Christine leaned forward obviously struggling, 'no it's not Carl. I almost wish it were Rosie.' She blinked, 'Rosie where are your kids?'

'Upstairs asleep.'

'All of them? Your daughter too Elaine?'

'Yes, all of them, Elaine said looking worried, 'I've just checked on them, they are all asleep. What's going on? I know it's serious.'

Christine sighed, 'there is no easy way to tell you this, but there was a fire...a serious fire...at your parent's house. Rosie...I'm so sorry but they didn't make it. A neighbour alerted the fire brigade and they were there in minutes but the blaze, it consumed the house.'

Rosie stared at the police officers, 'no there must be some mistake, my Dad he was meticulous about safety, they switched every socket off at night. Never ever would there be a fire.'

'Rosie I'm so sorry, but it is definitely them. I was on duty and I went out because my mum called me and told me it was your parent's house. I went out and I saw them when they were brought out, there is no mistake.' Rosie, they were asleep, if it's any consolation they didn't suffer. I don't know what happened, the fire investigation boys are in there now and as soon as its light they will begin an investigation. They will make the area safe and go through it with a fine-tooth comb. We will find out what happened, it does look like an accident though.' Christine looked at Elaine, 'Lainey...she began.

Rosie jumped to her feet. 'No, no, no, this isn't happening, I've lost enough people. I can't do this again, not mum and dad. Not like this, No, I don't accept this. Lainey tell her no...it can't happen.'

Elaine the shock on her face evident, looked at the police officer, 'my gran was in the house...she was staying there...it was the Boxing day party.' She took a deep breath and asked, 'is she...is she dead too?'

Christine nodded, 'I'm so sorry Elaine, there was no chance of anyone in there surviving. Apparently, there was some sort of explosion and the whole house just went up. Could be gas perhaps, we won't know until the fire investigators have finished their work. 'Rosie,' Christine said gently, 'we need to know who else was in the house. There are bodies of two other adults, they were in the downstairs room. I'm afraid they are badly burned, and we don't know who they are. Who else was likely to have stayed the night?'

'My aunt Lucy and Uncle Fred, they were here from Glasgow, they would have stayed I think, my cousin's little boy was going to be with them.' Rosie jumped to her feet, putting her hands on her head, she cried out. 'Oh my God . . . was there a child? He is seven,' same age as Toby. His name is Jordan, you asked about our kids when you came in Chris.'

'He was there, Chloe was playing with him.' Elaine said quietly. He is much the same age, it was one of the reasons I had to bring her, he was playing a bit too rough for her. Rosie please calm down, we need to not disturb the kids. Elaine put her hand on Rosie's arm and then gripped her friends hand. 'Sit down, try to breath, Rosie we have each other now.'

CHAPTER
THIRTY-FOUR

Greece 2018

Rosie was suddenly awakened by the tapping of her hotel room door. She sighed, remembering last night's events, thinking it would be madam Katsoulis back to try to match-make with her son. She stepped out of bed and called out 'Who is it?'

'Madam Gibbs, it is Michael, you left one of your bags in my taxi last night. I waited till this morning as I thought you may be tired and need to rest.'

Rosie put on the white fluffy robe from the chair in the corner and opened the door, Michael and the man she had mistaken for Wilson the night before, stood in the hallway. Michael handed her the bag.

'Thank you, Michael, I hadn't noticed it wasn't there.'

'Madam Gibbs, this is my friend Keith, you met last night, he would like to speak to you.'

Rosie sighed and shook her head, 'look I don't want to be rude, but I really just want to forget it all. Yesterday was a very traumatic day for me. If you are here to plead for him, please don't. You have no idea what your friend did to me and my family.'

'Please Miss Gibbs . . . just five minutes in private, I promise you then I will go. I need to talk to you. I'm Keith Arnold, I'm sorry about what happened last night, but I need to talk to you. I'm Jimmy's brother-in-law, and his best friend. Until tonight I didn't know you existed.'

'Why are you calling him Jimmy? That's not his name, nor it would seem is Wilson. He's a devious bastard Keith and I don't wish to be rude, but you have no idea what he did to me.'

'Miss Gibbs, there are things you must hear.'

'Okay five minutes, but please understand, I don't want to hear you plead for him? I really don't think there is anything you could tell me which will change my opinion.' Rosie looked around the doorway, 'he'd better not be here Keith. Please call me Rosie.'

'Rosie, you need to listen to me, tonight he told me everything, I understand why you are so upset. But there are things you don't know.' Keith looked sadly at Rosie, 'things you need to know. He's going to be at the ferry terminal in the morning to try to talk to you. So, I need to speak to you tell you some stuff, then you can decide whether you want to speak to him or not. If you don't, well, Michael and I, we will get you off the island without you having to see him. I give you my word.'

Rosie held open the door and Keith entered Michael raised his hand then went off down the hallway.

Keith lifted the wine carafe and looked at Rosie, she nodded and watched silently as he poured her a glass of the red wine. Lifting a mug from the tea tray on the sideboard he poured a generous measure in to it. Taking a gulp from the mug he sat down on the edge of the bed. Rosie continued to stand by the door as though ready to open it and ask him to leave. Keith could see she was emotional, and after the story he had heard from Jimmy earlier, Keith realised that this must be agony for the woman in front of him.

The Nightclub Owners Wife

'Okay so talk,' Rosie sighed, her eyes welling up, tell me why he did it? Why talk to me for nearly two years and not tell me one vital piece of information?' She shook her head sadly, 'I couldn't believe how understanding he was, how nice, it was as though he knew what I was thinking. I can't believe I fell for his lies. Then again, he lived a lie for years, so it would be easy for him?'

'Rosie, I know this is difficult for you to hear, and after the way he has lied to us all. I don't know why I still know this? Jimmy is the most trustworthy guy I have ever met. I need you to listen to this story. As I said, you can walk away. I will get my friend to take you across to the mainland on his boat, so you can avoid the ferry in the morning if that's what you want.' Keith sighed and looked at her, Jimmy was married to my sister. I thought she was the love of his life, I had no idea about his past. Him and Kim well it was pretty special, she knew about you though. He told you she was dead, didn't he?'

'He said she died in an accident, I know that is true because it was all over the news at the time. I'm sorry Keith, but if you know what he did to me, you'll realise I'm quite unsure as to what is truthful and what is fantasy. Firstly, will you tell me why you call him Jimmy, his name is Alex Lockwood I grew up with him I knew his mother, so that's definitely his name. I also know he is a famous architect now, and he was married to Kim Maldon. I'm sorry for your loss Keith, I know how it feels to lose people you love. Alex Lockwood left me without even a backward glance, to pursue his career, he uses his own name for that, so why call himself Jimmy?'

'You've been following his career then? If you know how well known his work is? You must also know how reclusive he is?'

Rosie shook her head, 'not especially, but he has been in the news, and our home town, well they do like local boys and girls made good. It's been on the Scottish news a few times and I own his first house, they wanted to put up a plaque to him. I turn the television off when he's mentioned. Rosie looked sadly at Keith, 'he didn't just hurt me, he walked out on my children too, they were devastated he was the only father they had known, and they had . . . they had just lost their baby sister.'

'I know that Rosie, he told me what he did to you.'

'My parents . . . my parents thought of him as a son Keith, he just walked away from us all. He didn't just hurt me. My parents died eleven years ago, they never understood why he did it either, they were bitter about him. Me . . . I just shut it all out. I stopped feeling you know?' Rosie sighed and looked at the man in front of her. 'I had to cope with my own and everyone else's grief too and he just left me to do it. That's why I'm so angry at what he's done, pretending to be someone else. He was my rock, I loved him, my child had just died, and my son was desperately ill, he just wrote a letter and walked out of our lives. So, forgive me for being bitter, Keith, I think I earned the right. You say he is honest and trustworthy you don't know him Keith. Just as I didn't know him.'

'I've known him for ten years Rosie, can you just spare me half an hour and I'll tell you what he told me last night? I wouldn't normally betray a confidence however this is important. Firstly, I'll tell you how he came to be my best friend, I first met him in 2007 when I commissioned him to design the hotel.'

CHAPTER
THIRTY-FIVE

New York 2007

'Sis, how are you? You are looking wonderful, like the hair.' Keith smiled at his sister and moved into the room dropping his case on the marble floor, he looked around. 'This house is amazing by the way.'

Kim Maldon hugged her brother, 'it's rented Keith, but I am buying, well actually I'm about to build my own house.'

'Yeah, great, where though? You surely don't want to stay in America?' He nudged his sister, 'wont building a house break some of those nails? I saw the film by the way, fuck you really are a good actress. I'm glad you got out of the soap though and took the chance, where's Freddy? He's usually lurking about. I saw you got him a part in the film?'

Kim's beautiful face clouded over, she sighed, tears welled up in her eyes, her brow furrowed, and she looked away from her brother. 'It's over Keith, he slept with one of the extra's on the film, I had to sort it out in my own head first before I told you. I knew you and Michael would say good riddance, I wanted to see you to tell you.'

Keith wrapped his arms around his sister and kissed her forehead, 'I'm so sorry sweetheart, I won't do all the big brother told you stuff, cos I know you are really hurt.' He kissed his sister on the top of her head then held her at arm's length. 'Do you want me to go and punch him or something? Cos, I really would love to.'

'He'll sue you and you would end up penniless and living off me too. Look I really don't want to talk about it, just another fickle Hollywood romance I suppose. I'm okay, mum came over, and she of course put it into perspective, at least I didn't marry him. I'm never having another man, that's it. I've decided to be a lesbian, being gay seems less complicated.'

'You do know that to be a lesbian you have to have sex with women?'

'Okay so I don't actually fancy women and that might be a teeny bit of a problem.' Kim smiled sadly, 'It's been a few months so I'm mostly over it. Let's just talk about something more interesting. What are you over here for anyway?'

'Great minds must think alike. Would you believe Michael and I are building a hotel sis!'

'In America?'

'No on Mykosis. We're selling the place in Cambridge and moving. His Dad isn't too good and Michael kind of feels he needs to go home. His Grandfather left him a plot of land in his will, it's prime land great position with its own private beach. The reason for this trip is to meet an architect. He's New York based.'

Kim gasped you are going to let an American design a hotel for you? Wow thought you said all American architecture was pretentious and wrong?' Her eyes narrowed. 'And where are you two getting the money from?'

'He's not American, the architect, he's British, Scottish actually. We've had an offer for the hotel, five and a half million sis, so Mikey-boy and I are looking at being millionaires. Even using an award-winning architect, we will have quite a bit of change after the build. Have you heard of Lockwood Aniston?'

Kim shook her head, 'can't say I have Keith should I have?'

'You just said you were going to build a house, I'm assuming even the beautiful Kim Maldon needs someone to do the plans? They are a new up and coming firm of Architects, New York based, but they have an office in Athens too, one of the partners is of Greek descent and they do some amazing stuff. It's expensive but probably worth it. They arranged to see us on Mykosis. Then the Aniston partner broke her leg in a jet skiing accident, so I'm seeing the Lockwood partner here, which I'm secretly pleased about. AJ Lockwood designed the new Museum of Scotland building. So, I'm getting an award-winning architect.'

'Gosh I visited that when I was in Glasgow last year, it's amazing. Anyway, where is Mikey? Why is he not here, you do know I like him more than you, don't you?'

'Michael isn't with me because he has gone to see his mother, she is trying to marry him off again, and that is so going to be our life now. But well I kind of knew that it would be difficult.'

'So, she still doesn't accept he's gay and you and him are life partners? Talk about complicated love life? Is it homophobia? She and Sandro well they were really nice to me when they were over in Britain and they appear to love you like a son.'

Keith smiled and shook his head. 'She doesn't mind him being gay, she just wants grandchildren. They keep saying that some of the Greek gods took men but then did their duty by producing. Achilles and Patroclus, you must remember from your rep days?' Keith giggled and shook his head, 'when he told his parents, they weren't too bothered about him being gay, they asked if he gave or took. He's a fucking coward he said he was the giver. I had to shave my fucking designer stubble off and he grew a beard.'

Kim looked puzzled, then smiled as the penny dropped. 'Of course, it's the penetrative part isn't it. Greek mythology, the gender doesn't matter, its masculine to do it and feminine to receive. Fuck sake Keith! What are you going to do once you are out there?'

I love him Kim, it's worth the charade for what we have together, so it's just something I must do. He loves me, but he also respects his parent's views, it's their culture and their religion.' Keith nudged his sister, and grinned. 'They've been more accepting of us than some British folks, remember how Gran reacted when she found out I was gay?'

Kim smiled, 'she isn't exactly a good example, is she? She also thought that being an actress was much the same as being a prostitute. Yet she loved Corrie, didn't miss it, remember the shock on her face when I visited her, and all the old dears knew who I was from Eastenders? She didn't like southerners either, so she never watched it.'

'Yeah, she had a bit of a bucket list of biases, didn't she? Must have been awful in her eyes, a queer and a hooker, then we both had partners who had...what was that horrible expression she used?'

'A touch of the tar brush.' Kim grimaced remembering.

She was a bigoted old git, wasn't she?' Keith laughed and nudged his sister. 'You also lived in sin with Ari so that was definitely up there with going to hell. She would have called Freddy a real man though. Look how that was? I hate bigots Kim, but fuck, when it's in your own family. Mum was always okay with it though, so I suppose that made up for some of it. She encouraged me to come out, she says she always knew. She loves Mikey too, he is so respectful and kind, what's not to love? Anyway, what're you up to today? Want to come to the architects with me?'

'Can't babe, I have to go see a director, I'm doing a remake of Helen of Troy would you believe, so if you are going to be in Greece next year I can catch up with you and Michael for a holiday. Not sure where they are filming, most will be around Athens, but Jackson is playing Paris, he has already said he's taking his yacht. He offered me a room, he plans to take it to wherever we are filming. Where is your architect based? I'm going to Manhattan?'

I'm seeing him at his office in Manhattan, so I could meet you afterwards and you can buy me dinner. Now you're a famous movie star you can afford to buy me a decent meal.'

'You just told me you are worth two and a half million you can afford my kind of dining, I'll do a reservation at the Four Seasons.'

'Okay text me when you finish your meeting and I'll do the same, so whoever finishes first, buys dinner. I'm not rich yet sis the sale doesn't go through until next month. So, you might need to pay it for me just now. Four Seasons? I've never been there. Have I? Is it expensive?

Kim laughed, 'yeah and then some, last time I was there the bar bill alone was well... it was into four figures. It is definitely the place to get noticed in New York though. You can also look at what is current for your new hotel.'

***

Kim this is A J Lockwood, hope you don't mind but I asked him to join us for dinner to discuss the hotel. You need to pay though, cos I finished first.'

'No, you didn't, you asked Mr Lockwood here to dinner because you wanted to win. There really is no end to your competitiveness you devious prick.' Kim put out her hand, it's nice to meet you Mr Lockwood, are you a good architect?'

'The best Miss Maldon, I'm hoping your brother and his partner give me the job. I quite like the Greek Islands and Kiri my business partner will do all the legal stuff, she's Greek so knows all about building there. She has a broken leg, but she is actually in Greece, so I can see her whilst I'm over there seeing the site, by the time it all goes through she should be fit and able to take over.' Alex shook his head, 'she got hurt in Greece visiting her parents with her husband who is our accountant, so I can kill two birds with one stone so to speak. Tell you what Miss

Maldon why don't I pay for dinner? Then you and your brother can call it quits.'

Over dinner Kim made it clear she liked the big Scotsman however he appeared determined to keep things on a professional level. 'How long have you been over here?' Keith asked as they ate desert. You're a long way from home, that's a west coast accent, isn't it?'

'Yip, well spotted, I grew up in Ayrshire. I've been out here about two years. I came over to join a firm in California originally, but the climate didn't suit, far too sunny all time. We Scots need a bit of miserable weather to feel alive. So, I came to New York, I met Stavros, he's an accountant he introduced me to his architect wife. Kiri and I share similar views on architecture so about six months ago we decided to take the plunge and set up on our own. It's going well, and we are building a good reputation.'

'So, what brought you here then? Surely, they need good architects in the UK. Keith says you designed the Museum of Scotland building, it's amazing. I was in Glasgow filming last year and I visited it.' Kim smiled at the two men. 'I wondered who A J Lockwood was, what does the A.J stand for?'

'Alexander James Lockwood. When I came here, Kiri decided because I didn't want to do the publicity thing, I should be known as A.J. I kind of like it, it's very American.'

'I think you look like a James, not an A J, I shall call you Jimmy, very Scottish.' Kim said smiling, like me, my name is Annabel Kimberly Maldon Arnold. I became Kim Maldon. You kind of need some privacy over here.' Kim looked at Alex, 'so what do you think? Do you want the job I mentioned, because I want to hire Jimmy, not AJ?'

'Jimmy, I shall be then, anyway it's been a very pleasant evening, but I have an early start in the morning.' Alex took his wallet from his jacket pocket and motioned to the waiter. He addressed the table as he did. 'So, Miss Maldon, Keith, if

The Nightclub Owners Wife

you'll excuse me, I'll pay the bill and then get us a taxi. I live in Greenwich, so you can drop me on route.'

'Is your wife Scottish?' Kim asked as she got into the taxi. 'The wedding ring?' She said pointing to his hand.

'I'm not married, I lost my wife and child two years ago, I live alone.' He looked down sadly at the ring, 'never been able to take it off.'

'Shit I'm so sorry, I didn't know, what happened?'

'I don't talk about it.' Alex held the door open for Kim to get into the taxi, he moved away to allow Keith to follow her. 'Look if you'll excuse me, I'm going to walk home. Kim it was great to meet you, I'll look forward to your next film, and if you want a quote for drawings, get in touch. Keith, I'll send you the initial drawings in a few days, you can let me know. Bye folks.' Alex took a deep breath and closed the door he patted the top and moved away. Watching the cab disappear he sighed and hailed a second taxi. He knew Kim Maldon was interested in him, she had made that clear several times during the evening. Alex had been out with a few women since leaving Scotland, however he never mixed business with pleasure. Alex felt lonely, he knew that a woman wasn't the answer, however he did know that he needed to move on and do it soon. He still longed for Rosie and her children, despite his best efforts never a day went by he didn't wonder.

'Well, that was very indiscreet sis, even for you. I think you scared him.'

'Do you think he's gay Keith?'

'Nah he's hetro, nothing gay about him. I think you might have upset him asking about his family. God, I wonder what happened to lose both wife and child? Maybe an accident.'

'Do you think I should call him and apologise?'

'No, I think you should accept that some men don't fancy you Kim.' Keith smiled and put his arm around his sister, 'you were practically on his lap, making it obvious you wanted him.

Wait and see whether he is going to be working for me and them maybe you can try a subtler approach. Maybe he's just shy.'

'God, I hope so, because I think I've just met my future husband and babyfather.'

Alex paid the driver and walked slowly up to his building, he unlocked the door of his loft apartment. His mail in his hands, as he closed the door behind him, he began to open the letters. An A5 envelope with a Scottish postmark and a do not bend sticker caught his eye. He quickly opened it, a photograph fell out as he shook the contents from the envelope, he looked at it, gasped, sat down and sobbed into his hands.

When he stopped crying he poured a generous measure of malt whisky into a glass. He pulled the white gold band from his finger, kissed it, threw it down the garbage chute.

CHAPTER
THIRTY-SIX

Eight years later

Jimmy, good to see you, how was your flight? I'm glad you changed your mind about the holiday. Keith Arnold smiled at the big man in front of him. He had been delighted with the design for the new hotel and with the help of Kiri Aniston, they had been able to have most of the building completed on time.

Alex had visited Mykosis several times over the years. His relationship with Kim had developed slowly, he had waited until he had finished both her new home in Dorset and her brothers' hotel, before beginning initially a casual relationship with her. His friendship with Keith Arnold and his partner Michael had also developed over the last eight years.

'Always a pleasure to come out here Keith. The place is my second home. New York is just so busy and it's good to get away from it. Now Kiri is back at work after her maternity leave, I can take a break, I've got a full two months off.' Alex looked around, it must be poker time? I have been playing a lot, so hold on to your shirt Keith cos I'm going to take it from your back.

Kim is going to be held up filming for a few weeks longer, so no distractions mate.'

So, you're back together, that must be a record for her, most men have got out by now. You've been on and off for what six, years? I should do the big brother thing, but much as I love her... Well, I'm not blind to her behaviour. You are taking on a lot mate, she's a fucking nightmare, a real diva. Michael is at his parents, so it's just you and me. Have you got my drawings for the extension done? Here let me get your bag. We can have a few beers and then we will see how good your poker skills are? Michael is really looking forward to playing with you, he's the best I've ever played with, so good luck Amigo, hope you've been practicing as much as you say?'

Oh, I have been practicing, now Kiri is back, once I did all the handovers I had some time on my hands. I read books, studied the internet. Seriously bro, you'd better look out, because I am dynamite.'

***

'Jimmy darling you look relaxed, did you tell them?' Kim Maldon whispered, as she wrapped her arms around the big man. She kissed him on the mouth standing on tip toes to reach. She was small, a natural UK size six, just over five foot in her converse skate shoes she reached Alex Lockwood's chest. Throwing back her long blond hair, she looked over at her brother. 'Did he tell you?'

'What that my sisters a psycho? I saw the film by the way you were amazing as usual sis, but this is your first with Jackson for a while. He's a real cutie, isn't he? Has Jimmy won another award is that it?'

'No, that he's about to make an honest woman of me, we are getting married.' Kim held out her left hand showing a large diamond ring.'

'Wow, there's a finger on your rock sis.' Keith grinned at Jimmy. 'You've been here three weeks and you never said a thing. Fuck sake mate, you are going to be my brother-in-law. Wow! Come and let's get wasted, celebrate. The hotel is quiet this week, so we can party. Can't believe you are going to marry my crazy sister.' Keith grinned at Kim, 'hey eight years it's taken you. I knew you fancied him that very first night, never thought he would be stupid enough to go out with you, never mind marry you.'

Kim giggled, 'it took me two years to get him to go out with me, the another four on and off to get him to take me seriously. I think I always knew. We want to get married over here though, just a simple tasteful wedding, nothing too Hollywood, just Jimmy me and our nearest and dearest. Hello magazine have offered me quite a lot to have the sole rights to the photographs. That means they will provide security.'

Jimmy stood up and motioned with his head, 'a moment Kim, in private?' He lifted Kim's two large cases with ease and walked towards the lift.

Kim shrugged and followed her fiancé from the room, Keith looked at Michael and smiled. 'The big man is a bit upset me thinks.'

***

Upstairs in their room, Alex shut the door behind Kim and glared at her. 'I told you Kim I do not want publicity. I want us to get married quietly without any razzmatazz. You promised, now you are telling me you have spoken to a magazine? Why Kim? I told you I don't want it. He shook his head and sat down on the bed. 'I just want to get married and go about our lives, is that too much to ask? I understand there is interest, but I do not want the press there. I don't have any family and you only have your mum, Keith and Michael. Can't we just do it quietly, say I'm shy or something?'

'I don't get you Jimmy, you say you love me, but you don't care about my career. It's okay for you, you don't need personal publicity. You know I need to stay in the news, and besides we are being offered a good deal. All you have to do is pose for a few photographs and they will do the rest. I haven't told anyone I'm pregnant yet. I've got the new film to get started and I've told Bess I'm taking a year off after this next one. I don't get why you don't want to shout it out?'

'You accepted the film? I thought we discussed this and you were going to knock it back? You are going to make an action film when you'll have just had a baby? Come on Kim you have a responsibility to our child here.'

'I need to do the film, I had already signed up when I realised I was pregnant, babe it will be fine I promise. They won't take any chances with me the insurance is too high for them to let anything happen. I have a stunt double and a body double, so I can just do it. Jimmy I'm getting thirteen million for this one, with what I got for the last one, it makes me the highest paid actress in the world this year.' Kim sighed and looked Alex in the eye. 'Jimmy, this is about us about you not wanting to admit we are a couple. I haven't even told my brother, your best friend, that I'm expecting. How long do you think I can hide it? I'm four months pregnant, I need to announce it soon.'

'Kim, this is my baby too, I just want you and the baby to be safe and healthy.' Alex looked at the floor, 'you knew when we got together I didn't want the Hollywood lifestyle and all that stuff. I worry about you, how the fuck can you finish a film when you will be what, eight months? You are going to have the baby and need to go straight back to work. I read the fucking script Kim, there's some pretty dangerous stuff.'

'Darling, I will be fine, I'm getting excellent healthcare, everything looks good you saw the scan. Jimmy, I know you are worried about it because of losing your wife and child. I just wish you would talk to me about it. I don't know why you keep it all to yourself? I'm glad you told me about it at the start. I knew there was something tragic in your past when I met you, I need you to trust me Jimmy. I try to respect your wishes, but you are not being fair to me. I'm going to be your wife, I'm having your baby, why won't you tell me what happened to your family? Don't you trust me?'

'Kim, please, it's just painful, I don't want to talk about it. I thought you had accepted I can't talk about it. We keep having this conversation, I told you when we discussed getting married. It's my cross and I don't want to share it. Kim, I never thought I could love again, but you changed that for me, and I want to be with you. I just can't explain. Alex started to walk away, he knew he should be able to tell the woman he was going to marry everything, but Kim, although she was loving and a great person, tended to see things from her point of view. Alex had always known that eventually he would have to provide some detail of his life before he had come to America, however he also knew Kim. He just couldn't find the words to describe all that had happened.

Alex had, for a long time, avoided becoming involved with the gregarious, attention seeking actress. He knew he loved her, however he also knew that he could never love her in the same way he had loved Rosie. There had been many breaks in their relationship. Alex had been considering ending the relationship for good, when she announced she was expecting his baby. In recent weeks the surge in her hormones had interfered with her medication for bi-polar disorder making it difficult. She had showed no real interest in his life before, now it had become an obsession. Alex was afraid of what the effect on her mental health would be, and although he tried, he had been unable to discuss his past.

'Jimmy, I can't compete with a ghost.' Kim began to cry, she looked at Alex and sobbed. 'Please Jimmy, what about our child, shouldn't he or she know about her brother, sister? ... I ... I don't even know if it was a boy or a girl? I know your wife was called either Rosie or Becca you talk in your sleep Jimmy, I'm guessing its Rosie, you say her name sometimes when ... ' I know nothing about you, those scars on your body, was it an accident? Was it your fault? Is that why you won't talk about it? You didn't ... you didn't kill your child? Is Becca your child? you cry out that name sometimes? You've also said other names, Imogen, Toby, who are they? Alex please just tell me, I need to know, the midwife asked me about you, she thought it was weird I didn't know.'

Alex sat down on the bed and stared out the window, suddenly weary. 'The scars are from a fight when I was a boy. My child? I had a daughter; her name was Rebecca she was one and a half and she got ill suddenly and died there were no suspicious circumstances Kim, it was natural causes. I got over it by not talking about it. I'm sorry Kim, I just can't darling, it was just too painful. I love you, you know I do, it was just a really difficult time.'

'What about her mother, Rosie, what happened? Please Jimmy I need to know. How did she die? Did she take her own life? Is that why you won't tell me because you know I've tried to kill myself when I've been depressed? Every day I compete with a ghost. Please talk to me? I know you loved her more than me, but I don't understand why you won't discuss it?'

'Because I fucking can't Kim, I don't discuss Rosie or Becca. I can't because the pain is as raw now as it was then. I lost everything, my children, the woman I loved and my home.'

'You loved Rosie more than me Jimmy admit it, I'm just the substitute I always knew that.' Kim's voice rose, Alex knew the signs of a row beginning. 'You owe me an explanation I've been patient not pushed, you said children Jimmy, who are they?'

'Oh, fuck off Kim, not tonight please not tonight? It's the anniversary of Becca's death eleven years ago today I lost her, so please, not tonight?' Tears ran down Alex's face and he lay back on the bed. Kim could see the pain on his face feel the grief he felt. She had never seen Alex this upset, he had told her about his mother dying, about his childhood, the absent father, the poverty, his mother's illness. She had ignored the fact that he wouldn't talk about his wife and child, she had always thought he, in some way, caused their deaths, now she felt betrayed and devastated at what he had just told her. Suddenly Kim realised she didn't want to lose this man, she looked at him sadly, her anger evaporating. 'What do you want to do? She asked, 'Jimmy what do you want? Do you want me? Do you want this baby? Do you want to marry me?'

'Of course, I do, you and I well, we are good together. You never asked any questions before. You let me have my privacy, respected my wish to keep it all to myself. Kim, I wanted to tell you, but I couldn't. For years it was so painful. The night I met you I knew I was attracted to you, but after Rosie I had promised I would never get so involved again. The pain, well it devastated me. I know I'm a fucking coward I just couldn't cope so I buried it. Kim, I promise I will be the best husband and father, but babe I can't live in your world... I'm the fucking Banksy of architecture, its who I am. I've never interfered in your working life, I've been there for you, helped you rehearse love scenes, love scenes you do with other men. Kim, I don't want to be Mr Maldon babe. I don't want people prying into my life, I'm a private person. You are a mega star, highest paid actress in the world. You are beautiful, talented and I love you. I love Annie Arnold though, not Kim Maldon, she is way out of my league.'

'We're good together Jimmy, look at us? 'We are a beautiful couple. You are so talented, it could help your career too?'

'I don't want to be the beautiful couple, I want to be Mr and Mrs Lockwood. I want to get married out there on the beach on this beautiful island and I want to be just you and me, the world can wait. Other actors do it Kim, you have made it now, you don't need all the other trimmings of success. Okay I'm not in your league when it comes to earnings, but I'm a millionaire now too. I'm in demand and getting into the history books with my buildings. I don't do the 'no one knows me' thing, but I don't look for publicity either, so they leave me alone. A.J Lockwood is just a designer of buildings and on this island, I'm just Jimmy. We are Jimmy and Kim, everyday people.'

'I'm still fucking angry at you Jimmy, I hope you get that? I think you could have told me sooner about Rebecca. I would have got it, I'm really hurt, and I need to understand why you didn't tell me. I remember that night, the first night we met. You said you lost your wife and child. You said you didn't want to discuss it, I respected you, I never asked. What happened to your wife and children?'

'Oh babe, I don't want to discuss it, it happened, time passed, and oh I suppose I didn't want to be that man, didn't want to grieve. When I met you, I had cried every night for two years. I met you and it changed, I resisted getting involved so I know it wasn't the bolt of lightning and I'm not exactly Romeo, but Kim, I swear I love you and our child. I never expected to feel this way again.'

Tears ran down Alex's face, he lifted a wad of tissues from the beside cabinet and held them to his face, now sobbing. Kim had never seen him be anything but strong, she knew she loved him. She sat down and wrapped her arms around him holding him, crying with him. She knew the rest could wait. 'Okay' she whispered, 'I love you Jimmy, and I want to be your wife, I promise I will never bring this up again, if that's what you want. Someday I hope you will talk to me about it all.'

'I don't deserve you being this understanding babe.' Alex sobbed. 'I'm so sorry I'm like this but I just can't speak about it, I can't cope. I really don't deserve you.'

'No, you fucking don't, look let's get married this week? Go see the . . . registrar? Have a civil wedding? I don't know what it is in Greek, but Michael will know?' Jimmy, does Keith know about your family?'

Alex shook his head, 'no and I don't want anyone else to know, he only knows what you knew. What I told you both that first night, guys don't discuss shit like that. We play poker, drink a lot and talk about who Michael's mother is going to try to marry him to next, and Keith's crazy sister.' Alex smiled through his tears and wrapped his arms around Kim. 'I tell him how much I love her, and he tells me I'm fucking mad. Know what you are mad babe, but mad for still wanting to take me on. I love you Kim.'

CHAPTER
THIRTY-SEVEN

Five months later, Christmas 2015

'Hey, you look wow, big, you are the size of a small house, thank God you didn't do the film. Are you keeping all right? Mum said you haven't been well?'

'Oh, I'm fine, my medication had to be changed again because it was affecting my blood pressure. I have been up and down mood wise. Jimmy has, as always, been great. He's just getting the bags out of the car. The house is nearly finished, got an entry date for next month. It will be good to have our own home here. Do you know I had to pay extra to come over so close to my date? I also had to take out extra insurance too in case I pop here.' Kim looked up as her husband came into the bar carrying a bag and pulling a trolley behind him.

'There you are Mr Lockwood, how are you? You made it? How long can you stay?' Keith said hugging his sister and smiling at Alex. 'By God must be twelve pounder you two are having, she's huge Jimmy. Your rooms are ready, I just realised this is probably the last time you two will stay here, now you have your own place you'll want to go there. Keith sighed and looked momentarily sad. 'I'm so glad you could come for

Christmas, it's difficult with Michael having to be the loyal son.' Keith sighed and shook his head, he looked his sister in the eye. 'Mums coming out tomorrow, so we will have the full house. I can't wait to show you what Michael bought me for Christmas. After lunch I'll show you, come take your bags up to the room and we can eat. Did Michael tell you he's helping Sandro drive the taxi now?'

***

'Wow a boat, it's amazing, we won't need to wait for the ferry now, when can we go out on it?' The large speed boat sat resplendent in the blue water its name *'Kimberly'* proudly emblazoned in purple on the side. You called it after me, I'm touched,' Kim said reading the name from the side, and you used my favourite colour too. Oh, you old romantic Michael, buying him a boat.'

Michael smiled and looked at Kim, 'he never even dropped a hint. I thought, *'what do you buy someone who has everything?'* The hotel is doing well this year, I bought papa another taxi and I am helping, so we thought we could start a water taxi round the bay too. I'm sorry not to be there on Christmas morning, but my mama, she wanted me to be at home. She is planning a picnic after church and well, she did invite you all.' He looked sadly at Keith then nodded at Kim. 'We thought with you being pregnant, the last thing you would want was a trip onto Bhionthys.'

Kim stamped her foot, 'why wouldn't I want to go?' She said angrily. 'Your little island is beautiful and if this weather holds up it will be amazing, you don't want me there do you that's it, isn't it?'

'Kim calm down,' Alex said quietly putting a hand on his wife's arm. 'You are being silly.'

'Oh, you can fuck off too Jimmy, stop fucking trying to wrap me in cotton wool all of you.' She look at her brother, 'you can go with your boyfriend and take Jimmy with you, I'd hate to spoil things for you.'

'No, no its just with your condition.' Michael said looking at Kim and then at Alex. 'We thought . . . you know? That you would want to rest? I don't mind, and Keith was going to spend it with you and Jimmy.'

'I'm pregnant Michael, not fucking disabled.' She sighed and shook her head sadly. 'Sorry Mikey, Keith, I didn't mean to snap at you. I've been a bit touchy recently.' I'd love to spend Christmas with you and Michael and his family.' Seeing the relief on her brothers face she took his hand. 'Keith, you spend your whole life trying to please other people, stop it and take the things you deserve.' She looked at Alex who was examining the boat, 'you like the boat Jimmy? Maybe I should get you one, so we can use it here. It would be an investment save all that waiting around for the ferry, and be cheaper than the helicopter.' She nudged Alex who smiled and put his arm around her, kissing her cheek. She looked at her brother and his partner. 'We are going to make this our main base once the baby comes. I mean where better to bring up a child? Now you have broadband on the island Jimmy can work remotely.'

'Really?' Keith said smiling broadly, 'I'd hoped that you would spend more time here. But your main base . . . cool, Michael and I get to be the favourite uncles. Wow, we are delighted aren't we Michael?'

'We can take you over to the mainland with our new boat, anytime you like, small charge.' Michael said smiling and looking relieved.

'With a boat of his own he can be on the mainland and in the Athens office in an hour. Kiri will be delighted. Wont she Jimmy?'

Alex nodded and smiled. 'Kiri wants to be back in the states so its suiting everyone.'

'I'm going to only do a film every other year, so we can enjoy life.' Kim rubbed her swollen stomach, 'and we can also enjoy what we made, with those we love around us.' I can't wait to have a go at driving the boat. What do you say, to me, as the only person who is tee total, bringing you back from Bhionthys on Christmas day? I'm sure I could with a little lesson on how to, it can't be much different from driving a car?'

'It's not, but there are a lot of rocks around here, they are mostly hidden in the water, so you need to do it carefully. I do it with my eyes shut, but you will need to be guided. Michael looked over at Keith. 'You think I should let your sister drive us all in the boat? What about you Jimmy?'

'It's nothing to do with them. I bet I could do it as well as you do Mikey.'

Michael has been steering boats in and out of Bhionthys all his life.' Keith grinned, 'before he and I met, he used to use it for clandestine encounters with men. He knew he was gay long before he met me. Contrary to what his mother thinks I didn't pervert him. So, picnic on the beach on Christmas day it is then? I would have done the whole turkey thing if I had to. I even had the bird picked out. Michael was going to kill it tonight. Hey Mikey, Catherina lives to fight another day.'

'No, no my love, Catherina is hanging in the kitchen I killed her this morning. She look at me and I say, *Catherina, this is your destiny.* She died bravely, her spirit will live on,' Michael smiled broadly, 'we can eat her for St Stephens feast now, yes?'

***

'Are you okay Jimmy?' Kim asked touching his arm as she watched him spread butter on to a slice of Michael's grandmothers home baked bread. 'This must be difficult for you with me like this?'

'Stop going on Kim, it's alright. I have to live with it, every year there are going to be memories. I am looking forward to meeting our baby sweetheart. It's just oh I don't know, kind of bittersweet, I told you Becca's birthday was in February, so it's been on my mind that ours could be born around then. Honestly I'm okay babe.' It was tea time; the sun was going down. Much to everyone's relief, the parents had grown tired of the sunshine.

The Nightclub Owners Wife

Michael had taken Kim's mother, his own parents and his grandmother on the short trip back to the larger island.

Michael had returned, thrown the boat keys across to Kim and opened a bottle of wine. 'I'll guide you, out of the cove my sweet sister. Yaya thinks it's a disgrace you are baring your stomach. She says, '*English women have no dignity*'. My mother of course she say she would not mind if it were my baby, you could show the world your body. Why didn't we think of that Keith, we could have used a surrogate maybe that would get her off my back, she's like the devil. I'm to meet a distant cousin of Gregory the baker next week.'

'What as a surrogate?' Kim laughed.

'No, another potential bride, she is eighteen and apparently very beautiful. I . . . oh, it is so difficult, I keep telling her, but she will not get it out of her head. She wants a grandchild.'

Kim looked at her brother and his partner. 'I suppose you could look after our baby, boys. Get some practice in, you could afford a surrogate so why not? I would imagine as long as it's your sperm you use Mikey she would be happy?' She took Alex's hand and smiled. 'next Christmas we will be opening presents with our unique golden-haired child babe. This is our last Christmas as a childless couple. Fuck babe, I'm sorry that came out wrong.'

Alex shrugged, 'I'm fine darling, Christmas is always particularly hard.' He gazed out to sea, the other three people could see the pain in his eyes. 'Can we talk about something else?' He said quietly, 'I have no intention of spoiling everyone else's Christmas by being maudlin.'

Keith jumped to his feet, 'come on Mikey, let's have one last swim before we leave? We can do things in the water now the parents have gone.'

'Gross!' Even worse than my belly baring that is.' Kim looked at Keith, Alex continued to stare out to sea.

Kim waited until the others had gone in to the water. 'What was she like babe, Rebecca? I've never dared ask but I kind of want to be able to tell our baby about her.'

Alex sighed, he gazed over at Keith and Michael frolicking in the waves, then reached over and took his wallet out of his pocket. He took a small photograph out looked at it longingly for a few seconds before handing it to his wife. 'That was a fortnight before she took ill, we were in Disneyland, then in the Caribbean. Three weeks days later she was gone.' Alex stood up and walked away towards the boat. Kim followed, she could see her brother and Michael in the water beyond it.

'Jimmy, I didn't mean to upset you babe, I just always wondered, if she looked like you or her mum? I shouldn't have asked. Now that I have though, the other children in the photo? Are they Imogen and Toby? Fuck I'm sorry, I don't have any right to ask, must be my hormones, its bothering me for some reason.'

'No, you have every right to ask Kim, I should have shown you this, told you about it all sooner. I just find it all so difficult, sometimes it feels as raw as it did then. Other times I can go days without remembering and then I feel guilty.'

'I'm so sorry Jimmy, I hope this baby here,' Kim put her hands around her bump as though protecting it from harm. 'I hope he or she can make some of this up to you.' I know another child can't take the place of one you lost. There has to be some comfort for you though?'

Alex smiled sadly, 'I love you and I will love our child too. I had two stepchildren, Imogen and Toby, they were only a little older. I loved them like my own. Imogen was only a baby when Rosie and I got together. She was pregnant with Toby. I was there from the time he was born. Rosie oh well she was married to my friend, he went to prison and her, and I . . . oh, there's so much I need to tell you.' He gently touched Kim and pulled her towards him, this is not the time babe. It's difficult for me, I keep trying to tell you all of it you have been so patient babe.'

'What about your wife? What happened to her? Did she kill herself, what happened Jimmy? Please tell me?' Sometimes you call out in your sleep, you say her name, Jimmy it's not normal the way you deal with this. I know you have demons, fuck sake we are married. I'm having your baby in a few weeks.' Kim put her hands back onto her abdomen and looked at her husband who was staring out to sea. She could see the pain on his face. 'Talk to me, I'll understand? How did Rosie die?'

'Kim it's Christmas, can we just not speak about it just now, it's really painful and today, well, I just want to enjoy it babe. I promise I will talk to you about it I promise, when we are alone. I don't want to talk about it today.' He wiped away a tear from his eye. 'Just leave it for another day!'

'But I need to know,' she looked at him and leaned in putting her head against his chest. 'You're not being fair to me Jimmy, I've been really patient'

'I'm sorry babe, can we leave it for now? Look here's Michael and Keith coming back out the water. Let's just go home and have an early night it's almost seven o'clock.'

'Hey, Michael thinks we should come back tomorrow, have another picnic with the leftovers? Keith said lifting a towel from the deckchair next to Alex. 'What do you think guys?' He looked at his sister. 'Mum is going to spend the day with Michaels Yaya, so we can just come back?'

'Yeah I think that would be good mate.' Alex said smiling, 'I love it here, it's so private and we can just chill. Now let's go, you promised me a game of poker tonight, my lovely wife is pregnant and tired. So, I'm all yours guys, must be about time I won.'

Kim noticed the immediate change in Alex's demeanour when he spoke to her brother. She said nothing however, an idea growing in her head.

CHAPTER
THIRTY-EIGHT

'You still awake babe?' Alex asked as he got into bed, 'I thought you would have been sleeping hours ago?' He threw a wad of notes onto the bedside table. 'finally managed to beat them, they are both drunk of course, not that I took advantage, I was on fire.' Alex began to take of his clothes, dropping them onto the floor at the foot of the bed.

Kim sat up and looked at her husband, 'I was doing some research.' She nodded at the laptop on the floor by the bed.

'For a part?'

'Hm Bernie Sheerer offered me a good role in a film he's producing. It's a great part.'

Alex shook his head, 'you said no more for a couple of years.'

'It won't start filming for about three months and its being shot in Italy so it's fairly close. Jimmy please don't start, we can we talk about it another time, I'm tired now and I need a cuddle so get in here.'

Kim lay back down, she sighed as Alex pulled her close and wrapped his arms around her. 'Did I tell you I'm in love with a gorgeous film star?' He whispered, kissing her neck.

'No is she hot?'

'Yeah and then some!' He slid his hand under her nightshirt and his hand moved to her breast. 'God, I love you Mrs Lockwood.'

The Nightclub Owners Wife

'As much as you loved Rosie?'

'Please don't start again Kim, please just let it go. You and I are together, I love you and that's it.'

'I didn't mean it to sound like that, but I can't compete with a ghost Jimmy.'

'You are the only one who thinks there's a competition Kim, please can we just leave it? This is one of the reasons why I can't talk to you about it.' Alex moved away from his wife and turned his back.

Kim knew he was crying, she felt the bed move. She sat up and switched on the bedside lamp. 'Stop it Jimmy, stop shutting me out ... you don't care about me, you wish that you still had your perfect little fucking family ... your fucking Rosie and perfect children. What happened to them? The other kids? If their father was in jail and their mother died? Did you just fuck off and leave them?'

Alex looked at her, tears now rolling down his face, 'Kim ... I ... please Kim, not tonight.'

'I'm sorry babe,' she gasped, I don't mean it, you know it's just so frustrating for me.'

Alex ignored her, he got up and went through to the en-suite. He shut and locked the door then sat down on the floor pulling a towel from the rail he held it to his face trying to stem the flow of tears. 'Go back to sleep babe,' he pleaded when Kim kept knocking on the door, eventually, afraid they would wake the other residents of the hotel he unlocked it.

Kim put her head around the bathroom door. 'I think I'm having some sort of hormone surge. I'm so sorry Jimmy, I can't do this anymore ... I need to know?'

He looked up, 'Kim just give me a few days, let's get Christmas out of the way, and I'll try to tell you the whole story.'

'Promise? You've said that before and then you change your mind?'

'Yeah, I promise, I'm scared Kim, frightened it will set you back and interfere with your illness.' He looked at his wife, 'you are going to change how you view me too babe.'

'Jimmy, I've loved you from the minute I met you, nothing you can tell me, will change how I view you. I've given you space for years, this has nothing to do with my mental health.' Kim held on to the door handle, she looked at her husband. 'Let me in to your head babe, I promise I won't judge you? Now dry your eyes you big woose and get back into bed.'

***

'Jimmy I'm sorry about last night, I really am, I don't know why it bothers me so much just now, it's got to be the hormones.' Kim looked at her husband as he sat down at the breakfast table. 'I suppose it's just that I want to share this pain with you, but you just won't let me in.'

'It's just, oh it's too hard to explain it all, there's things . . . like I said, let's just get this week over and back to England . . . I know I need to share it with you, its just hard.'

'Jimmy, I need to know!'

'Please Kim . . . not . . . today, just please give it a rest for today?'

Alex stopped speaking as Michael came in from the kitchen carrying a plate of food. He sat down and began to eat, seemingly unaware of the mood of his companions. 'You ready Jimmy? I want to go soon, catch the tide. We left all that food and beer on the island yesterday, so we don't need to take anything. He looked at Kim, 'Papa he says he be over for the next tide, will that be okay?'

Alex looked at his wife. He raised an eyebrow, 'where are you going?' He asked.

'Jimmy, you go to the island with Michael and Keith, I've asked Sandro to bring me out later.' Kim put the piece of toast in her hand down on the plate and picked up her morning cup of tea. 'I really need to speak to Bernie today. I'm not going to accept the role, you are right I need to spend time with you and the baby. I have to let Bernie know, he'll want to approach Margot Henley. She is reading for Karl Kloss, so he needs to speak to her tonight before she accepts the part in his film.' Michael says Sandro will bring me out in the small boat later. He's taking Mum over to Oyster bay with Michael's mum. He's going to bring me out first and come back for them.'

'Can't say I'm not pleased babe, I was hoping you would decide to stay at home with me and the baby.' Alex smiled, 'I know your career is important to you, but I've enjoyed having you with me these last few weeks. I think we need to get the house organised. You make sure you don't over tire yourself just now though. Kim, maybe I should just wait and come over with you?'

'No... you will just be sitting about waiting, and I need to have a very honest discussion with Bernie. He could sue me if he takes it into his head.' Kim stood up and moved towards her husband, he looked up at her and wrapped his arms around her. She kissed him gently and ruffled his hair. 'You go with the boys, I'll catch up later.'

CHAPTER
THIRTY-NINE

Seeing Sandro steering his boat into the little sandy bay, Alex left Michael and Keith in the water and swam back to the shore, he clambered on to the rocks and threw his mask and snorkel onto the ground as he walked towards his wife. Alex knew Kim well enough to realise just from the way she walked she was upset. 'What's wrong babe is it the baby?' He waved as Michael's father turned the small boat around and started back towards the mainland.

Kim looked at Alex, she shook her head, 'the baby is fine, she turned away from him. 'I can't look at you, I can't believe what I found out today. I knew there was more to you than what you told me.' She began to sob, and Alex moved in trying to put his arms around her, she pushed him away. 'don't fucking touch me you lying bastard, you told me she died Rosie, your Rosie. I have never questioned you. I let you . . . I let you fucking lie, never questioned what you were able to tell me.'

'Kim what on earth have you done? I asked you to leave it alone. I told you I love you, I don't want anything else, just you and the baby. I told you I would talk to you about it.'

You told me she died, I've spent fucking years thinking you were the most honest man I knew. You missed out lots of detail Jimmy, you told me she was dead. You never stopped loving her, did you? Fucking answer me Jimmy, it's always been her? Not me, not us and not this fucking baby.' You lied, you said your wife died.'

Alex sighed and looked at his wife, 'I never said she died Kim, I said I lost her. She wasn't my wife she was someone else's. After Becca... It was grief I suppose and oh please Kim, no good can come of opening old wounds. It was painful then, but I'm over her. I can never get over losing my child, but I live with that. I saw a counsellor for a while that helped me to find ways to cope. I've never forgotten her, I just don't want to talk about her all the time. I'm sorry Kim it's just how I am.'

'You let me believe you were a widower, you fucking lied Jimmy. The times you have called out for Rosie in your sleep... The times you've called me her name while we made love. I let it go because I thought you were hurting, and now I find you have lied about it all. What else did you lie about?' Kim stood up and slapped Alex hard on the face. 'You lying, devious, bastard. Who the fuck are you?'

Kim please sit down and listen, there were reasons! It was hard, our child died, Rosie wasn't coping, our son was ill. I fucking walked out on her the day we buried our daughter. Please Kim you need to calm down. Let's go back to the hotel and we can talk. I promise I will tell you everything.'

Kim however was too angry to pay attention, she took the large solitaire ring from her finger and threw it at Alex. 'You can shove that where the sun doesn't shine for all I care. I can't believe you lied. The woman you loved, the perfect woman, she's still out there and you didn't fucking tell me?'

'Kim stop this, please, I haven't seen her since Becca died, I walked out, and I've never gone back. It was over, we went our separate ways. It's just that I got hurt, I suppose I wore my heart on my sleeve, and I would have died for her, but it's not healthy that kind of love. I knew her all my life, she married someone else, then I realised I loved her. Her husband, well he did a bad thing and went to prison. He was away and her and I well ... we got together. When I lost Becca something in me died too.'

Kim however was too angry to listen, she ran towards the boat. 'Just fuck off with your lies.'

Alex followed her, 'please darling just calm down and we can talk. I promise I'll tell you everything.'

She turned and looked at him her eyes flashing anger. 'Stop it! I know it all, the murder the rape, you stealing her from her husband whilst he was in jail. The cruise ship and the food poisoning. I had a private detective working on it. I was going to see him when I got back to England, but I called him today and he told me it all ... the whole sordid story ... You bastard. I thought I was dealing with a memory, but she's a living breathing woman and you're still in love with her aren't you?'

'Kim please calm down, this isn't good for you or the baby. Please Kim, I just couldn't talk about it all. I love you, Rosie is not a threat to you. It's over, she might as well be dead.'

'You lying devious, bastard, she is alive, I've walked on broken glass for years and you fucking let me think she was dead? You don't fucking get it do you? You fucking bastard, is any of what we had true?'

Kim climbed on the boat Alex jumped in as she started the engine. He fell over and hit his head on the side of the boat as Kim accelerated out of the cove. Dizzy and disorientated he crawled towards his wife. 'Kim don't, please stop, be careful the rocks!'

CHAPTER

FORTY

When Alex opened his eyes, he saw Becca. She was holding his wife's hand. Kim held a golden-haired baby, they were smiling at him. Kim beckoned to him. 'Come with us, look your mother is here, she has been looking after Becca for you, they're here.' Alex saw his mother behind Kim. She was the mother he had known as a young boy, happy and well, not the shell she had been at the time of her death. There were other people behind them, but Alex couldn't see them there was a mist covering the area, but he knew there were people there.

Alex made to move towards them, but his feet were rooted to the spot, he tried harder to move towards the small group. Kim held her arms out. 'Come with us Jimmy, it's alright I know it all darling, I love you ... Please Jimmy, we can all be together.'

His mother shook her head and put her arm around Kim, 'no it's not his time, he must go back. She kissed Kim's head, 'he still has a lot to achieve, he must follow his destiny.' Rebecca smiled at her son over her shoulder as she led Kim and the two children away into the mist, he saw Becca run to a female figure who took her hand and led her away. Suddenly his mother appeared in front of him. 'Go on son, you make me proud every day, the man you have become, you are an inspiration.' She kissed his cheek, he felt a cool breeze and she was gone.

'Kim I'm sorry. Kim please forgive me . . . please Kim don't go . . . Mum, don't take them away . . . please, the baby just let me hold her . . . Becca, Becca don't go.'

***

'Jimmy thank God you are awake, we have been so worried my friend. Do you remember what happened?'

'Michael, where is Kim? Is she? What happened? We were on the boat, we were having a row. She jumped on and I followed her,' He touched his forehead feeling the heavy bandage. 'Did I hit my head? I don't remember anything else.'

Michael sighed and sat down on the bed beside Alex, 'I'm sorry my friend there was a crash. My boat, it was too fast . . . Kim she didn't know how to drive and the boat . . . ' Michael began to cry. 'I'm so sorry Jimmy, she didn't make it, the boat hit the rocks and it flipped . . . you were thrown clear, but Kim went with the boat, she died, the baby died with her, the boat it . . . oh, I need to just tell you. The boat it burned, she didn't stand a chance.'

'Where am I?

'Athens, your injuries are bad my friend, but your doctors will tell you all that. You need not to move, there are some injuries to your spine, and you have broken both legs.'

'Michael mate, thank you for being so up front about Kim and the baby, that can't have been easy. Where's Keith? Is he coping?' Alex tried hard to focus, he wanted to sound normal. He knew however this was his fault. He knew he deserved every moment of pain racking his body.

Michael sighed and then shrugged, 'how do you think he is? He is devastated, and of course it's world news. The place is crawling with people and camera's, they know there is a story. He is with Audrey.'

Alex nodded, 'there is no worse pain than losing your child, I don't suppose it matters what age they are?'

'Jimmy, what happened? My papa...he says she was in a foul mood when they were coming across to the island.'

'Mate can we just not talk about it just now, we had a row, and she just, oh I should have stopped her. You know what her and I are...were...like when we argue. It goes from nought to one hundred in three seconds.' Tears built up in Alex's eyes as he remembered the dream and realised she was gone, he turned to face the wall. 'Michael mate do you mind? I just need a wee bit of time alone. I just...oh fuck Michael I...I don't know what to say.'

Michael nodded, he put his hand on Alex's shoulder and squeezed. 'I understand my friend, I need to go call Keith let him know you are awake. You almost died too, when we got you out the water you weren't breathing. We couldn't do anything for Kim, but Keith, he saved your life. You have had many hours of surgery, you must rest now.' He moved towards the door and as he opened it he turned. 'Jimmy, I will come back in the morning. The nurses here, their English is not good, I will come and translate for you...yes?'

'Thanks mate, my Greek is getting better, but I still don't catch all of it.' Alex nodded and as Michael closed the door, he turned his head and sobbed into the pillow. Eventually a doctor came in to the room, seeing Alex distressed state he took a syringe and injected it into the cannula in Alex's hand. Alex felt himself drifting away from the pain.

Alex opened his eyes, he had no idea how long he had slept but he knew somehow it was a different day. The door was wedged open, a nurse put her head around it. 'Meester Lockwood the police, they are here to speak with you.' The nurse looked seriously at Alex, 'they need to know about your accident they say. Meester Keith, he over from Mykosis, he and Michael is speaking to the Police, they very good friends Mr Lockwood? Yes?'

***

The police officer took the statement from Michael and handed it to Alex. Michael nodded, 'it is just what you said my friend.' Alex moved slightly and moaned as the pain shot across his body. He had managed to tell what happened on the boat without crying. He had lied to them about the reasons for the argument saying it was about Kim's career and him not wanting her to return to acting after the birth of the child. No one appeared to question this, and Alex was disgusted with himself for lying. He couldn't say what Kim had been angry about. Alex knew he was a coward who could not admit that he had lied to his wife and her family about his past.

The Greek police appeared uninterested in the situation. They told Alex the witness statements from those who had seen Kim that day, corroborated his statement. She had been angry; Michael and Keith had provided eyewitness accounts of her slapping Alex and getting on the boat. Sandro and a local fisherman had also seen the crash. No one questioned in any depth the reason behind the argument.

The Doctor sitting by the door who had remained silent throughout the half hour interview with the police, stood up. He spoke in Greek to the two police officers and then in English to Alex. 'I am going to sedate you Mr Lockwood, you must rest you have surgery tomorrow yes? I tell the police officers you must go, yes.' The policemen nodded at Alex and then left the room.

Alex looked at the doctor. 'Can it wait for another half hour please?' He whispered, he was exhausted after the interview with the police. The frustration of trying to understand what they were saying to him, Michael trying to translate, had tired him out. Alex knew however that there was something he had to do. 'The pain medication is working, I just moved, if I lie still it is bearable.' Alex looked over at Michael, 'thanks for all that mate, I don't know what I would have done if you hadn't been here, my written Greek well it's not that good. I can understand what you are saying if you speak slowly, but reading it? I do try, but languages were never my strong point.' Alex took a deep breath, 'I need to speak to Keith, I know he is with you.'

Michael nodded and relayed this in Greek to the doctor, who looked at Alex and shrugged. 'As you wish Mr Lockwood, but the pain will be unbearable soon, you do not need to be brave here.' He sighed and followed Michael from the room.

The door opened quietly, and Keith entered the room, Alex on seeing his brother-in-law, bust in to tears. 'I'm so sorry Keith.' He sobbed, 'so, so, sorry, I can't imagine life without her but you and her you are . . . were so close.'

Keith sat down, his eyes were red and swollen, he was clearly fighting tears, 'Jimmy it's alright, I saw what happened. Kim . . . I loved her she was my sister and it was her and I against the world a lot of the time . . . I loved her more than anyone in this world. But . . . mate . . . I have no illusions about that temper of hers. I was on the receiving end of it many times my friend.' Keith lifted a wad of tissues from the bedside locker and after handing half to Alex, he held them to his face. 'Her mood was worse than normal recently, she was illogical at times. I know that was her illness my friend, bi-polar disorder, affected by the pregnancy hormones. You were the best thing that ever happened to her Jimmy. You were so calm and good with her when she was ill. I think that apart from me, you were the only person who got it. She didn't mean a lot of it, and I know what she was like.'

'Keith, it was my fault, I should have stopped her, should have told her some stuff. She found out something and I should have told her. She was angry because of me.'

Keith held up his hand, 'no, you don't get to take the blame this time Jimmy. That's your speciality isn't it?' He said bitterly, 'Jimmy saviour of the world. Fucking stop it, you are a man who has just lost his wife in terrible circumstances. You and I are much the same Jimmy, people pleasers. You keep your secrets, and I won't tell you what it was like pulling her from that boat . . . Jimmy it doesn't matter mate. She is still going to be gone. Kim was who Kim was, I loved her you loved her. The argument could have been about anything she would have still reacted that way and you tried to stop her. I saw her swing at you, I saw you fall when the boat started. She lived she died Jimmy, and you are still my friend. So, let's just mourn the woman we both loved and get on with it.'

'You are a wonderful man Keith, I was dreading seeing you.' Alex put out his hand and Keith gripped it, Alex looked at Keith, 'what are we going to do about a funeral?'

Keith shrugged, 'what did she want? Did you ever discuss it?'

Alex shook his head, 'It's not something you think about at our age is it? We never discussed it ever, even when she was suicidal, we talked about positives a lot of the time, she loved it here though. I'd like her buried on Mykosis.' Alex wiped away the tears now flowing down his face. He sobbed, 'I know she was a big star ... and if I'm honest I know she would want the whole Hollywood thing. I want her for myself here on the island we both loved.' He looked at Keith, 'is that selfish, to want to keep her here?'

'Yeah probably, but she was your wife, my sister and I think we get to choose what happens. We can always do a memorial service later. I'll check with her lawyer, and Bess, she's here by the way. She is still trying to milk her twenty percent out of Kim even in death.'

'Bess is okay Keith, she put up with a lot, managing Kim all those years and she looked after her health a lot of the time. I know you and Bess have some sort of history. 'Did you have a fall out? There's loads of pictures of you from years ago in a box in the London flat. Kim always said she didn't know why you and Bess disliked each other. You all go back a long way, don't you? You should really kiss and make up.'

Keith made a face and then smiled wryly, 'can't stand the bitch, she just grates on me. I'm just oh ... she used to say that I was as damaged as my sister. That was what I got from everyone for a while. 'The bi polar you know it's in our family, gran had it, and mum, but she only gets the lows the deep depression, her mum, our maternal grandmother, fuck she was unbelievable. I don't have it, but I had to live with their illness. I suppose that's where I developed the part of me where I try to please everyone. My father and mother met when they were in hospital together, so he had a mental illness too. You know Kim found him when he killed himself, she was just a little girl, nine years old, that kind of set her illness off. I had to look after all of them after that.'

'Must have been tough on you Keith, I think that why you and I are such good friends. My experiences are similar watching my mum die from the outside in.' Alex sighed, and shook his head. 'My dad fucked off when I was a kid, so it was me and her. At least your dad was selfish because he was ill, mine just didn't give a fuck about me or my mum. My mum, she was a beautiful woman, she had an illness which affected all her facilities except her brain, she knew what was going on right up until the last. You and I became carers at an early age, and I suppose have an over developed sense of empathy. Alex wiped away a tear and looked at Keith, 'so what's the story with you and Bess?'

Keith smiled slightly and leaned forward. 'If I tell you I'll need to kill you. You're out your tits on painkillers so you probably won't remember anyway. Before I met Michael, I did some fucking crazy stuff, some I can't even begin to tell you, but this I suppose is one of the saner things.' Keith grimaced, 'I once slept with Bess, and oh you don't need the details. You know she started out as an actress, and she was a good one. That's how they met, Kim and her, when she was in rep well she and Bess were in a play together and I was at that point where I was curious.'

'You are joking, I thought you were always a poof? Hey fuck sake? Bess? I wouldn't have thought she was that way either I thought she was exclusively gay too.' Alex shook his head. 'Fuck I always thought it was because she fancied Kim.'

Well Mr Lockwood you learn something new every day my friend. It didn't last long, I went to Uni, met Michael, my Greek God and that was it, my experimenting days were over. Kim, well, she didn't need to know about it, she would have made fun of me. Besides much as I loved my sister, if it wasn't about her then she never really was interested, was she? Bess well she became her agent, so I never said anything, and I doubt that Bess did. I think I really hurt her Jimmy. I mean to hold a grudge all these years?'

CHAPTER
FORTY-ONE

Ten months later.

'Hey, my friend, how are you?' Michael opened the patio doors and entered Alex's open plan living room. He put the bag he was carrying down. A freshly baked loaf peaked out of the top.

Alex quickly switched off his laptop and closed it. 'Good mate, in fact excellent.' He looked around and smiled at Michael. 'I walked to the bottom of the lane this morning, it's getting better. I reckon soon I'm not going to need this anymore,' he patted the arm of the wheelchair, 'or the nurses every day. I managed to shower this morning all by myself. I can't do all that being washed by someone. That wee blond nurse, I'm sure she keeps looking at my willy, said she needed to wash all of me.'

'Hey, don't be so impatient Jimmy, you look a lot better, and you are starting to work again my friend.' Michael nodded at the drawings on the table.'

It's been ten fucking months now. When I saw the consultant last month, he reckoned that by the time I see him again in December I will be able to be fully mobile. That last op was extremely painful, but they reckon that's it, all the pins are holding, I can feel the difference. So hopefully it's goodbye to the nurses and hello physiotherapists again.'

'You could have stayed at the hotel longer my friend, you didn't need to come back here.' Michael smiled and glanced out the panoramic window, 'you know you are welcome anytime.'

'It feels better to be here Michael, even if I can't do much. I'm going to try a walk along the beach tomorrow.' He smiled, 'Kiri is coming over on Friday, with Stavros. I want to surprise them by meeting them at the pier. She's been brilliant, I've finished the drawings for the new museum in Thessaloniki. So, she is going to do all the site management of it for me although they are not starting until January and hoping to have it finished in a year. We have to get the festive season over first, it's going to be hard. Have you and Keith discussed it?'

Michael nodded, 'we are going to keep the hotel opened this year, be busy that's what we think, we have a few American guests booked in.' He lifted the bag and walked towards the fridge in the corner of the large open plan kitchen diner. 'You want coffee, yes?' Not stopping for a reply Michael switched on the coffee machine on the worktop he had noticed Alex on the laptop when he came into the garden, he was smiling and typing furiously into it. He wondered but didn't ask. Keith had mentioned that he thought perhaps Alex was talking to someone on-line and both he and Michael hoped it was a woman.

As he drove back across the island, Michael thought about his friend. Alex had been through eight operations in the last ten months. The days after the accident had been difficult and he and Keith had crossed the sea and travelled to Athens weekly to see Alex. He'd spent six months in hospital initially, then returned to Mykosis for the summer. Staying in a wheelchair adapted room in the hotel, Alex had, when he designed, never dreamt that he would one day be forced to occupy. He's had what they hoped was his final operation six weeks before. It was hard for Alex's friends to see the big strong capable man reduced to a wheelchair and being cared for by a team of nurses.

However, his consultant was sure he would walk again, possibly he would always be disabled but would be on his feet. This remained Alex's only goal, to be independently mobile. Keith and Michael knew that Alex's grief and guilt at Kim's death had initially been overwhelming, however he appeared to be coming to terms with it.

***

Alex put his coffee cup down and switched the laptop back on, he glanced over at the clock above the stove and then logged on.

During his time in hospital Alex had discovered the Viking online game by accident. He had become interested in Vikings when the staff in the Athens hospital had continually referred to him as the Varangian. His blond hair and large stature giving them the impression he was Scandinavian. He had begun to research his family tree and had been amazed when he discovered his father's family had originally come from the Shetland isles, there was a Scandinavian connection to this. Stuck in bed in a hospital where very few staff spoke English, Alex had found escape in reading and trawling through the internet. He had become knowledgeable about all things Scandinavian. One of Alex's goals for his future, was to visit Norway.

The game had initially been for a few hours a week, he mainly spent the time online watching others play. However, as his interest grew he began to take part. Alex quickly became a major player in the clan wars. He also began to enjoy the daily chat online with others and loved the anonymity of being able to talk without anyone realising who he was. Everyone who visited him in hospital knew about Kim, online he could be someone else. Someone who had no secrets. He never really discussed where he lived other than that he was on one of 6,000 Greek Islands. Only a few of Alex's very close friends knew which of the 227 inhabited Islands he lived on. Alex had quickly discovered the game players were worldwide, which meant that during the many sleepless nights there was always someone available to play with or to chat online. He took the name Trygve which he knew meant trustworthy. He had years before in New York met a Norwegian actor acquaintance of Kim's whose name was Trygve and it was the only Viking name Alex knew how to pronounce. He liked the idea of being trustworthy. Because Alex Lockwood knew in the real world away from the fantasy world he had built up, he was a liar and a fraud.

Alex had many regrets, his love for Rosie had never died, and he resisted the urge in him to find out what she and the children were doing. He knew that if he saw her he would want her, and he knew that what he had done to her was unforgivable. Alex hoped she and the children were happy, that their life was fulfilled, and they were loved. Before he left Scotland, Alex had set up a fund with a florist and had flowers placed on Becca and his mother's graves monthly. He longed to return to Scotland, wanted to stand in front of the graves and grieve, however he had never dared to do this afraid of what it may unleash. The immense guilt about his past, about Rosie and the children was always there. Also knowing essentially Kim's death had been because of the lies he had told, ate away at him. He had grown to love the outgoing and gregarious actress and missed her greatly. Kim's bi-polar disorder had never been an issue for him, it had been mainly well controlled by medication, and he felt that it had added to her creativity. Kim's acting skills had he thought been one of the many positive results of her disorder.'

The on-line Viking game was a million miles away from Alex's hometown in Scotland and the small Greek Island he now thought of as home. He had moved into the house he had designed and built on the island. It had been almost finished when Kim died, Alex found comfort there. Designed to be bright and airy with a large open plan living area and balcony leading out to stairs and an infinity pool. Alex had made the house fit the rugged headland of the island and the view out to sea was magnificent. Despite his best efforts, it reminded him of the first home he built, the house built with love for Rosie and their family. Alex smiled as he saw a passing fishing boat head out to sea. He took a drink from his mug and then returned to his laptop. He was soon engrossed in the game, raiding a neighbouring village with his clan, he enjoyed the chat and he didn't notice the time passing.

The weeks passed quickly, Alex became stronger every day. He tried hard not to show his emotional pain as the physical pain left him. Christmas arrived and despite both Keith and Michael asking him to spend the festive meal with them, Alex declined and decided to remain at home. His thoughts drifting to long ago and recent holiday celebrations he poured himself a drink and switched on the television, idly flicking through the channels unable to find anything to view. He glanced over at his laptop sitting on the kitchen table and looking at the clock he sighed and switched it on. He logged on to the game site and to his amazement there was someone on. 'Sigrunn?' he typed 'I thought you would be in the middle of Christmas dinner it's what? 4pm? in the UK?'

Despite there being no one else on the site, Alex noted the message, 'move into a private room?' he did so and a few seconds later a message popped up.

Alex read it, 'quite sad, my kids are out partying and I'm on my own, feeling a bit low, so thought I would log on in case there were Americans, or Australians on so I had someone to talk to.'

'I'm much the same, Christmas is a difficult time, makes you feel like the loneliest person in the world,' he typed back. Alex sat back and stared at the screen, before he knew it he was in a texting conversation with this person in the UK. He had been aware of Sigrunn, she was the warrior of the clan, always fighting and he was unsure if the person chatting back was male or female. The handle used was female, however any previous chats had been impersonal and about the game. Over the next year as Alex returned to physical health, they chatted over the internet. Where ever Alex was in the world, the game was his main escape from his feelings. Sigrunn became the person he gravitated towards. For Alex it was anonymous and fun. They found many common themes and Alex found himself looking forward to their conversations, they talked about books, films, and hid their growing friendship from the others in the clan. They still played in the game, however they found they were spending more and more time in the chatroom speaking. In the game their characters worked together raiding villages, building an empire, working together. In the chatroom they spoke about their lives.

Sigrunn told him about her life as a writer, she never disclosed her real name, she had she said been an English teacher, but had stopped working after her divorce. She lived and worked in Scotland. She had children and they lived with her. Not wanting to go down that road, Alex had told her that he had no children. So Sigrunn never really discussed hers.

Alex knew that he was reasonably well known in the United Kingdom, but particularly in Scotland. He never asked Sigrunn whereabouts in Scotland. She was cautious he realised, about divulging anything. For a year as they spoke regularly, they became friends. The second Christmas day, Alex had dinner with Michael and Keith, he enjoyed the day, although they had invited a group of holidaymakers who were staying at the hotel. Keith apparently hoping Alex might be interested in one of them. Alex with the benefit of a few glasses of wine warmed to one in particular. She was an American widow who had come to the island with a group of married couples for the festive period.

***

'Hey this is nice? What an amazing house. Have you lived here long?'

Alex handed her a glass of wine, 'about eighteen months, I was building it when my wife died. So, it was supposed to be a family home.' He shrugged and looked at the woman sadly, all through the meal they had flirted, he had brought her home, encouraged by Michael and Keith, to show her his house. Something about her reminded him of Rosie and he hoped they were going to have sex. 'Hey, shit happens. How did your husband die?'

'Road accident, he was coming home from work on the freeway in a storm and there was a pile up. He was a good man, but it's hard being widowed young.' She sighed 'you'll know all about that though. I can't believe you were married to Kim Maldon, she was one of my favourite actresses. It was so sad, it must have been awful losing her and the baby? I can't believe it's been two years either, it doesn't seem that long. I was in London that Christmas, it was my first year after Buck died. Keith said you have been widowed twice, that's real bad luck. What happened to your first wife?'

'Karen do you mind if we don't talk about it? This time of year, well it's difficult for me. Look come over here and I'll get you another drink.' He had lifted a bottle from the wine fridge in the corner, she walked towards him and took it from him.

'Have you been with anyone since Kim died, Jimmy?'

Alex shook his head, 'as I said I was mostly laid up for the first year or so. I broke my back and my legs in the crash. So, I never even thought about it. Have you? Been with anyone?'

'Yeah, a couple of men, just for sex,' she looked into Alex's eyes and moved closer. 'I'm not looking for anything else Jimmy, I like my life as it is, but I am attracted to you. I think you are a handsome man and well, one of us has to ask this, do you fancy some hot, no strings sex?'

Alex smiled, 'thought you'd never ask,' he stepped forward and they kissed. Their kisses became more intense and he found himself moving against her, aroused he lifted her onto the worktop, and they had sex there. Afterwards he led her upstairs and they repeated it in his bed. His emotional hunger slated, Alex fell in to a deep sleep. He dreamt of Rosie and the children, in the early days, this had been a recurring subject of his dreams. He used to wait impatiently for night time, going to bed hoping to dream of them, Becca was always there too, but he never knew she was dead in the dreams. It had been a long time since he had dreamt of them. He wakened to the smell of coffee. Karen stood smiling, a mug in her hands.

'Hey there's some pancakes I've just made downstairs, you said at dinner yesterday you missed American food. I thought I would pay you back for the amazing sex. You're pretty good at it Jimmy, can't believe you haven't done it for ages though. Jimmy, can I ask you something?'

'Sure.'

'Who's Rosie?'

Alex sighed and looked away. 'Was I talking in my sleep?'

'No Jimmy, when you were making love to me I heard you whisper Rosie I love you.'

Alex's face reddened, he stammered, 'Karen I . . . I'm sorry, Rosie was my first wife, well not my wife, we were engaged . . . look I'm mortified about it. I didn't even realise I'd said it out loud, you kind of remind me of her and I'm afraid . . . fuck I'm so sorry I kind of was . . . thinking of her earlier.'

'It's okay Jimmy, I get it, sometimes I do that, pretend Buck is still here. I did that the first time I made love again, shut my eyes and tried to imagine it was him. It's okay, for the record, the sex was amazing, and you were great . . .'

'But?'

'No woman wants to compete with a ghost Jimmy, you need to get some help with that. Counselling, therapy . . . talk to someone. How come it's your first wife and not Kim?'

'He shook his head, 'it happened a few times with Kim too, she used to get in a right strop about it. I loved her, but I suppose I just loved Rosie more. 'I did love Kim . . . but Rosie . . . I'm afraid she was the love of my life, look Karen, I just don't speak about her, or that time of my life. I've never really got over her.'

'Where did you get the scars from? You look as though you've been stabbed, they are not from the accident?' Seeing Alex's puzzled look Karen smiled, 'sorry, I told you I'm a doctor? Well, I work in the ER, so I see lots of stab wounds I know what they look like, but also healing takes place over years, I guessed they were from before.'

'I used to be a bouncer, I was stabbed at work, was pretty serious lost a kidney and my spleen, but it was a long, long time ago. Another lifetime actually.' He smiled back at her sadly, 'do you mind if we change the subject please? I don't talk about myself, I tried counselling, but it wasn't for me. I much prefer to keep my thoughts bottled up. I don't want to forget, I don't want to lose the guilt I feel.'

'Well get dressed come downstairs and eat the pancakes before they get cold. I think you need a woman to look after you Mr Lockwood.'

***

'These are really good pancakes, I haven't tasted anything this good since I left the states Karen, you are a good cook.' Alex grinned then added, 'and a very sexy desirable woman.' They were sitting at Alex's kitchen table. Alex was now embarrassed, and he really just wanted Karen to go. He smiled and made small talk.

'Well if you ever make it to Chicago, Jimmy, look me up. Do you think you will ever come back to the States permanently? I had heard of you by the way, you design some amazing buildings, A J Lockwood. I also never knew you were married to Kim. So, you must like your privacy?'

Alex nodded, 'I value it, I never wanted the film star life Kim had, and I think she did, but wanted to make me happy. We were going to live here and raise our child.' His eyes filled with tears, 'it just wasn't to be.'

'I'm so sorry Jimmy, 'I can't imagine what it must be like for you to have lost so much.'

Alex put down his knife and fork and wiped his mouth with the napkin in front of him. He pursed his lips and shrugged. 'you become used to pain and longing, and you always wonder how it would have all panned out if things had been different. That's life I suppose. Most people have a hard luck story.'

When Karen eventually left, Alex returned to his lap top, Sigrunn was online, this was unexpected.. She had told him she was going to the states to spend Christmas with her sister. She told Alex she had missed her flight, so she was now travelling on boxing day. He wasn't sure why, but he told her about Karen and his having been with her. There was a long pause before she typed back. 'do you miss sex?' She asked, 'was it hard to be with someone else when you've lost the person you love? Did you miss sex, as much as you miss your wife?'

'I don't really know,' he typed back, 'I hadn't really thought about it till tonight, yeah, I think I do miss it. I enjoyed the comfort of being with someone, the physical release, but I think I miss the familiarity of being intimate with someone I know well. I never got bored with long term partners, relationships ended for reasons that had nothing to do with sex.'

'Have you had many relationships?' Sigrunn asked after a few moments pause. 'I know I don't know you, but you don't appear to be the type of man who has a lot of different women?'

'I've been with a few women, however there was a first love, and no one ever really measured up to her. I'm afraid I'm a bit sad that way. I guess I'm a one-woman man at heart. Bit strange for a Viking don't you think?' What about you? Is there someone special, I'm kind of guessing not?'

There was a further long pause, so long that Alex assumed that she had gone off line. When she replied, he realised he had touched a raw nerve.

'What makes you say that? She finally replied.

'You are on your own at Christmas.'

'That might be by choice.'

'Is it?'

'Not exactly, but it's safer for me, uses less energy and if I'm not in a relationship, I can't get hurt.'

The Nightclub Owners Wife

'What about sex? Don't you miss it?' Alex held his breath mesmerised by the conversation, he found he wanted to know what made this woman tick.

'Yes, a bit, I miss the physical act I suppose a bit like you I miss the release. I have had a few sexual encounters, but I haven't been with anyone in a long time. Now I just write about it. *(I'm good at writing about it!!!)* I also teach creative writing, so I help others to express their inner selves. I'm not too good at relationships, I was hurt when I was young, and I suppose if found it hard to trust anyone after that experience. I tried again and got hurt again. Time is only a healer when someone dies. I don't talk about it by the way, still too painful. Sex is different isn't it? I mean it doesn't have to be about love and trust to be fulfilling, that's a myth I think, made up by men to keep women under control. Men get to sow wild oats but when a woman does it she is a tart.'

'Do you really think that? I kind of don't see you as a radical feminist.' Alex realised that they were discussing intimacy and he wanted to see where it would go.

'Why not?' She typed back almost immediately. 'I consider myself a feminist, yes, why do you think I'm not?'

'Well for starters you are playing a game, and doing it well I must say, but you are involved in a pastime that involves very misogynist thinking. I mean the Vikings were not exactly respectful of women, were they? Last week when you and Ragnar did that raid on the coastal village, you were supporting that view. I got a bit jealous Sigrunn when you were joking with him about gathering wood.'

'That's escapism, the game, is it not?' There was another pause before the words appeared again continuing the conversation. 'If I thought about it sexually it would be a fantasy.'

'Do you think about it sexually? How do you deal with that, have there been no men you've wanted to keep doing it with? Do you think about sex?'

'Sometimes, it depends on what my current fantasy is. Fantasies are safe, they require no real contact. I mainly put my fantasies into my writing. Sometime the fantasy gets stronger and it needs something else. I'm not in the market for another man.' There was another long pause before the words continued on the screen. 'So, I control it mainly by masturbation, women do that you know? It's not just men who do that to their fantasy.'

Alex took a deep breath. 'Am I a fantasy for you?' He typed in, there was yet another long pause before she replied.

'Am I for you?

'If I'm honest you weren't . . . I just liked talking to you, but tonight I don't know, I think it might be.' There was no reply this time and a message popped up with her caricature saying '*Sigrunn has gone off line.*' Alex sighed and logged off himself. He stood up and smiled as he realised he was aroused. 'fuck it's like having a crush on Minnie Mouse.' He said out loud.

Alex felt restless, logged off from the game switched on the television then sat back down on the sofa. He normally enjoyed Greek television and over the last two years he had, with Michael's help, become fluent in the language. He couldn't concentrate, he was surprised at his arousal talking to Sigrunn, he realised he didn't know her real name. He was unaware of any of the players real names, in some ways for Alex that had been the point of playing. He could forget who he was for a few hours.

CHAPTER
FORTY-TWO

In her house in Ayrshire, Rosie stared at the laptop, not able to believe how aroused she was. She had enjoyed the Viking game and had made lots of friends on line. Safe friends who she never had to meet, she mainly played late at night meaning that most of the people she played with were in different time zones. She was careful not to share too much personal information, her work had in the past few years been successful, she was now the author of eleven published novels. Her first book had been adapted for a very successful television show and although not exactly a household name she was well known.

'What you up to mum?' Rosie looked up as her son standing behind her put his arms around her neck and kissed her cheek. 'You look guilty, were you talking to a man?'

'Oh, just browsing on line darling, why are you back early?' She sniffed the air, 'Toby, how much have you had to drink?'

'Mum don't start nagging, I've had just enough to be sociable, that's why I'm home. I know how precious my one kidney is, what it cost . . . the others have gone back to Chloe's they'll leave from there in the morning, meet us at the airport. I came back to make sure you and the cases get to the airport.' He looked at the pad of paper next to the lap top, 'who or what is Trygve?'

'What? Where did you hear that name?'

'You have written it one … two … five times on the pad, is it for your new book? Some of the girls were talking about your last one tonight. Apparently, it's very steamy. I'm kind of wishing I could read them mum, but well it's you and I suppose no one wants to think about their mum having sex.' Toby smiled his eyes sparkled, he moved around the table and sat down opposite her lifting a bottle of sparkling water from the fridge on the way. 'You shouldn't just be writing about romance mum, you should be experiencing it. I hate that you are alone, not all men are bastards mum, you were just unlucky.'

Rosie smiled, 'thought you didn't want to think about your mother having sex?'

'I don't, but I also don't want you to be alone. Imogen thinks you have been talking to someone online?'

'I'm allowed to have friends Toby, there is no law against it as far as I'm aware. If you must know, I've been playing an online game and I talk to the other players.'

'Online game? Is it safe? So, you are not on plenty of fish or something like that? Are you gambling mum?'

No of course not, it's just a bit of harmless fun. Okay if you are going to bed go. I have my word quota to do before we leave tomorrow. I have a deadline of January 20th for the first draft, and I don't want to have to work when we are in the states.' Rosie switched her laptop back on ignoring the message icon which popped up she opened a folder from her desktop.

'What's the new one called? Toby asked smiling at his mother. 'Is it steamy and sexy?'

'It's called, in to the abyss, and yes there are some sex scenes. Do you want to read it?' She grinned at her son, 'you could proof read it for me, six months in to an English literature degree? Actually, it's a murder mystery one, I thought I'd change genres a bit and go down the crime thriller route this time. 'A bit of Tartan Noir, William Mcilvanney with hot steamy sex, I'm not sure if it will work. Cathy is having kittens thinking I'm going to ruin my reputation, she wants me to use another name just in case.'

'She's probably more concerned about losing her twenty percent mum, she is a crap agent, b'list, everyone says so. You should be world famous by now, eleven best sellers, three major literary awards and a successful American network show. You can still shop in the local co-op without being recognised?' Toby stood up, Auntie Elaine says you need to stop hiding, come out and take the credit.'

'I'll leave the fame game to Auntie Elaine if you don't mind Toby. What has she got planned for next week? I take it you talked to her if you were with Chloe?'

'New year's party at her new pad in L.A, Bel Air Mum, wow. She says it's ready for us, we spoke to Beau and Ella too on FaceTime, like we promised, they said they were missing us they were really disappointed we didn't make it for Christmas dinner. Brian took them to Disneyland, and they got to be extra's in a film. Elaine is so well known in America now. Chloe says that the new house is amazing.'

'I spoke to them all this morning on Skype again, got the virtual tour.'

You miss her, Auntie Elaine, I mean, don't you? Funny how things turn out. I'm glad you and her sorted things out, Chloe is so much part of our lives now, isn't she? Carl, well he took so much from you both, mum, it's amazing you can accept it all without going mad?' Toby looked sad, 'I struggle to think that part of him is living inside me, I would be dead if he hadn't given me his kidney, but... mum I just can't.'

'Please don't Toby, I've been trying all day not to think about it. It's been eleven years now and I still can't deal with it all, it still scares me what your father was capable of.' Rosie stood up and put her arms around her tall son, so like his father physically but personality wise, nothing like him. 'You and your sister are the only good things that came out of my marriage, I've never regretted that. Now there is nothing else to say Toby, you know it all. I can never forgive what he did, but he was your father and if he ever was capable of loving anyone it was you.'

'What about Dad? You never discuss him? Have you ever heard from him? I loved him mum, but he just went off and left us . . .'

'Toby, how many times must I say it, he didn't care about us, he lied about most things.'

'Mum I know I was young, but, he was a great guy. Mum I remember more than you think? I think that there must have been more to this? Mum I'd kind of like to see him again. Are you sure you don't know where his is now?'

Rosie shook her head. 'Toby, not again, and not tonight please?' Rosie snapped her laptop shut and pulled the pen drive from the side port. She stood up and dropped a kiss on her son's head. 'Right now, I'm going to bed, tomorrow is a difficult day and I'm glad we are travelling most of it.' She glanced over at the sink where three wreathes lay, 'I'll do the cemetery in the morning first thing. If you don't want to come it's okay darling. We all deal with things differently.'

'Mum, I'm sorry, I can see I've upset you. Mum you might not want to know, but I do, I promised you I wouldn't go behind your back, but I want to know why he did it. I don't even know his second name. I've tried so many times to discuss this, so has Imogen. I asked Auntie Elaine she said I needed to speak to you. I'll come to the cemetery if you want,' seeing the tears gathering in his mother's eyes he sighed. 'I want to support you mum, I don't want to hurt you.'

'Please Toby? I don't want to speak about it, I just can't, do you not realise if he had cared, he would have come to us after the fire?' Rosie somehow managed to walk upstairs and into her bedroom, not the same room she had shared with Alex. She had swapped rooms after she decided to remain in the house he had designed. So many memories were contained in this house and she had never managed to move away. She closed the door behind her and grabbing her robe from the back of the door sobbed silently into it. She opened the patio doors and walked out onto the balcony. The sea roared splashing off the rocks to her right and she could see the lights of the houses on Arran. The light from what she knew was Ailsa Craig sparkled out at sea to her left. Rosie sighed, and her mind drifted back to that night when she had become the sole survivor of the Gibb' family. The horror never left her she saw it often, she looked at the photograph on her bedside cabinet her parents and Simon an ordinary snap taken by ten-year-old Rosie with her new birthday camera. They had been on holiday in Norfolk, Great Yarmouth, the summer before Simon was in the accident. Rosie loved the snap, a memory of the last time she remembered them being a happy family. Alex had been with them on that holiday, she remembered he had stood beside her as she took the photograph then he took one of all four of the Gibb's together. Rosie could see his shadow faintly on the ground in that picture, she could not bear to look at it.

Rosie picked up the photograph she kissed her finger and touched each of the three people then she lifted a second frame. Her parents holding Becca at her christening, tears began to flow, and Rosie lay down remembering.

CHAPTER
FORTY-THREE

27ᵗʰ December 2007

Rosie looked at the two police officers, 'what happened?' She sat down beside Elaine on the sofa, 'how did it start, the fire? When?'

'Never mind that right now, where is her cousin's wee boy Christine? Elaine said quickly, we know the adults are dead. The wee boy though?'

Rosie nodded. 'Where is Jordan? Oh my God, my mum and my dad, but wee Jordan is the same age as Toby.'

'He was there earlier, him and Chloe were playing together.' Elaine jumped to her feet, 'Christine you need to tell them to look for him? Are you sure they haven't found him?' Elaine sat back down on the sofa.

Christine Caven shook her head, she looked at the uniformed police officer, 'Bert radio that in. There was no child, we had it checked because one of the neighbours thought your kids were there Rosie. They said your mum told them you were coming later. The firefighters went through what's left of the house looking.'

The Nightclub Owners Wife

'We decided not to go over, oh there was some stuff with Carl yesterday and ... well we decided just to stay here.'

'I brought my daughter back here.' Elaine sobbed into her hands. 'I almost left Chloe there, but she has been so clingy lately ... thank god.' She looked over at Rosie, who was sitting quietly on the couch, staring at the television which was switched off. 'Rosie are you alright? Rosie, don't do this, speak to me? Please Rosie don't do this I need you to be here.'

Elaine moved over and nudged her. Rosie looked at her and shook her head. 'I'm okay, I just need to process this, I will be okay.' She repeated, looking over at Christine who also had tears on her cheeks. Rosie put her arms out to Elaine and the two women clung together, both crying, but finding comfort in the fact they were together.'

Christine looked up as her radio crackled, she went outside the living room, when she returned she looked over at Rosie and Elaine still huddled together on the sofa. 'A young boy has turned up outside Crosshouse hospital, he is about four-foot six, dark hair says his name is Jordan Thompson? I don't have any other details, but he is unhurt, and I need someone who knows him to sit with him. Do you know your cousins address Rosie? We need to inform his parents?'

'Beth and her husband are at a wedding they didn't come to mum and dads this year because their friend was getting married and their daughter Amy was a flower girl. Jordan was playing up because he wanted to come here; so, they let him. Thank god he is alright, but how did he get from Onthank to Crosshouse? He's not from here, he doesn't know the area?'

Christine shrugged, 'we need to question him, find out what happened? We can't do anything until we can speak to his parents and get permission. Can you sit with him Rosie, how well do you know him?'

'Well not too well, we see him a couple of times a year, he is not an easy child. Mine are reasonably well behaved and Toby kind of emulates Jordan when he's here. This is an awful thing to be thinking, but the last time they visited he was playing with matches?' Rosie sighed and looked up at Christine. 'I can't get it out of my head, he is the only one not hurt. What if? He's just a little boy, but if they were all distracted, and he was bored?'

'Rosie, we don't know anything yet, let the police and fire brigade do their work.' Christine sighed. 'We really need to speak to his parents. They say he is not upset or anything, but we really should not be speaking to him without their permission.'

'I have Beth and Kenny's address in my address book, they stay just outside Glasgow. Newton Mearns, so it's this side of Glasgow.'

CHAPTER
FORTY-FOUR

'Rosie the wee boy Jordan, he doesn't really know much. He says he was dreaming, there was a man in the bedroom. The man gave him an injection wrapped him in a blanket and carried him out to a car. He thinks it was a dream,' Christine Cavan took a deep breath, 'there was a sedative in his body according to the tox report. Thing is he was medicated because of his ADHD, the sedative worked against it. So, it took longer to work. The medics say that's why he remembers being taken out. Next thing he recalls is waking up at the side of the road he saw the lights of the hospital and walked to it.' Christine sat down on the sofa opposite Rosie. 'Hope you don't mind, but I volunteered to come over and tell you. I'm the D.I for the family protection team now, so it was my lot who interviewed Jordan. I've offered to do the family liaison with you. I thought it might be easier for you, given I did it all those years ago. Jordan's parents have taken him home, but we'll interview him again, and we have a psychologist standing by to talk to him about the fire.'

Rosie nodded, 'my cousin, Beth, called me. I had been thinking that, someone had to have taken him to the hospital, he wouldn't know how to get there.' Rosie looked at the door as Elaine came through it. 'Are they all settled?' She asked.

Elaine nodded, 'finally, I think Chloe was just a bit overwhelmed by everything that's happened. She is not too pleased about my pregnancy either. Sorry about her tantrum, to be honest she can be a bit of a diva. I think I've spoiled her quite a bit.' Elaine smiled, 'Imogen was brilliant with her, she is such a sensible little thing, isn't she?'

Rosie nodded, then sighed. 'I just wish sometimes she would tantrum like Chloe. I want her to enjoy her childhood, not be a mini adult. I think it stems from when Alex upped and left, she sort of became an adult overnight. She's barely in double figures yet he acts like she is thirty.'

'She's very like you Rosie,' Elaine said quietly, 'you were always infinitely more sensible than everyone else our age. I think I would have been even more of a wild child if I hadn't had you. You kind of kept me grounded. I think though, Imogen is even more sensible than you were.'

'Yeah look where it got me being sensible. I wasn't sensible I was naïve.' Rosie put her hand out and took the glass of wine from Elaine. She looked at Christine, 'now the kids are asleep, can you tell us what is going on. Have they found out anything?'

Christine Caven sighed she looked from Rosie to Elaine and lifted the wine glass from the table, she looked at her watch and took a gulp from the glass. 'I'm officially on duty,' she said quietly looking at Elaine. 'I wouldn't have a drink with anyone else. I told the boss I would break the latest bit of news to you, I needed the kids to be asleep.' Christine gulped the wine down and looked down at the empty glass. 'Thing is girls, oh I don't think this is going to come as a shock, but, well . . . the fire it was deliberately started.'

'Was it Jordan?'

'Not unless he doused the place with petrol first.'

'What?' Rosie gasped, 'who would do that?'

'Oh, for fuck sake Rosie, you are so fucking right about being naïve, grow up, who do we both know who is capable of that?'

Elaine said shaking her head, 'wake up and smell the coffee. The wee boy was drugged.'

'Carl? No, he wouldn't, his kids could have been there, he wouldn't have known they weren't.'

Christine sighed, she put her hand on Rosie's shoulder and looked into her eyes, 'we are looking to speak to him to find out what he knows, but... there's no sign of him. He withdrew a lot of money from the bank on Christmas eve, then took all the takings from the pubs on Christmas day. He's been moving money about since he got out, and well... he's vanished. Rosie, Jordan looks like Toby, he was in the room alone where Toby normally sleeps... you told me that yourself. This is hard, but we think someone took the child thinking it was Toby, then doused the house with petrol. Jordan had been drugged, injection of a sedative. I'm so sorry Rosie, but we think it was either Carl, or he paid someone to do it. He must have thought you were all at your parents. Rosie, he meant to kill all of you. We know from the post mortem that they were all asleep when the fire started. The forensics prove it was a deliberate act.'

Rosie stared at the police officer, she shook her head, 'he meant to kill my entire family, except for Toby?'

'Of course, he did,' Elaine snapped, 'do you think he is not capable of it? He's a fucking psychopath Rosie, you know he is, think about it?' Elaine turned to Christine, 'and your lot, the police, they didn't want to believe it either. I fucking told them on Christmas eve, something would happen. They didn't arrest him after what he did here.'

'Please Elaine, no one could have forecast this, all his risk assessments pointed to him being a reformed character. There was also not enough to hold him, at best it was a breach of the peace. The police when they spoke to him said he seemed genuinely upset and embarrassed about the way he had behaved. I'm so sorry this has happened to you all.'

Elaine shook her head, 'Christine, I'm not getting at you. You are the only cop who listened to my concerns and tried to take action. This could have been prevented if they had arrested him, but they said he was not in breach of his licence! They preferred to blame her for his behaviour. Femme fatal, going with other men, causing their little bruised egos to make them do things. Do you know what Christine? I am going to make sure that there is an enquiry into this, all of it. We could all have been dead.' Elaine turned her back to Rosie, her voice breaking, the pain in it unmistakable. 'My gran, she was seventy, helped people all her life, Davie and Maggie, they were good people.' She looked around again. 'Your aunt and uncle coming for a party, and that bastard killed them, all because you had dinner with another man! They'd better throw away the fucking key this time.'

'Elaine, I'm so sorry,' Rosie sobbed, I never thought he would harm the children. Or my parents, I'm so sorry about your gran.'

'No Rosie, no, you don't take the blame for this, our children were fathered by an animal. But its nurture not nature, we bring them up to be good people. Carl is a spoiled little fucking boy, he can't have so he takes. He knows exactly what he is doing Rosie, he has no feelings. I hope he's driven his fucking car off a cliff somewhere.' Elaine stood up and walked to the window, she stared out at the darkness. 'One thing I do know if he has, it would be an accident, he is too fucking devoid of feelings to have any remorse for what he has done.' Elaine looked at Christine, 'that's why you put the police guard out there, why you are here, isn't it? You know we are all at risk, he meant to kill us. The people who died were just innocent bystanders. It was us, Rosie and I and our children he took his son and heir.'

Christine nodded, 'we think when he sees it all over the media, he will come out of hiding. Thing is it was really well done, the fire, well thought out. We only discovered it because of Jordan being taken, your dad had petrol in a can lying at the garage, he had the patio heaters on at the party, for the smokers outside. You know he was careful Rosie, and wouldn't have left it right at the door, however everyone at the party saw him use it for the old greenhouse heater and put the can down. There was also a little cut in the gas supply pipe outside. Professionally done we think. Planned and premeditated. Carl won't know we know all that, the press is concentrating on the tragedy element, so he will I think, wait a few days and re appear. We deliberately fed them the story about Jordan wandering into the hospital lost.'

'You think he will come here?' Rosie asked, 'to harm me and the kids?'

'No, the forensic psychologist thinks he might use this to try to endear himself to you. Offer his support, we didn't think we could tie him to it, however his DNA is on Jordan's clothes, so we can put him at the scene. He bought tickets to fly to Lanzarote, someone using his passport left the country on Boxing day. We are waiting to arrest said person on their return. We don't think it was him. Not sure why he spared Jordan when he discovered he wasn't Toby? Maybe he does have some compassionate feelings after all? He is a very damaged man Rosie. You must understand how dangerous he's become. Now it's all safe outside, everyone is in position, there is no way anyone will get in here.' Christine nodded at the plain clothes policeman sitting on the other sofa, a gun holster over his uniform. 'Gary here will entertain you, and of course he will disguise his firearm under something in case the children get out of bed.' She stood up, 'I'm going to get some sleep, I suggest you two do the same. Is it ok to use a spare bedroom?' She nodded at the police man who was putting his gun under his sweater. 'I'll get up around five and let you sleep for a few hours.'

'You can have the downstairs guest room,' Rosie said quietly, I changed the sheets this morning. I usually use it as my office, I write there, it looks over the beach, Elaine and Chloe have been using it, but she's in with Imogen tonight. Elaine do you want to sleep upstairs?'

Elaine stood up, 'can I sleep with you tonight Rosie?' She looked at Christine and smiled sadly, 'my confession here is, I'm a shocking parent, as you may have gathered from the tantrum earlier. I usually allow Chloe to sleep with me, especially if we are away from home on our own. Plays havoc with my love life. Gran was much stricter, she came and lived with me after Chloe was born as you know. That helped me get my degree finished. When I went to Canada she came with us. I have a nanny, as I told you, Grace, she has been with us since Chloe was a toddler. I think that's part of the problem, Chloe is missing her. She will be due back off leave the day after tomorrow, is it okay to call her Christine? She was coming here. I'll give her a few days extra leave.' Elaine sighed, 'she is part of the family actually, I will need to call her and tell her about Gran. She's from Plymouth, so it's unlikely she will have heard about the fire on the news there.'

'I think I'd like you to bunk in with me Elaine, if you want?' Rosie looked at her friend tears building in her eyes. 'I think I'd like to sleep with someone else tonight. It will make me feel a bit less anxious.'

Christine nodded. She looked over at Elaine. 'Call your nanny in the morning, however, please don't tell her about the investigation, just that there was a fire.' Christine looked around the room. 'There was surveillance equipment in the house. Not in here, but in your bedroom and the kid's room. One of the kids had put a toy in front of it. So that's possibly why he didn't know you were here. Christine smiled, 'the boys have accidentally thrown your coat over the one in your bedroom. It's not an audio one they are much bigger, so he wouldn't have risked it.'

'That's what those guys were searching for this morning?' Elaine said wearily.

Christine nodded, 'Carl Ranmore is not a stupid man, and he is also a very rich one. If there is a way of monitoring you, he will have done it. The boffins have done a thorough sweep of the building. There was nothing else that we can see.'

'Spy equipment? Surely not? I'm sure there will be a thug somewhere watching the house, but surveillance equipment that's a bit MI5 is it not?' Rosie said her face reflecting her confusion. 'I can't believe that this is happening, it's like something in a movie, or a nightmare I'm going to wake up from an discover everything is normal.'

***

The telephone rang, it was ten o'clock on New Year's eve. Christine lifted the receiver, 'hello, Gibbs residence.' She said confidently, she listened intently. 'Oh, thanks Frank, that's grand, we will all be sleeping a bit easier now, Happy New Year to you too.' Christine looked over at the others and nodded, she smiled wryly, Rosie and Elaine realised that something important had happened. 'That's fine, I realise that Frank, but we will sit tight just now.'

'What's happened? Is it Carl? Have they arrested him? Rosie asked. 'Have they got him?' She repeated, Elaine also stood watching intently, she sat down on the sofa beside Rosie looking up at Christine.

'They have him, he is at this moment helping us with our enquiries. Now ladies I don't want to alarm you, but we will keep the guards in just now, because he has worthies who work for him. I'm going to have a few hours' sleep and then I'll go into Ayr and watch him being interviewed.' She looked up, Rosie and Elaine were wrapped in each other's arms on the sofa sobbing. 'I think however you two can now get on with the business of grieving for your loved ones. Frank says Carl was very subdued, he was trying to come through the airport check, at Prestwick. We know he wasn't on the flight, so we can tie him to the crime. I think he was planning to take Toby and go abroad Rosie.'

'Why? How do you know?'

'He had Toby's passport Rosie, how did he get it? Carl can't leave the country without telling us, so he was willing to break the law, God only knows where he was going to go.'

CHAPTER
FORTY-FIVE

The days passed quickly, Carl was remanded in custody, Elaine and Rosie buried their respective loved ones and then got on with the process of learning to live without them. Rosie was to feel later the only positive thing in this time was that it had brought Elaine Lamont back into her life.

Rosie missed her parents every day, she felt responsible for their deaths and this caused her overwhelming pain. The children however needed her, and this combined with Elaine and her supporting each other helped her to deal with her grief. Rosie published her first book and started her second, the writing of it had she felt helped her to deal with the trauma around her.

Elaine and her daughter Chloe became family to Rosie and her children. Elaine was a much sought-after journalist, her looks and quick wit developed her career into celebrity status. She and Chloe moved back to live in London around the same time Carl's trial ended and he was convicted and returned to prison. Rosie and Elaine re discovered their relationship, and with Elaine in London they saw each other frequently. Rosie was maid of honour when Elaine married her long-term lover Brian. Rosie was also Godmother to Elaine and Brian's son Beau.

Rosie initially again considered moving out of the house on the beach. After a lot of soul searching she and the children remained there. Elaine, Brian, and their growing family were frequent visitors to Scotland, the two women needed each other, feeling a sense of a shared belonging. Rosie did have a few boyfriends over the years, however she could never commit, never trust a man.

It was Elaine who told Rosie of Alex marrying Kim Maldon, the only person who understood the pain and confusion around her past relationships was Elaine. When the architectural society wanted to put a plaque to Alex on the house, it was Elaine who dealt with them. Elaine knew that the pain left by both Carl and Alex betrayal, burned away at Rosie and prevented her from moving on. Rosie however never discussed it and Elaine learned to support her without attempting to talk in any depth about either man.

Rosie completed her post graduate teaching qualification and carried on writing whilst teaching English for a few years. When her divorce from Carl was complete, she began to concentrate on her writing, teaching part time. Rosanna Gibson romantic fiction quickly became part of the best seller lists in many countries.

Rosie discovered the Viking game whilst researching for a historical novel. She began playing using the name Sigrunn which was the main character in her book. She continued playing the game long after the book was finished. She loved the anonymity of online game playing. Even in the chat rooms no one knew who she was. Rosie resisted any attempts by the other players to talk on the telephone, she concentrated on online chatting, she was Sigrunn, she did say she wrote, and that she was an English teacher but that was all. Most of the players had put photographs of themselves. When she saw his photograph, Rosie had immediately realised that Trygve looked friendly and happy. Knowing what he looked like helped her to imagine what he was like as a person. He wasn't the type of man Rosie had been attracted to, he wasn't handsome or macho. Rosie had never put up a photo, instead she used a female Viking caricature, no one knew what the mysterious British woman looked like.

That Christmas when she had begun speaking to Trygve privately, she did not log on until she returned from America. The festive season was always difficult and because of the time difference she was travelling on Boxing day. Elaine however was an excellent hostess. Brian like Rosie had given up practice and become a very successful writer, they lived a very ostentatious life and moved between London and California. Elaine had secured a post as anchor woman on a major news channel but now had her own political chat show and was extremely well known in both America and the UK.

Before she left for the airport Rosie visited the cemetery with the wreathes. One for the Gibbs plot, her parents, Simon and Becca. One for Rowena and of course the wreath Elaine had asked her to lay on her Grandmothers grave. She no longer read the tributes from Alex, but she always removed the card, so the children never saw it. She had worked out the day of the month they arrived. Screwing up the small memoriam card she threw it into the bin at the cemetery gates.

Throughout the three-week holiday, despite being happy to be with Elaine and their respective families, Rosie's thoughts kept wandering to thoughts of the Viking game and Trygve. She resisted the urge to log on whilst in the states, however on her return home, whilst her children went to bed suffering from jet lag. Rosie sitting up in bed unable to sleep logged back on the game.

***

In Athens Alex looked at the screen of his laptop. He had gone to spend new year with Kiri and Stavros who were over for the festive period with their three children. Alex stayed on to visit a site where there were problems with one of their designs. He enjoyed the company and felt a bit less sad than he had for a while. He was a little confused by Sigrunn logging off the way she had and then not being on again, but he supposed that she had her reasons. Every day for three weeks he logged on but Sigrunn was never on line.

Rosie was about to log off when the man she had been thinking about logged on. She saw his icon and typed on 'hey are you having a good day? You have been busy since I've been away.'

'Were you on vacation?' Another player, Pac asked, 'we have missed you Sigrunn. Freya took over for you, and we have done well. Trygve has added fifteen villages and now we own a lot more gold. We are going to be the richest clan in the game at this rate.'

'Well done Trygve,' Rosie typed, hoping she was sounding casual. She had been searching for him since she had logged back on to the game site. 'Yes Pac, in fact I've been in your neck of the woods, California, my sister lives out there,' she lied.

'How was it? Have you been over here before?'

'Yes a few times but not for a while. It was good we spent New Year's there, very different from here, the weather was amazing. Anyway folks, I just wanted to say hi I'm just back and very tired so I'm going to bed.'

'Goodnight everyone said.'

'Thought you had gone for good.' Alex typed, as he and Sigrunn entered the chat room. 'I thought I might have upset you with the sex talk.'

'No, my son walked in and well it's not something you want to be talking about in front of your kids is it? I was leaving in the morning, so I didn't get another chance.'

'So, can we resume where we left off, or is that why you didn't come back into the game? We were having an interesting conversation and going off in a particular direction. I was worried that you didn't like where we were heading?'

'Fantasy is an interesting thing; can I ask you something Trygve?'

'Yeah of course, what?'

'Were you turned on that night?'

'Why were you?'

'Just answer.'

'Yes, there was a certain movement in the trouser area. That's never happened to me before.'

'Did you masturbate?' Rosie typed in she waited a few seconds before he eventually answered.

'Did you?'

'Yes,' she admitted, 'I had never done that before, thinking about someone I had never met. I do have a photograph so I could imagine you doing it.'

'When did you last have sex with a man.'

'A long time ago. What about you?'

'I had a one-night stand about a week ago I was away on business. I had sex with a woman I met at a friend's party. She wanted more though, and I didn't.'

'Was it good?'

'I was thinking about you, if I'm honest. Imagining what it was like.'

'What is it like?'

'With you Sigrunn?

'Yes.'

'Very loving, you are adventurous but shy with it, not confident in how hot you are.'

'Hmm not bad, so you don't think I would be ripping off my bodice and making a lot of noise?'

'No, you would be soft and warm, very loving, you kiss a lot and you like to be held. You don't care if your man is well endowed as long as he holds you. What about me, what do I like?'

'Rosie suddenly found herself remembering sex with Alex, she remembered the earth-shattering orgasms, the way he made love to her, his consideration, his body, muscular and well endowed. His mouth on hers kissing down her body. She began to type the words in, describing moments with Alex. When he responded she felt the type of passion she normally just wrote about these days.

As the weeks passed Sigrunn and Trygve became lovers they spoke most days, not just about virtual sex, they talked about politics, religion, current affairs, people. Both went through the motions of everyday living but found that they lived for the nights when lying in bed they talked. They didn't always talk about sex, but when they did the fantasy was there. Trygve told her about the island he lived on, he told her about his life leaving out the identifying factors. It was Easter when Alex finally found out he was speaking to the woman he had loved most of his life.

He had been asking her to put up a photograph, and eventually she agreed. She said however, that she only wanted him to see it, so they logged in and she put her photograph on.

In Greece, Alex was shocked to the core, he realised it might be someone using Rosie's photograph, after all he had used Keith's. He had been about to own up to the fact he wasn't Wilson Anderson and that he had put a false photograph on, when Rosie put hers on.' Alex had switched his laptop off and pretended it had stopped working. He had no idea what he was going to say to her. He knew enough from his talking to her online that Rosie had never forgiven him. He suspected there had been no man in her life since he had left. Alex knew he needed to find a way tell her why he did it, what was going through his mind that day, the day he left her.

He googled her name, there was very little online, he did some research and realised he was talking to Rosanna Gibson. She was a mysterious women's fiction writer. By some detective work he discovered that her sister in America was Elaine. He had followed Elaine Lamont's career, she was another person who Alex knew he owed an apology. Rosie had told him her parents were dead, when he asked what happened to them, not knowing he was talking to Rosie, she had told him they died in a house fire. Alex became like a detective he found the newspaper article and the story of the court case. Alex wept as he read what Carl

Ranmore had done. He was sad when they referred to Rosie as a mother of three in the article, knowing that the third child lay in the cemetery overlooking the estate where they had all grown up. Lying in the ground with all the other members of the Gibb's family, across from Rowena Ranmore and his mother Rebecca, the graveyard Alex had never visited in the years since Becca had died.

Alex wanted to go to Rosie that night, hold her, make it all better for her. It had been at that point he had begun to ask her to visit.

He started to ask subtle leading questions and if he was honest he began to woo Rosie on line. Getting her to agree to come to Greece took him four months. He promised she could stay in his friends' hotel, let her see the booking. He thought if he could just get her on to the island he could explain. Thing was he knew it was madness. He knew what he had done was unforgivable, but he was unable to stop, he had to see her. Now he knew, he had to make one last attempt to see her again in the flesh.

As he was to admit to Keith later, he knew if he went to Scotland she would never speak to him. He didn't want her children to know. He had opened a floodgate, he knew about Imogen becoming engaged to a local businessman, he scoured face-book looking for pictures of the children. However, he realised that their pages were not public. He supposed that this was because of Carl Ranmore and the interest in the murder of their Grandparents.

CHAPTER
FORTY-SIX

Greece 2018

Keith watched as Rosie took a drink from the wine glass and sighed. 'Okay,' she finally said, 'so he's had a hard time, he never stopped loving me. He had a fight with his wife on the day she died. That doesn't explain why he walked out on me and my children. Why he left me to deal with our child's death.'

'I'm just getting to that part of the story Rosie, as I said I had no idea you weren't dead. We all thought his first wife had died. Today, I learned some stuff that was hard to hear. I learned why my sister went off on one that day, the day she died. She found out you were alive.'

Rose her face white, her eyes tearless looked at the man in front of her. 'So, he lied, to you and his wife? That's what Alex does, he's so good at it, he can take everyone in.'

Keith nodded, he knew this woman was deeply hurt, after what his friend had imparted today he understood why. 'Yes, I understand why you are so hurt, he told me what he did to you, about your little girl.'

'Did he tell you about his two other children? The two kids in Cyprus with a woman old enough to be his mother. One of each, so he had no need for my child or the one your sister was having.' She said bitterly. 'I have a knack Keith, super power really, of getting involved with men who have personality disorders.'

'You have no idea how wrong you are Rosie, you need to hear this. Hear what happened all those years ago. Yes, he has lied, but he has had good reason. 'I lied too Rosie . . . he is downstairs, Rosie, please? I know you don't know me, and you have no reason to trust me but please listen to what he has to say, hear him out and then Michael who is my husband, incidentally, will take you back to the mainland.' Keith put his hand on Rosie's arm, 'you must need closure on this too.'

Rosie looked at Keith and nodded, 'I don't want him in here? Is there somewhere I can meet with him? Somewhere public but private?'

CHAPTER
FORTY-SEVEN

Rosie walked out on to the small rocky outcrop, despite how she felt about Alex. It wasn't like Carl, she did know instinctively he wouldn't physically harm her. She walked towards the figure, familiar even after twelve years. The golden hair cut neatly but still the man she had once thought she knew inside out. All the harm other men had done, Ronnie Muir, Carl, all the hurt and fear paled in to insignificance. The pain she felt looking at Alex Lockwood as deep and penetrating as it had been that first day in the hospital. She wanted to hate him, but more than that, she wanted to know why he had abandoned her.

As she approached, Alex turned to look at her, she saw his beautiful eyes, knew he had been crying. '*Crocodile tears!*' She thought to herself. She walked past him and sat on the bench staring out to sea. Alex walked around the bench and stood in front of her. 'Don't look at me Alex,' she whispered, I don't want to look into your eyes and see you lie. I can't stand to think I never knew you.'

'Rosie, I don't expect you ever to be able to forgive me, I realise I was living a fantasy. When I discovered it was you I had been talking to, when you put up that photo. I wanted to see you one last time, in the hope ... I could show you I never stopped loving you. I asked to see you because I just want you to know why? I know from talking to you online that what I did, more than anyone, has made you who you are. I don't want you to be alone. I need you to know it wasn't out of not wanting you I left. It wasn't anything you did.'

'Then what was it Alex? How could you have done it, not the walking away. I kind of get that, we were both grieving, that kind of pain forces you apart, you do things. What I really don't get was how you did it, not a word, I know you never get over losing a child. I know you loved her, I know you are still grieving for her. I am too. I know you have also lost your wife and child, I know how it feels to lose people you love. But us Alex ... Why didn't you have the fucking guts to tell me why?'

When he spoke, she had to lean forward to hear him, his voice was raw with emotion barely a whisper. 'I didn't mean to stay away Rosie, I had to go. I came back, but you and Carl had gotten back together.' Alex sobbed into his hands, 'I had lost my child I didn't want to cause another man to feel what I was feeling. Carl was the kids father.'

'What? Have you been in a fucking vacuum Alex? Carl Ranmore murdered my fucking parents. I never went back with him. Why did you think I took him back?'

'I saw you together, in the hospital you were kissing him and then there was this? It came about two years after Becca died.'

He pulled a faded torn photograph out of his pocket and handed it to Rosie. She could see the pain on his face, she couldn't understand how he had come by the photograph. Carl, her and the children. Rosie looked at the date on the back then turned to Alex. 'You'd better tell me what happened? All of it? I'm looking at you and I think there's something bad here. Something he did. What happened that day, the day of the funeral?'

I went to see him. He had asked to see me Rosie.' Alex stared out to sea remembering.

CHAPTER
FORTY-EIGHT

2005 Kilmarnock

Alex sat in the prison visiting room, he watched as the guard brought Carl towards him. 'You asked to see me Carl? What can you possibly want? They told you what's happened?'

'Yeah I heard you and Rosie's little bastard died. Does it hurt, leaving your kid in a hole in the ground? Does it eat away at you? I hope it hurts Lex, because you deserve every fucking wakened night, was it a fucking slow painful death, did you watch?'

Kicking back the chair, Alex stood up and made to walk away, he turned his back on Carl and gestured to the guard to open the door.

'I hear my boy, the boy you kept from me Lex, I hear he needs a kidney, and I am the best match.' Carl laughed, 'you fucking need me Lex. I hear you love those kids like they are your own. I hear you treat my wife like a princess, love her to death. Sit back down Lex and we can talk?' He laughed, 'let's test how much you love her? Hear you have a job in the States too? How much do you love wee Rosie, Lex? Will she still love you if another kiddie dies?' Carl laughed out loud, 'I have the fucking power.'

'Carl, that wee boy is going to face years of dialysis, even death, you can help. You can do one fucking good thing in all this. Yes, I love Rosie and the kids, yes maybe losing Becca is our punishment. I thought, despite everything you loved Rosie, Carl, you loved Imogen, yeah maybe she should have told you that Toby was yours. She was scared, scared that Ronnie Muir fathered him, so she never did the DNA.'

'Oh, my fucking heart bleeds, despite everything I still want her Lex, and I am going to have her back. With you Mr fucking knight in shining armour not able to help her, she will want me. Especially when I save our boy.'

'So, you are going to let him have the kidney?' The relief on Alex face and in his voice was obvious. Alex didn't care, he had come here to the prison to beg and he wasn't going to let pride get in the way of saving Toby.

'Oh yes, of course I am, he is obviously my son and I want to get to know him.'

'Thank you,' Alex stood up again and turned to leave.

'Sit down Lex, there are conditions?'

'Conditions?' Alex looked blankly at Carl.

'Uh Huh, conditions matey, and the first one is you get to fuck away from my family. You hear me, mine, not yours. I'm out of here soon, and I want my wife back.' He smiled, 'let's just say you have been keeping her warm for me, teaching her how do be a woman. You don't need to worry Lex, I will take really good care of all three of them. I would never hurt my Rosie. You know I love her, Imogen not so much, I had her to get my boy, now that I'm sure he's mine I am going to win my woman and son back. Don't worry I won't be bad to Imogen, she is my daughter. You Lex are going to write a wee letter, then you are going to fuck off to America and your new life without them, tell her your grief is overwhelming.'

The Nightclub Owners Wife

'You can't be serious? Are you fucking mad? Rosie will never have you back. She doesn't love you Carl, not sure if she ever did. She won't let you donate the kidney if she knows those are the terms.'

'Only if you tell her, she will, I guess, do anything to save the boy. I will win her back Lex. I've waited years for this revenge, I can wait as long as it takes. I will be her saviour; her friend and I will have her.' Carl laughed bitterly, 'I get rid of anyone who comes between me and what I want.'

'I could go and tell her this, what you've said.'

'She hates me anyway, so nothing will change, but she could hate you too, have you ever told her about your other kids? Oh yes, I know you didn't tell her Lex. The two wee ones in Cyprus with Dougie and Moira, can't believe that soft bastard accepted your fucking brats as his own. I hear the wee boy is a dead ringer for your one that died. I hear you love my son like your own? Do you want to take a chance Lex? Here is your chance to fuck off and know that the boy will get my parts into him. Your choice Lex, what is it to be? You leave the field clear for me to comfort her, I'll deny this conversation by the way, if you ever repeat it.'

'You are a sick bastard, Alex spat, he stood up and walked to the door.'

'Just phone the prison when you have written the letter and get on the fucking plane Lex.'

CHAPTER
FORTY-NINE

Greece 2018

Rosie stared at Alex's back, she could hear the grief and pain in his voice. His shoulders shook as he sobbed.

'Rosie, I wrote the letter left it in the weans bag, then I went to Cyprus to see Moira. I told her, and she said I was fucking mad. She said I should go back and tell you the truth. All of it.'

'Why didn't you tell me about the kids Alex?

'Rosie, the thing with Moira? Oh, it was about Dougie firing blanks. We came to an arrangement, I was young and fucking stupid Rosie. I was with Lainey and it wasn't serious, I got drunk with them one night, her and Dougie, and they asked me to father a child. I got sex with Moira whilst Dougie was away, no strings. I liked her, we were friends, the sex was good for both of us. Soon as she got pregnant it was to be over, we had one last session when she told me she was pregnant, that was when . . . when Elaine caught us. They went to Cyprus and that was that. It wasn't my kid it was Dougie's as far as I was concerned. Then when the baby, a little boy, was born, Dougie came back and asked if I would do it again. They wanted both kids to have the same father. It was around the time of Carl's trial, I thought about it... they are great parents. I was starting to have feelings for you and thinking there might be a chance for me and you, so rather than sleep with Moira again, I offered to donate sperm. Turkey baster in their house in Cyprus, when I went over with Norrie, remember just before Toby was born. Dougie inseminated her not me.'

'Do you ever see the kids?' Rosie asked. 'They are adults now? Do they know?'

'They both know I'm their biological father, Dougie and Moira always told them the truth.' Alex sighed, 'obviously Douglas doesn't know that I actually had sex with his mum, they think it was artificial insemination, somethings are best left alone. I should have told you about it, but I suppose it kind of got lost. After Becca died, I started to go to Cyprus once a year. I'm just uncle Lex to them. Oh, I know it's a bit weird and everything, but, I was young and daft, Rosie.'

'Alex, I kind of get it, why did you hide it from me?'

'Moira told me to tell you all about it, she knew Bobby was still seeing Carl, and she warned me. I never saw the kids till they were school age. I sent birthday presents, but I didn't know where else to go after Becca died. I just wanted to see them. Luckily Moira and Dougie were, well still are, grateful to me. Moira told me to come home and fess up and then tell you about what Carl had asked? As she said, he could hardly take the kidney back, could he?'

'So why didn't you? You know I didn't want him to give Toby the kidney?'

'I got to the hospital, you were snogging Carl in the room.' Alex looked at her, 'I didn't come in I saw you through the glass. I went to the states, and I just couldn't get over you. Even after I met Kim I kept her at arm's length. Every woman I met I compared to you, I never got over you. I was with her on and off for years before I married her. I only went out with her when I got the photo, I don't know who sent it, maybe Bobby. I thought you had gone back to him. Well you know what I thought?'

'What about Kim? You must have loved her?'

'It was I suppose a bit like you and me, I kept putting off marrying her, then she got pregnant, so we did it. I did love her Rosie, not the way I loved you, but I loved her. I lied to her too though, I told myself it might make her ill if I told her. Kim had a serious mental health issue, she had bi polar disorder. She kept relatively well, but that kind of illness, well there were highs and lows. I didn't tell her about you, I couldn't, I knew she would realise how much I loved you. She knew about you; well knew I had been with a woman called Rosie and we lost a child. She thought you had died too.'

'How did she know? What did she know?'

'She knew because I used to cry out in my sleep for you, call you and the children's names, Rosie, our family.' Alex looked at the ground. There were times when we were intimate, I shut my eyes and pretended I was with you. A couple of times I called out your name. I really hurt her Rosie, all because I'm a fucking coward.'

'What happened to her that day?'

Alex turned around and looked at Rosie, she could see the distress on his face, feel his pain. 'How do you tell someone . . . someone who loves you, someone who thinks you are a great guy, how do you tell them you walked out on the woman you loved when you had just lost your child.' Alex buried his face in his hands. 'The day Kim died she found out you were still alive, I had let her believe I was widowed. I never lied, she assumed, and I let her. As I said Kim had an illness, because of the pregnancy and her hormones it unbalanced the drugs she took, so she had bad highs and lows. She went off on one, jumped onto Michael's boat. I went after her and there was a crash then a fire. I was thrown clear, I had a lot of injuries and was laid up for nearly a year, but she died as you probably saw on the news our baby died with her, it was a little girl.'

'Alex, I know how it feels to lose people you love, I'm sorry that happened to you. I wanted to hate you, but I never could. I suppose it was because I had got it so wrong with Carl too. I just thought I was a lousy judge of people. What you did left me more damaged than anything he did Alex. Now I need to go home. I need to go away and try to sort this out in my head. Can you tell your friend thanks, but I will wait and get the ferry in the morning?'

'Can you forgive me Rosie?'

'I don't know? It all seems so obvious now, it was out of character what you did. Oh, maybe this is the closure we both need. Hate is a wasted emotion Alex, but there have been so many times, when I've wondered what if? When the fire happened, I fantasised you would come back, don't know why but I kind of wanted you to offer. It did bring Elaine back into my life.'

'I never knew about your parents either, I thought you and he were living happily ever after. I don't know if Moira knows, she doesn't have any connections there now. Not after Bobby telling Carl about the kids probably being mine, they moved to North Cyprus after that. Oh God Rosie, I just thought you were playing happy families. You poor wee thing.'

'Don't patronise me Alex, I'm not wee fat Rosie anymore. I am Rosanna Gibson, writer, strong woman, and I am Rosie Gibb. I don't need anyone to feel sorry for me. Do you know when Carl died he left me everything, he told his lawyer he trusted me to share it equally with the children. Apparently, he found God in his last year or so.'

'What did he die of?'

'Suicide . . . hung himself in prison, he left me a letter, telling me he was sorry for all he did and was ready to stand in front of his maker and take what was coming to him. He had been ill, heart problems the same as his dad. He thought that he would die, then he didn't, so he helped it along. He had just admitted to murdering Julie Muir. Alex, I felt nothing. The kids too they didn't even grieve, they say that you were their father.'

'I can't feel sympathy for him Rosie, I still hate him. He took you from me. All these years, I spent them thinking you and him were sailing off into the sunset with our kids. I loved the kids all of them, you know I did.'

'Oh Alex, why didn't you trust me? You should have known I would never have taken him back. My kids thought you died, a bit like you and your wife. They thought you died with Becca. I didn't tell them until they were adults that you had just up and left and I didn't know where you were. If we had just stopped and thought, what we had was pretty special.'

'You didn't trust me either Rosie, all those years you would not divorce him, you wouldn't marry me. When I saw you together I just thought that you had lied, you still loved him. I saw you and him, I don't know? I wanted to kill him, I had never felt like that. Well I would have killed Ronnie Muir. When I saw you kissing him in the hospital, as usual I was a fucking coward, I ran away.'

Rosie looked sadly at Alex then she turned and made her way back up the beach leaving him watching her walk away.

CHAPTER FIFTY

'Well? How was it? I take it the fact that you are home after three days it didn't work out. You didn't say much in the text and didn't answer my calls.'

'I used our safe word.'

'I'm assuming you just didn't fancy him as much when you saw him in the flesh?' Elaine asked she pushed a glass of wine in front of Rosie. 'I thought I'd come over and see you.'

'I was just going to stay away for the next three days, I knew you would do this. Want to do a post mortem. Where are the kids? I wasn't going to tell you I was back, but when you called... I needed to talk to someone. Where are the kids?' Rosie repeated, 'I don't want them walking in on this.'

'The girls are at Loch Lomond, party at Cameron House, they told you they were going, its Annie Dexter's 18th.'

'Toby?'

'At the cinema in Glasgow, he's taken Beau with him they are at my flat. Okay we are all alone, Brian is in New York, so let's discuss this? Did you get a shag?'

'Wilson wasn't Wilson... he was Alex.'

'What? You are fucking kidding? Did you?

'Elaine, I am fucking dying here.' Rosie's face crumpled, 'I didn't do anything, he did explain all of what happened.' Rosie burst into tears, Elaine took a gulp of her wine, finishing the glass, she could see Rosie was distraught and must have been holding in tears for hours.

Elaine let her sob and then sat down beside her friend she put the bottle and glasses on the table. Waiting until Rosie contained herself before speaking. 'Okay, tell me it all Rosie, what happened?'

***

Elaine shook her head in disbelief, she had let Rosie talk, tell her everything without interruption. 'Oh, fuck Rosie, what are you going to do? You need to tell him all that happened when he left.' The two women sat on the sofa, two bottles of wine lay empty on the floor. Rosie had told Elaine everything she had learned in Greece. 'What are you going to do?' Elaine repeated.

Rosie very drunk and still sad shook her head. 'Nothing I think, maybe it's best left this way. His brother-in-law Keith, he said I needed closure, and I suppose so does Alex. I never stopped loving him you know? Even when I hated him I just wanted to understand. I think it might help me move on now, at least I know I didn't get it all wrong.' Rosie smiled through her tears, 'suddenly the pain I feel is different Lainey. It's like, what might have been. I used to wish I had never met him, now I think, if we hadn't gone on that cruise. If I had just admitted that I feared Carl getting out and hurting Alex, rather than letting him believe I still wanted to be with Carl. What a fucking mess.'

Elaine took a large gulp from her wine, 'are you going to tell the kids? Imogen has always talked about him, always said to the others what a wonderful man he was. She says he was her real dad not Carl. Rosie, I will help you do it. I think you should.'

Rosie nodded, 'I know, part of me wants to just go back to Greece and take the kids with me. It's too late for me and him but perhaps the kids and him can have a relationship.'

'Is it too late for you and him?' Elaine looked thoughtful, 'You've never got over him babe, how did you feel when you saw him? Could you forget what happened?'

'I can't even begin to think about that Lainey, I need to digest it all. A couple of years ago, Imogen wanted to try to trace him. Toby asked me at Christmas about him. I kind of blocked it, they don't even know his second name.' Rosie sighed and sipped her wine, she looked at her friend eyes full. 'I feel that they could have a relationship with him. You think I should take them out there? Don't you?'

'Why don't you?'

'I've got a lot of explaining to do, haven't I? All the way home I was thinking about him, about how it was. How he was when we were together.'

Elaine smiled. 'You know when you think about it Rosie, Lex he loved you and the kids a lot to do what he did. To walk away so Toby could get the transplant, and then to not fight when he thought you were with Carl.'

CHAPTER
FIFTY-ONE

Six weeks later

'Wow!' Imogen said nudging her mother, what an amazing hotel, you say he designed this too. I can't believe that you never told us that he was A.J Lockwood, you said that he was a friend of A. J's and got him to design the house.' Imogen put her arm around her mother. 'Okay mummy dearest, take a deep breath. You say his friend is going to make sure he is here. How is he going to feel when we all walk in?'

'I have no idea, I didn't want him to know in case I couldn't go through with it.'

Toby and Imogen's fiancé Stewart lifted the cases out of the boot with Michael, and they walked up the steps of the hotel Angelica. Michael followed them in. Alex was serving behind the bar. Michael led the way into the room, Keith saw them and lifted the bar flap.

'These people are here to see you my friend' he said inclining his head in the direction of the doorway, 'you might want to see them.'

The Nightclub Owners Wife

Alex saw Toby first and straight away he realised who he was. Toby so like Carl now it was unmistakable to think he was anyone else.

'Alex these are my children.'

Alex walked around the bar, his face showing the shock he was feeling. 'Rosie!' he gasped, 'I don't know what to say.'

'Say hello to Toby, Imogen, her fiancée Stewart and this is Ella, Alex,' Rosie put her arm around her twelve-year-old daughter and kissed her blond curls. 'Ella this is your father,' she said quietly.

Keith nudged Alex, 'Rosie asked me not to tell you, she is going to go to the blue oyster with Michael and the kids are going to stay here.'

Imogen came forward and minutes later she was in his arms, both of them sobbing. Rosie, crying herself, followed Michael from the room. Toby watched her go, he was aware of Alex watching her over the top of Imogen's head.

Michael his arm around Rosie led her from the bar and out to the taxi. 'My mother is so happy you decided to stay with us, she is still trying to marry me off by the way, so you will be asked of course. How like Alex your daughter is, you must see him in her?'

Rosie nodded she wiped her eyes as she got in the cab. 'I almost never had her. I was in the hospital, they were going to give me some drugs and once I had them then I couldn't go back, needed to have the termination. I was sitting there waiting I picked up my file and on it they had written a confinement date, that's the date the baby is due and then suddenly I couldn't do it. The nurse came in with the tray and I had my clothes back on and was phoning a cab.'

'So, you had been going to abort her? What was the date?'

Ella was born on what would have been Becca's second birthday. When she was born she was so like Becca, who did look like Alex. Rosie looked sad for a moment remembering her lost baby, then she smiled. However, the physical resemblance to Alex is where it ends.'

'What do you mean? she is his child? There is no way her father could be anyone else?'

'She is a flaming nightmare, a little madam, a real drama queen. Oh, Imogen and Toby are great with her, so is Chloe who is my friends' daughter, and my older children's half-sister. Ella is oh she is beautiful and lovely, but she is hard work. The egocentric tweenie is one thing. Our lovely Ella takes it all to yet another level. I'm being a bit facetious she is actually a lovely wee girl. It's my fault she is so spoilt, mine and the kids. I felt I had to make up to her for having no father. Of course, Imogen was like a little mother to her she was nine when Ella was born.'

'Did you never think about telling Alex about her?'

'I was too scared. For a little while I thought that my husband was accepting of my decision to have her. He even arranged a big christening party. Then he waited over a year and sent a photograph of us as a family him holding Ella with our kids to Alex. Happy families, he wrote on the back with the date. That's when I realised that what Alex was telling me was the truth, I recognised Carl's writing on the back. It was sent to Alex after my parents died.'

'That was so sad, so awful Rosie, Keith told me about it all, how he set fire to the house. I can't believe anyone could be that evil.'

He meant to kill us all except Toby, he thought we were all there. He broke in drugged my cousins' son, it was dark, and he didn't realise it wasn't Toby. He wrote me a letter before he took his own life and told me. I think at the end of his life Carl really did feel remorse for what he had done. He admitted to most of the things he had done. Except he never admitted what he had done to Alex. I guess he carried on hating him. When Carl died, he left everything to me. I've sold off all the clubs and pubs and put the money in trust for the kids. My two elder kids both work, that's who they are. Despite the money, they all earn their way in life.'

'Do you think you can forgive Jimmy, he really does love you, always has. Keith and I just want him to be happy Rosie. He is a good man.'

'I know, yes, I have been able to have closure and it's all academic now isn't it? I hope Alex and I can be friends.'

CHAPTER
FIFTY-TWO

One year later

The musicians began to play the wedding march, the door to the hotel Angelina opened and the bride walked towards the alter on the beach. It was a beautiful sunny day. Some tourists stopped to watch, and the wedding guests looked back as Alex Lockwood like the other men in the party, wearing full highland dress, escorted Imogen down the aisle. Behind her walked Chloe and Ella in their beautiful dusky pink bridesmaids' dresses. Flowers bounced on top of Ella's blond curls. At the altar, Alex kissed Imogen and placed her hand in Stewart's as she handed her bouquet to Chloe. Ella glared at Alex and then turned and did the same to her mother.

Alex walked backwards and into the front row of seats beside Rosie, Toby, Elaine, Brian and Beau. 'You look amazing too.' He whispered more like their sister than their mother, what's up with Ella? She is in a right huff, what is it this time?'

'You are such a bullshitter Alex Lockwood I look every one of my thirty-nine years and you know it,' Rosie hissed, she reached out and took his hand. Her other hand moved to her four-month baby bump. 'Ella is horrified at us being pregnant. I had to tell her. I know we said after the wedding, but Imogen noticed I wasn't drinking champagne and asked.' Rosie smiled, 'everyone else is delighted though. She'll come around, Ella, I mean, she always does that, she's a little madam, she has been spoiled since the day she was born. I get it though, she is right, by the time this one is born Imogen will be twenty-three. We are going to end up with kids and grandchildren going to school together.'

Alex smiled, and his fingers moved to the white gold wedding ring on the third finger of her left hand. Put there just six weeks previously. 'I love you Mrs Lockwood. He looked over at Ella who stopped glaring, rolled her eyes and stuck her tongue out. Then she smiled and mouthed, 'congratulations, but I'm not babysitting.'

Toby standing on the other side of his mother leaned forward and hissed, 'wow dad, there's life in the old dog yet. Congratulations. Don't worry about Ella, she will come around, she was hoping to be an auntie and she gets to be a big sister instead.'

Other Books by Maggie Parker

Black Velvet: Living the Dream
ISBN: 978-1-910757-69-7

The Rock band, Black Velvet, are living the dream. Five musically talented childhood friends from a small Scottish town, they are catapulted to international stardom under the direction of their controlling manager Tony Gorman.

Black Velvet Out of the Ashes
ISBN: 978-1-910757-78-9

The Story of Black Velvet continues, as the band carry on with Simon Forsyth as their new manager. They continue to live as a family at Brickstead manor, and move on to a new chapter in their careers.

The Politician
ISBN: 978-1-910757-82-6

When MP Caoimhe Black attends a wedding in her native Ayrshire, she runs into Tony Carter. Many years earlier Tony and Caoimhe had a secret affair which resulted in tragedy, they have not seen each other since their relationship ended. Neither have been able to forget the feelings they once shared.

The Lighthouse
ISBN: 978-1-910757-94-9

When Social Worker Stephanie Wilson attends a conference, and meets a former colleague, she has no idea her life is about to change. Grieving from the death of her policeman husband four years previously, Steph has thrown all her energies into her growing family, the business she and her late husband developed and renovating a disused lighthouse.

The Doctor
ISBN: 978-1-79674-000-4

When family doctor Carrie-Anne meets Calvin a handsome oil rig worker, on a North Sea Ferry during a storm, they quickly become friends. He travels with her to her Shetland holiday home, and a relationship develops as he waits to be returned to his oil rig. When her daughter and son-in-law find her in a compromising situation, Carrie-Anne discovers that Calvin has been pretending to be an ordinary person, he is in fact a Hollywood Actor. Carrie-Anne hurt and angry, sends Calvin away but she is forced by her feelings, to examine her life, and a web of deceit and lies is revealed.

Printed in Great Britain
by Amazon